HOME-GROWN
TERROR

HOME-GROWN
TERROR

PATRICK GORMAN

Library of Congress Control Number:		2013918675
ISBN:	Hardback	978-1-4931-1688-1
	Softcover	978-1-4931-1687-4
	Ebook	978-1-4931-1689-8

This book was printed in the United States of America.

Rev. date: 11/25/2013

To order additional copies of this book, contact:
Xlibris LLC
0-800-056-3182
www.xlibrispublishing.co.uk
Orders@xlibrispublishing.co.uk
516722

Dedications

This book is dedicated to my loving daughter, Yasmin.
She has been a source of inspiration throughout.

Special thanks to a true and dear friend, Levina Mapuli
who also encouraged me to complete the manuscript.

Gratitude for the friendship of Bruce Curran a seasoned and
successful writer residing in Makati, Manila, Philippines.

To my late grandfather who was my hero and role model
a 22 years serving soldier with the British Army.

Company Sergeant Major **H .A. Adlam** Royal Hampshire
regiment (disbanded)

Finally, to the Victoria Travel Hotel, Ggaba, Kampala, Uganda, where I
enjoyed the hospitality, peace, and serenity, to complete the book

INTRODUCTION

THE PRISONER IDLY counted the thick glass window bricks once again, forcing his mind to focus on something. There were twenty-eight glass bricks in total. Seven ran lengthways and four in height. The density of the thick glass only allowed daylight to penetrate their depth. The ten-by-eight-foot cell was very basic, and contained only essential amenities. A stainless steel lidless toilet stood in the corner of the room. Positioned beneath the thick glass window bricks stood a rigid enclosed wooden bed frame that was fixed firmly to the wall and floor. A thin green plastic mattress covered the top of the fabrication. The walls of the cell were painted a drab green colour, interrupted only by crude graffiti from former inhabitants.

A strong steel grey reinforced door was the only way in and out of the alien space. The door's austerity was interrupted only by a small round glass inspection window, and an oblong sliding grille. There were two odd things about the room. There was no handle on the inside of the door, and the toilet was un-flushable from inside the room. 'Must be to check on druggies,' the man idly thought. He lay down on the hard thin plastic sponge, closing his eyes. Every time he did so, he saw her sweet smiling face, and then the horror and the realisation of what had happened returned.

His heart was pumping. His head still ached from the fall. He could not concentrate on anything. He had been released from hospital, and brought back into police custody. A doctor had been called to the police station and had administered a mild sedative, but that was an hour before. His heart raced as the adrenalin surged through his veins and arteries fighting the numbing effect of the tranquillizer. He heard a noise, idly turning round he saw a police officer peering in at him through the round inspection window. Peter glared at the intrusion. The man turned and walked away.

The prisoner lay still on the bed for a short time willing sleep to rid him of his living nightmare. As he did so, his mind became tormented once again. Swivelling to a sitting position, he put his head in his hands, and moaned aloud.

The tears welled up in his eyes once again; and his body shook as he wept uncontrollably. He felt weak, broken, defeated, and robbed of the woman he loved.

After all that he had been through. The innocent victim had now become the accused!

The allegation was too much to bear. The penalty for murder and the repercussions were an even worse fate to consider. His memory of the incident was so vivid, and yet he could not accept the reality of the situation or his present demise to a police cell. It was all so surreal.

With mixed emotions, he stood up and paced round the room.

In frustration, and anger, he punched the walls until his knuckles became red and sore; it was almost as if the walls were responsible for his present confinement. The man wanted to feel some pain. His future prospects were bleak. He knew the police had found the weapon. He was aware that his finger and handprints were on the barrel, and trigger of the high-powered semi-automatic rifle. Unless the truth came out in full, and the police believed him, and events leading up to his wife's death, the prisoner was looking at a life sentence at the very least. Time would have no meaning in the confined surroundings of a Category 'A' prison such as HMP Belmarsh.

The present detention to a police cell was only a taste of what he could expect. 'Prison could not be an option,' he thought, as he sat down heavily on the bed.

In his tormented mind, he decided that he would kill himself if he were sentenced to life imprisonment.

A tangled web of despair engulfed his troubled mind once again, as he tried to grasp the situation and make sense of it. The man was unable to comprehend, or apply any logical thought with his emotions running so high. Rest was the only cure. He needed to recuperate, and have the chance to regain his strength, also his logical thinking. In the morning he knew that he had to be sharp at the interview. He would need a clear mind.

The sick feeling returned to his stomach once again. It was the same feeling he had when the bullet struck his wife. It had been over an hour after the incident before he phoned the emergency services. He had not been able to bring himself to report the incident immediately. His mind had been in turmoil, hampered by his injury. If there was ever a time that he needed her, it was now.

'Krissie' he called out in despair, softly at first and then again, slightly louder, as if she could hear him and would return to his side.

The custody sergeant heard the woman's name being called out. He took no notice. It happened all the time when prisoners were in custody.

The man knew that the interview would start in earnest sometime in the morning. He imagined the police were searching for evidence in order to find him guilty or not guilty of the serious crime. After all, he was the prime suspect. In the meantime, the processes of the law would be run by the book, but then again, he thought, probably not by the book. How many times had the police evidence been fabricated in order to frame a suspect, so that a case could be closed, especially by the Met (Metropolitan Police in London)? James Hanratty sprang to mind. He was an innocent man that had been sent to the gallows in Bradford, Yorkshire in 1962.

He imagined men and women in white one-piece suits, hands and shoes covered in plastic, trawling through his house. They would be searching through his personal possessions and those of his late wife. They would be taking photos, and piecing the whole tragic incident together.

As he sat alone with his thoughts, the coming day stretched ahead of him like an expanse of featureless desert. The engineer knew that he would be questioned and cross-examined by professional police officers who were used to dealing with murder suspects and serious crimes. He would be no match for them in his present state of mind. The custody sergeant had advised him to get a good lawyer.

He lay back on the bed tormented once again by his thoughts.

An hour later, when the policeman checked on him, the prisoner was sleeping peacefully.

The tranquilliser had finally overcome the adrenaline coursing through his veins.

PETER MAYNARD STOOD thoughtfully, gazing out of the open glass doorway leading to a small patio and an ornamental garden plot. He and his wife had so lovingly and painstakingly worked on the decorative plants and features of the back garden and were more than satisfied with the results.

The cottage was small, cosy and detached. It had previously been a farm worker's dwelling many years earlier. The small house was nestled in the quiet woodlands in a much sought after part of the Cotswolds. The couple enjoyed both the seclusion and serenity that the surrounding countryside had to offer.

At the bottom of the garden was a high brick wall. This was now hidden by a large shed. Peter had built the structure and tastefully converted it into a small but adequate office.

On the other side of the wall there was a footpath, with a large grass verge, and a road that linked Brinsham Park to the town of Yate.

Peter was a very talented and contented individual who enjoyed both his work life as well as his home life.

As the early morning dappled sunshine filtered through the great spreading canopy of a cedar tree, his thoughts came back to his present dilemma.

'How am I going to tell her?' he asked himself.

His gaze fell on the red stone Buddha with a bright golden sash running diagonally from shoulder to waist. The Buddha was seated high on a mound of stones at the right-hand corner of the garden. He appeared to have a wise serene expression carved into his face. Peter stared at the figure for some seconds as if for inspiration or for an answer to his predicament.

Although a practicing Catholic, Krissie had wanted the Buddha from the moment she saw it. Her husband succumbed and bought it for her at a garden centre in Wroughton near Swindon. The Buddha stared back over the open Cotswold pebbles at the man, with unseeing eyes.

The couple had been married for two years, and planning to have their first child.

Krissie loved England very much. It was a great improvement on the impoverished shanty town dwellings where she had grown up as a child on the island of Cebu, in the Philippines.

'Here my love,' she said walking past him and interrupting his train of thought.

'Here's cup of coffee for you. I only put one sugar in because you're getting fat,' she teased him, laughing. Her beautiful smile lit up her face. She placed the Mickey Mouse coffee mug on the green plastic patio table.

Stepping down onto the paving the engineer pulled back a chair and sat down saying softly, 'Sit with me for a minute Krissie.'

The early morning sun was pleasantly warm on his back and shoulders. 'There's something I want to tell you, my love.'

His wife did as she was bid. As he reached out for his coffee she instinctively put her hand on the back of his.

Her olive skin was smooth and soft. He smiled at her. She was so full of life and love for him and showed it in so many ways, including her simple tender gestures.

'Now what you want to say?' she asked. Her English had improved, but some sentences were still clipped and her words were often miss-pronounced. Peter found this both amusing and colloquial.

'I have been offered a job to work as a consultant in the Middle East for a short time. I don't want to turn the offer down because the money is so good. On the other hand, I don't want to leave you here on your own.'

'Can I come with you then like last time?' she asked a smile still playing, but fading on her pretty face.

'No, not at this time my love. I will be travelling a lot. The work is in Saudi and I will be living in hotels, not like before when we had a villa in the compound.'

'Will you be safe sweetheart?'

'Oh! Yes! I'll be quite safe,' he assured her.

'Then when I come back we'll have a short break together and look for a place in the Philippines like we planned. So you can be sure of a bit of fun and sun. I know how much you miss the sunshine and it will be our holiday home; and a sort of Shangri-La for later life, when we're old and grey,' he joked.

'Well as long as you'll be OK. I have my friends here,' she said half-heartedly with a sigh, trying to be brave and remain cheerful. 'There's Cherry and Nell, and then there's always the church and Father Thomas and I have my little job. I'll be fine. Don't worry about me. I just worry about you, my husband and want you to be safe.'

She took it better than he first thought, although he knew she was hurting inside. He looked at her for a moment. She averted his gaze and stared down into her Minnie Mouse mug of tea. A tear clouded her vision. It was then that Peter made a vow that he would never ever leave his wife again for months at a time. This would be the last contract that he would take without her. When he came back, he would find a job in the UK.

As he sipped his coffee, he consoled himself with the thought that time would pass quickly due to his busy schedule, and he would be back home in no time.

Peter Edward Maynard was a mobile telecoms consultant engineer. He worked on a self-employed basis for many different companies and organisations throughout the world. Usually, his assignments were obtained through recruitment agencies and the salaries were very attractive. His work took him to many different countries, some of which were Third World, whilst others were quite prosperous. The forthcoming project would start in Riyadh and cover Jeddah on the Red Sea and Dammam on the eastern coast of Saudi Arabia by the Gulf. His base would be in Riyadh and he would travel out from there as and when required. He comforted himself with the thought that once the contract was completed and the money was in the bank, he and his wife would take a well-earned break.

Peter had looked up Al Hammed Telecommunications on the Internet, the company he would be working for. The information on the website was sparse. The recruitment agency and the interviewers of Al Hammed had stressed the need for diplomacy. A confidentiality agreement had been signed before his commencement with the company; and after signing it, he received the three-month contract.

This was not unusual; the engineer had worked for Saudi Military Intelligence on a mobile telecom network some years before. He held the position as Head of Communications for the army on a two-year assignment for a telecoms operations and maintenance contract based in central Riyadh. As a result his experience of overseas working was one of the reasons why he had been shortlisted and selected for the consulting role. His qualifications, military experience and working knowledge of the Middle East, were the main factors that had determined the decision of the three interviewers. Peter was immediately offered the position with full benefits and a tax-free salary.

The information at the interview was sparse, and the job was described as a new start-up 4G GSM Network which was a division of Saudi Telecom Systems. This was the second largest telecoms company in Saudi Arabia.

Peter would be running the project from the Riyadh office and answerable directly to the sheik. He would liaise with the project directors for each of the three regions for technical matters on a day-to-day basis. This would ensure an up-to-date good working relationship with the client and local staff. The sub-contractors would be made up of Egyptians, Saudis, Pakistanis, Indians and Filipinos. There were only four other British ex-pats on the project. They held senior management roles in site construction, project co-ordination, RF and transmission planning, optimisation and integration.

Peter's main responsibilities would be for the installation, integration and commissioning of all the new sites. He would also be accountable for the implementation of the network roll-out to become operational on time. The project was scheduled to be completed by or before the programmed launch date. By then the network would be integrated and 'on air.' This would be a 4G VIP mobile telecoms project, and considered to be the most advanced and discreet venture in the Kingdom of Saudi Arabia. The VIP part of the network would be used by members of the Royal House of Saud, Ministry of Defence and Aviation, and senior officers of the Saudi armed forces.

*   *   *

On arrival at King Khalid Airport in Riyadh, a blast of the midday heat hit Peter Maynard full in the face as he emerged from the Saudi Arabian Airlines plane, and on to the mobile metal staircase. 'Like someone opening the oven door,' he thought as he felt the blast of heat.

Peter followed the procession of people across the tarmac and into the arrivals hall, and then made his way towards the immigration desk. A Saudi airport policeman ushered the Westerners to a queue that was marked in English and Arabic "Non-Saudi Nationals."

The straggly line was extensive. He put his black laptop carrying case on the floor together with his briefcase, and then looked along the row of people leading to the desk. The traditionally attired uniformed immigration officers appeared to be in no hurry to allow people into the sovereignty, and apportioned everyone with a generous part of their working day. They glared at the untidy crocodile of humanity. One by one the non-Saudi nationals were allowed to pass through the gateway and enter the border of the Kingdom of Saudi Arabia having had their passports stamped with a visa.

'This could take some time,' Peter thought. He felt tired; as impatience crept over him whilst he stood impassively in the slow-moving queue, waiting to shuffle forward.

His mind returned to Kristine. She had come to London Heathrow Airport to see him off. She would return to Bristol by coach and then take a local bus back to the Cotswold village where they lived close to Chipping Sodbury. She would return to an empty house with all the memories . . .

Kristine had been so tearful that morning and had tried really hard to be brave. Turning to wave at his wife as he made his way to the security and executive departure lounge, he couldn't help noticing her tears. He felt such a rat, leaving her like that. Once again he pictured her in his mind, standing there as he walked through to the departure area. She had dabbed the little white handkerchief at her eyes. She tried to be strong; she was so sweet, so sensitive, so loving, so caring. How could he do this to his beautiful, gentle young wife? He felt a lump come to his throat as his mouth went dry.

Suddenly, his thoughts were rudely interrupted by someone loudly calling out his name.

'*Maynard! Peter Maynard!*' An Arab in a crisp white dish-dash and headdress was shouting his name whilst holding up a white A4 piece of paper with his family name printed in thick black bold type.

'Yes. That's me,' Peter answered, from the middle of the queue, turning round and raising his arm instinctively as if he were back in school.

The well-dressed Arab gentleman advanced towards him. The two men shook hands briefly and then the Saudi said with an air of authority, 'Come with me.'

'*Follow me, please*' he insisted as if Peter hadn't heard or understood him the first time. The engineer followed the man to the front of the queue. He discovered later that the Arab was a government official employed by the Ministry of Telecommunications.

As they jumped the queue, the Saudi executive instructed the bored immigration officer to process the passport of Mr. Peter Edward Maynard immediately. A rubber stamp banged down heavily as the entry visa was entered into the burgundy red-covered United Kingdom identification. The official gave Peter a cursory glance with his heavy eyes as he handed the passport over. The look was as if in disgust for the man's Western importance that the infidel had in the Kingdom. Peter smiled in defiance muttering, 'Shukran,' (thank you). He knew that many Saudis bitterly resented Westerners working in their country, also the military US forces occupying the Holy Land since the Iraqi wars.

The two men made their way to the baggage reclaim area. When Peter identified his suitcases, the Arab motioned to a Pakistani porter indicating for him to put the cases onto a trolley. Then the unlikely trio ambled towards the customs check-in. Once again, the Arab exercised his authority. The suitcase and hand luggage passed through the X-ray machine and each case received a white squiggly chalk mark on emerging. None of the cases had been opened for inspection.

In no time the engineer was back out in the hot afternoon sunshine once again. He felt the heat beating down on him, penetrating his light grey suit jacket. The three men then made their way to a waiting black Lexus saloon car. The Pakistani porter struggled with the trolley as he tried to push it forward in a straight line. The porter had a problem with negotiating the trolley as it had a wonky wheel and appeared to have a mind of its own as to where it wanted to go.

On arrival to the roadside, Peter observed the Lexus driver was arguing with an airport policeman. The officer was not happy that the car had been parked in the "Arrivals" bay for so long. The Pakistani porter lifted the cases and placed them into the open boot of the luxury car. The Arab gave the Asian two, 100 Saudi riyal notes and waved him away. Then showing the policeman some ID the officer lost interest, nodded respectfully, and walked away, looking for another obstruction. Possibly, he would have the chance to earn some extra Saudi riyals by allowing someone to park and wait.

Peter got into the back of the vehicle. 'Talk about VIP treatment,' he thought.

The reception from the Arab had been rather hostile towards him initially. 'Maybe someone's stolen his camel,' he deliberated, trying to cheer himself up.

Thirty minutes later, the car pulled up outside the Radissons Hotel. This was formerly the Hyatt Regency Hotel on Prince Abdul Aziz Street. He recognized his whereabouts almost immediately. The place was close to the Old Batha in the town centre in one direction. Also known as the Rembrandt of Riyadh, and the opposite way was close to the Ministries, The Southern Sun, and Rafah's Turkish Restaurant

At the hotel entrance the car was stopped by security. They checked the car, under the bonnet, the boot, and then finally beneath the car with the use of a mirror on a long metal handle.

The concierge came out of the hotel and opened the door of the car as the engineer alighted.

The boot lid sprung open and a young man hurried down towards the car. The bellhop reached into the boot of the car and retrieved the cases. He also relieved Peter of his briefcase.

Then the bellhop proceeded to struggle with the revolving doors, laden with the cases and followed closely by the Englishman.

'*Maynard!*' Peter turned on hearing his name being called out for a second time, 'Rest for a while. Be ready to meet with the minister and some of the team in three hours. There is an important meeting. I will send a car for you,' and with that he was gone.

'The Ministry of Telecommunications is quite near here,' Peter thought, 'I could walk it. Oh! Well, here I am, just arrived and virtually having to hit the ground running!'

* * *

The car arrived at the predetermined time, and soon the occupants were entering the gates of the Ministry of Telecommunications. Peter checked his watch; it was ten minutes past five, in the evening. The engineer was met at the Ministry by the same Arab who finally introduced himself as 'Abdul bin Ageel.' Once inside the building the men entered a lift and descended to the basement. There was a babble of voices from the throng of people waiting outside the conference room.

Peter was introduced to the assorted assembly by the Arab.

The engineer warmed to the only Englishman in the crowd. The man was of smart appearance and stood erect. He was very dapper and had a well trimmed grey military style moustache. The once black hair was now silver grey. The man had a distinguished air about him. He was wearing a dark blue blazer with shiny yellow metal buttons. The shirt was white and neatly pressed, and the tie bore the Royal Signals' insignia—"Mercury" (the messenger). The tie stood out from the crisp white background of his shirt.

The trousers were light grey, with sharp creases, and the man's shoes were shiny black patent leather.

'Hello old boy,' he said to Peter extending his right hand as he introduced himself. 'Welcome aboard. Yer must be the new consultant engineer, call me Dudley! Colonel Dudley Coburn-Smythe retired.'

'Pleased to meet you, Dudley,' Peter replied cordially. The colonel's refined voice suggested that he was ex-public school, and that he was an ex-Sandhurst officer. Peter then introduced himself in a similar manner, 'Peter! Sergeant

Peter Edward Maynard, ex-Royal Signals, retired also,' he joked. 'I couldn't help noticing the corps tie and insignia, Dudley. May I ask what your position is here with the company?'

'Consultant Project Control Manager,' Dudley replied. 'Basically, I interface between the government officials, and the client, Al Hammed Telecoms, or AHT as they prefer ter be known. All *yer* have ter do, dear boy, is ter make sure we hit our targets. Feed the information back ter me then I enter it onto our database. Bit of a doddle really. Yer will have a pretty tough job on here, with a mainly Paki / Gypo crew. Yer will need ter chase the buggers from ear holes ter breakfast so as ter make sure we hit our deadlines or milestones as they like ter refer ter 'em. The sheik is paranoid about us launching the network on time, so that we please the Princes. If anything goes wrong, we get the blame. When all goes well, they take the credit. Same shit different day, if yer understand me!

'The contractors will try every trick in the book ter get away with whatever they think they can. Watch 'em like hawks, that's my advice to yer. The Flips (Filipinos) are great; yer'll have no trouble with them.'

'Thanks for the advice,' replied the engineer, 'and point taken. It's always good to know the makeup of the troops,' he said with a wink of the eye to the senior soldier.

Suddenly, the lift doors opened again.

A large, wide built, bearded Arab gentleman emerged wearing flowing white Arabic robes and a white hatata (head dress). He walked hurriedly towards the mass of people. Everyone made way as he ambled his way through the crowd, nodding to both the Europeans, and Arabic employees alike. There was a resounding of 'Salaam alaikum,' (Peace be with you), and followed by the response 'Alaikum salaam,' (peace be on you also). The sheik was accompanied by two other Saudi's, one of whom hurried in front of the entourage in an effort to unlock the conference room door.

Then the three Saudi dignitaries made their way into the large room, as the waiting assembly dutifully filtered through the narrow doorway.

The meeting was fairly brief and very much to the point. Sheik Allah Abdul Al Bakra, the minister for telecommunications, sat at the head of the table. He welcomed Peter to the project and stressed the urgency to get the new network operational by the launch date. The sheik announced that many sites in Riyadh had been built and were ready to be powered up and made operational. They only required final alarm checking, and then test and commissioning on a few problem sites. This was to be Peter's main priority. The dignitary also intimated that there were a few problems with the line of sight equipment, but the engineers were busy working to close all critical issues.

Another Englishman arrived, although a little late, and gave his apologies. This was the transmission engineer. After being introduced to Peter the engineer informed the sheik, whilst occasionally glancing at Peter, that his department was busily engaged on the last phases of the fine tuning in the Riyadh region. This would minimise interference and ensure good coverage across the network continuum, then all the sites would be fully radiated. The Sheik raised his hand and announced for the newcomers benefit:-

'You see Maynard; everyone is mushrul, very busy, busy.' Peter nodded respectfully, and mumbled something incoherent.

Only the sheik and the RF engineers had mobile phones for radio access on the VIP network.

The RF engineers required cell phones for test purposes only. There were two test handsets that were required for checking the coverage and monitoring the network performance by the drive test teams.

When the meeting ended, Peter was formerly introduced to the sheik. They shook hands and made good eye contact. The sheik smiled. His handshake was firm which indicated friendship. The engineer was informed that the sheik had studied in England and graduated in the States where he had received a doctorate. It was then apparent as to where the sheik's American accent had come from. They exchanged pleasantries including family matters. Then after a farewell handshake, the assembly dispersed and left the room.

Some people took the lift, and others ascended the stairs to the foyer. Peter followed Dudley towards the stairwell, considering him to be a friend.

'Hey, Dudley,' he called in a hushed voice as they moved to a quiet corner. 'Is there anywhere I can get a drink here? I know it's banned and all that, but I could always get a snifter without any worries when I was working here before. I just need something to calm me down. I guess I am missing the wife and all that.'

'Not a problem old boy. Do yer have a car?'

'Yes! A car *and* a driver,' the engineer replied.

The two men trudged up the stairs, through the lobby and then out into the warm evening air. Dudley pointed towards a silver grey four wheel drive Toyota Land Cruiser. 'Just follow me. My place is only a few clicks up the road from here. Let's see what we can do for yer.'

Peter's vehicle followed the 4WD and very soon they were entering a European compound by the name of Arabian Homes. Peter got out of his vehicle instructing his driver to wait for him, and then entered Dudley's 4WD, as the security did not permit visitor's vehicles to enter the complex.

Once through the strict security checks, they alighted from the vehicle.

The two men walked along a path and past a swimming pool. There were several European bodies lounging around the poolside. Most were in swimming attire or shorts. The scene had a slight Mediterranean feel about it. The remnants of a bar-b-cue were in evidence.

A few tired balloons lay shriveled on the ground in the still evening air. The children were too tired, too hot or too bored to get any further enjoyment from them.

Dudley said 'Hi!' to a few Western individuals, and wished one young lady with a small baby in her arms, 'A Very Happy Birthday!' Peter nodded and smiled to those that Dudley had spoken to.

The colonel entered a corner villa. 'Come on in,' he cordially invited.

'Oh! Here she is!' he announced once inside. An attractive Filipina lady of about thirty-five years of age, and around five foot two in height, walked from the kitchen towards them. She had a huge welcoming smile on her face.

Absentmindedly, she had forgotten the red chequered tea towel in her right hand. Her long black hair was slightly ruffled, and added to her pleasant appearance.

'This lady is my wife—Lisa. Actually it's Mona Lisa, 'cos she's always moaning at me.' The Filipina placed the tea towel on the back of a chair and extended her right hand to Peter, giving him a coy smile. They briefly said 'Hello' and then Dudley announced:-

'Oh! Look out! Here comes trouble.' A pretty, half English, half Filipina girl of about nine years of age entered the room. She wore a set of fashionable pink denim dungarees over a white tee shirt.

'This is Peter,' he said to his daughter, 'and this is Clarita,' he informed turning to the engineer, 'Or Clarrie as she prefers to be called.'

The young girl extended her right hand furtively at the introduction, smiling shyly in doing so. Peter took her small soft hand in his and shook it warmly.

'So, what have yer been up ter terday dressed like that young lady,' Dudley asked.

'Cleaning the windows?'

'Da-aad!' his young daughter stressed the word. 'It's called fashion. You wouldn't understand.'

'Daresay I wouldn't understand, if that's what they call fashion these days,' retorted the colonel.

He had a wry smile on his lips and gave a wink of his eye towards his guest.

'You always teasing Clarrie, Dudley,' scolded Lisa good-naturedly. 'Leave the poor girl alone.'

Peter immediately warmed to the family. They were happy, contented and he enjoyed their good natured banter. He hoped that one day he and Krissie would also be like them and blessed with having a son or daughter.

'Sit down old boy, no need ter stand on ceremony here. Now then, let's get down ter business. What's yer poison, beer, Sid or old sock red wine?'

'I think I'll try the Sid,' (an illicit drink made from a root vegetable. It is illegally distilled in Saudi Arabia and sold to Westerners on the black market).

'What is old sock red wine?' Peter asked with a grin.

'Well, it's wine of a sort, but when I make it; I never know how it's going to turn out. So I experiment. Sometimes I add extra sugar; other times I put in extra blackberries, but it always seems ter come out tasting of old socks. Well, how I think old socks would taste anyway. It's a bit hit and miss really, every time I brew it.

'I've got some Jeddah gin on the go at the moment, as well. That's stuff's really strong, bags of fruit and potatoes. I mean old socks' is OK if I'm desperate or I've run out of the other stuff. It doesn't taste that good—but it delivers the same effect. The only trouble is, it makes yer mouth rather dry in the morning! Sometimes yer need a drink at the end of a stressful day, working with the ragheads.

'Yer sit down, darling, take it easy and entertain our guest. I'll see ter the drinks,'

Dudley joked, noticing that his wife had already settled on the sofa and left the chore to him anyway. The colonel went into the kitchen and came back with two tall straight glasses. Both glasses had large measures of the prohibited substance and tonic water. A slice of lemon and two blocks of ice in each of the glasses completed the drink.

'Here y'are old boy Sid and tonic and a slice of lemon, and two blocks of ice, just what the doctor didn't order. Get stuck in, I'm going upstairs ter change inter something more comfortable,' he said. At the same time he removed his tie and unbuttoned his shirt. The colonel left the room and briskly ascended the green carpeted staircase.

Peter made small talk with Lisa. She was both surprised and most interested to know that he also had a young Filipina wife. Lisa came from Cagayan de Oro, about eight hours by ferry to the island of Cebu. They sat and chatted about family life as they waited for the host to reappear.

The Sid had its desired effect on Peter. He was feeling mellow and more relaxed. He was also happy to be with the present company. It was just what he needed, on his first day—a booster being away from his loving wife.

Dudley came down the stairs wearing a dark blue T-shirt, bearing the slogan "No Worries" and a pair of faded blue jeans.

'What's that you're wearing Dad?' Clarita asked cheekily.

'Yer wouldn't understand,' replied Dudley cheerily. 'It's called fashion.'

'Old fashioned, more like,' she responded giggling loudly.

'Touché,' remarked her father grinning broadly. He picked up his glass and raised it in a salute to his guest.

'Cheers all, and welcome to Saudi Arabia and the company, Peter. By the way, when were yer last here in Saudi?'

'In the year two thousand and seven, I think it was and before that, the year two thousand.'

'Hmmm! Things have changed quite a bit since then. It's a more security conscious country now, especially since nine-eleven, in two thousand and one.'

'Yes, I noticed the chicane, the security and armed soldiers on the gate of the compound as we drove in.'

'That's the Saudi Arabia National Guard. It is double standards, old boy.

'The Saudi's don't really want us here, but they need our technology and for us to improve their infrastructures. Also they need us and the American forces ter fight their battles and ter win their wars and safeguard their oil fields. Conversely the Americans and British need the oil and are willing ter pay the price ter protect it. It's very much a marriage of convenience and a sort of catch twenty-two situation. If Saudi was only known for growing carrots and asparagus, none of us would be here. It would still be Arabia, and as poor a country as it was before the oil was discovered.

'So yer see the Saudi's have gone from camels ter Cadillac's, so ter speak in a very short space of time.' He beamed above the top of his glass as he was about to take another swig.

They rambled on for over an hour, discussing life in Saudi, the project, the compound, and what it had to offer . . . .

Peter spoke about Kristine and his hopes and ambitions of investing in a property in the Philippines and raising a family . . . .

When the young engineer finally left the villa he had a warm glowing feeling inside. He also had a bottle of Sid in a mineral water bottle inside a plastic bag as a parting gift.

'In case of emergencies,' Dudley had joked, with a wink, a nod and a wry smile.

Peter's Indian driver was sleeping as he respectfully waited for his "master." They drove back to the hotel in relative silence.

The engineer was pleased to know that he had made such good friends in such a short space of time.

Suddenly, he remembered that he had to call his wife before going to bed.

*   *   *

As the days passed Peter threw himself into his work and enjoyed the ambiance and camaraderie of the people that worked in the company's offices. He had got used to his hotel accommodation and had set up a basic office in his room.

There he composed reports for the company in the evening and managed to chat online to friends and family.

The project was going very well and the Riyadh operation was on schedule for the launch date. The engineer had regular weekly meetings with the minister, or one of his aides.

On one occasion he had been invited to the sheik's palace near Olaya, (in Riyadh centre) for a party. These were grand affairs with a plentiful selection of food, soft drinks, mineral water and an all male guest list including, military officers, high ranking police officers, diplomats and dignitaries.

The weekly meetings always took place on a Saturday morning. Peter had met with the RF team, the project team and the sub-contractors. He informed them of what he expected, and gradually built up a good working relationship with his team.

*   *   *

Everything was going extremely well; until one Friday morning, three weeks into his contract.

It all started when Peter visited a rooftop site with the identification prefix "Site 262." He went to the location that day to carry out some routine alarm testing. Friday is the Islamic holy day, and a non-working day for Muslims. But Peter wanted to ensure that everything was ready for the engineers visiting the site for test and commissioning the following day. The site was about to be integrated into the network and powered up. The engineer had to ensure that all the alarms were working correctly back to the Network Operations Centre. He also wanted to be certain that there would be no failures and for the client to sign the acceptance certificate. Site ID 262, was a rooftop site and a main hub station. It was therefore important to its neighbouring base transceiver stations, and essential to get "on air."

When he reached the rooftop, he noticed the guard lying on a large piece of a flattened brown, cardboard box, asleep. This was not an unusual occurrence. Peter didn't like to disturb the man from his slumber and continued on his way.

He had not visited the site before, and as he gazed over the parapet, he was amazed at the incredible view from across that part of the city.

He then observed the radio room, but wanted to check the other outbuildings on the flat rooftop. He needed to see if they housed any spare parts for the radios. There were three small stone buildings in front of him. He entered the nearest room, and observed that it was being used as a hardware store. There were spare antennas, coils of cable, tower cross members, nuts and bolts, old cardboard boxes and general superfluous scrap material. These were all leftover from the build of the site installation. The items were strewn across the floor in an untidy fashion.

Peter was specifically looking for spare radio parts, such as printed circuit cards, processor boards, and so on. When he entered the third building, he thought at first it was the guard's room. He came to this assumption because there were some sleeping bags on top of flattened cardboard boxes on the floor. He idly picked up what he mistakenly thought was the site log book and opened it. The book was not the log book at all—but something a lot more sinister!

Flicking through the pages he was amazed at what he saw. There were anniversary dates with pencilled notes next to them. These were earmarked for some time in the future. Also September the eleventh, the anniversary of George Bush's New World Order. October the twelfth the Bali bombing. The American Embassy bombing in Nairobi, The London bombings. The Kampala, Uganda bombings . . . . The list was extensive.

There was a register of prominent English politician's; their names and addresses were neatly jotted down. There were also well-known place names in both the UK and the United States. Many of these the engineer instantly recognised. There were prominent airfields listed, control towers, and radar stations. Many had references with rough sketches and GPS coordinates. Further examination revealed gas and power stations, one of which was in Battersea, London, and main water reservoirs, along the River Thames.

A cold shiver ran down his spine.

If this was what he thought it was, then the security authorities had to be informed. This was a matter of security. 'Could these be terrorist targets?' he asked himself as he flicked through the pages.

In addition to the place names and possible target locations, there were dubious names and addresses of a foreign nature. These were probably lists of safe house addresses. There were phone numbers in Bradford, Slough, Birmingham Manchester, Leeds, Liverpool and London. There were names of mosques in England, assigned presumably for the training of terrorists in the techniques of bomb making, chemical warfare, and suicide bombings. Finsbury Park Mosque was identified with a red line drawn through it. Peter remembered that some time ago, this had been known as a school for terrorists. The notorious Abu Hamsa had been detained by Her Majesty's pleasure for preaching hatred against the West and its allies. Another page displayed times and dates identified for some covert activity in America for the future.

The engineer rightly assumed that these were to be intended potential targets. Peter would need to study the book closer to get a better idea of what the manual was really all about. There were also a lot of notes written in Urdu or Arabic, which Peter could not understand.

At the back of the book were some newspaper cuttings showing prominent people. Their faces were clearly visible. Notes in ink were written by the edges of the newspaper again in an unfamiliar scrawl.

On the table was a black covered book. He hastily picked it up and turned it over He observed the printed capital dirty white lettering for the first time, it read; "Training Manual!"

He looked around the room, both nervous and curious. He walked to the left hand corner of the small space. A coloured blanket concealed a mound of something. He gingerly lifted back the cover. There to his utter astonishment, was a cache of ammunition, and two AK-47 assault rifles. Peter broke out in a cold sweat.

There were also some suspicious looking packages. He thought they could be explosives.

There were timing devices, wire, a soldering iron, solder, a digital voltmeter and a spectrum analyser. Peter assumed this was for listening into and the monitoring of mobile phone conversations. There were a dozen small cartons of children's "Silly Putty." The engineer wondered about that . . . In addition there was a satellite phone user's handbook.

He froze; momentarily, instinctively knowing that he had stumbled upon an Al Qaeda, or similar, terrorist cell.

'What the Hell am I to do with this?' he asked himself looking back at the book.

The engineer peered outside cautiously and walked to the wall. He warily peered down below. Everything was as it had been when he first came to the location. His 4WD was parked by the side of the road. Both the vehicle and driver were waiting for him. He glanced at the guard and observed that he was still away with the fairies. There were no unusual activities taking place outside. The street was relatively quiet. No one appeared to be entering or leaving the building. Seizing the opportunity, Peter ran back to the dirty whitewashed outbuilding. He picked up the book that contained the disturbing evidence. His mind was confused, he was acting on instinct. Holding the book with the hand written contact details and addresses, the engineer hurriedly unzipped the laptop case and placed the book inside. His next move was to get away from the building as quickly as possible.

He tiptoed noiselessly past the guard, who was snoring loudly. Rather than take the lift the engineer decided to make for the stairwell that circled the lift shaft. He ran down the spiral of uneven concrete steps, almost falling on two occasions. Steadying himself on the loose handrail he finally reached the ground floor. Nonchalantly Peter ambled out of the building at a normal walking pace, so as not to arouse suspicion. A few women in black abayas sat on a long bench seat just inside the open doorway. Children played and chased each other mischievously around the centre doorpost of the main entrance. Nobody appeared to take any interest in the casually dressed foreigner.

When Peter got to the roadside he fell into the car out of breath and instructed his Indian driver, 'Gopol take me back to the hotel and please hurry. I have forgotten something.'

'*Aamma. Sare, sare, Iya!*' (Yes. OK, OK, Sir), the Indian driver responded in Tamil, engaging the car into "drive" as he sped off along the open road.

* * *

Back at the Radissons Hotel Peter hurried towards the business centre.

'I need to do some photo-copying,' he said to the desk clerk urgently and nervously out of breath.

'Certainly sir,' the obliging employee replied with a strong Arabic accent. 'Give me the documents sir, and I will have them copied—'

'No!' Peter interrupted firmly. 'These are restricted documents. I have to copy them myself for my company and immediately.'

'Yes, sir! Of course! I understand. If you will come this way please . . . .'

Peter removed the red covered notebook from his computer case. In the relative privacy of the room he copied the pages of the book. The photocopy machine seemed to be working very slowly. As he copied the pages he discovered more drawings and sketches with loose notes on chemicals to be used for gas attacks. There were biological warfare techniques and the making of explosive devices. Reading the words hastily, reminded him of a ballistics course that he had once attended some years before, when he was in the army.

After twenty-five copies on A4 sheets of paper, Peter carefully inserted them under his laptop. Remembering the addresses and contact numbers in the UK he was about to make more copies when two smartly dressed hotel employees entered the room. There was no time to make further copies. He felt certain that there was enough photo-copied evidence for the British authorities to be interested in.

The engineer was certain that something sinister was being planned. Hurriedly, the book was replaced under the laptop.

The engineer made a hasty exit from the hotel and returned to the waiting car.

'OK. Back to the site, Gopol, and please be quick. *Jeldi, jeldi*,' Peter instructed the driver. He had ter get back to the rooftop before the book was discovered missing. The driver did as he was told and made the journey in record time.

Just as the car pulled up by the rooftop site, Peter observed four men entering the building. 'Four men, four beds of cardboard, and four cases,' he thought. 'Could these be the occupants of the small outbuilding?' They were wearing round white caps and loose-fitting Pakistani-style clothing. He presumed they had just returned from Friday prayers at the mosque. The men were facing towards the counter as he entered the foyer. They were busily engaged in conversation.

* * *

Peter checked the lift; it was on the ground floor. Deciding not to take a chance and risk the lift stopping en route to the eighth floor, thereby causing a delay, he decided to climb the stone steps two at a time. When he finally reached the ninth floor at the rooftop he was once again breathless, and feeling slightly dizzy. He had taken two weeks exercise in under two hours! On arrival to the flat roof he noticed the guard was still sleeping soundly, and appeared not to have stirred since the engineer had left the building around an hour earlier.

Just as he was about to make his way towards the outbuilding with the makeshift beds, to return the book, he heard men's voices trudging up the stairs. They had evidently taken the lift.

The elevator stopped short by two flights of stairs on the eighth floor. Peter realised that he would not have time to reach the far building, return the book to its rightful place, and then enter the radio room without being seen. There was only one option left open to him.

The master key opened the lock of the transmission room easily. The door swung outwards. On entering the room, Peter turned the light on and closed the door. Then he removed the laptop from its case and pressed the on/off button. The computer went through the process of starting up. There was a collapsible table that had been left ready for use. Peter placed the laptop on the table and hastily removed the manual from the laptop case and searched for a suitable hiding place. There was a tight space at the top of the BTS transmission cabinet. Peter wedged the book between the metal casing and the inner shelter wall. It was hidden from sight.

'No one would ever think of looking there,' he said to himself confidently.

Swiftly, he turned back to his computer, and plugged it into the radio cabinet to make it look as though he was industriously employed. Peter's mind was racing. He was breathing heavily. There was no way that he could do any work, and no time to check the alarms. He hoped the technician's reports were correct and accurate. In hindsight, there was no real reason for doubt, but the engineer was a perfectionist when it came to work.

The noise of the four men walking towards their room grew louder as they walked past the radio room. They were laughing and joking. The Asians were speaking excitedly in English, but the words were muffled from outside the shelter with the heavy door closed.

Then someone shouted something indiscernible. Peter could hear the men speaking in their own language, and was unable to decipher what was being said.

The men had entered the small building, when the loud babble of voices suddenly died down.

An uneasy silence descended on the group. Peter sensed that there was definite cause for concern.

It was obvious to the Asians that someone had entered their room.

Their precious book was missing!

Then there was an excited and heated exchange of words coming from across the rooftop.

The men walked back towards the sleeping guard.

One of the men kicked the security man. He instantly woke from his slumber.

Peter heard the Asians speaking very excitedly and loudly in Urdu.

The guard had replied, presumably, that he hadn't seen or heard anyone coming or going. The Asians sensed that there *was* or had been someone else on the rooftop, of that they were certain.

One of the men observed that the radio room door was slightly open. Peter had been observing the four-man gang through the narrow opening. Then the voices grew louder and more excited as they advanced towards the shelter. The engineer busied himself pretending to download data. Suddenly, and without warning the door opened fully. Peter felt the hot blast of mid-morning air fighting with the cold controlled temperature discharging from the air conditioning unit.

'Salaam alaikum.'

Peter turned and saw a Pakistani man standing in the doorway.

'Alaikum salaam' he replied in return, immediately recognizing the man from the foyer of the building.

'Sadiq, what are you doing working here on a Friday, it is the holy day?'

'I am here to get this equipment ready for tomorrow morning,' the engineer replied.

'Have you been to any of the other rooms on this rooftop?' the voice certainly had a distinct Yorkshire accent, and the man was dressed in Pakistani clothing.

'No! What rooms? I've never seen any rooms other than this one,' he lied.

'Then if you have not been in my room, someone else has. Some stuff has been disturbed. Is there anyone else here with you?'

'No! Only the guard,' replied Peter. 'Maybe it was him.'

'Where are you from?'

'I am from England, the same as you by your accent!' The Asian ignored the remark.

'Why are you working on the holy day?' The accent was definitely broad Yorkshire.

As the man got more agitated, the Pakistani accent became more pronounced.

'I told you already. I am here for the Ministry of Telecoms. As I said earlier, I have to get all this radio equipment ready to go on air for tomorrow morning. I am sorry. I have a very busy schedule and not a lot of time to spare. You'll have to excuse me.' He turned his back on the Asian and made to look as if he was once again busily employed.

'I have to get off the rooftop and quick,' he told himself. Then looking behind him again, he saw that the Pakistani man hadn't moved, and was still standing in the doorway observing him. The Asian looked at the engineer, somewhat perplexed, and unsure as to what to do or say next.

'Look, here's my card with my details. If you have any doubts about my credibility, or if you're concerned about my being here, give the office a call,' Peter advised, in an effort to break the pregnant silence. The engineer hoped that he sounded convincing, by giving the impression that all was well and that he was on the rooftop, just doing his job, which indeed he was initially. This was the sole purpose of his visit.

The Pakistani looked disinterestedly at the printed business card and shoved it unconcernedly into the pocket of his long coat. He was clearly unimpressed.

The card gave nothing away, other than the engineer's name, the name of the Saudi company he worked for, his company email address, and company mobile phone number.

The Asian descended the three steps and walked back towards the guard. He argued vehemently with the security man. Both their voices rose in anger. Again he spoke in Urdu. Peter couldn't understand a word that was being spoken. But he could hazard a guess as to the nature of the conversation. The Pakistani was obviously infuriated that someone had intruded into the room, and that a valuable item was missing. Also the guard had been sleeping and not doing his job. The watchman was probably arguing that it was Friday, and it should be his day of rest.

While the heated exchange continued, the engineer unplugged the laptop, turned it off, and once again placed the computer over the sheaf of photocopied papers in the case.

He then looked through the open doorway, and checked that no one was coming back to the shelter. Frantically the engineer made a grab for the book. It was an effort retrieving it from its tightly sandwiched position. The book was wedged very tightly between the metal casing of the BTS radio cabinet and the prefabricated wall. Eventually, it came free. Placing the hardback book in the back of his trousers, Peter pulled his long shirttail out in order to cover any sign of the object. The photocopies were hidden from view by the body of the computer.

'If I get caught with the book,' the engineer thought, with the weaponry in the building in mind, 'it will be the worse for me.' Peter turned off the light, locked the door, descended the three steps, and walked towards the exit. He was conscious of the volume tightly pressing against his buttocks. He knew that he had to front the situation out if he was challenged.

'Ali,' someone called out. Peter turned and saw another Asian calling the one talking to the guard. The Asian indicated that the stranger was about to leave. It was the same man that had spoken to him earlier. 'So his name is Ali,' Peter thought.

'Wait!' instructed Ali.

Peter turned. Being a very hot day the sun was bright and blinding. It was difficult to see clearly as he squinted at the Asian. Ali stood in front of the stone stairwell thereby blocking the path of the engineer's intended descent.

Peter took this to be confrontational.

'What have you got in that bag?' Ali asked the engineer. His colleagues moved forward as one, presumably in case there was any trouble.

Peter found himself assessing his chances if there was to be a fight. He positioned himself so that his back was to the wall as he slowly unzipped his case. He weighed up the situation, his chances of escape and the opposition. They were all about the same height as him. The Asians were of a slightly less build but were young. They looked fit and agile. The terrorists had probably received some form of combat training and self-defence.

Peter was well versed in martial arts; although a little rusty and slightly overweight, he was also aware that he was unfit having not trained for a long while.

'However,' he thought, 'I could push Ali down the stairwell while the man was distracted.'

But there were four of them, five if he included the guard.

Deciding discretion to be the better part of valour, he replied, 'My laptop and the manual.'

He then opened the case cautiously. The metal flat blue lid of the Toshiba laptop was exposed to view. The papers were well hidden out of sight.

'What manual?'

'This manual, it is for the BTS radio equipment,' he replied in a matter-of-fact tone of voice, as if they were interested. Removing an Ericsson instruction paperback book from another pocket of the case, Peter handed it to the Asian. The others edged forward, but realised it was unrelated to their quest for the missing book. Dismissively, they backed away and just stared at the Englishman.

Ali looked at him again; his eyes were narrow and sinister. There was no doubt that he was by now even more suspicious of the engineer now, than he had been before, but nothing could be proved.

'Why were you in such a hurry to get past us in the hallway? You seemed to be in a bit of a rush.'

His English was perfect. This suggested to Peter that he had grown up in the UK. The Pakistani had probably been brought up in the Bradford area. The engineer smiled nervously in an effort to appear both casual and friendly.

'I left something in the car that I needed in the radio room for my work,' he lied. 'Not only that, but today is Friday and I wanted to get the job finished. I need to have some quality time to myself, the same as you guys.' He again made a pitiful attempt at smiling. Replacing the technical folder carefully inside the pocket of the laptop case, he stood uneasily waiting for the next question.

There was a far from companionable silence hanging in the air.

'What?'

'What do you mean what?" Peter asked the Pakistani again trying to sound casual.

'What did you forget when you went back to the car?'

'Oh! I see what you mean!'

He zipped up the laptop case and placed the bag on the ground between the wall and his leg.

Then reaching into the map pocket, in the leg of his khaki denim mock army fatigues, he bent down slightly and felt for the object.

'This,' he replied, pulling out a yellow Fluke digital multi-meter. Again, the Asian looked nonplussed. Peter replaced it back in the pocket.

'Well,' he began with an air of well-being, 'It has been really nice meeting you guys although why you are here on the rooftop I have no idea. You obviously don't need to sunbathe. Ha! Ha!'

The remark fell on deaf ears.

Peter then nodded to the small assembly once again. 'And now I really *must* be off. *Masalama, sadiq*,' (Goodbye my friend), he said in Arabic.

Again, he tried to appear as laid-back and casual as he could. Slowly he moved away from the wall and edged towards the stairwell. His heart started to beat faster.

Ali asked him for a third time;

'Are you sure that you have not been in our room?'

'Positive!' Peter lied. 'The only room I entered is the one you saw me in—that one there.' He indicated to the radio shelter. 'That's the room I'm interested in. Why would I want to go into any other room? What is in there? Why do you keep asking me the same question? My work is with the radios and equipment, that's why I am here. I am not a building inspector. Those outhouses are of no interest to me!'

The Englishman had had enough of parleying words with the Asians for one day. With his back to the wall, he sidled determinedly past Ali. At the same time, he was hoping that he wasn't going to get a shove in the back as he was about to descend the concrete steps. Brushing past the man, the engineer sauntered down the stone stairway. Outwardly, it looked as if he hadn't a care in the world. Deep inside, his heart rate was double what it should be.

The Asian and the guard stared incredulously after him. The lift was still in its top floor position.

Apparently, nobody had requested it since the Asians had used it last.

The engineer again decided not to take it. Out of sight, he hurriedly ran down the stairwell that circled the lift shaft for a second time that day. Peter pressed the lift buttons as he descended each of the floors. 'That will slow down the Asians if they decide to use the lift to follow me,' he thought. When the engineer finally exited the building, he was out of breath for the third time that eventful day, and his heart was racing. Reaching the ground floor, he walked as casually as he could towards the waiting car. Daring not to look up towards the rooftop, he felt sure four pairs of eyes were watching him from above.

*   *   *

Back in the hotel room, Peter was shaking with fear and trepidation. He realised the importance of his discovery, and was suddenly overcome by anxiety. Reaching into the minibar, he hurriedly poured himself a large glass of Sid from the plastic water bottle that Dudley had provided.

There was no tonic, but he found a can of coke in the back of the small fridge. Placing a lump of ice in the glass, he took a large gulp of the contents to calm his nerves.

Unexpectedly he heaved, coughed and spluttered, choking on the near neat contents of the glass, the strength of which he had not previously sampled. He sat doubled up on the bed. His face became red. His eyes watered, he coughed again as he tried to regain some form of composure. He took a mouthful of fizzy coke from the can in an attempt to dilute the substance that had burnt the back of his throat.

Having partially recovered, he stood up, coughed again, and removed the book from the back of his mock denims. Peter sat quietly on the bed for some moments contemplating what to do next with regard to the red-covered article and its contents.

He flicked through the pages, and once again was amazed at what he found on closer examination.

Unintentionally, he had both the photocopies *and* the book with *all* the information in his possession. He knew both the Home Office and Foreign Office in London plus Special Branch, Counter Terrorist Squad, SAS, SIS, Sabre Team, and the American CIA would be more than interested.

Getting the manual back to the UK was going to be the biggest problem.

'How can I keep it hidden until my departure date?' he asked himself.

He stood up, and instantly felt more assertive. His mind raced as he paced around the room like a caged animal, whilst deep in thought.

He added a drop more coke to the near empty glass in his hand, and looked around the room for a suitable hiding place. The adrenaline coursed through his veins, and this drove him onwards to do something positive. Unable to risk taking the photocopy papers anywhere, even less the book, he contemplated what he should do next. The British Embassy in Riyadh was an option. No! They had been useless in the past. Years before in 1995, he had requested a security update from the British Embassy in Riyadh after the bombings in Alkobar. Due to the Consulate's lax security updates for British expats, all the British citizens dialled the American Embassy for security status information. The Americans were more forthcoming and efficient in these matters than the British High Commission. The security levels had been, green, yellow, amber, or red.

Peter's mind drifted back to something he had once read. "It is both naïve and a fallacy to believe that British diplomatic missions abroad exist to help out their nationals who have got themselves into trouble. Rather, they exist to promote good relations with the ruling government in whichever country they are located. Whether the government is made up of very nice people, or brutal sexual deviants, murderers or torturers, the British Government tries to make the best of the situation they are in without getting too politically involved."

'Hmm, what a bunch of chinless wonders,' the man deliberated.

Peter's thoughts once again returned to the problem in hand, and again he searched the room for a secure hiding place.

Eventually, he found what he was looking for, and managed to conceal the book in a place where he felt sure that no one would discover it. Then placing the photocopies in the room safe, he felt certain the documents would be secure for the time being.

Peter decided to rest and sleep on any further decisions as to what he should do next, and with whom he should make contact.

*   *   *

It was Saturday morning. The car stopped at the gate of the Ministry of Telecoms. Gopol, handed the iqamas, (identity work permits), of himself and Peter to the armed, uniformed guard. Peering inside the car, the guard stared at Peter seated in the back, and checked the physical resemblance to the photograph. Then satisfied, he returned the ID's and waved them through.

On entering the building, Peter observed the lift doors were open, so he quickly entered.

The elevator descended to the basement. He made his way to the open conference room. Many people had already arrived and were seated around the huge oval wooden table; their notepads were open in front of them. Some meeting members raised a hand in acknowledgement when they saw the Englishman enter the room. He nodded in return and noticed a spare seat next to Dudley. Placing his folder on the table, he pulled his chair up and sat down.

'Hello, old boy. How are yer getting on? Are yer sites ready fer the launch yet?' the colonel asked in a hushed voice.

'They're coming on very well thanks, Dudley, and I have quite a busy schedule today. Listen, Dudders, can I see you on a highly important matter a bit later?'

'Gosh! This *does* sound intriguing. Does it involve Sid?'

'It is extremely important, and I am deadly serious, Dudley,' Peter interrupted. Then, not wanting to offend his colleague, he replied with a half smile, 'Yes! Sid could well be involved!'

'OK! Where do yer want ter meet, yer place or mine?'

'Better make it mine,' replied the engineer. 'I have something I want you to see.'

'Hmm, it sounds intriguing. OK. What time? Six-thirty this evening would suit me. I can't stay fer too long. I want ter take Lisa out ter the compound restaurant fer dinner tonight. It's our dreading anniversary, don't yer know? He ha! She thinks I've forgotten about it!' he said.

He gave Peter a wink of the eye and a grin.

'You old toad!' replied Peter playfully. 'OK that's perfect, it won't take long, Dudders, and then you can continue with your agenda.'

The sheik entered the room and everyone stood up as a mark of respect. The dignitary then took his place at the head of the table. When he had seated himself, the others followed suit.

The meeting was mundane. Peter stood up and gave a progress report, and a forecasted projection of deliverables. He handed a written account of project progress to the sheik, and was informed that he should go to Jeddah for about three days. It would require a complete evaluation of the readiness of the sites in the western region. A detailed progress report would be required for the Jeddah operation to include critical issues, on his return. The account had to be ready by or before the following Saturday morning meeting. Peter replied that he would present it on a spreadsheet for easy reading and clarity, plus both a soft copy and a hard copy would be provided. The sheik nodded solemnly in approval.

* * *

Dudley was as usual five minutes early. Peter was pacing around the hotel foyer, head down and deep in thought. He was sub-consciously walking on the off-white colour of the carpet, as if to walk on the red pattern would bring bad luck. Dudley stood for a moment by the revolving glass doors and observed his friend's strange behaviour from a distance. As he did so the duty manager from behind the reception desk also observed the strange antics.

The two men exchanged glances. Dudley shrugged his shoulders, and extended his arms outwards, smiling at the administrator. The manager nodded, returning the gesture, smiling in return, then continued with his work. 'Crazy Brit's,' he probably thought.

'Penny for 'em,' Dudley said, eventually, walking over to the engineer.

'Gosh! Yer were miles away, old boy. Where were yer, back in the UK?'

'No not really, although I wish I was there now,' Peter replied.

'OK, Peter, what's all this cloak and dagger stuff about?'

'Cloak and dagger are about right,' declared Peter. 'I think we should go to my room to discuss the issue.' He walked away from the carpet not caring about which colours he trod on, and led the way towards the lift. 'The matter is a little delicate to say the least, Dudders.'

As the two men entered the hotel room, Peter reached into the minibar removing the half empty bottle of Sid. He poured two generous measures, placed two cubes of ice into the glasses and then removed a can of newly purchased tonic water.

'This conversation has to be in the strictest of confidence,' Peter informed his guest. 'I think you are a man that can be trusted.'

'Yes, understood, old boy! Gosh! Covert stuff, eh! Are yer sure that yer want ter disclose yer business with me? Are yer in some sort of trouble?'

'It is of the highest national security importance. No I don't think I am in any sort of trouble. Well, not yet at any rate. Although, I think I could well be in trouble soon. That is why I have to let someone know about it.

'Look,' Peter continued, 'you are ex-military, same as me. I only achieved the rank of sergeant in the Royal Signals. Being an officer, you moved in different circles to me. You obviously know people in high places. That's why I need your help and advice right now.'

'Absolutely, anything I can do ter help, dear boy. Please go on.' The colonel edged forward in his chair, eager to learn more.

The engineer placed Dudley's glass of Sid, ice, and a slice of lemon together with a chilled can of tonic water, on the table next to him. He once again resumed his earlier pattern of slowly and deliberately pacing around the room, head bowed. It helped him to think. His mind was searching how to best describe the events earlier that day.

The engineer needed to choose his words carefully, as he was about to confide in his friend.

Dudley slowly raised his glass, breaking both the silence, and Peter's train of thought, and said, 'Cheers!'

Peter looked up, nodded, picked up his own glass and raised it in salute, and replied, 'Cheers!' He then took a large gulp from the chilled glass.

'OK, silly question number one, are you or your colleagues aware that Al Qaeda or similar are or have been operating here in Riyadh, or Saudi? I mean, have you heard anything on the grapevine since you have been in the country?'

'No, not that I can recall, but the buggers could be here or anywhere. Does this have anything as ter why yer called me here this evening?'

'Yes Dudders! It has everything to do with why I called you here this evening.'

The engineer then went on to elaborate to his colleague about the visit to Site 262, and the discovery he had made on the rooftop earlier the previous day.

Dudley sat in stunned silence, totally attentive, and completely immersed in the incredible story. He intermittently sipped at the Sid and tonic. He concentrated on every word of the verbal account. As he did so, he idly watched a lemon pip rising and falling in the glass of the effervescent drink. He pondered, 'Why is the pip rising and falling in this way? Maybe it is gasses or trapped air.'

When Peter completed his account, Dudley again sat in bewildered silence, deliberating and trying hard to make sense of what he had been told. The colonel had to admit that he did not know the engineer that well, and maybe, just maybe, this was a fictitious tale; but for what purpose?

'Hmm!' he mused. 'It sounds almost too incredible fer words. Where are the photocopies now? I mean yer must have some sort of proof. What yer say sounds so far-fetched ter the point of being unbelievable, especially on one of our sites.'

'Oh! There's proof alright. Do you think I asked you here because I made it all up?'

'No, no, old boy, please calm down. I just wondered where is the proof of all this?'

'In the room safe,' Peter replied.

'What about the book?'

'It's well hidden,' the engineer responded

'Do yer mind if I take a look?'

'You can look at the copies by all means, but I am not letting either the book or the copies out of my sight. Not just yet, anyway. Plus, I don't want the book's hiding place known. Not that I don't trust you, Dudders, but I have to safeguard myself at this time.'

'That's fair enough,' Dudley remarked, feeling that maybe he wasn't trusted quite 100 percent by his colleague. He moved back in the chair, and crossed his legs in an effort to get comfortable. He was not quite sure as to what to do or say next.

Peter stood up as if sensing the colonel's uneasiness of the situation. He felt there was an element of doubt in the colonel's mind as to the reliability of what sounded like a yarn. Purposely, he strode towards the built-in wardrobe, and drew the sliding door across. Punching a four digit code into the keypad of the hotel safe with the forefinger of his right hand, he waited. There was a whirring sound as the safe door obeyed the command, and swung open. Peter then removed the sheaf of copies, and returned to the table. He sat on the bed opposite the colonel and placed the copies on the table between them.

'Here, tell me what you make of these,' Peter began.

Dudley picked up the A4 papers and pored over the contents in relative silence except for the odd 'Hmm!' finally, he looked up at his colleague, and uttered, 'Incredible!'

Then after a while, he said, 'In my view, it looks as though yer have stumbled upon a terrorist sleeper cell, waiting ter strike when the time is right.

'Come ter think of it, what better place could there be fer a hideout than on a rooftop? It has a good vantage point. The guys could be airlifted by helicopter. I expect the security guard is in on the act as well,' he continued, 'and as yer know, there have been a number of European compounds blown up here in Saudi in the past. Many expats have been killed and maimed. There was the explosion at an American Marine accommodation block at Alkobar in Dammam region. That was about 1994/95?' he raised his eyebrows and looked at Peter as if for confirmation.

The man nodded in agreement.

'Then there were three hits here in Riyadh, including Al Hambra compound, off the airport road.

'That resulted in many lives lost, and serious injuries. Then attempts were made in Jeddah, at the American Embassy, and then there have been the odd drive by shootings, and car bombings in the past.

'Nowhere is safe since the farcical 9/11, old boy. Obviously, we don't know where or when these bastards are going to strike next. Not until now, that is, with this book of yours. Did yer manage ter take any photos of the room?'

'No! I never had my camera with me. I only just got away from the four Asians without causing any trouble for myself. I am sure they suspect that it *was* me that entered their room and took the book. At the moment, they can't prove anything.'

'Hmm! Pity we don't have photographic evidence.' Dudley mused. 'Look, I'll have a discreet word with someone I know at the British High Commission here in Riyadh, if I have yer approval. Leave it ter me. I am not sure what ter say about this or how ter broach the subject, old boy. I need ter go away and have a quiet think. Rest assured yer secret is safe with me. I'll probably be lost in thought on this all evening now.'

'Don't let it spoil your wedding anniversary dinner, Dudders.'

'No! No! That won't happen. Most intriguing though. Hmm! Well, must be orf, I've got to take memsahib out, or I'll be shot and no nookie for a year. Ha! Ha! Ha!'

The colonel stood for a few moments apparently lost in thought. Peter tried to decipher what was going on in his colleague's mind.

Then Dudley asked, 'Does anyone else know about this apart from me?'

'No!' replied Peter, 'and that's the truth. You are the only one privy to this.'

'Good,' the colonel replied. 'Let's keep it that way fer the time being. Leave it ter me ter make contact with our man at the Embassy. That's if I have yer approval?'

'Yes! Yes! If you can be sure he can be trusted?'

Dudley handed the papers back to the engineer, drained his glass, and placed it carefully on the table. 'I think so,' he replied, then confirming, 'I know so.' They briefly shook hands, and the colonel left.

* * *

Ali made the dreaded call on the satellite phone. The Arab leader, at the receiving end of the link on the Pakistani borders, was silent all the while Ali was speaking, taking in his every word. When the Asian had finished his delivery, the silence was suddenly broken as the terrorist leader erupted into a rage, and began shouting in an extremely agitated manner. The cleric told Ali, in no uncertain terms, that the engineer had to be found. The book, with all the contact details had to be recovered immediately.

After the document had been retrieved, the English infidel was to be killed in order that he could not impart any information to the American or British authorities.

This action was *not* to be carried out *until* the book had been repossessed, and back in "safe" hands.

The notorious Egyptian terrorist leader Ahmed Mubarak was on his way to Riyadh to collect the priceless document. There had been months of planning and research gone into the manual. Mubarak's task was to oversee the fanatic's terror activities, both in England, and Saudi Arabia. Mosques would be used as a shield to cover the planning and attacks. It would also be a very bad thing for the imam in Pakistan, if the book was not recovered, and fast.

The cleric continued to tell Ali and the others not to be so careless in the future. If the book was not found, the cell members would be severely punished. Ali was given strict instructions as to the course of action that was to be taken, in order to repossess the work.

The cleric's instructions were to be followed to the letter, and without question.

After the call, Ali pulled out Maynard's visiting card that was still in his loose-fitting jacket pocket.

He looked at the name in bold mid blue printing on the white background of the Saudi Telecoms Systems business card. The letters AHT were discreetly printed on the top right-hand corner. The initials meant nothing to him. He was only interested in the name *Peter E. Maynard*, BSc. MBA, Consultant Principle Engineer.

* * *

The phone rang on Abdul Hakim's desk. *'Salaam alaikum.'*

'Alaikum salaam,' replied Tariq, one of the four terrorists.

'Kabul Hal'

'Humderella'

With the greetings over, the voice that had answered said, 'Hakim, Saudi Telecommunication Systems, AHT division. How can I help you?'

This is Tariq Mohammed from your company,' Tariq impersonated. 'Is Mr. Peter Maynard there? I need to talk to him urgently.'

'No! Maynard is not in the office today. Can I help you?' Hakim replied innocently.

'I need to contact him immediately about a technical matter. Do you happen to know which compound or hotel he is staying at?'

'Wait. I will check with HR, sadiq,' (my friend).

Arabic music played in the background while Tariq waited. A few minutes later, Hakim's voice came back on the line, 'sadiq?'

'Aiwa!' (Yes).

'Maynard is staying at the Radissons Hotel here in Riyadh, in Prince Abdul Aziz Street.' Not suspecting anything untoward the receptionist had also given Maynard's room number.

'Baaraka Allahu fik,' (God bless you). Then the line went dead.

* * *

Peter had decided to travel from Riyadh to Jeddah by road. He left at four o'clock in the morning, and his anticipated arrival time in Jeddah would be around two o'clock in the afternoon. He drove a dark green off-road Cherokee Jeep. The journey would take him approximately ten or eleven hours. He chose to drive rather than fly as he needed more time to think. Peter was still undecided about some things. He knew he had to make a decision, and it had to be the right one. He had studied the manual in depth. There were times, dates, and references in the book that were for covert activities two to three months hence. There were also references to US bases at Lakenheath, Mildenhall, and Marwell in the UK. 'Too close to home.' Peter thought.

In addition, a list of names of American nationals that resided at the Al Reim compound, and Palm Court in Riyadh, were also included in the back of the volume. Peter thought the names could be of Americans working at the American Embassy in Riyadh, or Jeddah. The listed compounds were probably another two of the terrorists intended targets.

The planned attacks were calculated for maximum impact against America and her allies. One such operation was set for the Fourth of July, the American Day of Independence at Al Hambra compound. The engineer shuddered at the thought.

Another date in the book had been set for Palm Court Compound. This attack was intended for 'Thanksgiving Day' in November. Peter figured the reason the dates were so far ahead was for the terrorists to plan their evil furtive activities in finite detail, well in advance. Many of the extremists had only achieved success as a result of their careful planning in the past. There had been careless security from the British and American authorities before, probably due to a lack of intelligence gathering. This was evident, like the bombing of the American Embassy in Nairobi, Kenya. There was also the bombing at Dar es Salaam in Tanzania (Arabic translation, House of Peace); also there was Kikambala Hotel near Mombasa, Kenya, where 250 people lost their lives. There were the London bombings, and the Marriott Hotel bombing in Islamabad, Pakistan. Then there were the bombings in Kampala, Uganda, at the Kyandondo Rugby Club, and the Ethiopian Village Restaurant on 11 July 2010 where seventy-nine people were killed in total. Then the Westland's Shopping Mall in Nairobi, Kenya, September 2013, where over seventy people were killed. Since then the security services in the relevant countries were a lot more alert.

Thankfully, there had been many failings on the terrorist's side. On a number of occasions, mercifully, their attacks did not go according to plan. This was due mainly to detonators not firing the explosives. More attention was now being paid to intricate detail by the insurgents before planting their destructive devices. The planned attacks would certainly be carried out if the terrorists were not stopped.

'They probably intended to train even more suicide bombers, and extremists in Afghanistan, or Pakistan. This would almost certainly be close to the borders,' Peter deliberated. These dark thoughts and many more accompanied him on his journey along the wide five-lane highway towards Jeddah.

Peter stopped twice on the journey to refuel, and freshen up. He walked around his vehicle at the gas station while the truck was being refuelled. Once the vehicle was parked up, the engineer drank the horrible, sweet, milky coffee that the highway cafes provided, in order to stay awake. The food and drink at the cafeterias were basic, and not hygienically handled to Western standards.

On arrival at Medina, the engineer came to a familiar T-junction. He looked to his right and observed the famous arched entrances to the holy city of Makkah.

"Muslims Only" the sign read both in English and Arabic. There was an armed police presence at the archways. Many red-and-white-painted oil drums were strategically placed outside the entrances. This is for security checks and to monitor the traffic flow into the holy land of Makkah.

Peter turned the vehicle to the left and continued his journey towards the once ancient Arabian capital city of Jeddah.

On arrival, he drove directly to the Red Sea Palace Hotel where he had previously made a reservation.

The engineer intended staying there for three nights whilst engaged in his work programme, prior to his return to Riyadh on Wednesday.

* * *

Meanwhile, back at the Radissons Hotel, sinister moves were afoot.

There was an unanswered knock at Peter's room door. Two Asian men stood passively in the quiet carpeted, corridor outside.

'Room service!' one called out. There was no reply. One of the men knocked on the door again, and called out for a second time. The strangers using a stolen housekeeping master swipe card entered Maynard's room.

* * *

Peter met with the Western regional engineers in the STS-AHT offices. He analysed the status of the network in the Jeddah region, and confirmed the number of sites that were ready to go "on air," and made notes in the meeting room for reasons of delays on the sites that had deficiencies. The engineer decided to visit a number of building locations unannounced in order to assess the work activity of subcontractors. Issues needed to be addressed. Problems needed to be solved, and solutions had to be found, and then implemented.

Quality, time scales, and budget, these were the three main criteria for the operation. Peter looked at each item in turn, and made entries into a spreadsheet on his laptop. To his delight, he observed that in the main, progress was good. The project was more or less on target for kick-off in the

Jeddah region. There were only minimal non-service-affecting deficiencies to be cleared up, such as buildings, and groundwork. All the alarm tests had been carried out successfully back to the Network Operation Centre. Most of the sites were ready to be radiated, and just waiting for sign off, and site acceptance from the client. The engineer also checked that the site documentation was up to date and correct, which it apparently had been.

* * *

Peter was by now halfway into the contract, and his thoughts continually returned to his planned homecoming. Dutifully he phoned his wife every day. Some days Kristine appeared happy, and other days she sounded sad, depressed, and even tearful. He knew that she was aching inside and missing him badly.

'Don't worry, darling. I am halfway through the contract. It's only another six weeks, and I'll be home. I'll call my mother and sister to come to visit you,' he had said in an attempt to comfort his wife on the phone.

It was no good, she was not easily consoled. It wasn't his mother and sister she wanted; it was *him* she needed. Peter decided to buy his wife some bangles at the gold souk, (market), in the centre of Jeddah. He pictured in his mind the fine, shiny bands of gold on her delicate, olive wrist.

* * *

'You say you think your man stumbled across what he took to be a sleeper cell whilst carrying out his work?' George Fotheringaye of the Foreign Office sat opposite Dudley on a green leather captain's swivel chair behind a matching green leather-topped teak desk. The walls of the room at the British Embassy building were of oak wood panelling. Book shelves ran along one side of the room. Books and folders littered the shelves in no particular order.

George was a tall, well-built man in his mid-forties. He wore a dark blue pinstripe suit and a starched white shirt. His tie had the wide diagonal maroon and dark blue stripes signifying the Brigade of Guards. His shiny patent black leather shoes mimicked those of Dudleys. The man from the British Embassy sat with both elbows on the desk. He rested his chin in his hands, making a steeple with the fingers of both hands as he listened intently to the colonel's account.

Absent-mindedly, he lightly touched his lips and nose with the tips of his fingers, looking as if in prayer.

'Yes, old boy. I actually saw the photocopies meself. Peter hadn't enough time to copy everything. He had to get back to the site and return the book before it was discovered missing. Unfortunately, or fortunately, depending how yer look at it, he never had time ter put the book back from where he got it. The Pakis, or whoever they are, were back on site. Some of the wording he feels is written in Urdu.'

'How does he know it is in Urdu?' the man from the embassy asked, removing his hands from his face. 'It could be in Arabic or Hindi.'

'Yes! It could well be. It was just an assumption. He felt they were Pakistanis by their accents and the way they dressed. Urdu, as yer know, is their national language. Also he has worked in Karachi, Islamabad and Lahore in the past for several months. I guess he has some knowledge of the language.'

'Hmm!' George deliberated. 'Where is the book now?'

'He wouldn't say. I only saw the photocopies.'

'If your man has the book in his possession, London needs to get their hands on it and PDQ. All the time that this Peter guy has it, his life is in great danger. That is *if* what you're telling me is the truth. I have no reason to doubt you, Dudley, and this could be quite a find. Now we don't want to get the Saudis or the Americans involved. I think it is best if this is handled by us, and London. I would like to examine the papers, also the book. I would also like to visit this rooftop place to see for myself.

'I do not want to cause any suspicion or to draw attention to ourselves. When is your man due back from Jeddah?'

'He is expected back tomorrow afternoon,' Dudley replied.

'Ah! Yes, Wednesday,' declared George Fotheringaye as he scribbled down some notes.

'I have to say that I am not an expert in these matters, Dudley. We don't want to get too excited and jump to any wrong conclusions, but I do need to examine the contents of this, er, book, as I mentioned. OK let us set up a meeting for say, Thursday afternoon?

'Let's say, fourteen hundred hours? How does that fit in with your work schedule?'

Dudley nodded his head thoughtfully. 'Yes! I should think that would be OK. Peter will have to deliver his report to the sheik, by Saturday,' he said, thinking out loud.

'Thursday is a half day here so, I suggest we meet downstairs and then travel to this office block, or whatever it is, together. It will be best to dress down, if you understand me. We should look and act as if we are "part of the team," or whatever you call yourselves. We must, er, try and blend in so that we don't draw attention to ourselves, as I said earlier. Now, what does Peter wear when he visits these sites?'

'He normally wears a T-shirt or polo shirt, jeans, CAT industrial boots, and a hard hat, on occasions.'

'OK. I don't have industrial boots, or a hard hat. I suppose jeans, trainers and a T-shirt would be the next best thing for the sake of appearances.

'I am concerned that you say he found *weapons* there. We will have to play the softly, softly approach. If this book contains what you say it does, then it will be a significant advantage to our winning the war against terrorism. It will also be a very bitter blow for Al Qaeda, or whoever these suspected terrorists represent.'

The phone on the desk suddenly burst into life. George picked it up,' 'Fotheringaye,' he snapped into the receiver. 'Right, two minutes.' He put the receiver back into its cradle.

'Sorry, colonel, I have to go. I have an urgent meeting.' The man from the ministry unfolded his six foot five inch frame from the swivel chair. 'I thank you for coming to see me, and most of all, for bringing this matter to my attention. I will follow it up from here with the appropriate departments in London. Right, that's about it; until Thursday then.'

He smiled broadly at the colonel, stood up, and was by the doorway of the room in three long strides. He opened the door for his visitor. Then with his foot against it, he shook hands warmly, and Dudley found himself out in the corridor. He was escorted back to the foyer by a young man in a dark blue suit, waiting for him in the corridor.

*   *   *

It had been some years since Peter had last visited Jeddah. He spent his time on the first evening walking around the familiar narrow streets of the old part of the city. With a feeling of déja vu, he sauntered through the large souk, (market), in the old part of the ancient capital of Arabia. Just about everything and anything could be purchased in the marketplace. Among the items on display were brightly coloured silks, drab black abayas that the women had to wear to cover their bodies. There was children's clothing, Indian and Pakistani handmade merchandise, leather goods, such as wallets, purses, handbags, belts, cases, suitcases, and footwear. There was an assortment of silks and scarves which added colour to the stalls. Sweets, herbs, spices, rice, nuts, grain, fruit and vegetables were also on display. The engineer took his time to look at the variety of goods on display.

After a while, Peter walked out of the souk and crossed to the large shopping mall opposite in Balad district. By contrast, the single-storey mall was contemporary. Both the souk and Balad were in walking distance of the Red Sea Palace Hotel. He peered inquisitively into the shop windows, the goods displayed were modern. There were CD and DVD players, pocket TV's, laptops, I-pods, iPhones, miniature radios, minicomputers, GPS's, digital cameras, video cameras, and many other gadgets and electronic devices.

'The Saudi import business must be booming,' he thought as he strolled through the shopping mall. Then stepping out into the warm afternoon air, he made his way to the gold souk area of the old town. He saw the imposing STC offices that faced the ancient historic seaport and remembered his time there in the past when STC were known as MOPTT.

On his arrival, he was amazed to see the array of gold ingots, rings, necklaces, headbands, ankle bracelets, earrings, nose rings, nose pins, body piercing adornments, and wrist bracelets. The selection was vast.

There were so many male and female body adornments that were not available on his last visit.

Finally, he decided on buying Kristine three intricately patterned fine gold bangles. Each wristlet was weighed individually, and a certificate was given for the bangles in exchange for payment.

Peter retraced his steps back to the Balad shopping mall, where he bought a gold Citizen watch for his wife.

He then returned to the hotel, pleased with his purchases, and went back to his room. He lay on the bed idly watching the television. Feeling tired, he turned the volume down intending to give his wife a call after a short rest. As he lay on the bed, sleep finally overtook his good intentions.

Peter awoke with a start. He was still fully dressed. In his drowsy state, he was trying to figure out where he was. The television was flickering. Then he regained full consciousness and control of his faculties.

He looked at his watch; it was three in the morning. He had slept for five hours. A sudden urge to phone his wife came over him. She would be worried sick waiting for his call. It would be gone midnight in the UK by now. He checked his mobile phone for missed calls, but the battery had gone flat! He needed to use the hotel landline.

'Another three hours, and I will be back on the road for the long drive back to Riyadh,' he thought as he grabbed the receiver.

*   *   *

She never heard the intruder. She was sleeping soundly huddled under the duvet cover cuddling a pillow for comfort, having taken an herbal sleeping tablet.

His rubber-soled boots were covered in cling film. He wore a black woolen balaclava that covered his face, except for his eyes and mouth. His trousers and sleeves were taped at the ankles and wrists. On his hands, he wore surgical gloves. Silently he had made a forced entry through the patio door. The spade lifted the sliding door from its runners easily, thus bypassing the lock. He then silently eased the glass pane door back onto the runners and back in place, leaving it wide open for a quick exit. It was just past midnight, and the house was in darkness. Moving silently around the room he looked for a suitable location to plant the device for maximum audible effect.

Removing a Maglite torch from his pocket, he played the beam around the area as he searched.

He was just about to execute his task when the telephone suddenly let out a shrill ring. The high-pitched tone startled him in the stillness of the night air. 'What diabolical timing,' the intruder thought.

He heard a noise upstairs. Small feet landed on the wooden-carpeted floor above him.

The phone continued to reverberate close to where he was standing.

The upstairs hallway light came on, and partially illuminated the room below. He saw what he was looking for. He placed the object carefully and deliberately in a secure hidden position, and then left through the open doorway.

Small feet were padding unsteadily down the wooden-carpeted treads of the stairs.

There wasn't time to close the door behind him for fear of making a noise and being seen. He left as silently as he had entered, and disappeared towards the back of the garden. Silently he heaved himself up on top of the shed roof, and then rolled his body over the rooftop in order not to be noticed. He then dropped to the ground on the other side of the wall. The motorbike engine roared noisily into life, and then man and machine disappeared into the enveloping darkness of the night.

'It is cold downstairs,' Kristine thought as she hurried to the phone.

'Hello darling.' She said expectantly into the landline mouthpiece.

'Krissie, how are you, my love? Sorry it's late. I fell asleep watching TV. I've got to be up and on the road in three hours. I had to call you to make sure that you are OK.'

'Yes, my love, I miss you, and-' the noise of a motorbike accelerating noisily away interrupted her train of thought. 'Strange,' she thought, 'the outside traffic noise sounds louder than usual.'

'What's wrong?' Peter asked sensing something was amiss.

'I don't know. Wait! I'll be back.'

She put the receiver down on the table. At first, she hadn't noticed the glass patio door wide open. It had been pulled back to its fullest extent. Then she felt the wetness from the carpet on her bare feet. She stood at the open doorway. The wind and drizzle played on her face and tickled her nose, and the top of her bare feet. Kristine peered out into the black gloom of the night.

'So that is why the motorbike noise sounded so loud, and the reason why it is so cold in here,' she thought, 'but how is it that the door is wide open?'

There was no apparent movement in the garden, and in fact, no one was there as far as she could tell. There was a garden spade near the patio that she had not remembered seeing before. She dare not venture outside. With effort, Kristine slid the door across, but it did not click into the lock. Deliberately she unlocked the door from the inside and tried again to slide it into place. This time, the door catch engaged the lock. The Filipina turned the key. The house was secure once again.

Something was wrong. Something was *very* wrong, but she was not sure what it was.

Still drowsy from sleep, Kristine walked back to the phone. She was puzzled as to why part of the carpet was wet, and other parts were dry; then she blamed it on to the wind having driven the rain inside.

Peter, from his hotel room in Jeddah, was overly concerned as he held the phone to his ear. He tried to decipher the noises that he heard from the phone microphone in the UK.

Impatiently, he waited for his wife to return, having no idea as to what was going on.

'Hello darling. I am back.'

'What is wrong?' Peter asked, interrupting her with an unusual urgency in his voice.

'I don't know, sweetheart. The patio door was wide open. I am sure that it was closed and locked before I went to bed.'

'Is it locked now?'

'Yah! And it is bolted!'

'Good girl. Are you sure that you locked it?'

'Yah! I think so.'

'Well, if you only think so, then you cannot be sure,' he exclaimed. Frustration and exasperation were mixed in his voice together with concern. 'Go and check.'

'Darling, please don't let us argue. It's late. It was my fault. I am sorry.'

'Well, it seems a bit strange the door being open like that, if you say you locked it. Anyway, just as long as you are safe, that's all that matters. Make sure all the doors and windows are locked day and night. Something strange could be going on. I don't want to worry you, but please take precautions in the future.'

* * *

It was no good. No matter how hard he tried, Peter could not get back to sleep. He tossed and turned as he lay in the bed. The night nadgers were gnawing at his brain, teasing him, and keeping him awake. The thoughts put fear and doubt into his troubled mind. He knew that Kristine was a bit of a scatterbrain at times, but she had always been very careful about locking up at night. It was not like her to go to bed without checking the security of the house.

Peter was uptight, and he knew that he must relax before the long, monotonous drive back to Riyadh.

Realising that sleep was no longer an option, he got out of bed and ran the water for a bath, adding shower gel. His mind was racing once again. He picked up a complimentary Nescafe sachet and emptied the contents into a cup. The water in the kettle was boiling as the bathwater ran in the tub.

Adding sugar and powdered milk, he then took the cup of hot mid-brown coffee into the bathroom. The warm foamy water in the bath was both welcoming and relaxing as he stepped into the bathtub, sinking deep into the bubbles. The luxurious water lapped around his body and felt good. He sat up slightly and sipped at his hot coffee. Laying back into the soothing lather once again, he tried to apply logic rather than emotion to the situation back in England.

'There is nothing worth stealing in the house,' he thought. 'The other possibility will be vandals or a rapist!' The thought sickened him. 'Supposing the person is inside the house and Kristine had unknowingly locked him *in?*'

He was becoming paranoid. Common sense told him that there was most certainly a simple explanation for the occurrence.

After he finished bathing, Peter spent the remaining two hours of the morning, prior to his departure, keeping busy. He wrote up the Jeddah reports on his laptop computer, and then sent off some personal emails to his family and friends back in the UK. An hour later, still concerned, he phoned his wife again, waking her up for a second time that night.

'Thank the Lord,' he said out loud into the mouthpiece. 'You are alright!'

* * *

It took ten hours to drive back to Riyadh; the journey was both mundane and uneventful. Memories of the phone call kept returning to him during the long drive in the darkness of the early morning. 'How could it have been that the patio door had been open?' Kristine had told him that she thought she had locked it before going to bed. This was now an additional worry to him, and he was too far from home to do anything about any personal problems.

Peter still wasn't quite sure what he should do with regards to the book issue.

He laughed at himself. There always seemed to be something for him to worry about. The engineer had read somewhere that "worrying is negative, and never gets positive results." He tried to put the thoughts out of his mind and concentrate once more on his driving.

As he drove into the dawn, he observed, as he had done on his way to Jeddah, the monkeys on the jebels (mountains) at Taif. He had dreaded the long, arduous drive down the long winding chicane, spiralling steeply away in front of him. Cars were dangerously overtaking on what appeared to be blind bends, despite the double yellow lines and warning signs. The open side of the mountain had been reinforced with heavy metal crash barriers.

Many drivers had lost control of their vehicles and ended their lives, and the lives of others, at the bottom of the ravine. Their belief that Allah was protecting them had proved wrong, many times.

Once back onto the main highway, Peter again observed the overturned, crashed and wrecked vehicles along the side of the freeways. They served as reminders that one had to be vigilant, and alert whilst driving along the tedious wide highways. Many drivers had ended their lives falling asleep at the wheel on the long stretches of the open five-lane public roads.

Finally, the Jeep entered a service station and was refuelled. The oil and water was checked.

Peter drank some more of the horrible sweet milky coffee in the service station, hoping what little caffeine was in the cup would assist in keeping him awake. He walked around the car park, yawned, stretched, and paid for the fuel and then drove off.

Tired and weary, Peter eventually arrived back at the Radissons Hotel in Riyadh. It was two o' clock in the afternoon.

For the second time that day, he ran a bath. He lay soaking in the soothing hot foam-covered water. This time, instead of coffee as a stimulant, he was accompanied at the bath by a large glass of Sid and tonic, with added ice and a thick slice of squeezed, shrivelled up lemon from the fridge complimenting the drink. Mercifully, Dudley had kindly renewed his stock of Sid on his last visit to the hotel.

The water was relaxing as he lay in soak once again. He turned over everything in his mind as lay in the soothing hot water.

The report was ready for the sheik, and senior management. Peter had re-read the account, cross-checked and edited it on the spreadsheet on his laptop. After that he had carried out the final read through, and was pleased with the result. It accentuated on the positive, giving solutions for the issues and possible risks. It was accurate and informative, short and to the point— just what the sheik would expect to see, with no unexpected unpleasant surprises.

Then his mind again wandered back to Site 262, the rooftop site, and the discovery of the book, and the possible sleeper cell.

'Had Dudley made contact?' he wondered. 'What was the reaction from whoever it was at the British Embassy that the colonel was going to meet with?'

He would look at the scribbled notes in English and Urdu, or whatever it was, once again when he got out of the bath.

The incident at home with the patio door being wide open returned to his mind continually. It was like a bad dream. It was very rare that the door was ever fully opened, especially for the time of year, and time of night!

His mind was racing, and the urge to do something positive came over him very strong, almost like an obsession.

He had an uneasy feeling in his mind. Something disturbed him. Almost like a sixth sense telling him that "all was not well." He was getting these premonitions more frequently now. It was weird.

'Maybe I am becoming a psychic,' he thought. The feeling was still there, something was not right; but what was it? What could it be that was wrong?

Hurriedly he washed, and then eased himself out of the bathtub.

He yanked at the chain attached to the plug, thus releasing the water. Grabbing a neatly folded, clean, white towel, from the chrome rack on the bathroom wall, he hastily rubbed it over his chest and back. Then wrapping the towel around his waist, he walked towards the wardrobe.

Pulling back the sliding door, it exposed the wall safe—the engineer's eyes widened in total disbelief.

The safe door was not fully closed, and when the door was completely opened, the safe was empty! It had been forced open.

'*Shit!*' He walked over to the bed and dragged it away from the wall. Then lifting up the carpet and underlay, he found the remaining pages. They were still undisturbed exactly where he had hidden them three days previous.

After his meeting with Dudley at the hotel, Peter had decided to divide the photocopies into two lots as a precaution.

One half he left in the safe, and the other papers, he had placed under the carpet. At that time he was not one hundred percent certain with regards to Dudley's trustworthiness. He felt at the time that he could not afford to take any chances. The engineer wanted to trust the colonel but, to trust someone is to take the greatest risk of all.

'Then again,' he contemplated at the time, 'without trust, nothing would ever get done! No one would get married, businesses would not be started, and banks would certainly not lend money.'

His gut feeling was that the colonel *could* be trusted, or he wouldn't have confided in him.

The man that he was referring to was "old school!"

A sick feeling encompassed him. He checked to ensure the room door was locked from the inside Peter took the chair from the desk, and placed it directly beneath the air conditioning maintenance hatch. Then pushing the panel upwards, he slid it to one side. Easing his body up and into the confined space, he was relieved to find what he was looking for. The book taken from the terrorist hideout was where he had left it before heading to Jeddah. The volume was firmly wedged in a tight space between the bathroom wall and the air conditioning unit. It was invisible to anyone that for whatever reason would enter the cramped compartment. Leaving the book in place, he returned to the open hatch, and dropped back down onto the chair. Reaching up, he replaced the cover, and returned the chair to the desk. Peter then picked up the phone and without dialing, he returned it to the cradle.

'I know I locked the safe before I left for Jeddah,' he thought. 'Who could have taken the papers? Only Dudley knew that they were hidden in the safe. No! It couldn't be him, but then who else *could* it be?' His mind was once again in a troubled state of confusion.

The engineer picked up the phone for a second time; he asked the reception desk for the duty manager.

On answering, the engineer explained briefly, that some of his things had been removed from the wall safe. The manager appeared concerned and informed his guest that he would be at his room immediately.

While he was dressing there was a sharp rap at the door. Heaving his T-shirt over his head, Peter opened the door. The duty manager was standing framed in the doorway. The man was a Saudi national, impeccably dressed in a dark blue Western-styled suit, white shirt, and dark blue tie. Accompanying him was two security men in fine blue and white-striped shirts, and dark blue trousers. Each security man held a walkie-talkie radio. On invitation, the trio entered the room. The manager asked what the problem was. Peter pointed to the open safe. The chief security man asked in broken English if anything had been taken.

'Some papers,' replied Peter.

'What papers?'

'Just papers for my work,' he lied.

'Is there anything else?'

'Yes, a photocopy of my passport, my English driving licence, a return ticket to London.

'Oh! And my travellers cheques. Thank you very much!'

'How much money was taken in total?'

'I don't know, around 500 hundred US dollars I think,' Peter replied irritably.

'You should be able to get compensation for the travellers cheques from your insurance or travel company, the duty manager advised.

'Has anything else been taken?' the head of security, asked.

'Well, if they could open the wall safe without damaging it too much, they could certainly get into my suitcase,' Peter responded.

'Let's take a look, sir shall we?'

Peter returned to the wardrobe and removed a small bunch of keys from his jacket pocket, and then returning to his valise, he unlocked it. The side locks sprung open easily, and the engineer lifted the case lid.

The hotel staff nosily peered inside the suitcase as Peter searched through his belongings. There was a jumble of underwear, socks, phone and digital camera charger leads, and some technical papers. The engineer hastily pulled the contents about, still observed by the manger and his aides.

'Oh, no,' Peter moaned.

'What is it, Mr. Maynard?' the duty manager inquired.

'My camera has gone.'

'What was on the camera?'

'There were pictures of sites for my work, my wife, and photos of our house back in the UK.'

'Again, you will be able to claim against the insurance company,' the manager proffered.

'That's not the point,' Peter protested in exasperation. 'It's not the camera itself that is so important. It's the contents that are stored in it that I'm worried about. Also, I am annoyed to think that someone was able to get into my room and steal from me, that easily. Now, someone has my driving licence with my UK address on it, my passport copy, and pictures of my wife and house. 'But it's a forced entry, can't you see?'

'It looks like the work of a common thief. Crime here in Saudi Arabia is very rare. It is probably the work of a foreigner. Do you have any enemies here, or do you suspect anyone?'

'Well, no. No enemies that I am aware of.'

The question was unexpected, and it played on his mind. On reflection, he thought, he didn't have any enemies; that is not until he had discovered the dreaded book with its alarming contents.

Suddenly everything pointed to the terrorists!

'But how could they have got into his room?' The question hung over him like the sword of Damocles, on a very fine thread.

He was not able to give any formal explanation to the strangers in his midst. He also needed time to think.

'We will interview the hotel staff that visited your room during your absence. Where was it you went? Jeddah, was it, sir?'

The head of security seemed well informed of the engineer's movements. 'Could it be that these men were somehow involved?' the engineer mused.

'I strongly advise that if you have any valuables that need to be kept secure, you should leave them in one of our safe deposit boxes at reception in future.'

'It's a bit late for that now, isn't it? My valuables have been stolen. Well, is that it then?' Peter asked slightly irritated.

'*Aiwa*,' (yes), that is all for now, Mr. Maynard.

'We will talk again once the staff has been questioned.' The duty manager did his best to reassure and appease the guest. 'In the meantime, if I or any of my staff can be of further assistance, please don't hesitate to make contact.'

'Yeah!' the engineer thought. 'You were no use before the items were stolen, and you're not much use now.'

*   *   *

'Hi, Dudders, Peter here,' he said speaking into his mobile phone.

'Hello, old boy. How did yer trip go?'

'The trip was OK, but I have a problem.'

'Oh! Peter. Not another problem. Yer seem ter attract problems like a magnet attracts ferrous metals. Ha! Ha! Ha! Anyway, I've got some *good* news fer yer. When can we meet?'

'As soon as you like,' Peter answered, 'in fact, the sooner the better and it's by no means a laughing matter.'

'Right ho! I'll finish sorting out the paperwork here, and I'll be right over. Say in about an hour?'

*   *   *

Further down the corridor, in another hotel room, Asif and Tariq were bent over a digital transceiver listening to every word that had been spoken by the engineer and hotel staff. They had also recorded the telephone conversations for analyses should it be necessary for a later time.

'The missing documents and Peter's personal losses could have been the work of a common thief, or the hotel employees!' That was what the hotel management had said. So there was no suspicion on the terrorists for the moment.

Dudley arrived at the hotel and presented himself at Peter's room on time. He was his usual cheerful self. The colonel's finely trimmed grey moustache bristled over the top of his upper lip as he smiled, when greeting his friend. The two men shook hands.

Taking a comfortable armchair by the window, Dudley observed, with approval, the engineer administering the ritual Sid and tonics. The host did the honours and then handed over a tumbler complete with all the contents. The colonel raised it cheerily, observing two blocks of ice, and a slice of lemon floating at an acute angle in the glass.

'Cheers, old boy!' he proffered.

'Yes. Cheers!' replied the engineer, raising his own tumbler slowly and deliberately.

He was deep in thought once again.

The colonel noticed that something did not appear as it should be, and his friend seemed visibly disturbed and stressed out about something.

After a short while, the engineer composed himself. Then he began to explain the discovery of his losses, and the events that had occurred earlier that afternoon in his hotel room on his return from Jeddah.

Dudley was nonplussed and could not give a credible explanation, or any reason as to the theft. Both men independently came to the same conclusion.

After a brief pause, and a few more sips of the ice cold diluted forbidden substance, Dudley informed the engineer about his meeting with the British High Commission at the DQ (Diplomatic Quarter) in Riyadh. Finally, the colonel concluded his report by saying, 'So George Fotheringaye suggests that we meet up tomorrow afternoon at fourteen hundred hours sharp, and then visit the rooftop site so he can see for himself. Is that OK with you, Peter?'

'Yes! I am at your disposal, but can we trust him? I mean, I know he's probably Foreign Office and all that. MI6 is my guess, I don't know much about these things. On the other hand, how do I know that it wasn't one of his guys that took the copies of the book? Only you were privy to this information.'

'Steady on, old boy. What *are* yer suggesting?'

'Sorry, Dudley, I do not mean to imply anything bad. Dear God! My mind is so confused right now.' He ran his fingers through his hair and stared down at the carpeted floor once again deep in thought.

'I just need to get out of here, what with the long drive, personal problems at home, and now this.'

'Yer stressed out, old boy. Yer wouldn't be any good in the trenches like that,' the colonel joked, trying to make light of things.

'I'm not in the bloody trenches, am I, Dudders? I'm stuck here for my sins, in this damn place . . .

'Saudi Arabia, the biggest open prison in the world.' A trace of a smile crept over his face but did not remain there for long.

'OK. Let's take a look at the facts,' the engineer continued. 'Someone unknown to us must have had proof or assumed that I have the book in my possession. They were probably the ones that entered and searched my room. They broke into the safe, found the documents, and removed them. They took other items and stuff from my suitcase. My guess is they did that as a cover to make it look like the work of a common thief.'

'What about yer book?'

'That's safe!'

'Now, I know this might seem hard to grasp, old boy, but according ter George the buggers will stop at nothing ter get the information yer have. It is my gut feeling that it was them that paid a visit to yer room. Yer can forget George, and the Brit Embassy interfering. That's not their style. Well, not in this case anyway. But then I am not an expert in these matters.'

'But don't you see,' interrupted Peter, 'even a layman like me can work out that if it was only the photocopies that were taken, it would point to the terrorists. They or the British Embassy guy or Foreign Office or whatever you call them, would be under suspicion also. But if more than one item is taken, like money and personal things, then it looks like the work of Ali Baba—a common thief? That is what whoever took the items wants us, and the staff here, to think. It removes the suspicion from the real thieves, who I believe *are* the terrorists.'

'Hmm, yes, yer certainly have a point,' said the colonel. 'I think yer can definitely rule out the Foreign Office anyway.'

'With respect Dudley, I can't really rule out anyone or any organisation at this present time.'

'Hmm, perhaps yer right, if as yer say, more than the documents were taken, then that may have been done deliberately ter make it *look* as if it was the work of a thief, as yer say, and from within the hotel. Like a staff member.'

'Yes!' replied Peter. 'That is what I mean, and that is what they *want* us to think. Gosh! This is such a mess. The other thing that bothers me is that my address is on my driving licence, and the pictures in my camera are of Krissie and the house.'

'Hmm!' Dudley said thoughtfully. 'I see yer predicament clearer now. Let's see what George makes of all this tomorrow. Fer the moment yer need ter relax.'

'I wish I could. I probably won't get any sleep tonight now.'

'Hmm maybe a nightcap would help,' Dudley replied with a wry smile.

'Sid appeared to be the remedy for everything,' Peter thought

'Anyway, how would anyone know where I am?'

'Simple, yer could have been followed ter the hotel, followed to yer room, and spied on from a distance. Reception may have given someone yer room number with good intentions. Housekeeping also, they can't be ruled out. I really don't know. I am not a policeman, but it wouldn't be too difficult fer someone that is determined ter find out what yer movements are, and so on.

'Getting back ter the book, yer say that it is still in yer possession?'

'Yes!'

'Where is it exactly?'

'Somewhere safe, and that's all I'm saying for the moment.'

*　　*　　*

Tariq and Asif's eyes met as they listened in to the conversation in their hotel room along the corridor.

So Maynard *did* take their book, and has it in his possession. Despite the infidel's lies that he *had not* entered their room on the rooftop that day, and removed it. Now this Dudley and George from the British Embassy were involved. They also planned a visit to the rooftop the following day. The men would have to warn the others, to vacate the site, and go to another location. The situation was becoming more complex and critical by the day. The radicals continued to listen to the conversation in Maynard's room.

* * *

'Try not ter think too much about this. Sorry to hear about yer wife.'

'Thanks Dudders, I guess you're right on that score!'

'Well, must be orf and see memsahib.' The colonel stood up. 'Sorry to hear that yer wife's been so upset. It was strange that she found the patio door open during the night, maybe she fergot ter close and lock it. Look, old boy, don't put two and two together and make five. Maybe yer letting yer mind run away with yer. The matters here, and the issues at home, are probably not related. Try and look at this whole thing objectively, from a distance, not subjectively as yer are doing now, perhaps yer thinking too much.'

Dudley finished his drink, draining the contents of his glass, and placed it gently on top of the minibar, and then walked to the door

'Until tomorrow morning then. I'll pick yer up at fourteen hundred hours. Oh! And fer *goodness* sake, do get some rest, and try and relax, old son!'

The colonel seemed to give Peter's hand an extra hard squeeze concluding with, 'Everything will work out alright in the end, yer'll see,' and with a wink of the eye, and a broad grin he was gone.

* * *

The terrorists heard Peter sigh as he sat down heavily in an armchair. Grabbing the hotel phone, the engineer punched the buttons on the hotel telephone with his right index finger. He was in the process of making another call.

'Hello, darling, it's only me. Are you OK?'

'Yes quite well thanks. I'm fine. How are you, my love? Are you OK?'

'Yes. I'm OK thanks.'

'Something is wrong? Tell me what is it?'

'No nothing's wrong,' Peter lied. 'I'm just a bit tired after the long drive, that's all. I just wanted to make sure that . . .'

It was a routine husband and wife conversation, and of no interest to the terrorists as they crouched intently over the receiver. They sat diligently waiting for news and clues as to the whereabouts of their precious manual.

Asif made a call to the clerical leader on the Pakistan borders. He then confirmed to the imam that it *was* Maynard that had taken their precious book. He informed the cleric that a man named Dudley and a man from the British Embassy called George were also now involved. Asif advised the cleric, that they would be leaving their hideout on the rooftop that evening as a visit from the three men was about to take place the following day.

The cleric from his base, felt that the net was closing in on the cell members. He then gave strict instructions as to what the men had to do next.

Maynard had said in his conversation that the book was 'somewhere safe.' Asif told the cleric that the search of his room had revealed nothing, apart from the papers that were in the room safe. There were no clues given as to the whereabouts of the book.

The voice at the other end of the phone spoke slowly and deliberately in Urdu. The tone of the mullah was low, level and even. He was clearly trying to keep himself in control. Finally he said, 'Clean up after you in the place you occupied, and make sure everything is cleared away, and leave no traces. Ahmed Mubarak will be in Riyadh the day after tomorrow, he is expecting to pick up the book, and then return to London with it. He is not aware as yet that it is missing.

'Search Maynard's room again, and this time be more thorough. You know what you have to do now, and this time, *do not* mess things up. It will be the worse for all of you if you do.'

With that threat hovering in the air, the satcom link was cut.

* * *

At fourteen hundred hours on Thursday afternoon, Dudley drove the metallic silver grey Toyota along King Khaled Road, and eventually into the Diplomatic Quarter in Riyadh. He steered the vehicle into the grounds of the British Embassy. Peter sat apprehensively beside him. They were stopped at the gate by two armed, uniformed policemen. A call was made to George Fotheringaye's office, and the man confirmed to the policeman that he was expecting the visitors. The vehicle was checked and the men's iqarma (work permit) were taken by security, and both men were given a visitor's badge in exchange.

Dudley drove to the parking bay, and the two men were escorted by an armed security guard to the reception area. Dudley and Peter presented themselves to the front desk, where they were requested to sign the visitor's book. They were then shown to an adjoining waiting room area.

Almost immediately after they had sat down, George Fotheringaye entered the room. Peter was surprised to see such a tall, fit, well-built man. He was expecting a small dapper chinless wonder! Also, the man was not dressed as Peter had expected. He wore faded blue jeans, a white non-descript T-shirt and Reebok trainers. Dudley made the introductions, and the two men made eye contact and shook hands firmly, and briefly. Peter felt both the strength and the warmth of the man that was to accompany them to the site.

'Rather have him on our side than not,' the engineer thought.

Dudley had dressed in a similar manner as the men had previously agreed. If questioned, the trio would say that they were field engineers on a routine visit to the site. Peter was pleased about their dress sense, but he felt uneasy about visiting the site again. He understood the need to do so, but if things got nasty, he felt the Asians would use the weapons against them as a last resort. They would stop at nothing to escape, and there would be no independent witnesses other than the rooftop guard. The three Englishmen had no armed back up, and their only defence was that they were there on company business.

* * *

On arrival to the building of Site 262, the three men sat in the vehicle for a few moments in silence. They observed the traffic flow and people going about their everyday tasks. Satisfied that everything appeared "normal" and that there were no obvious lookouts, neither on the ground or on the rooftops, George suggested that they enter the apartment block. The men took the lift to the top floor and trudged up the remaining two flights of uneven concrete steps that led to the rooftop.

There was a change of guard on duty, and this time he was very much alert. He viewed the three men with suspicion, and did not appear overfriendly. They nodded to him, 'Salaam alaikum,' the guard greeted them.

'Alaikum salaam. Engineer! Engineer!' repeated Peter, indicating himself, Dudley and George. 'Teletra.' (Three).

'Mafi mushkela,' (no problem) the guard replied in Arabic, he appeared unruffled by their arrival and allowed the men through the archway. His English appeared very basic, and he pointed to a log book for the visitors to sign. Peter and Dudley signed in as themselves; the engineer observed, with a grin, that George had signed himself as George Washington! For obvious reasons, as he did not want to reveal his true identity.

They purposely ignored all the other buildings, and Peter led the way to the radio room. He climbed the three steps leading to the door of the shelter. With key in hand, he was about to insert it into the lock when he noticed that there had been a forced-entry. Turning the handle, the door opened freely. The lock had been broken in order for someone to enter.

At first, the engineer was puzzled as to why the door had been forced. Then it dawned on him. It was a feasible assumption that the terrorists "may" have thought the book was hidden in the small radio equipment room, and had made a break-in to retrieve it. He breathed a sigh of relief that he had had the good sense to remove the volume from its hiding place when he did.

On entering the shelter, Peter turned on the light and placed his laptop case on the small table.

He pulled the door towards him and closed it. He had brought the empty laptop case to make it look as though he was on business, to anyone observing him from outside.

The three men stood inside the cramped air-conditioned room.

'This door has been forced open, since I was here last!' he explained to George and Dudley.

'It was not like this before.'

'What does that tell you?' asked the man from the Embassy.

'Well,' began Peter with a slight laugh in his voice, 'it tells me that someone has broken in to this room!'

'Yes! Yes! I know that. But what I mean is *why* would anyone *want* to break in here?'

'Well, my guess is that someone, maybe the terrorists, was trying to find the missing book containing all their contact details. Perhaps they thought it was hidden in the room. I don't know for sure. I'm an engineer, not a policeman or a psychic. That's what my logic tells me anyway. Nothing's been taken, so it wasn't thieves. Nothing's been damaged, so it wasn't vandals, and the guard will have to answer for the damage.'

'What about your own people?' George asked. 'Maybe they made a visit.'

'Good point, but highly unlikely,' interjected Dudley. 'All our engineers have pass keys to the sites.'

'What about the guard?' George enquired.

'No. It is not normal for them to have a key, or they will move their bed in the room to keep cool,' replied the engineer.

'Has anything been disturbed, since you were here last, that is obvious?' George asked looking at Peter.

'No! I already checked. The microwave radios are working as they should, and there are no alarms showing. Everything's fine, except for the door. But an intruder alarm would have registered at the NOC, (network operations centre). I will have to check that later.'

Peter picked up the site log book that he had taken from the guard on arrival and scanned the signatories.

'Look. I was the second to last entry in the book on an engineering site visit. The BTS engineers were here on Saturday last. They were expected.' Then pointing to an entry, he said, 'That is the date I discovered the cache and the book, almost a week ago!'

'Can we see the building where yer discovered the ammo, and weaponry from here?' Dudley asked.

Peter gingerly opened the door. He peered outside; the building was partially hidden from view by two other small buildings.

'Look there. The far one,' he said, pointing. 'Not the first building or the second one!'

'Right,' began the man from the Foreign Office. 'I need to take a look. Can you create some sort of a diversion or distract the guard's attention?'

'No problem, I need to ask him about the forced entry anyway. What if there's someone there in the room?'

'I'll cross that bridge when I come to it,' George replied. 'While you're dealing with the guard, I'll make my way over there,' he informed, pointing to the dirty white stone building.

'If the room is occupied, just apologise and say that you are looking for the room where the spare parts are kept.' Peter advised.

George nodded in agreement, not really understanding what the engineer meant by "spare parts."

Peter and Dudley descended the three metal steps. The man from the Ministry remained in the shelter, hidden from view until the time was right.

'Sadiq,' called Peter to the guard while waving his right arm, and holding the black site log book. The guard was standing thoughtfully a short distance away. He looked bored, as he slowly turned his head.

'Aiwa!'

'Mushkela.' There is a problem with the door, sadiq.'

Peter guided the guard round the corner and into the shade. He indicated towards the sun, using that as the excuse to move. The real reason was so that George would not be seen leaving the radio hut and entering the suspected terrorist's outbuilding.

Dudley nodded to George that the coast was clear. From where the colonel was standing, he could observe both parties. George sprinted across to the small outbuilding, and he was out of view by both Peter and the guard.

The guard nodded. Peter demonstrated with a levering action on an imaginary crowbar on the guard's room door. He then pointed to the radio room.

With the man from the Embassy now in the outbuilding, Peter indicated for the guard to follow him.

They made their way back from the guard's quarters to the radio room. Peter pointed out the problem on the closed door. The metalwork adjacent to the lock was buckled. He indicated to the guard that an amateurish intrusion had taken place, maybe with the use of a makeshift crowbar. The guard was about to open the door and enter the room.

'Nehey,' (no) advised Peter using Urdu. 'Telecom engineer mushrul' (busy).

He gave the impression that George was in the room. The guard nodded, he half smiled for the first time, not fully understanding English. He then shrugged his shoulders, raising both arms away from his sides, demonstrating that he knew nothing about the damage to the door. Peter stared into the guard's eyes. The guard did not hold his gaze. He knew something, but he was not going to give anything away to the Westerners.

'Mafi mufta,' (no key), informed Peter. He indicated a levering action again. The guard was clearly not interested and walked back to his station.

Peter followed the security man. Dudley had taken up his position once again. The guard sat on his makeshift bed. He picked up a worn green leather-bound book. It was the Koran.

He ignored the two engineers, and then proceeded to read silently from the open pages.

Dudley saw George peering out of the far building. The colonel nodded to him, this indicated that it was safe to return. George emerged from the building, making his way hastily back to the radio room.

Peter left the guard, and he and Dudley walked back to the shelter.

'Well?' asked Peter on arrival inside the radio room.

'There's nobody in the room, and there's nothing there,' replied George.

'Impossible! What about the bedding, weapons, and all the stuff that I saw?'

'There's nothing there I tell you. The room's empty—no beds, no weaponry, no nothing except for a makeshift wooden table!' The man from the Embassy explained.

'But that's impossible,' the engineer repeated. 'I must see for myself.'

'Wait a minute, Peter. Smell this.' George raised the fingers of his right hand towards Peter, and then to Dudley's nostril

'What does that smell like?' asked George.

'Marzipan or almonds,' replied Peter.

'My word, plastic explosives!' declared Dudley.

'Precisely, so there may have been some suspicious goings-on in that room, and you were probably right, Peter.'

'I still need to take a look for myself,' the engineer insisted.

He checked on the guard who had just laid out a small prayer mat. He was standing for a moment solemnly with his head bowed. His back was to the trio. He was facing towards the east. Somewhere a mosque burst into life and then another. '*Allahu Akbar.*' (God is great). It was the call to prayer. Now was the time to walk to the building.

He arrived at the small brick structure. The rickety wooden door squeaked on its fatigued rusty hinges as it was forcibly pulled open. George was right. The table was there as it had been before, and that was all. The place had been thoroughly cleaned out. The middle outbuilding was again empty apart from a few superfluous cables. The small pull along suitcases had also disappeared.

'Where were the terrorists hiding now? Where was their cache?' he asked himself. 'The book must be of more importance to the activists than he had first thought. Maybe they were tipped off—but how and by whom?'

He then checked the other two concrete buildings. Nothing had changed. They still housed the same redundant tower cross members, and superfluous materials as before. There was no weaponry or suspicious looking packages anywhere to be seen. The fanatics must have cleaned up, and maybe fled in panic.

Peter returned to the shelter.

'Well?' asked Dudley.

'George is right. They've done a bunk, and we've drawn a blank. There is no sign that the extremists were ever here. The only thing we have is a forced entry, and the smell of Semtex on George's fingers. It's only supposition that it was the Pakis that tried to enter the radio room.'

'OK. So what do we do now?' queried the colonel.

'All I can do, as far as this site is concerned, is to make out a damage report on a forced entry. I'll let the office take up the issue to install a new door. They'll probably get the contractors in to fit it!'

'No! I'm not talking about the blasted damage to the door,' responded the retired army officer in exasperation. 'I'm talking about these damn terrorist types. It all seems a bit shambolic and farcical now.'

'Oh! Sorry, Dudders. I really don't know. All I can say is the bastards had got wind that we were on to them. We seem to have underestimated their intelligence. I have an uneasy feeling now about my own safety, unless they've cleared off for good.'

* * *

Asif and Tariq entered Peter's room for a second time. They surveyed the furnishings once again. The room had just been cleaned, and the bed was neatly made. They lifted up the mattress. There was nothing under there. They lifted the pillows, looking for a hard oblong shape. They searched his suitcase once again. They removed the minibar; they looked behind it and underneath. They checked the safe for a second time—it was still empty. They moved furniture, opened drawers, lifted the top of the water cistern, they read through his reports. They lifted the television set and removed the back, then replaced it, having found nothing. The bath panel was removed and replaced. Their search proved futile! The Asians were clearly irritated. The two men firmly believed the book was hidden in the room somewhere, but where? The second search had again revealed nothing.

Finally, the terrorists came to the conclusion that Maynard either had the book with him; it was in his vehicle, or with a third party.

Worse still, if it was now in the hands of the man from the British Embassy, it would be almost impossible to recover. If that were the case, it was imperative that they get the notebook back at all costs, and quick. Now was the time to act. They had waited long enough, and time was now their enemy, and it was running out for them fast. It was necessary for a confrontation!

* * *

There was an uneasy silence in the vehicle as Dudley drove his truck back to the Radissons Hotel. Each man sat alone with his own thoughts. To break the uneasy atmosphere, the colonel suggested they all dine at the hotel restaurant. 'Hot food and a full belly would put things right,' he thought good-naturedly.

The bill would be charged to his AHT expense account.

As the three men entered the foyer, they were observed by one of the Asians.

Sohail had observed them entering the lobby. He was seated facing the door with an English version of the Arab News on his lap. He picked up his walkie-talkie and spoke quietly into it, 'The eagles have landed. They are going to the restaurant.'

Tariq and Asif remained in their room. Tariq called the fourth member of the gang. 'Ali, go to the car park. Check the silver grey Land Cruiser, the silver grey Toyota, and the green Cherokee Jeep.' He then read out the Saudi index plate identification for each of the vehicles.

* * *

To the right and at the rear of the hotel foyer was a restaurant. Twenty-five tables were draped with parrot green damask cloth. As the trio entered, they were met by the Filipino maitre d'hôtel. He enquired whether they had booked a table. Dudley answered in the negative. Not that it appeared to matter whether they had booked or not, as the bistro was empty. They were guided to a table near the entrance. George declined, and opted for a table set for four in the far corner of the room.

A Filipino waiter came to the table and presented each man with a large leather bound menu.

The colonel instantly ordered a large bottle of water.

The waiter returned with the water, pouring each man a generous amount, and then proceeded to take their orders.

Peter kept it simple, ordering warm artichoke to be followed by a chicken salad.

Dudley and George selected minestrone soup followed by a spicy grilled salmon fillet, vegetables, champ potatoes, dill oil, and wasabi crème fraiche.

The assembly made small talk until their meals arrived.

During the meal, Peter, Dudley and George consumed their food in silence. Their minds returned to the episode on the rooftop. Each man had an individual interpretation as to the disappearance of the terrorists and their proposed activities. A "where do we go from here?" question remained unanswered.

Peter decided that he was not going to hand the book over to Dudley or George, not yet anyway. He needed time to think. Nevertheless, the events would not affect the planned Saudi assaults for a few months. There was plenty of time for the authorities to act, and intercept a proposed attack. They could follow up the addresses in the UK, and then make arrests. Peter felt a strong urge to return to England, and make contact with the Home Office, the Foreign Office or whichever the appropriate intelligence organisation was. The book contained issues affecting both national and international security.

His immediate intention was to make enquiries with the AHT HR (human resources) department in the morning to see about getting an exit visa stamped in his passport. He planned to return to the UK for a brief visit. 'I'll use compassionate grounds, also personal family matters as the excuse. That should do the trick,' he thought.

Again, Peter looked at both men as they tucked into their meals. He had a warm feeling about the present situation. The two men appeared genuinely concerned about the issue. The engineer needed friends he could trust at this time. On the other hand, he also had to safeguard himself, and that meant being ultra-cautious with regards to the book.

Other diners came into the restaurant and were seated near to the front. When George finished eating he leant forward. He placed his spoon and fork neatly together on the plate, and then looked at Peter.

'So,' he began in a quiet voice, 'we have no photocopies, no suspect's hideout, and no knowledge as to the whereabouts of these er, terrorist suspects. It is almost as if what you saw never happened.'

'I saw the photocopies,' Dudley reminded George in support of the engineer.

'That's not good enough. I need to see the original notebook.'

'Well, you're not getting it,' Peter thought, as he scooped up the last of the fresh fruit salad and ice cream, finally complementing his meal.

He was deep in thought about leaving the Kingdom, at the time, and getting himself and the manual safely back to the UK.

'Then there is the plastic explosive, George. Yer experienced that first-hand, so ter speak. Ha! Ha!

'Pardon the pun, but it was on yer fingers,' Dudley looked at Peter, and winked his eye, a half smile spread across his face. Peter couldn't help but smile also at the remark. It appeared as if the two of them had scored a point in their favour.

'I apologise, George, if you think I have been wasting your time. I only know what I saw, and I have experienced the losses taken from my room. I will say that I am sorry if you feel that I or we have led you up the garden path. Maybe you consider the whole episode some kind of fabrication or charade.'

'Not at all, Peter. I believe that *some* covert activity took place in that room. Dudley rightly diagnosed the Semtex.

'OK,' continued George. 'Let's look at the facts as I see them. Best case scenario, you were mistaken in what you saw.'

Peter was about to protest. George authoritatively raised his right hand. His palm was facing the engineer in an effort to silence the irritated man.

'I know you weren't mistaken, Peter. *Worst case scenario,*' he stressed, pausing as if in thought for a moment. 'By removing the book, your life *could* now be in very grave danger. That is, if the book is still in your possession, or even if it's not, if those guys know it was you that took it, they will be after you, make no mistake about that. You are probably the number one suspect on their hit list.'

The man from the British High Commission paused once again, letting his words sink in. Dudley fidgeted uncomfortably with his near empty glass of Saudi champagne, wishing it were Sid and tonic, or something of an alcoholic nature.

'If the book contains documented information representative of clandestine activities, names, addresses, dates, safe houses in the UK, and Saudi as you say it does, then the terrorists will stop at nothing, and I mean absolutely *nothing* to get their grubby hands on it and repossess their precious information. That means that you could be followed. Your phone could be tapped. Your room could be bugged. You could be followed, watched, photographed from a distance, monitored as to who you are in contact with, the list goes on. Do you understand what I am getting at, Peter?'

The engineer nodded his head silently and thoughtfully. He swallowed hard. His thoughts returned to the patio door incident, in England. The reality of what George was saying rang true.

'Even your loved ones *could* be affected,' George continued as if reading the engineer's mind. 'We can do little or nothing here to protect you. Back in the UK, well, it's a totally different ball game. You will be well protected 24/7 by the Special Protection Unit, usually authorised by the CPS (Crown Prosecution Service). You will not be able to go anywhere, or travel without some form of an armed escort. It will affect not only you, but your family also. Is that how you want to live your life Peter?' His words hit a nerve with the engineer.

Again the engineer was about to venture a verbal contribution, and for a second time, he was silenced before he could utter a word.

'Terrorism is an international business. It knows no boundaries. It has no borders. There are no barriers.' His gaze shifted between the two men, including them both in the conversation. He spoke quietly and informatively.

'There is no known deterrent to stop these fanatics. Suicide bombers don't give a hoot about anything, other than killing for their Cause. They cannot be deterred in any way. Military invasion is not the answer. Look at Vietnam, Iraq and Afghanistan, for example; what a balls up, the Yanks made of that. Pardon my language! They tried bombing all and sundry into submission, but it did not work, and now the Yanks are talking about hitting Syria, and getting involved in other Middle East countries where trouble is brewing?

'When the terrorists are caught and exterminated, or incarcerated, they are seen to be martyrs. They are laughing at us, at our futile laws, and Christian beliefs, every step of the way.

'Have either of you ever heard of ITS?' Both men shook their heads.

'It is the Islamic Terror Syndicate; and it is a general title of terrorist groups like Al Qaeda, Al-Shabab, Hamas, and so on. These organisations put fear into the people of a nation. Fear then makes the populace anxious, worried, nervous, uneasy, on edge. Is it safe to go shopping? Is it safe to travel? Is it safe to take the kids to school? Is it safe to go to work? Look at Libya, and Syria. It affects the mind as well as the economy. It affects national security, the everyday way of life; it changes things as did, for example, 9/11.

'No one knows when or where these evil fanatics will strike next. That is why; *we* need the information you have, as much as they do, Peter.' He emphasized slowly and deliberately letting his words sink in. 'Terrorism is designed to destabilise a government, it causes loss of confidence with the masses against the regime of the day, and it is shrouded in religious beliefs.

'Therefore, whatever decision the government makes, you can bet your sweet life that it will be the wrong one! This in turn leads to re-elections, and the whole unhinged nonsense starts all over again with another set of elected puppet politicians attempting to solve the issues of the day by introducing new laws. This is the reason why governments have to be strong; they need to take tough action against these forces of evil. And evil is what they are.'

Dudley nodded his head solemnly, as George realised that he was getting through to the men.

'The British and American governments kid themselves that they are winning the war on terror. They are not. Look at the mess Iraq is in. Again look at Palestine, Afghanistan, Pakistan, Syria, and Egypt, as I said. Iran is standing up to the West, but for how long, and at what cost? But they are clever, and have the backing of China, Russia, Cuba, North Korea, and Venezuela. The last American president cocked up big time. George Bush put a ban on body bags containing the remains of American soldiers and marines being shown on American TV.

'Why? Because he didn't want public opinion to go against him.

'The present president doesn't want public opinion to go against him either, or his Islamic beliefs. If America turns into a Muslim State, then where will we all be?

'It is getting on for over 5,000 American troops that have been killed in Iraq alone. Numerous members of the army and marines are injured, both mentally and physically. They don't publish the number of soldiers, and marines that desert, and then migrate to Canada. You will also not see any mention of the countless innocent Iraqi and Afghan civilians that have been annihilated, and wounded by American and British forces. One wonders why there is no public outcry!

'Sanctions won't work against any oil producing nation, like Iraq or Iran. They have us by the balls. They only have to squeeze a little bit harder, and up goes the price of oil per barrel. We feel it in our pockets, as it is reflected at the pumps in the UK and the States.

'It is my guess that if there was to be a strike on Iran, it would come from Israel. They are fearful of the instability, as are the Americans. Iran is manufacturing uranium isotopes for nuclear warheads. If they are used for aggressive purposes in an air strike, it will be catastrophic!'

Dudley fidgeted in his chair. 'This is turning into a lecture of a lifetime more than a quiet chat,' he thought.

'Al Qaeda is like a virus,' George continued twirling his empty glass round in on one hand. 'New terror groups and terror cells start up frequently, just like you described on your rooftop site.

'Sudan, Somalia, Algeria, Bangladesh, Pakistan, Mali, Turkey, and you can bet your life Britain. Many countries have sleeper cells that lay dormant. They collect and collate information and feed it back to their leaders, usually by the use of satellite phones, and now by what you have discovered, Peter, there appear to be infiltrators in Saudi Arabia.

'The terrorists are trained on the roughest terrains on both sides of the borders with Iran, Afghanistan, and Pakistan. Baluchistan is a sort of no-man's-land. It is owned by Pakistan, and uncontrollable by the Pakis. It is an ideal training ground. That much we do know. In the cities, they are well organised. They use mosques or madrassas, as they are called, as a cover to train their recruits. They lay low, just waiting until they are given instructions to strike. Very often, they only work in a group of two or four members. Often, one cell will not be aware that a neighbouring cell exists, unless instructed to join forces. Many activist cells work independently of each other with a specific task to do.

'As I said, this is the reason why something that you may have in your possession, and that belongs to the terrorists, is so important for us to have, Peter. It is also something these guys will die for, and ultimately kill you for. We, the British, need this evidence in order to be one step ahead in this war on terror. We have to fight this evil, in order to stop it from spreading. The terrorists masquerade under their religious beliefs inciting the Islamic masses into rioting.

'Another example, look at what happened when the Danish cartoonist depicted the Prophet Mohammed. It was what those Islamic extremists wanted. It caused the Muslim world to rise up in anger, and voice their outrage in the West, and the Christian world, calling for a jihad (holy war). 'All these extremist Muslims need is an excuse, any excuse. Yet if you read their holy book, the Koran, nowhere does it say to kill and maim innocent men, women and children. Only to rise up and oppose those who are against Islam, the infidels, that's us, by the way—Christians.

'But if a sentence is taken out of context it can be misinterpreted to mean something completely different, like for instance, a reference in the Bible. Do you understand?'

Peter nodded, feeling like a small schoolboy in front of the headmaster. He was bored and restless having sat in the chair for nearly an hour and a half. The engineer was waiting for the punch line.

But he could not see it coming. It appeared still some way in the distance. George was obviously very well informed, and making a point.

'Hmm!' contributed Dudley thoughtfully.

'That is how these fundamentalists work. This is what Abu Hamza at the Finsbury Park Mosque was doing. The bastard was inciting racial hatred against British Christians. He succeeded, but where did it get him? He has now been extradited to the States. He is seen by many Muslims as a martyr to their cause. We, the British taxpayers are keeping people like him and his family in relative luxury. He still has his houses in England by the way. The State is still paying out, but his property should be confiscated for what he has done. The do-gooders in the UK stuck up for him and reminded the government of his human rights. It makes me sick to be honest.

'His family should be deported, but the nanny state (Britain), does not want to upset ethnic minorities.'

Dudley uttered another thoughtful 'Hmm!' Peter glanced up at him, and took the utterance to mean some sort of an agreement as to what George was saying. The engineer took advantage of the brief respite in conversation.

'Do you think my wife could be in danger in the UK?' He asked.

'Not wishing to pour oil on troubled waters, Peter, but quite possibly, yes. These people are fanatics. They believe their activities are righteous. They become sacrificial lambs to the ultimate slaughter, and eventually as I said, martyrs to their cause, or mujahedin.' (holy warriors).

'Well, my wife's pictures were on my camera that was stolen. My address is on my UK driving licence, my passport copy taken. These items were stolen from my suitcase, and in the wall safe in the hotel room, the photocopies of the book were also taken. That's why I'm worried about the loss of my things.' Peter emptied the remnants of the (non-alcoholic) Saudi champagne from the glass and again swallowed hard. His mouth was dry.

George sighed.

'Also, the patio door at our home was found to be wide open a few nights ago, after she had apparently locked up and went to bed. I was in Jeddah at the time.'

'That does not sound good to me,' remarked George showing concern. He looked at Dudley, and then back at Peter. 'Did she report the incident to the police?'

'No I don't think so,' replied Peter. 'I never thought about that. I never told her about the book.'

'I don't want to worry her.'

'It may be an idea to inform the local police in the UK so that they can keep an eye on the place,' George suggested. The colonel nodded his head again solemnly in agreement.

'Keep this book thing between us, that's my advice. Do not tell your wife anything about it—she doesn't need to know. Do not tell anyone else either, in case you are overheard.'

'Thank you for the advice, George,' Peter replied. Then in an attempt to lighten up the atmosphere, Peter unexpectedly raised his arms in the air, and placed his hands on the table.

'Anyone fancy a Sid and something, to conclude our discussion in my room?'

He looked at Dudley and winked. Then hastily added, 'don't worry, Dudders, I was given a plastic water flagon of the stuff from someone I know at British Aerospace while I was in Jeddah.'

Dudley looked at George, and then looked back at Peter, then not giving George a chance to decline the offer or protest, he said, 'OK Why not? Come on George, what d'yer says?'

The conversation wasn't really over as George was trying to steer the tête-à-tête back towards him He was also hoping to leave the hotel with the terrorist's manual. Dudley called for the bill, paid it, and the three men alighted from the table, making their way to the lift, and ultimately to Peter's room.

* * *

Sohail made a call on his hand held radio, 'It looks as if the three men are going to Maynard's room. Stand by!'

'*Acha. Shukria.*' (Good! Thank you) was the reply from Asif in his hotel room. He would be listening in to the men's conversation.

* * *

Peter unlocked his room door, and the two men followed him inside. The engineer suddenly stopped in his tracks. He immediately saw that something was wrong.

The bed had been made, but it also appeared as though the covers and pillows had been disturbed.

The housekeepers were normally very meticulous, and tidy in their daily tasks.

Thoughtfully, Peter removed three frosted glasses from the minibar. He prepared the drinks giving the usual generous measures. The engineer picked up his glass and drank a generous mouthful. He felt that he needed a strong drink.

Dudley anticipated having a few Sid and tonics, and did not want to take a chance driving back to the villa. He took his mobile phone from his jacket pocket and called the driver informing him that he and George would like to be collected from the hotel in about an hour and a half's time. He needed the driver to take him back to the villa, and then George to the DQ, (diplomatic quarter).

When the two visitors were settled, Peter picked up the ivory-coloured landline phone by the bedside cupboard. Once again the duty manager was called.

'I want you and the housekeeping manager to come to my room *right now*,' he instructed the manager.

'*Aiwa.* We'll be with you immediately, Mr. Maynard.'

Dudley and George looked at each other in wonderment, not knowing what was wrong.

Shortly after the call, there were three loud raps at the door. Peter paced hurriedly across the carpeted floor towards the door and opened it. The duty manager stood outside the room with a tall man of dubious origin. Both men were smartly dressed. Peter ushered the men into the room.

'Salaam alaikum,' they said in greeting to Peter and his guests as they entered the room.

'What is the problem now, Mr. Maynard?' the manager enquired in a somewhat jaded manner.

'The *problem* is the state of my room. Look at the bed. The pillows and covers are not properly arranged. The drawers and furniture were not in this untidy fashion as you see now when I left earlier. The safe has been opened once again. What is your explanation for this?'

The duty manager turned and looked at the tall man for some sort of an explanation. He received only a blank expression, and a shrug of the shoulders in response to the question. The housekeeping manager looked at Peter and asked if he could use the hotel phone; Peter nodded.

The manager spoke to someone in Urdu, and then replaced the receiver.

'The houseboys are on their way,' he informed the guests. Then, sensing the tense atmosphere in the room created by Mr. Maynard, the duty manager advised the three guests, 'We will wait outside.' He touched the housekeeping manager on the arm, and nodded his head, indicating that they should leave.

'Calm down, Peter,' advised Dudley once the door was closed. 'Yer are stressing yerself out again.'

'*Calm down? Calm down?*' mimicked the irate engineer by now seated on the bed and running his fingers through his hair in frustration.

'Look! I'm pissed off with what is happening here. I don't think this,' he indicated with a sweep of his left arm to the bed, drawers, and furniture, 'is any fault of the housekeeping people?

'My wife thinks we've had intruders in the house back home in England but nothing's been taken.

'George says that my family could be in danger. My life could be in danger also. I saw something sinister on the rooftop, and it's not there anymore. I found a book, made copies and placed some in the safe. Someone entered my room, and opened the safe, and then removed the papers, my driving license, and a copy of my passport, plane ticket, and my travellers cheques have all disappeared. My suitcase, which was locked, has been broken into. My digital camera with pictures of my wife and cottage in England has been taken, and now this and I am being told to calm down! How do you think I feel Dudders?'

'Right Doubting Thomas,' said Peter without giving his friend a chance to reply, and by now angered, he stood up. Then looking directly at George, he walked forcefully towards the bed, and then pulled it away from the wall. Kneeling down, he lifted the carpet. Rummaging beneath the underlay, he found what he was searching for. Retrieving the photocopies, he dropped them on George's lap and said, 'Here, take a look at these and see what you make of them.' He then pushed the bed hard back against the wall.

* * *

Tariq and Asif were again listening intently to the VHF receiver. The digital chip was recording everything that was being said.

The Asians mistakenly thought that it was the book that Peter had passed to George.

The two men stared at each other.

'*Infidel*,' Tariq spat the three-syllable word out in hatred. So the book *was* in one of the three men's possession. They wondered if it had been in the laptop case all the time. The two men continued listening in to the conversation further down the corridor.

* * *

'Bloody hell! This *is* interesting. Do you have any more copies?' asked George.

'No.' said Peter in despair. 'The rest was stolen. I told you that. After I showed the whole sheaf of notes to Dudley, I split the papers into two small lots. Sorry, Dudders, I didn't know you that well at the time. No offence meant.'

'No worries, old boy, none taken.'

The colonel swirled the contents of the glass round creating a mini storm in the tumbler as the ice chased the lemon around the glass.

Peter went to the minibar once more and poured another double measure of Sid from the large plastic container labelled "Pure Spring Water" written in English and Arabic. He felt his heart thumping as the adrenaline coursed through his veins.

'Yes!' he thought, 'I need to calm down. Dudley is right.'

'I understand yer reasoning, or at least, I'm trying ter. Daresay I would be feeling the same way in yer shoes,' the colonel replied smiling, and slightly embarrassed. He twirled the glass around in his right hand once again, hoping that Peter would notice that the contents were getting rather low. Taking the hint the engineer put two cans of lemonade and one bottle of water on the table for the sake of appearances. This was so as not to arouse suspicion to the staff that they were drinking alcohol. He then poured two generous measures, inserted ice with a spoon, and topped the drinks up with tonic water.

'OK, George,' Peter continued, 'one pile I put in the safe, and the others I hid there.'

He indicated downwards towards the carpet at the headboard. 'I did that as a precaution. Obviously, I never expected to have a break-in.'

'Can I have these?' George asked.

'No!' replied Peter defiantly, taking the papers out of George's grasp. 'I think I need to remind you that up until now . . . .' his voice trailed away.

George's huge frame shifted slightly menacingly in the armchair. He leaned forward and looked directly at Peter who was again seated on the edge of the bed. The engineer stared into a pair of bottle green eyes beneath a twitching sun tanned forehead. George said in a hushed, and even voice, almost threatening, 'And I think I need to remind you, Peter, under the circumstances-'

The man from the British Embassy's authoritative words stopped short in mid-sentence.

There was an urgent rapping at the door once again. It was the two managers, accompanied by two house boys, and the head of security.

Peter opened the door, and returned to the table as the entourage trailed into the room behind him.

The engineer was still holding the sheaf of papers in his hand. He folded the wad of papers in half, and handed the copies to George.

'Here, see what you make of these. Sorry, I wasn't thinking straight.' He turned away focusing his attention on the managers and housekeepers.

George opened the papers, and re-folded them, hiding the writing, and then put the bulky twelve pages into the back left-hand pocket of his faded blue jeans.

The staff exchanged agitated words in Tamil. The houseboys protested vehemently to their manager that they had not left the room in that condition.

Peter believed them as the housekeeping manager interpreted from Tamil for the sake of the Englishmen.

The three men instinctively knew that it had been the work of an intruder. The person had probably been disturbed and not had time to make the room tidy before departing.

The head of security asked some mundane questions, and stated that he and his staff would be extra vigilant with regards to the security of Mr. Maynard's room in future.

Again, Peter expressed his disappointment, stating that he thought it was a bit late. He mentioned something about bolting the stable door after the horse had gone. The manager didn't understand what an untidy room and a possible intrusion had to do with horses.

The houseboys busied themselves tidying the room, and then sensing a slightly tense atmosphere they looked at the housekeeping manager, he nodded his head, and the entourage hurriedly left.

*   *   *

It was early Friday morning, the holy day, and Dudley did not have to go to the office. He awoke early and looked at his lovely wife asleep, lying on the crisp white bed sheets. Her head was to one side facing towards him. Her flowing long black hair was spread over the pillow. Lisa's left arm was raised, and was curled around her head on the pillow. She looked a picture. He gently pulled back the bed sheet to get out of the bed, and as he did so, his gaze fell on her small, firm, perfectly formed breasts.

They heaved ever so slightly up and down as she breathed.

He felt his manhood straining against his Calvin Klein boxer shorts.

'I had too much of the old sock red wine last night,' he reminded himself. Red wine always gave him an erection during the night, and early morning. Lager and beer had the opposite effect, and gave him what he referred to as "brewer's droop!" He looked at Lisa again. She lay there so peacefully; such a loving, devoted wife and a wonderful mother to Clarita after all the years of marriage.

He was torn between waking his wife and making love, thereby relieving his animal instincts, and carnal desires, or letting her sleep. He reluctantly decided on the latter, and went to the bathroom, and took a near cold shower.

After washing, Dudley dressed, and went downstairs to prepare breakfast. As the eggs were boiling, Clarita wandered into the kitchen in her red Minnie Mouse dressing gown. She yawned, and stretched, dropping a worn out teddy bear on the floor as she did so

'Good morning, princess. I see yer've got Fred Bear with yer again,' her father joked.

'Stop it Daddy, you're not funny,' she said, picking up the soft worn toy from the floor.

She hugged the Harrods Teddy Bear to her chest, and held it to the side of her face, protectively.

'OK, sweetheart, what would you like fer breakfast?'

'Orange juice and coco pops please, Daddy,' she replied.

'And Fred?' he again teased.

'DA-Ady! Stop it.'

'Shh! I am making breakfast for sleeping beauty so that she can have a lie in and give her a nice surprise.'

*   *   *

Peter's room phone rang. It was Dudley on the line.

'Hello, old boy, Dudley here. I've arrived at the hotel to pick up the old jalopy.

'Lisa wondered if yer would like ter come over fer brunch. Well, it's a barbecue of sorts, and snorts,' he jested. 'It'll be a twelve ter one o'clockish kick-off. I can wait and give yer a lift now, if it's convenient, ter save yer driving over.'

'Thanks, Dudders, that's so kind of you. I must admit I am not that good at patio and paving events, but I'm sure it will be most enjoyable.' The engineer stretched, and then yawned, having just awoken from a fairly deep slumber.

'What time is it? Wow! Eleven-thirty! I think some food, drink, and pleasant company would do me the world of good.'

'Well, yer've had a bad week, and yer don't have ter do much. Just sit there and shovel the grub in and wash it down with a drop of the old yer know what? I'm sure yer can manage that without too much effort. Also, yer can splash around in the pool when it gets too hot.' Dudley joked.

'Sorry, I haven't got my thinking head on yet. Just woke up from a good night's rest. OK, Dudders give me twenty minutes, and I'll be with you.'

The colonel was in good spirits as he waited in the hotel lobby. He picked up a copy of the Kuraish Times, and idly read the headlines, as he stood in the hotel foyer waiting for his friend. He was quite tranquil, and looking forward to a relaxing afternoon with his family, Peter, and friends.

After a while, the engineer appeared looking fit and well. He was wearing a clean T-shirt bearing the words "No Money No Honey," and a pair of faded blue denim jeans, and trainers.

*　*　*

It was Ali this time sitting in the hotel entrance hall, and keeping watch. 'The bird has flown,' he informed the other two Asians over the radio. This was the signal for another room search.

After a discreet period, and with no further calls from Ali, the two men walked along the corridor and entered Maynard's room for the third time.

*   *   *

It was Peter that noticed it. If Dudley had been on his own, he may not have noticed the damage for several days.

As he stood by the passenger door, he saw a bulge of rubber trim around the front passenger side window that had not been there before. Peter also observed small scratches or marks on the paintwork. These indicated that a metal instrument of some description had been inserted into the rubber seal.

'Dudley, has the car had a break-in recently?' he asked.

Dudley walked round to the passenger side of his vehicle.

'No! Not that I am aware,' he replied. Then noticing the deformity of the rubber; he exclaimed, 'Damn! Someone's tried ter break in. They may have succeeded fer all I know,' he exclaimed. Both men had tried to push the bulge of rubber back in place, but it wouldn't retract as it had been when factory fitted.

'Check underneath the car; just in case an explosive device has been planted. Make sure there is not a box or timer in the engine compartment also.' Peter instructed. 'If it's clear, then check inside and look to see if anything's missing. Check under the driver's seat but *do not* sit on the seat, until you have checked first.

'There may be a pressure switch fitted. I'll do the same with my vehicle,' Peter advised.

These "goings-on" were all very alien to Dudley. After all, he was an engineer, employed on a telecom project, not a secret agent. What with Peter's room having been broken into, and items removed, and now his own vehicle. The colonel felt that he had been unwittingly drawn into the saga of the terrorist's missing manual. This web of intrigue only happened in James Bond movies, as far he was aware.

Dudley lifted the bonnet but was at a loss to know what to look for, not being a mechanically minded person. There was the battery, the distributor, radiator, air filter, spark plugs, and other electro-mechanical apparatus. Nothing appeared to be out of the usual. He got down on his hands and knees and peered under the truck, again not sure what he was supposed to be searching for. Everything appeared as he thought it should. There was a film of sandy dirt over everything.

Nothing had the appearance of newness about it.

When Peter got to his Cherokee Jeep, he searched for scratches around the doors and windows. The rubber trim of the passenger door, in this case, had been cut, and it had slightly shrunk back as the two pieces of rubber did not meet flush any more.

He checked underneath the vehicle, under the bonnet, inside the cab, and finally under the seat.

Apart from the cut rubber, and a scratch made by a blade, there was nothing untoward.

Both vehicles had nothing missing or added. There were no apparent electronic devices installed, and no suspicious wiring. He checked the other vehicle. The passenger door was unlocked but nothing had been taken or introduced to the truck as far as he could tell.

'Why didn't the alarms go off?' Dudley asked as he walked over to Peter.

'Good question. It was because the door lock was tripped. As if the door had been opened with a key,' explained Peter. 'These guys, whoever they are, know what they're about. It certainly reflects well on their training. That's if it *is* the terrorist bastards. You can see what we're up against now, can't you? These dickheads are still about—somewhere.'

He turned and nervously looked in the distance to see if there was a pair of binoculars trained on his every move.

'Well, there are no explosives or timing devices fitted that I can see. We should be alright to make the journey back to your place,' then he added, 'but then again, I am not an expert in these matters! It's just what I learned when we used to do vehicle checks when I was in the army in Northern Ireland.'

'I shouldn't think they would want yer *killed*,' informed Dudley, as the two men entered his vehicle, 'not until they get the damn book back. Once they have the book, yer are no longer of any use to 'em. They probably assume that yer will inform the authorities. I really do think yer should leave Saudi for yer own safety, Peter, and PDQ.'

'Thank you for those few well-chosen words of encouragement. Yes! I intend to leave here as soon as I can. I have to check on the progress of my exit visa next week, to see how it's progressing. I will probably be in just as much danger in the UK as I am here.'

'Not according ter George, yer won't. Yer would get armed protection. The Foreign Office, or whoever yer going to meet with, wouldn't want yer dead. Yer have too much valuable information. The Embassy here won't offer yer any protection. By the way, George is an MI6 agent. He answers to London. Well, I am afraid yer are pretty much on yer own on this one.'

'Thank you again, Dudders! That's exactly why I need to take the damn thing back with me to the UK. There are too many extremists here,' he sat idly looking out of the window. 'Hopefully, I'll be in London before they know I've gone, and by this time next week with any luck,

'I have to meet with whoever is responsible for home security, and then get back here to finish the job off.'

'This business is extremely important as it involves both national and international security by the looks of things as yer say, and according ter George.

'Well, that's according to George's lecture of yesterday.' He gave a nervous laugh at the thought.

Dudley raised his hand to the security men at the gate of the residential compound in greeting.

The guard motioned for him to stop and proceeded to check underneath the vehicle with a mirror. They then checked inside the vehicle. Soldiers of the Saudi Arabian National Guard (SANG) sat idly watching the man with the mirror in blue uniform.

'We've already checked all that,' Peter said to Dudley, with a smile.

When they arrived at the parking bay, the two men sat in the vehicle for a few moments deep in thought. It was the colonel that finally spoke as they sat contemplating.

'I think we should both independently document *everything* that's occurred. If something happens to one of us, the anti-terrorist squad, MI6 or whoever, can carry out a crosscheck.'

'That's a pretty morbid thought. Anyway, it is a good idea, Dudley. Like a sort of diary, you mean?'

'Exactly,' the colonel replied, 'and fer now, Peter, let's put this nonsense behind us. We'll enjoy the rest of the afternoon with family, friends, a few beers, and our good old mate Sid!'

*   *   *

This time when the intruders entered Maynard's chamber, they observed the room had not been made up. Therefore, it wouldn't make any difference if they disturbed anything or not. The housekeeping staff started work later on a Friday, as many guests preferred to take brunch instead of breakfast. Asif and Tariq moved the bed away from the wall. They were certain that was the noise they heard on the receiver. Tariq noticed that the fitted carpet had been pulled away from the wall and floor at the centre of where the headboard stood. There was a space, and he got down on his knees and put his hand into the opening as he fumbled underneath the carpet, and underlay.

'There's nothing here,' he announced. 'This is probably where the book was. The carpet has been torn away from the wall.'

'The case,' Asif suggested. He pointed to Peter's black leather and canvas carrying case for the laptop. Tariq pushed the bed back in place.

The other option the terrorist agents were concerned about was this guy called George. The question was, "Had either he or the Dudley man the book in their possession, or the photocopies?" In which case, they needed to get hold of one, either or both of them, without further delay.

Peter's laptop case revealed nothing of interest. The laptop was on the desk. It was still turned on.

The engineer had checked his emails, but in his haste to leave the room, he had forgotten to turn it off.

Tariq rubbed his finger on the touch pad. The laptop was on standby. After a few seconds it came back to life. A spreadsheet came up with a list of sites, and the progress report. Tariq ignored that and went to Yahoo and checked the emails, they revealed nothing. There was only work-related stuff, mundane family, and friend's correspondence, and a few work related attachments.

Both the in and out boxes of the laptop were nondescript. He then checked Peter's address book on the computer. Again, it revealed nothing of interest. Next, Tariq went into Internet Explorer and scrolled through the websites. He checked what search engines, and websites Peter had contacted. Nothing of any significance showed up. Maynard hadn't contacted anyone in London, the British Embassy, or other authorities in Saudi Arabia by using the internet as far as he could tell.

Asif suggested he click on Skype for phone contacts. This once more revealed nothing untoward.

Neither did Yahoo Messenger.

Everything was clean, clinically clean, and the Asians still had nothing to go on.

The search in the vehicles had also revealed nothing. The conclusion the men came to was once again the wrong one.

'If it's not here, then maybe this Dudley guy or George guy has got the book.'

'It will be easier to get to the Dudley man than to the George man. Do we know where this Dudley lives?' asked Tariq.

'Sohail does. He followed him back one night. It's a place close by to Mursalat called European Homes, Arabian Homes, something like that. I'm not sure but I know it's in the Mursalat district near to STC main offices. You'll have to ask Sohail.'

'That's not far away. I think we should pay this Mr. Dudley a little visit,' suggested Tariq.

All four terrorists were getting a lot of unpleasant pressure from their clerical leader back in Pakistan, due to the loss.

The two men left Maynard's room relatively undisturbed, feeling certain that the hardback was not there. The houseboys would straighten everything up before Maynard got back. No one would be aware that the Asians had entered his room this time.

* * *

Ahmed Mubarak, the leader, had arrived in Riyadh a day early, and was staying at the Marriott Hotel, waiting to receive the book before his intended onward journey to London.

* * *

Later that day, after a pleasant afternoon, Dudley's driver took Peter back to his hotel. The engineer was feeling happy, although slightly light-headed. His thoughts always returned to his wife, and the time when they could be back together again.

The intrusion into his room, the invasion of his privacy, and the things that had happened were overshadowed as a result of a relaxing time by the pool, and barbecue.

He felt a slight depression every time he entered the hotel foyer.

For all he knew, the hotel staff could also be involved. As he walked in the direction of the lifts, he could not believe his eyes.

Sitting a few metres in front of him and momentarily caught off guard, was one of the four terrorist suspects.

Ali, on seeing Peter, hurriedly lifted a copy of the Arab News, and pretended to be reading it. He was, in fact, using the paper as a screen to shield himself from Peter's view. But it was too late!

Due to the amount of alcohol Peter had consumed, it had given him a fair amount of "Dutch courage." He quietly walked over to where the Asian was sitting, and silently sat down opposite the man. A long low light-coloured marble topped coffee table stood between them. After a brief spell, the terrorist lowered the paper, thinking that Peter had taken the lift, and gone to his room. His gaze was averted at the time as he was looking down at his two-way radio. Just as he was about to speak into the mouthpiece, Peter leant forward in the chair across the low dividing table. 'Salaam alaikum, you fucking wanker!' he said quietly, and with venom in his voice.

The Asian was both shocked and clearly embarrassed. He looked around him as if for an escape route or help. His cover had been blown. Without saying a word, or looking at Maynard, he got up and proceeded to walk towards the main entrance.

Peter jumped out of the chair and followed the man raising his voice as they walked.

'If I ever see you in here, outside, or ever again, I'll kick your fucking head in,' the outburst was out of character for the engineer. Now fuelled with Sid, and emotionally angered by recent events, the alcohol had taken over his mind, and his rational thinking. He wanted a fight and had a job to control his words, feelings, and actions. The Pakistani tried to appear casual and dismissive, but it was difficult with Maynard shouting at him at such a close proximity.

Ali walked as quickly as he could towards the entrance, giving a smile to the alerted clerks standing behind the reception desk, shrugging his shoulders as if he was the innocent party. He tried to make it look as though it was the engineer that was the one out of order, as he hurriedly made his way to the front entrance. He was by now a few paces from the revolving doors. Peter's barrage of words continued mixed with expletives. Ali was a naturally aggressive person, but managed to keep himself in control for the sake of anonymity and appearances. He was desperate to get away from the embarrassing situation that he found himself in.

The reception desk staff, and guests at the desk, were all staring as Peter continued his verbal abuse on the Asian. Other guests milling around the lobby were following the disturbance. Peter was walking beside the Asian, pointing his forefinger at the side of the man's head in a threatening manner. He was almost goading the Asian into doing something physical. It was all the engineer could do to restrain himself from actual physical violence against the Pakistani.

Both men approached the revolving glass doors of the foyer at the same time.

'Keep away from me you scum, or you're dead meat. You can tell that to your Paki mates as well!'

As the terrorist entered the revolving doors, Peter grabbed hold of one side of a door as it came into view, and gave a hefty shove. Ali felt the thick plate glass door hit him on his back, and the back of his head. He spun out of the doors like a spinning top, and fell down onto the paving stones on one knee with such force that it tore the thin cotton material of his light coffee-coloured trousers, and cut into his knee. Both his pride and his leg had been injured. The man brushed off the offer of help from the concierge as the man rushed over to assist the injured man. Ali was in considerable pain as he limped away from the hotel. He made an urgent call on the radio.

* * *

'I would not expect that sort of behaviour to be allowed in a five star hotel such as this.' Peter emphasised to the duty manager as he approached the reception desk. The manager had got to know the unpredictable Maynard quite well by now. He was never sure of what to expect next with the complex Western guest.

'What is the problem now, Mr. Maynard?' the manager enquired in a concerned and irritated manner.

'The problem *is* that the man is a homosexual. He was making lewd, suggestive remarks, and sexual advances towards me. You should keep him and his friends out of here. I have a good mind to report the matter to the GM!' (General Manager).

'That won't be necessary, Mr. Maynard. Please rest assured, sir, it will not happen again. Kindly accept my sincerest apologies. He will not be allowed to enter this hotel in future. We cannot have our guests harassed in this manner. Incidentally, he is not a resident guest here, but merely a visitor.' He motioned to the concierge to come forward.

'Well, a visitor that we can all do without, I should think.' The sentence hung in midair. There was no further comment, as the manager finished off some paperwork.

Peter walked to the lift feeling assertive. He turned just before entering the elevator and saw the manager and concierge deep in conversation.

* * *

Ali was the one that had confronted Peter on the rooftop. He appeared to be in charge of the four-man operation.

Peter had no proof, but he had a gut feeling that Ali, and his colleagues were responsible for the missing items and the intrusion to his hotel room.

Unbeknown to him, Ali was the most evil of the four terrorists, and was already plotting his revenge.

* * *

Peter took the lift to the fourth floor, and the relative sanctuary of his room. Feeling tired, well fed, and lubricated, he fell onto the bed, and was soon deep in the arms of Morpheus.

Suddenly, and without any outside disturbance, the engineer awoke in a cold sweat. The effects of the Sid were starting to wear off. The full reality of his actions flooded back into his mind like a tidal wave.

Mentally, he sensed that his life was now in imminent danger.

An unseen force was compelling him to leave the Kingdom of Saudi Arabia immediately. 'I have to be more vigilant from this moment on,' he told himself. He was now both anxious, and disturbed by earlier events.

The engineer then consoled himself with the thought that he would be leaving Riyadh by the end of the week. His exit visa should be finalised by Thursday. He walked to the minibar, and took out a chilled glass, and poured a large Sid and tonic. His hands were shaking. He sat on the bed breathing deeply. After a while, he unsteadily placed the glass on the bedside cabinet. He wearily turned over on the bed, returning to a near normal sleep.

*   *   *

It was Saturday afternoon, and Dudley was taken aback when he received a call from Lisa at four o'clock in the afternoon on his iPhone. The project had reached a crucial point as the first phase was coming to a close. The mobile telecom launch was imminent, and needed his undivided attention. The colonel had a vast amount of work to log into the computer database that day. There were reports to write, and now Lisa was begging him to come home. She had urgency in her voice that Dudley had never heard before. She would not tell him what the matter was about over the phone, but was very distraught.

'Something's come up,' he said to Peter as they passed each other in the corridor. Dudley's light grey jacket hung over his shoulder, and was hooked over his back by the forefinger of his left hand. In his right hand, he held his laptop case.

'I have ter go back to the villa, old boy. Lisa has just called me. I'm not sure what the problem is. She wouldn't say over the phone, but it seems pretty urgent. I will work from home and have everything completed by tomorrow morning. If the sheik asks about my whereabouts, be a pal and explain that I've had to dash orf. Just say I have urgent family matters ter attend ter, which in truth—I do have,' he made a half hearted attempt to smile.

'Yes, of course, Dudley. Do you want me to drop by this evening, when I finish work?' he asked.

'That's very kind of yer, but no thanks, that won't be necessary. I should be alright. I must dash. Sorry, old boy.'

Peter was concerned, and checked Dudley's office to see if there were any clues as to why he had left in such a hurry. He even looked in the rubbish bin, and checked the screwed up balls of paper. It was very odd about his colleague having to leave for home so early.

The colonel usually worked in the office until six-thirty or seven in the evening. Peter wondered if Clarita had been involved in an accident, or had gone missing.

The engineer reflected on the day's events. There was nothing untoward that had happened to suggest Dudley's haste in leaving the office. Therefore, it had to be of a personal nature, he concluded.

The meeting earlier that day had dragged on longer than usual. The sheik was again pleased with Peter's progress report from Jeddah. He said he would instruct the Jeddah Project Manager of the engineer's recommendations, and would insist the PM concentrated on getting sites on air with the engineer's suggested changes. In addition, he was not to allow non-service affecting problems to get in the way of the planned launch programme.

At the end of the meeting, the sheik requested that Peter visit Dammam next, to check on the progress of the project in the Eastern Region. Peter was pleased for a chance of a break from Riyadh once again. 'It will be good to be away from the web of intrigue that encompasses me,' he thought. 'Dammam will be a welcome change of scenery also, and one step nearer getting home.'

The engineer had already informed the sheik that he needed to take a mini-break of about four days at the end of the coming week. The sheik had merely nodded his consent, and all that Peter had to do was to provide a progress report on the Eastern Region.

There hadn't been a chance to discuss with Dudley, the events on his arrival back at the hotel.

Peter consoled himself with the thought that within a week, he would be back in the United Kingdom, and in the arms of his doting wife. His passport was at the Ministry of Interior and should be ready by the time he got back from Dammam on Wednesday. All he needed to do was to book a flight with British Airways, Saudi Arabian Airlines, or BMI. A four or maybe five day break at home would give him ample time to see Kristine, and meet with the Ministries of Intelligence, (MI5 and MI6). He would then hand over the documented evidence, and then return to Saudi in good time for the launch. That was his plan.

The project would be completed, and he could relax during the short time that remained on his contract.

The engineer parked the vehicle, and then wandered into Al Jarir Bookstore in Al Olaya Street.

Browsing through the vast range of technical books, he purchased one on satellite communications. He then scanned the huge range of the non-fiction section. Finally, he found a book that interested him called *Fallen Hero*. The engineer took lunch at Yamal Ash'am, which is an Arab shawarma fast food restaurant close by. He enjoyed two large glasses of freshly squeezed orange juice and a chicken shawarma.

Returning to work, Peter began to prepare for his journey to Dammam. After making a series of phone calls, he sent an email message informing the project director for that region, of his intentions, and his estimated time of arrival.

A meeting had been arranged for the afternoon of the following day. Peter had also made a hotel reservation for himself at the Dammam Sheraton.

When Peter Maynard left the office that evening, he decided not to return directly to the hotel as there was something that he had to do. He drove to Site 262. This time the guard showed no interest in his arrival to the site.

As he was about to insert the key into the lock of the radio room, Peter noticed that the door had been replaced.

He removed an item from his laptop case, and then concealed it in what he considered to be a safe place. Fifteen minutes later, Peter emerged from the room. He never bothered to sign the log book as it was an unofficial visit. He gave a cursory nod to the guard who at the time seemed disinterested with life in general, and said 'shukran' (thank you), and left the site.

At the back of his mind, the engineer could not help feeling that something was wrong. He decided that before he returned to the hotel, he would check on his friend and family to ensure there were no problems. The engineer just hoped that Lisa and Clarita had not been involved in an accident.

* * *

During the drive back to Arabian Homes, Dudley was very worried. There was a big question in his mind as to why he should have to be home at such an early hour. He opened the door of the villa with his key as usual, then walked into the lobby calling out as he hung up his jacket, 'Hello, darling.'

He lowered his laptop case to the floor, and placed it tidily by the wall noticing the door to the living room was slightly ajar.

'Hello, darling,' he called out again, pushing the door open wide. Framed in the doorway, the colonel stood and stared in disbelief at what he saw before him. The room appeared to have been ransacked. There was a large bed sheet covering something in front of him. As he walked forward into the room a heavy blow landed to the left side of his head. Dudley's legs buckled, and the crumpled, lifeless body fell to the floor.

The colonel gradually returned to consciousness. He was aware that water was being splashed on his face. Further encouragement was aided by light slaps to the face. Slowly, he came round.

He lifted his head slightly: there was a throbbing pain in the temple where he had been struck.

His eyes were a little unfocused. His upper body was soaking wet. He could not move his arms or legs as they were strapped to the chair

Suddenly, his eyes opened wide at what he saw in front of him. He stared in awe and disbelief. The sheets had been removed, and he saw his lovely wife sitting in a carver dining chair opposite him. Her mouth was covered with canvas tape. Her wrists were bound with adhesive tape to the arms of the chair; and her ankles were taped to the chair legs. On Lisa's right-hand side, and about one metre away from her, sat their daughter. She was sitting in an ordinary dining chair, and bound similarly as her mother. Her wrists were secured behind her, to the wooden slats at the back of the chair.

Both the female's eyes were streaming with tears.

Dudley sat facing his family. He was restricted in his movements the same as his wife and daughter were. The only exception was not having his mouth taped. His head was throbbing, and continued to give him pain. Then the colonel became aware of two men in black balaclava woollen helmets.

They came from the extreme sides of the room; one from the left, and the other from the right of the females. They wore loose fitting Pakistani style clothing. One was positioned behind Dudley's wife, the other man stood at the back of his daughter's chair. Both men were facing him, and their eyes looked menacing. This was the picture they wanted him to see on his full recovery to consciousness.

Slowly, the colonel became aware of the harsh reality of events. He and his family had been kidnapped, and were being held hostage in their rented accommodation!

One man walked a few paces away from Clarita, and then stood behind her again. For effect he removed a very long-bladed sharp knife from under his loose-fitting jacket. Immediately, Dudley recognised it as being a twelve inch, (30 cm), KA-BAR. A vicious knife favoured by the Special Air Service. The man held the knife at Clarita's throat. Her movements were restrained by her taped limbs. Her body went rigid with fear. Her eyes were bulging wide open in fright.

She looked directly at her father for help.

'Bastards.' Dudley managed to utter in a hoarse voice. He showed his anger and disgust through clenched teeth. He struggled to get free of the chair, but the bonds were too tight, and restrained him.

'Now, now! That sort of talk will get you nowhere. Nowhere at all, Mr. Dudley;' the voice had an unmistakable Yorkshire inflection, with Pakistani overtones on some words . . .

'Now, the destiny of the lives of you and those of your family remains entirely in your own hands. Your responses to our questions will determine our actions. We are merely the instruments of torture or liberation. You have the power, and er, the force that will decide what actions we will take. We are merely the tools in the game show.

'So you will determine your family's fate. Therefore, it is up to you as to whether they are injured, if they are to die, or on the other hand, if you comply with us, you will all be free to carry on with your lives. Everything is dependent on your answers to our questions. Their fate is in your hands, so to speak. So you see, Mr. Dudley, you are the decision-maker. We are the executioners or the liberators. We will act on your response to our questions. Everything is entirely up to you.'

'What cowardly bastards,' Dudley thought as he strained his wrists against the tape.

'Now, what you have to do is very simple. Just tell us what we want to know and then this unpleasantness,' he said waving his hand encompassing the disarray 'will come to an abrupt end. You will not be bothered by us ever again. You will be able to continue with your lives. *But* you need to answer our questions honestly and accurately. If you cooperate with us, we will cooperate with you. Your lives will be spared and there will be no injuries, but if you do not . . .' The sentence remained unfinished as he turned to the man holding the knife.

The Asian drew the point of the blade across the fitted, back cushion of the sofa. The stretched material opened, and then white foam stuffing emerged out of the slit.

'See how sharp is the blade of the knife, Mr. Dudley?'

The man held the knife in front of Clarita's throat, 'Razor sharp, innit?' the man holding the knife said, laughing mockingly.

Dudley stared in stunned silence. He noticed the man with the knife had a pronounced limp, and it appeared to trouble him when he walked, or put pressure on it.

The colonel was witnessing a living nightmare. He tried to make sense of the situation, and searching his mind for the best course of action to take. There was only one option left to him. He was not in a position to negotiate or argue with these terrorist fanatics. Neither was it time for bravado. He had to consider the safety of his family. He knew these evil men meant what they said, and would carry out their vile threats! It was no loss to them what happened to him or his family. They would just walk away, and disappear.

'What do you want with us?' Dudley asked.

'All will become clear in a short while, Mr. Dudley,' the man that was doing all the talking informed.

George's words came back to him, "They will stop at nothing . . . ."

'Now,' continued the speaker interrupting Dudley's thoughts, 'you, or your friends, have something that we want, and it belongs to us. In other words, it is *ours*. *You understand?*' he emphasised.

Dudley painfully nodded.

'I will begin by telling you all that we know, so that you are aware of our intelligence gathering.

You will help us by filling in the gaps and tell us what we *need* to know in order for us to get it back. Your family will be the ones to suffer if you tell us any lies, and we will know if you are lying to us.

'So it is a bit like a quiz show, or game show, so popular with you English bastards. Now think carefully before replying to each question, and take your time, but not too long. OK, game on.

'Number one, a manual with sensitive information inside was stolen from our hideout by one of your colleagues.

'Number two; some papers were photocopied from the manual that was stolen.

'Number three, we have in our possession the copies that we got back from your colleagues.

'Number four, we know that some of these papers had been handed to someone in the British High Commission at DQ here in Riyadh, a Mr. George.

'Number five; we have now recovered these copied documents from that office.'

Dudley was startled at this news. He wondered if they were bluffing, but how could they know? Up to number four, they were spot on, but how did they know about George, and the photocopies?

'Number six, we know who took the book from our base. Maynard, a Mr. Peter Maynard.

'This is what we *do* know. Now, number seven, is what we *don't* know, and this is where you are going to help us, Mr. Dudley. I must remind you again before you answer the questions, that if you do not tell us *exactly* what we need to know, and truthfully, that is, and if you lie to us; it will be the worse for these two ladies, *innit?*'

The colonel sat passively, but the last shouted word, made him jump. If this was a military interrogation, he would have held out to the last possible moment. But this was a different story. This wasn't about giving away the number of troops you had, or the positions of the men on the ground, or by which means you came to be behind enemy lines. This was about his loved ones. He didn't want his family harmed in any way.

His wife and daughter were so precious to him, and now they were pawns in this crazy terrorist's game.

The spokesman in the balaclava was in no hurry. His speech was slow, clear, precise, and measured. His sentences and actions were calculated. He wanted his words to have the maximum effect—and they did just that. The man had been well trained, and this scenario had been well thought out. The colonel realised what he was up against, and this was not the time for heroics.

'OK, game on, as I informed the man in the balaclava, pausing for effect.

'Now let's start so we can all move forward, and then leave you in peace, rather than pieces!' He laughed at his crazy joke.

The other hooded Asian gave a short laugh as he waved the knife about over Clarita's head. Lisa visibly shuddered, as Clarita burst into tears once more.

'Question number seven, for the freedom of the family, where is the manual? Or the book as you may call it? Where is the book that we are searching for, Mr. Dudley? The book that was taken from the rooftop, where is it?'

'The buggers know too much,' the colonel thought playing for time.

'I honestly do not know where the book is and that is the honest truth,' replied the colonel genuinely.

It sounded pathetic, and he knew it was not what they wanted to hear. His mind was racing. Their English was perfect with a hint of Pakistani or Indian mingled with their Yorkshire brogue.

His head throbbed. How could they have known about George, and that he had some of the photocopied material in his possession? How did they manage to get the documents back? Was George lying in a ditch somewhere?

Or were they pretending to know more than they did? Nobody could have told them.

Only two people in the hotel room knew that George had taken the photocopies with him that evening. It only pointed to one thing—Peter's room must be bugged!

'I honestly do not know, is not good enough, Mr. Dudley. Not good enough at all. OK, let us have an easier question to start with. Do you know this man?' Dudley was shown a photograph of Peter Maynard, taken from a distance. It would be no good denying his knowing the engineer. He had already been mentioned in conversation earlier.

'Yes! I know him,' the colonel replied truthfully. His mouth was dry. He licked his lips and he tried to swallow but the saliva seemed to have dried up.

'And do you know that he removed this book from a room on a rooftop here, in Riyadh?'

'I er, heard something about a book being taken. Yes!' He looked at his wife. Her eyes were filled with terror. She shook her head in despair. He tried to lick his dry lips again.

'If yer know he took the damned book, why don't yer ask him where it is? Why are yer bothering my family and me?'

'Oh, we will, make no mistake about that, but you have more to lose than he does. He may also lie. to us, and we want to hear the truth from an independent person.

'OK, now we are getting somewhere with the questioning, and you are familiar with what we are talking about; very good. We are making a little progress, not a lot,' he said, his eyes were smiling, almost mocking, 'but a little,' he continued.

'So where is it now, this book of ours?' Sohail sprung the question; his tone was suddenly a little more aggressive.

'I honestly don't know. Please believe me.'

The speaker nodded to the man holding the knife at Clarita's throat. It was Ali who was the most menacing of the four terrorists. He limped away from the young girl and towards Dudley.

He pulled the rolled up sleeve of the colonel's shirt further up to the elbow, thus exposing the man's left forearm. Ali then slowly pushed the point of the blade down, penetrating the dermis and epidermis.

Intentionally, he drew the point of the blade from near to the bend of the arm, and it was making a cut towards the wrist. The knife stopped at where the tape secured the limb to the arm of the chair. Dark red blood seeped through the skin and mingled with black hair of the forearm.

The blood overflowed and trickled down towards the red and gold wide stripes of the chair, and the polished dark wood. Clarita fainted. Lisa's eyes opened wide at the sight of her husband's wound. She gave out a muffled cry, she wanted to be sick. Tears rolled down her cheeks as she watched helplessly. Dudley winced at the burning sensation, holding his breath for an indeterminate period. He fought against the vicious sting of the cut; baring his teeth. He was not going to show the cowards that he could not take the pain, by passing out.

'Bastards!' he managed to gasp again.

'I warned you already. You see, and feel, Mr. Dudley, how easily it cuts?' Dudley gave a look of contempt to the Asian.

'Understand how easy it would be for this man to use the knife on her neck,' the terrorist's eyes looked towards Clarita. Ali hobbled back towards the young girl. His knee was giving him a lot of pain. He wiped the blade of the knife on the sofa and took up his position behind the young girl once again.

'Would you want to sit there, and watch her bleed to death? It is your choice, innit?'

'No damn you! No!' shouted Dudley hoarsely. His teeth were clenched in fear for his daughter's life. The cut on his left arm was giving him pain, and cause for concern. The wound was bleeding freely now. It dripped on the edge of the wooden seat frame. As it gathered on the arm of the chair, finally dripping onto the green shag pile fitted carpet.

'Good! So we have an understanding. Yes? The answer to the question is very simple and straightforward. You tell us what we want to know, and we will leave you alone, and no more injuries. OK. I will ask you for the *very* last time. This is your last chance to win your family's freedom without injury.

Where is the book?' he shouted the words so loud that Lisa jumped in her chair, having just come back to consciousness.

'How can I tell yer what I do not know? I don't know where it is! I am not protecting anyone. I want to protect my family, but I cannot. *I do not know where the bloody thing is! I only ever saw photocopies. He would not tell me where it was.'*

At the time Dudley would tell what he knew, for the sake of his loved ones, 'to hell with the consequences to Peter, for getting him involved and to the terrorists or anyone else for that matter,' he thought. It was more important that his family were protected, and not injured in any way.

The man asking the questions moved away from Lisa, and came round to Dudley. He stood in front of him. Bending down, he stared directly into the colonel's tired eyes. The man thought he saw fear there. The fear was misplaced. It was fear for the colonel's family; not for his own life. Dudley looked into the man's eyes. He tried to communicate, and search for a glimmer of compassion deep in the man's soul. Reasoning was the only solution left, that and a little psychology.

'Look, all I know is that a book was found by one of our engineers. He showed photocopies of the book ter me. It meant nothing, nothing at all. I called a friend of mine at the British Embassy, and he came to the hotel, and we had lunch. We discussed the matter. The Embassy man, as yer say took the photocopy documents. I saw some wording but only briefly. None of it made any sense ter me. I wasn't even interested in the damn thing. I never, ever, at any time saw the book in question,' he tried to rationalise. 'I don't know what it looks like, what colour the cover is, how thick it is, what size it is. I know absolutely nothing about the blessed thing, or its whereabouts. If I knew where it was, I would tell yer. That is the truth. I can only tell yer that it is securely hidden somewhere. I know not where. That is all I know. Believe me. It is not here, in this house, or in any of my possessions, if that's what yer thinking. Yer can cut me up inter tiny pieces, and I still won't be able to tell yer where it is. D'yer think I want ter sit here and watch my family suffer? If I knew I would tell yer.'

He had told the activists all he knew, and what they already knew.

'What you say is quite correct, Mr. Dudley. Maynard's room was checked thoroughly. The book was not found. No, Mr. Dudley, we started the cutting up with you and it will end with the ladies.'

'*You evil fucking bastards,*' Dudley's words were spat out with venom. '*May you rot in hell?*'

'Tut! Tut! Tut! We know you are involved, Mr. Dudley. You are the one that got the British authorities here drawn in.' Sohail took from his pocket a small electronic device. Suddenly the small machine came to life:'

'What about the book?'

'It's well hidden.'

'Do yer mind if I take a look?'

'Where is it exactly?'

'Somewhere safe, and that's all I'm saying for the moment.'

The recording was switched off.

The voices were of Dudley, and Peter Maynard, of that, there could be no doubt.

'Now, game over, I think, and time to start on the cutting and carving.'

The man again nodded to Ali. The Pakistani leveled the knife once more at Clarita's throat. This time he lightly pressed the blade into the area of skin close to the jugular vein. Thankfully, Clarita was unconscious once again. Her head was to one side, exposing the side of her neck to the terrorist.

The colonel frantically searched the archives of his mind in an effort to appease the kidnappers. Tears welled up in his eyes. He felt useless.

'Please God,' he thought. Then finally Dudley screamed the word.

'*Wait!*'

Lisa was startled by his sudden outburst.

The captive had eventually remembered something. The recording reminded him that when he had asked Peter where the book was, the engineer had replied that it was in a safe place. Subconsciously, as Peter Maynard spoke those words, he looked up towards the air conditioning unit in his room. It was as if to make sure the hatch was still closed, and in place. Maynard was probably unaware of the involuntary gesture at the time, and the colonel had forgotten about the incident until now.

'Did yer check by the air conditioning unit area in the room when yer searched it, just inside the door, and near the bathroom?'

'There is a removable cover in the ceiling for aircon maintenance. I think it could be in there. I saw Peter look up towards that part of the ceiling when he spoke about where the book was hidden. I never thought about that until now.'

Dudley was exhausted with both concentration, and anxiety. Sweat poured down his face. He had frantically searched the archives of his mind for the merest hint of something that would save the lives of his family, and he had eventually found it!

The two terrorists exchanged glances. They had not checked the false ceiling above the small entrance hall of the room. It was the one place they had overlooked. Of course; that must be where the book was hidden. They spoke rapidly in Urdu.

How many times had they walked underneath the hatchway when they were searching the room?

The Asians realised that Dudley did not know any more than he had told them. It was futile to carry on further questions or unnecessary mutilation. Sohail, (the kidnapper asking the questions), nodded his head that they should leave. Ali, holding the knife, mistook the gesture and made as if to cut Clarita's throat. The speaker shook his head violently. '*Nehey. Nehey!*' (No! No!)

Dudley fainted at the action. He had held on for too long. He was exhausted and totally drained, plus dehydrated as a result of the ordeal.

Ali put the knife back in its scabbard, and then placed it under his long coat. Tariq took a roll of tape from his pocket and tore off about fifteen centimetres. He placed it roughly over Dudley's mouth.

'Thank you, Mr. Dudley. You have finally told us what we needed ter know' Sohail said.

'Good night and sleep well. We will leave you in peace.'

The colonel was out for the count, and had not heard a word that was spoken. Lisa was the only one that could hear the words. She was relieved that the ordeal was over. She was confused, not knowing why this had happened in the first place, and what it was all about? Something about a book—what book? What was her husband involved in? It must be serious for men with masks to come into their home with knives and make threats. She stared at the inert body of her husband as he lay slumped at an awkward angle in the chair. Blood still dripped from the injury, but at a slower rate as it congealed with the hair of the forearm.

The Asians closed the door quietly behind them. In the lobby, they removed their black woollen balaclavas, then making sure there was no one about; they casually walked out of the villa and into the warm evening air.

*   *   *

At seven o'clock that evening, the security guard at the gate had phoned Dudley's villa in order to let him know that he had a visitor. There had been no reply.

'Maybe he's taken the family to the restaurant,' Peter suggested. The guard agreed. It was plausible. The security man had seen Dudley arrive earlier. He had also seen the engineer in the company of Dudley in the past. He asked for Peter's iqarma, and in exchange the guard gave him a visitor's badge.

Peter arrived at the Coburn-Smythe's front door. Dudley's metallic silver land cruiser was positioned at an angle as a result of being hurriedly parked in the bay.

The engineer rang the doorbell and waited. There was no answer. He then knocked on the door several times with his bare knuckles. There was still no reply. The impression he got was that the villa was empty.

It took a few minutes to walk to the small shopping complex in the compound. He checked the hairdresser, the travel shop, supermarket, library, and finally, the restaurant.

Dudley and his family were nowhere to be seen. He returned to the villa, and again knocked at the door. There were no barbecues or other activities by the poolside taking place, even though it was a warm and pleasant evening.

A door opened two villas up; and a heavily pregnant English woman appeared. Her swollen belly was exposed between a sleeveless pink top, and a pair of light grey jogging shorts.

Peter recognised her as one of the people at Dudley's barbecue.

'Hi! Have you seen Dudley or his family this evening?' the engineer asked.

'No! If they're not at the villa, maybe they are visiting friends,' she replied, 'or they could be at the shops.'

'No! I tried there.'

'Sorry, I can't help,' the expectant mother replied with a friendly smile.

Peter thanked her and walked slowly back towards the main gate. He stood for a few moments twirling his car keys around one finger. He took out his mobile phone and dialled the colonel's number. Thankfully, the phone rang but was not answered. Twice more the engineer rang the number. Something was wrong. He decided to check the villa one last time, and walked back towards Dudley's home. Maybe the family had returned while he was looking for them at the shops. He rang the doorbell again, and rapped on the black painted front door with his knuckles as he had done before. There was still no sound from within.

Peter had an instinctive feeling that something terrible must have happened. He tried using logic.

The vehicle was there signifying that the family or at least his friend was around. It was badly parked, indicating that the man was concerned about his family, and not bothering about parking prettily. Clarita would have to be at the Saudi British School early the following day. Therefore, she should be either having her tea, doing her homework, or getting ready for bed. Dudley had said that he would be working from home that evening. He said that he would clear the backlog of work that was mounting up, and had the company's laptop with him.

They weren't at the shops, and everything appeared fairly normal. So yes, maybe everything was satisfactory, and they were with friends.

But why did he leave the office in such a hurry? Why was he not answering his phone?

Were they at the hospital? Perhaps someone had given them a lift, or they were taken by ambulance to the hospital. Even the security guard had not seen the family leave. If they had visited friends, they should be back home fairly soon. No, there had to be another explanation.

He walked round to the back of the villa and checked to see if anyone was in the kitchen, and maybe had not heard him at the front door. He peered through the space of the half-closed blind of the back window. The kitchen was unusually untidy. Returning to the front of the house the engineer tried to contact the family by calling Dudley's mobile number once more.

The phone rang. He held it to his ear; then he heard a faint ringing coming from inside the villa. So maybe Dudders was inside, but why did he not answer. He tried again, still no response, as the faint ringing continued.

Peter put his face close to the glass of the living room window.

Placing his hands either side of his head to block out the light from the setting sun, he peered into the room. The net curtains gave some privacy as he stared into the gloomy interior.

Gradually his eyes adjusted to the darkness of the room. He was immediately surprised at what he saw. The living room was in a mess.

'Maybe they were moving house,' he thought.

Then gradually as his eyes became more adjusted to the dimness of the interior, he saw her. It was unmistakably Clarita. She was sitting in a chair with her head resting awkwardly on her right shoulder. Her long mousey dark hair flowed down her right arm, partially covering her face.

Peter banged on the window; there was no response from the young girl. 'Why is she sitting at such an odd angle in the chair?' he asked himself.

Instinctively, he ran round to the back of the villa, and tried the door and window. They were both locked. He looked for something to smash the thick glass with. There was a heavy terracotta pot by the fence. A bush of coriander flourished on the moist earth that Lisa was cultivating. Hurriedly and unceremoniously, Peter emptied the contents of the pot on the small patio area.

The glass in the door was reinforced with wire. There was no way that he could force an entry there. He then used the pot to break the glass of the kitchen window.

Suddenly, there was a loud smashing of glass. Shards and fragmented splinters flew in all directions into the room. He put his arm through the window frame, and lifted the latch. Then he hauled himself up through the opening and clambered over the stainless steel sink unit, and then onto the floor. His CAT boots crunched over the glass as he made his way into the living room.

On entering the area, Peter could not believe his eyes as he took in the disorder of everything.

At first, he thought there had been a robbery. All three family members were tightly bound and gagged, but thankfully, they all appeared to be alive. He observed Dudley and the wound to his left arm. He went back into the kitchen, and found a sharp meat knife. Peter walked to the chair, where Clarita was sitting with her head at an awkward angle.

He carefully removed the tape from her wrists, ankles, and mouth and then gently lifted her limp body from the chair, and laid her on the damaged sofa, placing her head on a cushion. She had thankfully blacked out when Dudley's arm had been lacerated, and had still not regained consciousness, therefore being completely oblivious to earlier events.

Peter then released Lisa from the chair. By this time, she was wide awake, and very distraught.

Tears streamed down her cheeks in rivulets once again. Peter could not understand what she was saying. It was a mixture of Cebuano and English, interspersed with heavy sobbing. Lisa went over to her daughter; she sobbed uncontrollably into Clarita's white school uniform blouse. She hugged the motionless body tightly for comfort.

Finally, Peter removed the tape and bonds that were restraining Dudley, who was by now slowly returning to consciousness, and becoming aware of the ordeal. The engineer was alarmed at the amount of blood that was on the chair and carpet. The gash on the colonel's left arm looked serious.

'What, what are yer doing here? Howja get in? Thanks, old boy. Oh, my head,' he wheezed.

He struggled for breath, his mouth and lips still very dry. Lisa wailed as she sat diagonally opposite him on the damaged sofa, still hugging her daughter, thankful that she was unharmed, and the ordeal was over. She looked at her husband.

Peter went back into the kitchen his CAT boots once again crushing and crunching on the broken glass that was scattered on the tiled floor. He found a clean tea towel and placed it under the cold water tap.

He then returned to the living room and washed away the dried blood off his friend's arm in an effort to clean the wound, and to see how deep the cut was.

The family was in a state of total shock. Clarita gradually regained consciousness. She took in the activities around her thankful to be safe and free. Then, as she became fully awake, she sat up and fell into her mother's arms. She sobbed freely as the memory of the trauma came flooding back to her. Lisa and Clarita went over to Dudley and hugged him. All three embraced each other. It was an emotional, personal, family moment.

Peter turned away feeling they needed a few moments alone, and went into the kitchen once again. He poured water into the kettle, plugged it in, and, while the water boiled, he found a dustpan and brush, and started to sweep up the debris from the kitchen floor. Tiny pieces of glass appeared to be everywhere. He had just cleared the floor, and emptied the last dustpan load of glass into the waste bin when Lisa walked into the room.

Suddenly, and unexpectedly, she threw her arms around Peter's neck. She hugged him tightly, and thanked him profusely for coming to their rescue. The engineer felt that this sudden expression of hero worship, and emotion was totally misplaced. Whilst patting her back and upper arms in an effort to comfort the woman, his feelings were confused, not knowing the full circumstances that had led to their predicament. He had an uneasy feeling that he was in some way responsible for the family's dilemma. He urgently needed to speak to Dudley in order to find out what had happened.

Lisa released her hold, and tried to smile through the tears.

Peter stated that he was about to make some hot sweet tea to help them get over the shock of the trauma.

'Well, old boy,' Dudley said wearily, and slightly tearfully as he walked unsteadily into the kitchen. 'Time ter get out of these wet clothes I guess.' He clutched the damp tea towel to his arm. The cloth had already changed colour from its original checkered blue and white, to a pale crimson. He took water from the fridge, and drank the contents from the plastic bottle. The colonel needed an excuse to leave the room.

'This is of yer making, yer know that don't yer? That blasted book has resulted in this.'

He indicated to the damage with a nod of his head.

'In the meantime, thanks fer coming round when yer did. We could have been tied up all night.'

'Don't thank me, Dudley,' Peter had an awful feeling in the pit of his stomach, by now knowing full well that he was definitely the root cause of the family's impasse.

He dreaded the thought that the family unit had received a visit from Al Qaeda or whoever.

'Well, whatever. I need ter talk ter yer in a while. I am bloody furious, but I don't want a scene here in front of the girls. I'm just thankful that no one is injured in any way; the bloody cowardly bastards.'

'OK, Dudders! I am so sorry. Do you want me to leave?' Peter asked, looking at the colonel sheepishly, and feeling as guilty as sin, and intruding into the family's privacy.

Then, he looked away, not able to hold the older man's gaze, and feeling embarrassed.

'No yer are better off staying here fer a while. I might need backup with memsahib. I will have ter make up a story!'

'What happened, Dudley?' Lisa asked as she entered the kitchen. 'Why did those men come here? What is going on? What are you involved in? What's all this about a book? What book?' Lisa was understandably, very distraught.

The small determined woman stood in front of her husband just as he was about to climb the stairs.

She had never experienced anything so terrible in her innocent life before.

Dudley looked helplessly down at Peter as he continued to make his interrupted way up the stairs.

Lisa followed anxiously and determinedly behind him.

The barrage of questions continued in the bedroom, in the bathroom, and in the upstairs hallway. Peter could tell that she was mad at her man, and understandably so. Lisa was not easily placated. She was taking out her frustration and anger on her husband. The little woman demanded some sort of an explanation. Peter heard the word book mentioned a number of times by her.

'Had Dudley told her about the terrorist's manual?' he contemplated.

The bedroom door closed, and the voices became muffled. The colonel did his best to appease his hysterical wife, but she remained terribly upset by his answers.

'There was no way that Dudley could tell his wife the truth at this time, surely?' Peter thought.

The colonel informed his wife that there had been a terrible mistake over something that had been found by Peter. The men thought he had a holy book in his possession, but they were mistaken.

They were Muslims, and it was a religious thing, he told her. There was no way that Dudley could ever explain the truth without further implicating Peter. Although, in all the confusion, Lisa's feminine intuition "told" her that her husband *was* in some way involved in something disturbing.

She came downstairs, clearly distressed. Gradually, she managed to compose herself enough to get on and clean the kitchen.

In the meantime, the engineer had moved the furniture back to where it had originally stood, and tried to clean the living room as best he could.

Lisa banged around in the kitchen taking her anger and frustration out on inanimate kitchen objects, as if they were in some way responsible. She drank the cup of tepid sweet tea that Peter had prepared twenty minutes earlier. Sensing Dudley's pent-up emotion, and his shocking part in the ordeal, she began to prepare some alcoholic beverages. Lisa knew that would be the first thing her husband would want when he returned downstairs to the living room. Her mind was totally bewildered. She was not capable of rational thinking as there were too many questions that remained unanswered.

'Why would anyone want to do such a thing? What was Dudley involved in that she did not know about? Who were those men that carried out such terrible deeds against the family? What was her husband hiding? What was it that they were after? What religious book was her husband talking about? Why would Dudley have such a thing? Why did the men have their faces covered?' These questions and many others flooded through her innocent mind as she tried to make sense of the situation whilst busying herself.

Dudley emerged making a strong effort to be calm, cool, and reasonably in control.

He descended the stairs slowly. A clean, damp, disinfected cloth was wrapped tightly around his arm.

Lisa scolded him by saying that he must go to the hospital immediately. The wound was open, and appeared deep and wide.

The colonel expressed that he didn't feel that the cut needed stitches as it was only a surface wound. The disinfectant had stung painfully as it made contact with the open flesh. In reality, the colonel felt he deserved whatever pain he suffered.

'It's just a scratch darling,' he tried to make light of the issue. Then he saw the tray of drinks.

'Strange,' he thought, 'why three glasses of Sid?' He handed Clarita an effervescent glass of coke with a knob of ice bobbing on the surface that was being bombarded by bubbles. His daughter took the glass gratefully, sipping the contents, whilst still suffering from her ordeal. She sobbed occasionally, as she hugged her Teddy Bear. Dudley gave his guest a glass, and he lifted the second glass of Sid to his own lips. Shaking slightly, he uttered a brief, but quiet, 'Cheers.'

He took a long, hard mouthful, and made a face as the contents hit the back of his throat.

Peter noticed a bruise that had formed at the side of the man's head. Dudley had suffered a lot more than he was letting on.

Then the colonel said in a raised voice, 'Darling, who's the other glass of Sid fer?'

'Me,' announced Lisa from the kitchen, and with that, she purposefully stomped into the living room, picked up the glass, lifted it to her lips, and drank greedily.

Suddenly, and unexpectedly she gasped. Her hand went to her throat; she then clutched her chest, and bent forward. She gulped in the air, exhaling noisily. She coughed, choked, coughed again, and spluttered. She held on to the back of the sofa for support.

Dudley and Peter made direct eye contact for the first time since the engineer was chastised. Watching Lisa hurriedly drinking the alcoholic beverage was a total surprise for both men. Spontaneously, they burst out laughing. Lisa straightened up, gasping slightly, not being used to alcohol. When she recovered, she raised the glass, and carefully took another gulp.

'Ugh!' she declared, 'it's horrible, but I needed it!'

Dudley smiled. His wife's amusing actions had diffused the tense atmosphere in the room. The lady of the house wandered back into the kitchen a little unsteady on her feet, but still quite compos mentis, and then she became very talkative.

'You gotta' go to the hoshpiral, darring,' she called from the kitchen, her speech slurred. 'You don' wanna the blood poison. You tell him Porter.'

'OK darling, anything you say,' Dudley winked at his guest.

'Porter!' he repeated with the hint of a smile.

'Lisa's right. You must go to the hospital, Dudders. You could have delayed concussion, and or blood poisoning.' Peter was in agreement with Lisa on that score. The colonel made a face.

'You should at least have an anti-tetanus injection for the knife wound, and stitches for the arm. It is a deep cut. Why not let me take you now, Dudders? We can chat on the way.'

'Yes, later on,' said Dudley dismissively. 'Please Lisa darling, don't fuss,' he called. 'Right now all I need is a drink.' He pointed to another freshly poured

Sid and tonic, using his right hand while the other was slightly elevated against his chest. He awkwardly squeezed a slice of lemon into the glass, and then dropped a cube of ice into the tumbler from the ice bucket. Dudley then removed four paracetamol painkiller tablets from a packet, and washed them down with Sid and tonic.

Peter stared at the colonel in disbelief.

'You've got to be kidding,' he protested.

'Bit of a headache, old boy. Cheers!' he said raising the glass in salute for a second time.

The colonel again made a face, 'Memsahib is not a happy lady?' he said in a low voice to Peter; the alcohol had started to kick in.

'It is hardly surprising with what you have all been through and the mess.' the engineer indicated to the wet carpet. It was still soiled with dried blood, and had already turned brown. He then pointed to the sofa that had previously spewed forth its contents. Peter was still wondering as to what had happened

'She'll be OK soon. Bless her. It's Clarrie I feel sorry fer more than anyone, poor little mite. Must have been scared half out of her wits,' he mused. The Sid, and maybe the tablets had finally calmed his nerves, at last the colonel was more relaxed, and back to his old self.

'So what happened? You had some uninvited visitors?' Peter asked in a low voice, when the females had left the room. 'Is that what the phone call was about earlier?'

'Yes, yer and the damned, blasted book.' Dudley showed the anger in front of his guest for the second time that evening.

'They came here, and tied up my wife, and daughter. Lisa made the call. I came back here, not knowing what ter expect. Then one of the bastards came up behind me and landed a blow on my blind side. I passed out. When I came round I was sitting bound to a chair. They threatened that if I did not tell them what they wanted ter know, my family's lives would be in danger, and threatened to mutilate the girls.

'They are cowardly bastards! They were very threatening and demanding. I must have passed out at some point. The next I knew was when I woke up as yer found me. What have yer got us involved in, Peter?' Dudley asked. He took another large swig of the spirit and tonic in his glass. Peter looked down at the green bloodstained carpet. The dark red to brown mark had been purposely missed in the cleaning up operation as a "spot and stain" remover would need to be employed.

Peter felt both guilty, and ashamed that he had brought this misfortune upon such a lovely, previously happy family.

'We underestimated them. The buggers have got yer place wired up, d'yer know that?' he asked.

'They came here thinking I had the damn book, or at least they thought I knew of its whereabouts. They know yer took the wretched thing. As George said, "these insurgents will stop at nothing." They also know that George had the photocopies. How else could they have known all this information if yer room wasn't bugged? They came here deliberately with the sole intention of torturing me and my family into submission. They asked where the damn thing was, and to let 'em have it, if not they threatened ter injure the girls.

'Sorry, old boy, but my family means more ter me than anything else in this wretched world. They played a short recording of our conversation, when yer first found the book. That reminded me of something. I told the buggers that I thought it could be in the aircon inspection hatch in yer room.' Peter shrugged his shoulders and nodded.

'I had to tell them something. One of the bastards had a knife to Clarrie's throat.'

'How did you know it was there Dudders?' Peter asked in a quiet voice.

'A hunch, I guess. Yer looked up there when yer told me it was in a safe place. Be prepared fer another visit. The best thing yer can do is get the hell out of this place. Yer a marked man, my boy, and make no mistake about that. He rubbed the side of his head. He then peeled back the TCP-soaked cloth from his left forearm. The long cut looked painfully sore and open.

'Well, it's stopped bleeding at last,' he observed.

'Yes, I know, and what you say is right, Dudley. I've made arrangements to leave Saudi.'

Then he went on to say that he wasn't bothered if his room was searched again. The book that had caused them all so much grief wasn't in that hiding place anymore.

He then elaborated on the events in the hotel lobby the evening of the previous day in graphic detail. It was the second time he had seen Dudley smile that evening. The pain in the colonel's head was easing slightly due to the combined numbing effect of the mixture of paracetamol tablets and Sid.

'Look, old boy, I really don't want any more association in these shenanigans. I am retired from the army, and today was a good indication that I am not up to it any more. The most precious thing I have in life is my family. I don't want any further connection with yer book. I mean just look at this place. How am I going ter explain this ter the site manager here?' he asked, nodding towards the sofa.

'Look at the distress that all this has caused my family. Now I have got ter account fer what has happened, to the Lisa, and Clarrie when yer've gone. It ain't going ter be easy, old boy, I can tell yer that. She's putting a fairly brave face on things at the moment, but, hell hath no fury . . . and all that!'

'I am so very, very sorry, Dudders. No one could have foreseen that this would happen to you all. Do you think we should give George a call?' Peter asked.

Dudley nodded.

'Yes, I should have thought of that earlier, although it's getting a bit late.'

'It may be worth letting him know,' Peter advised.

The colonel stood up, and walked slightly unsteadily over to his mobile phone that was on charge. He dialled George's number.

Peter wasn't listening to the conversation. He was too preoccupied with his own thoughts. Guilt, anger, frustration, and a tinge of fear for his own and Kristine's safety, crept into his mind.

Lisa came back into the room.

'Could I be the next victim for a visitation?' Peter asked himself. The answer came back to him loud and clear, 'Most definitely yes!'

'He's coming over,' Dudley informed Peter as he replaced the receiver, interrupting the engineer's train of thought.

'Whoo'sh comin' over?' Lisa asked still a bit tipsy.

'George. You know the guy from the embassy? The big chap! He was here for the barbecue.'

'No more of thish Dudley. I am shaying nooo more. We go. Poor Clarrie, look what you've put ush throo.' Lisa started crying again. The drink was making her emotional.

Dudley walked over to his wife, and put a comforting right arm around her shoulders.

'There, there, old girl, it's OK, darling. We have to talk to someone in authority. The police won't be interested,' he tried his best to reassure her.

'Why? Why?' she wailed.

For the second time that evening, Peter felt that he was very much in the way. Then he thought maybe Dudley needed him there for moral support, as had been previously suggested.

It was a catch 22 situation. He stared down at the carpet once again. Lisa wandered back into the kitchen still sobbing. The colonel sat back heavily in his chair. The finger and thumb of his right hand pinched the top of his nose between the corners of his eyes.

'Do you feel that your life and that of your family's are in any danger after what you have been through?' Peter asked.

The colonel took a moment to compose himself before answering.

'It's hard to tell. But my gut feeling is no! I do not think so; no not now. They know that I don't have the bloody thing. They will most definitely look fer it in yer room again. So expect another visit.

'I think I passed their test. But yer life is most definitely in danger, Peter.'

He took a sip from his glass as he was feeling slightly emotional.

'I think we underestimated those buggers, big time. They are so well organised, and very professional. The fact that yer threatened, and hurt one of them in the hotel will not go in yer favour. As I said, yer room is bugged. Those blighters know yer every move, and they know that George has some photocopies of the book. They told me many things that we discussed in yer room,' he repeated. 'Yer must move to another hotel or compound, and soon. Better still—*leave this damn country fer good!*"

'Well, let's see what George makes of all this,' Peter suggested.

Suddenly, the vacuum cleaner burst into life startling both men. They looked across at the source of the noise. Clarita was busily pushing the nozzle on the hard end of the flexible hose between the wainscoting and the carpet. The hose sucked the remaining glass particles trapped by the wall. The tiny pieces clicked as they were drawn inside the vacuum nozzle and then into the bag.

Meanwhile, outside, Lisa had managed to rescue the coriander plant. She replanted it in the terracotta pot that remained relatively undamaged despite its ordeal.

This boisterous and industrious activity of the females was their way of dealing with the situation. The girls were trying to get their lives back to some sort of normality, and they needed to forget the events of the evening, by keeping busy.

When Lisa had finally completed her gardening task, she returned to the kitchen, washed her hands, and organised some small snacks for everyone, although, not feeling hungry herself. Busying herself, and her first taste of Sid, had helped to take her mind off the incident, for the time being.

She had telephoned the maintenance office informing the Filipino manager that there had been an accident, and the back kitchen window required a new pane of glass. The maintenance manager wondered how the thick glass could have got broken, and speculated that there had been an attempted break-in. He thought Lisa sounded slightly drunk when she spoke to him in Tagalog.

The manager wrongly assumed there may have been a domestic argument.

The maintenance manager sent one of his men to the villa, and on arrival the man proceeded to board up the window area by securing block board to the window frame. The window would be replaced the following day.

In the meantime, Lisa left Dudley, and Peter talking and took Clarita upstairs to get her ready for bed.

It was quite late when the man from the British Embassy finally arrived at the villa.

George announced his arrival by three loud raps on the thick black wooden door. His huge frame filled the doorway as he entered the room.

'What the hell's happened here?' he asked, looking at the brown-stained blooded carpet, and the damaged sofa.

'We had a visit from the terrorists,' Dudley replied in a hushed voice. Then George noticed the colonel's left arm.

'*What?* My word—what happened?'

The three men spoke in hushed voices about the family's previous ordeal. After Dudley's account, Peter relayed to George about the hotel confrontation.

'And now,' George began, 'I have a piece of news that I know will upset Peter.'

'What's that?'

'The copies of the documents that you gave to me in your hotel room-'

'Yes! Well, what about them?' Peter interrupted.

'This is so *embarrassing!*' George emphasised the word and looked down at his shiny shoes.

He thought before he spoke.

'Well, I took them back to my office at the BHC, as I told you I would. I left them in the drawer, and now they're missing!'

'Oh! Nice!' Peter exclaimed. 'Well, just as well I never gave you the bloody book then, isn't it?

'What total and utter incompetence.' He stared at the man from the Embassy in total disbelief.

George averted Peter's gaze.

'I've reported the matter internally.' He was aware that Peter's eyes were almost burning into his very soul, and continued speaking, but could not make any further eye contact for the present.

It was Dudley that spoke next.

'That's exactly what one of those bastards told me. One of them said that they had recovered the copies from the British Embassy. I thought they were bluffing at first. They also mentioned they removed some copies from yer room, Peter,' Dudley said while briefly looking at the enraged engineer. 'They have the copies, *but* it's the bloody book they're after. That was the sole purpose of their visit *here* today!'

George made an attempt to cover things up as best he could.

'Peter, there's nothing I can do about the loss. There must be a sympathiser, a spy, or a mole in the British Embassy.' He paused briefly.

'It could be a cleaner, or a clerk, who knows? Their intelligence is better than we first thought. What I do know is that your life is now in *grave* danger. Grave being the operative word, pardon the pun. I agree with Dudley. I don't think they will go after him or the family again. No; it's *you* they're after. The sooner you can get out of this country, and back to the sanctuary of the UK, the better it will be for all of us.

'I spoke with some, er; let's say diplomatic guys that carry out covert operations, just before I left the office this evening. I informed them of the problems that you have been experiencing, Peter. I mentioned the content of Dudley's phone call this evening also. They are convinced that your hotel room is bugged.'

'Yes, that is what Dudley said earlier.' The engineer was trying to regain control and composure.

'Think about the conversations we had in that room, Peter. The terrorists know you have their book. They are aware you had the photocopies. They also knew that I had taken some of them. That is why they asked their mole in the embassy to retrieve them. Well, that is my guess. They obviously know of Dudley and of me from what was said earlier. They know every move you make. Every spoken word in your room is probably being listened to, recorded, and analysed. You say you chased an Asian guy that you recognised from the rooftop, out of the hotel lobby?'

Peter nodded.

'And that he had a walkie-talkie with him? It is our belief that the terrorists are operating from *within* the hotel, don't you see? It has to be somewhere fairly close by to be in the range of the listening device?'

'Anyway, following the discussions I had with our agents, we want to send someone to do a sweep of your room. I shouldn't think you'll object to that, will you?'

'Well, no!' Peter replied. He was still stunned that someone had removed the papers from the British High Commission. He thought that was sacrosanct ground, and a most secure place.

'We have to get you out of Saudi Arabia, and back to the safety of the UK, sooner, rather than later.

'We are talking days, and can help you with this through our diplomatic channels. Forget your project, someone will come out and carry on in your absence, of that, I am sure. The main thing is that you know too much. You've blown their cover. You can identify at least one of the men, and you've seen the terrorist's manual. You have it with their entire cell's underground operations, plus contact information.' Then he sprung the question unexpectedly, 'Do you still have the book, Peter?'

'Yes and no!'

'What sort of an answer is that?' George had finally regained his confidence. He was once more his usual self, and back in control and in the driving seat.

'Do I have it, you asked me? Well, if they have found it, no! If they have not found it, then the answer is yes! I will have to check.'

'What are your plans for the next few-?'

'Good night, Daddy.' Clarita interrupted the conversation having crept down the carpeted staircase unnoticed. The three men were leaning forward, and engrossed in quiet conversation. The young girl had quietly entered the room, and had climbed onto her father's lap for a brief moment. She gave him a long kiss on the side of his bruised face. In her left hand, she held the worn out Teddy Bear by one of its arms.

'Mummy says that you *must* go to the hospital. Promise me you *will* go, Daddy.'

'Oh! Yes very well, princess.'

'*Promise?*'

'Yes I promise, princess.'

'We mustn't break our promises, must we, daddy?' Then without waiting for an answer, she asked, 'Daddy, will those horrible men come back here again?'

'No, darling, they won't be back.'

'Good, I don't want any nightmares. Will you read me a story?'

'No not tonight, sweetheart, Mummy will read to you. Daddy has to talk to these nice men. Sweet dreams. See you in the morning, my love.'

Clarita kissed the other two men briefly on the cheek. 'Thank you for freeing us, Peter,' she said, not having any understanding of the true situation.

'No worries, little one. God bless.' She left the room, in her colourful pink nightie, clutching the worn out Teddy Bear to her chest and plodded up the stairs.

'Sorry, what were you saying, George?'

'I asked about your movements for the next few days,' he repeated.

'Ah! OK! I have to go to Dammam for about two days, and I'll be back probably on Wednesday.

'My passport *should* have the exit visa stamped in it by then. I hope to leave for the UK on Thursday night, or Friday morning. It will depend on the visa, also flight availability. I intend to be in the UK for three days, and meet with your counterparts. Also, I will need the contact numbers from you, George.'

'OK. No problem. I will give you the information about the man you are to meet, and to make contact with at the London office In the meantime, and in your absence, I will organise the sweep of your hotel room at Radissons as discussed. I hope you don't have any plans for coming back here afterwards, Peter.'

'Well, as I said, three or four days in the UK and then-'

'Forget it, Peter,' Dudley and George chorused, interrupting him.

'If you come back to Saudi from the UK, you're going to end up on a marble slab. When you get back to England, you make sure you stay there. If you see or hear anything suspicious, report it to the number I will give you.'

Dudley nodded solemnly in agreement to George's advice.

Lisa came down the stairs. Dudley put a finger to his lips indicating to Peter and George that the conversation was over for the moment.

It was eleven-thirty at night when everyone left.

Dudley ordered a taxi to transport him to the local hospital, and asked the driver to wait.

The wound was again cleaned, and secured with sutures that were clipped along the line of the cut. The male Filipino nurse had been as gentle as he could. He then gave Dudley an anti-tetanus injection to prevent any infection from the knife wound. Dudley refused local anaesthetic as he felt he was anaesthetised enough from the Sid. Everything was a blur to him, and dreamlike.

An Irish doctor had peered into the colonel's eyes with a light to check that the retinas had not been dislodged, and to ensure the pupils of the eyes were dilating as they should. All appeared normal. The physician advised that Dudley may suffer from delayed concussion, also headaches for a few days, and advised him accordingly as to which medication to take.

When asked how he had sustained the injuries, Dudley replied, 'There had been an accident!'

That was typical of the man as he never wanted to make a fuss.

The doctor remained unconvinced, and without further questioning, made an entry in his patient treatment log.

* * *

It took Peter a little over four hours to cover the journey from Riyadh to Dammam. The road had many radar checks for speeding vehicles, and there was an abundance of highway police patrol cars as they travelled up and down the motorway. The road to Dammam, he noted with approval, was better than the highway from Riyadh to Jeddah.

On arrival to the eastern province, he checked into the Sheraton Hotel, took a shower and then ate a hearty lunch.

Two hours later, he was driving along the Cornice to the offices of STS and AHT for the pre-arranged meeting.

On arrival, he met the field engineers of the Eastern region for the first time. The project director for that region was unable to attend the pre-arranged conference with the engineer that day. An unscheduled visit from the senior partners from one of the equipment suppliers had arrived unannounced. After a brief phone conversation with the PD, a meeting was agreed for nine o'clock the following morning.

Peter then made a call to a friend in Al Kobar that was contracted to Saudi Aramco, the oil giant. They arranged to meet for dinner that evening at the Sheraton Hotel.

* * *

It was early in the morning when Tariq and Asif paid yet another visit to Peter's room at the Radissons Hotel. The men were careful on entry to the room, and placed a DND (do not disturb) notice on the outside of the door. As a further precaution, they locked the door after them. Asif stood on Tariq's shoulders, then pushing the heavy air conditioning maintenance hatch upwards, and then over to one side, he pulled himself into the cramped space, cautious to keep to the reinforced framework of the ceiling as he did so.

Asif searched all around the air conditioning unit, but the book was not to be found. He lifted the fibre glass between the wooden framework.

They checked again around the bed, under the carpet, beneath the bathroom fittings, in the cistern, and under the wooden shelf that supported his suitcase. They rummaged inside his suitcase once again, and looked everywhere possible, where a book of that size could be hidden in a hotel room.

'Infidel!' Asif uttered the word in a rage. They were now in deep trouble with their clerical leader Ahmed Mubarak. He would be far from pleased at the bad news.

Finally, they were both satisfied that a more thorough search had been carried out this time than before, and the search still revealed nothing.

The conclusion they came to was that the engineer must have taken the book with him.

Asif made a coded call on the satellite phone to the imam on the Pakistan borders. He informed the cleric that the hotel room had been thoroughly checked, and was clean.

Asif also reported on the incident the day before at 'Mr. Dudley's villa.' He was asked as to the whereabouts of Maynard, and was informed that Maynard had gone to Dammam on business for the company.

'You know what has to be done. I don't want him killed at this stage,' the voice of the leader advised. 'But you *will* get the book back . . .' his voice concluded with a string of threats. The imam concluded that if the whereabouts of the valuable manual was not found, then certain unpleasant things would happen to the cell members responsible.

Asif was reporting on behalf of Ali and Sohail, who were also on their way to Dammam.

* * *

Two hours after the Asian's visit to Peter's room, two Englishmen of smart appearance arrived at the hotel. One of the men was carrying a large briefcase. They reported to the reception desk.

'I understand Mr. Maynard left instructions for us to be allowed to enter his room. We are collecting some important papers on a private company matter,' the man advised the receptionist.

The desk clerk checked the entries in the book, and confirmed this was, in fact, correct. The bell captain was summoned, as he was the only person available, and instructed him to escort the men to Maynard's room.

Once at the room he opened the door with a pass swipe card to allow the men entry. One man stood in front of the door whilst the other man, carrying the case, stepped silently inside. There was no way the bell captain would be allowed into the room as they needed silence, and secrecy. The man on the outside whispered '*Shukran*' to the porter, then produced two 100 Saudi riyal notes for the bell boy's help. The hotel employee gratefully pocketed the money, bowing slightly, and then hurried happily away.

Once inside the room, neither man spoke. They communicated to each other by sign language. The detection equipment was silently removed from the briefcase, and the detector turned on.

Many sophisticated listening devices (or bugs as they are more commonly known) have built in anti-detection safeguards. The men from the Ministry assumed they were dealing with the latest in hi-tech surveillance technology. They therefore had the most advanced equipment with them to deal with all eventualities. The receiver antenna was pointed in various directions as it swept the room. Slowly, and deliberately the frequency range was varied. After a short while a low audible whistle emanated from the handheld VHF device. The man pointed the antenna in various directions until a position was found where the sound was at its optimum. He nodded towards the telephone landline unit. The second man unscrewed the mouthpiece, and removed a small modular device powered by a tiny battery.

There was almost certainly a second transmitter somewhere else in the room, maybe set at another frequency in case one failed or was found. The process was again repeated. Sure enough another loud audible whistle emanated from the electronic apparatus. The tiny transmitter was barely visible to the untrained eye. The device had been placed above the mirror by the wall over the fitted desk. One of the men picked up the second electronic module, and hastily immobilised them both by removing the tiny batteries.

* * *

Even though Tariq and Asif knew that Maynard was in Dammam, the receiver had been left switched on. It was tuned in to the frequency of the tiny transmitters in Maynard's room.

Tariq had been lying on the bed deep in thought. The activist was pleased that he would not be returning to the terrorist training camp on the Pakistan-Afghan borders. Despite protests to the religious leader, it was decreed that it *would* only be necessary for Ali and Sohail to attend the training for further instruction. The cleric had decided they were responsible for what had gone wrong.

They were the two most senior activists of the four, and therefore had to be made an example of.

* * *

Ahmed Mubarak appeared briefly in a mosque in Olaya district. Sohail and Ali sheepishly presented him with the photocopies recovered from Maynard's room, and the British Embassy.

The man was very annoyed that he did not have all the information that he had come to collect.

Assurances were given that the book would be recovered in a matter of days.

The pre-planning of the terror attacks were based on the painstaking intelligence gathering over a long period of time. The attacks had to be accurate, and carried out with precision timing in order to gain maximum effect. The element of attack is surprise. Now that others may have this information, it was doubtful if their planned attacks could go ahead.

Promises were again made to the leader in the Pakistan region that the book would be back in safe custody very soon, and if not handed to Mubarak in Saudi, then it would be ready for him on his arrival to the UK. Arrangements were under way to capture Maynard, and interrogate him into submission before his being able to hand the manual over to the British authorities.

* * *

Asif was reading the Koran. The room was quiet. Suddenly the VHF receiver burst into life. A low whistle, barely audible at first, abruptly radiated from the receiver. Gradually the noise increased in volume then decreased, finally increasing again.

The operation was repeated for a second time.

'Someone's in Maynard's room. They're doing a sweep. The infidels are on to us. I thought you said you had removed the bugs,' Asif said, turning to Tariq.

'I was going to do it after the rooms had been cleaned,' replied Tariq. 'I didn't think there was any urgency as Maynard has gone away for a few days!'

'Correction,' Asif began. 'You did *not* think, full stop, innit?'

'Don't worry so much. He'll be taken care of in Dammam by the others.'

'That's not the point,' Asif continued, 'it's negligence like this that's caused Ali and Sohail to return to the training camp. It will be us next if we carry on messing up like this.'

'OK then what do we do about the guys in Maynard's room?' Tariq asked.

'There's nothing much we *can* do. Our function here is history as far as Maynard is concerned. The operation in Riyadh has been a flop, so it has been transferred to Dammam,' he deliberated. 'I have to make another call to our leader, which I am dreading.'

*   *   *

Earlier that morning, Sohail and Ali had met outside Radissons Hotel, and proceeded to drive to Dammam.

*   *   *

The two Englishmen nodded to the desk clerk, and politely thanked him as they walked briskly towards the revolving doors of the hotel. Their task had been successfully completed.

*   *   *

Peter was pleased to see Jim Grundy again. They had been neighbours in Al Kobar Villas in the year 2006. At that time, Peter was regional manager for Ericsson, and project manager of that region of Saudi Arabia for the telecoms giant STC. He had been in charge of a telecom/installation change-out, and build programme.

'Good to see you again after such a long time,' began Jim, shaking Peter warmly by the hand as they stood in the lobby of the Sheraton Hotel. Then jokingly he said, 'What brings you back to this yellow and barren land?'

'Money, bills, the bank manager, the wife, the list goes on.' Peter then went on to briefly elaborate on the work he was engaged in across the Kingdom.

'It sounds great,' Jim responded.

'Yes, it's not a bad deal, and it is going better than I could have imagined. OK, shall we eat first?' Peter asked.

'That sounds like a very good idea,' replied Jim. 'I am famished. The food here is very good I'm told although I've only ever dined here once during my four years in Kobar.'

After dinner they went to Peter's room, and Jim opened his briefcase and handed the engineer something in a brown paper bag.

'I've brought you a little present, sort of welcome back gift,' said Jim, handing over the package with a broad grin on his face. Peter gingerly removed the contents from the bag. It was a bottle of Johnny Walker Black Label whisky. His eyes bulged in disbelief. In English money, that would be the equivalent of about 100 pounds on the Saudi black market.

'Thanks, Jim. We'll have to do some serious damage to this!' Peter said, laughing. He opened the minibar and removed a can of soda water, and two frosted ice cold glasses.

'Would you like ice?'

'No, no thanks,' declined Jim. 'It killed my grandfather.'

'What? Killed your grandfather, how?' the engineer asked incredulously. 'How did that happen?'

'He was on the Titanic,' Jim joked. The two men laughed. 'I never trust the water anywhere I travel, apart from either bottled or in the UK.'

'That's very wise,' agreed Peter in return. He ignored the advice of his friend, and in so doing, dropped two ice cubes into his own glass.

When they had finished just over half of the bottle, Jim announced that it was time for him to leave the hotel and return to his compound.

'My driver will be getting impatient,' he informed the engineer, 'and I really must let my wife know that she has a good husband.'

Peter smiled, and said, I intend to go back to the UK by the end of the week, I am not sure if I'll be back again, but if I am, then I will most certainly give you a call, Jim. I'm hoping to get a flight without too many problems. I trust the dreaded exit visa has been stamped in my passport by now. I can't wait to get back and see the little woman.'

'I bet you can't. She sounds really nice. You are a lucky man, Peter; I don't know how you do it.'

'It's easy really, Jim, charm, charisma, good looks, personality—'

'Not to mention modesty,' Jim interjected with a grin

'Ha ha, yes, that as well. I sometimes wonder how it is that I lived so long without her in my life.'

*　*　*

The two Asian men sitting in the lobby were facing the lift doors at a discreet distance. It was getting late when they observed the Englishman exiting from the lift. He walked into the foyer, heading towards the exit. They had noted his arrival. Also the men's initial meeting as they stood by the reception desk. They then monitored the meeting of the new man and Maynard in the hotel restaurant. The Asians noticed that the man was still carrying a briefcase with him. They nodded one to the other, stood up, and followed the Englishman out of the hotel, and into the car park.

*　*　*

Meanwhile, Peter was feeling extremely relaxed as he sat back in the chair by the closed curtained window. For the first time in Saudi, he was happy, and contented with life. This was partly due to the whisky, and his relaxed state of mind, also knowing that he would be leaving KSA before his official departure date.

'Only a few more days,' he told himself, 'and I'll be back on British soil with the dreaded book that has caused my friends and me so many problems. Probably, I will never return to the Kingdom,' he mused.

'Once the authorities get hold of it, the planned attacks will be intercepted, thereby saving many lives and injuries.

'It was always good to renew old acquaintances. Good old, Jim,' he thought, as he drained the remaining dregs of whisky from the glass.

Peter attempted to make a call to Kristine, the international line was busy. He would try again later. He poured a modest measure of the amber nectar into the empty glass for a final nightcap, and took a swig. It remained in his mouth for fifteen seconds, and then he swallowed hard.

He changed into his pyjamas, and went into the bathroom. Just after he had applied toothpaste to the brush, there was an unexpected knock at the door. He looked at his watch; it was ten thirty-five.

'Hello!' he called through the closed locked door.

'This is housekeeping, sir. I have a gift for you on behalf of the hotel management, sir,' informed a brown faced man with a strong Asian accent.

'Probably a bowl of fruit or flowers,' Peter thought.

'OK, hang on a minute,' he replied cheerfully as he removed the internal lock, and detached the security chain.

In the instant the two men on the other side of the door saw the handle turning, and the door opening a fraction, two boots slammed simultaneously, kicking at the centre edge of the door.

The door swung back with such a sudden force, that the edge of the door struck Peter a stunning blow to the left side of his forehead sending him sprawling backwards. The back of his head struck the corner of a wall, near the fitted wardrobes. His lifeless body fell to the floor beside the open wardrobe. The accumulation of blows rendered the unsuspecting man unconscious.

The Asians entered the room, closed the door behind them, and locked it. They pulled out their black woollen balaclava helmets from inside their pockets and put them on. Together the two men roughly picked up Peter's heavy, limp, body, and threw him unceremoniously onto the neatly made up bedcovering. The Asians then tightly wrapped his body with the freshly laundered bedcover, rolling his lifeless form over on the bed.

One of the men turned on the television. He selected a music channel, and then increased the volume in order to suppress any extraneous noises coming from inside the room.

Together, the two men gripped the tightly rolled bedspread, keeping a hold on the open end, and a secure part of the rolled counterpane. They then pulled the inert body to the end of the bed, and let the counterpane with the dead weight drop onto the carpeted floor.

Then it started in earnest. Kicks and blows rained down heavily on Peter's motionless body. If he had been conscious, he would not have been able to move as both arms were pinned to his sides by the tightly wound bed cover. The movement of his legs was similarly restricted.

The punishment continued to the unconscious man for ten minutes.

'Infidel! Christian bastard! Death to America! Death to Britain! Praise be to Allah! Long live the Islamic nation.' Each chant was punctuated with either a kick or a punch.

Suddenly and without warning, there was a loud knocking on the room door. The noise from the television, and the shouting had woken up the person in the adjoining room.

'Turn the bloody noise down!' It was an irate Geordie oil worker that had to be at the Saudi Aramco de-gassing station early the following morning.

The beating had finished. It was now time for questions and answers from their battered victim. The volume of the television was turned down to a more acceptable level.

Brutally, they each grabbed the open end of the counterpane, and then yanked it upwards. Peter's lifeless form rolled over as the bed cover was unfurled. His body finally came to rest against an armchair.

He lay unmoving. Blood was flowing freely from his broken nose and lips.

Sohail went into the bathroom, and filled a plastic bucket (used for washing purposes after using the toilet), with cold water. The two men got either side of Peter then lifted him into one of the two armchairs. His body was about to slump forward. Sohail roughly pushed him back. Then picking up the opaque plastic bucket, he threw the cold contents at the victim's face. Peter turned his head, and let out a low groan.

Ali moved forward and slapped his face.

'Wake up! Wake up! Infidel, wake up! Bastard! Fucking bastard! Fucking English bastard,' the Pakistani ordered.

Unlike Dudley, and his family, Peter was not strapped into the chair. There was no need. The intensity of the beating had restrained him sufficiently to suppress any sudden movement, or plans of fighting or escape.

Peter was a mess. His face, hair and pyjamas were soaked. There was an open wound on his forehead, where blood trickled down his cheek. His left eye was closing. His nose was broken. Blood flowed down into his mouth it joined the blood on his lips that had now become badly swollen. Blood ran down his chin, and onto his light blue pyjama top.

There was a deep open wound on his forehead, which was bleeding. His ribs ached so much that it was hard for him to get comfortable, and he had difficulty in breathing. The side of his head was swollen, and throbbing, due to a combination of the severe kicking that he had received, and the blow from the room door. His arms and legs were also badly bruised.

The pain in Peter's head, face, chest, kidneys, and testicles was excruciating.

Apart from the throbbing, he was aware of dryness in his mouth as his mind gradually returned to consciousness. The engineer was in a state of total shock, despair and disbelief.

His right eye flickered open for a second whilst the left eye remained closed due to the swelling from the kicking to the face and head.

'So, infidel, you are with us now!' It was Ali speaking again. Peter recognised his voice, height, and noticed the slight limp as he walked about. There was no need for the men to use balaclavas, other than themselves appear more menacing.

The engineer sat doubled up in pain, and was gasping for breath. Each inhalation was agonisingly painful due to the damage sustained to his ribs.

Whilst in the army, he had been taught that the element of attack is surprise. The same philosophy had been applied by these masters of terror, torment, and torture. Nothing could have prepared him for the unannounced vicious onslaught that had taken place in the relative sanctuary of the hotel room.

'You bastards!' he managed to whisper hoarsely. His breathing was rasping like the last gasps of a dying man. It was almost impossible for him to speak.

'I think we overdid the beating,' Sohail said to Ali in Urdu. Ali had been too remonstrative as usual. Then he remembered their leader, and his previous instructions. The militants were *not* to kill Maynard "at this stage." That would come later, when the manual had been repossessed. All the time Maynard was alive, and able to speak, and tell of the book's whereabouts, he was of use to them. The beating was supposed to be a softening up process in order to get Maynard to talk.

'You know why we are here, sadiq (my friend), and you know what we want?'

It was Sohail speaking in a low voice with a broad Yorkshire accent. Peter was looking down with one eye at the mixture of blood, and water that had soaked his pyjama trousers, and the dark blue hotel room carpet. One of his teeth was loose. He was again doubled up in pain.

Sohail picked up a glass that had been used earlier by either himself or Jim. Then grabbing the whisky bottle, he poured a generous measure into the glass, offering it to the victim.

'Here,' he said, 'drink this. It might help ease the pain, and get you to talk.'

Peter took the glass between his two trembling hands. It was a huge effort to drink the contents. He had to tilt the glass at such an acute angle, due to the restricted movement of his neck, and swollen lips. Some of the whisky trickled out of the glass, and down his chin ending up on his pyjamas.

'Your ordeal will be over just as soon as it began. But you must tell us what we want to know so that you can get relief from your pain and suffering. You control your own destiny, Mr. Peter. You just have to tell us what we want to know, and we will leave you in peace. Now then, where is the book that you took from us?'

Peter realised that he had to hang on for as long as he could. If the terrorists had the information leading to the book's whereabouts, he would be of no more use to them. He would never see his lovely wife again. Knowing that he couldn't endure much more pain, the engineer tried to think of Kristine. He needed her. He had to get strength from somewhere. She would be his source of inspiration, power and energy. She was only a little woman, but she had a big heart. He tried to concentrate his mind on her. His hands were still shaking uncontrollably. The remnants of whisky swished from side to side in the held glass, like a mini-storm. The pain in his head was considerable. His vision was impaired, and he saw two of everything.

Peter attempted to take another drink from the glass.

He needed to kill the pain, also steady his nerves, and he needed time. Blood had mingled with the whisky in the glass. It didn't matter. Nothing mattered anymore except staying alive. He had too much to live for, and too much to lose.

'Fuck off!' he gasped both venomously and defiantly between clenched teeth. His jawbone ached. He felt the pain in his chest getting worse, his head and lips throbbed.

Ali unexpectedly delivered a blow to the side of the victim's head. The room started spinning.

'Tut! Tut! Tut! Mr. Peter; you are making life extremely difficult for yourself, and for us.

'Are you being brave or foolish? Foolish or brave—which is it?' It was Sohail speaking again.

'You do not realise the danger you are putting yourself in. It would be so easy for either one of us to snuff you out like the flame of a candle, innit? Make it easy on yourself, and just tell us what we want to know, and then we will leave you alone. If you don't tell us, then the pain and suffering will begin all over again. It will get worse and worse until you beg for mercy. Eventually you will tell us what we want to know, so it may as well be now.'

Ali stood up from his seated position opposite the injured man on the bed. He was about to deliver another vicious swing, and was physically restrained by Sohail.

'I—don't—have—it,' Peter wheezed slowly, painfully, and truthfully through clenched teeth.

His voice was little more than a hoarse whisper.

'Then where is it? If you don't have it, where can we go and find it?' asked Sohail.

His manner was almost friendly.

'It—is—not—with—me,' the reply was a broken whisper.

'OK, but then where is it *exactly*? Where is it *now*, at this precise moment in time?'

Peter remained silent.

'Maybe this will help,' it was Ali, the man at Radissons that Peter had shouted, and sworn at in the hotel lobby. The action happened so quickly that Sohail had no chance to hold back the Pakistani. Again, Peter never saw the blow coming. Even if he had, there would have been nothing he could have done. A well-aimed kick from a military boot struck the engineer's left shin bone.

Unexpectedly, the beaten man screamed out loud in agony. The glass fell from his grasp, and rolled across the carpeted floor. The remnants of the golden liquid spilled out freely. He blacked out again, falling forward. Ali shoved him roughly back into the chair. Peter's head lolled back on the cushioning.

The man in the room on the other side of the wall was again awakened, this time by the scream.

He sat up in bed startled, and angered by this sudden outburst.

'It was either the television, or someone playing about,' he thought. It never would have occurred to him that a man was being beaten up, and tortured by terrorists in the adjoining room.

For the second time that evening, the irate Geordie got out of bed. Wearing only his light grey underpants, he stood in the corridor hammering, and kicking on the door of Peter's room.

'If yow boogers don't shut yower bloody noise, I'll break the bloody door down and sort yews out. This is the last time I'm telling ya. Now shut it!'

The Asians ignored the Englishman's utterances and threats.

Peter was out for the count.

Sohail severely chastised Ali. There had been no need for the unprovoked attack. The victim was in enough pain. Sohail had figured that Peter could have been about to tell where the book was hidden, if coaxed. Ali had screwed up the chance of knowing its location due to his own personal revenge. Sohail returned to the bathroom, he refilled the bucket with cold water. He was fuming at the action Ali had taken. Carrying the large opaque plastic bucket from the bathroom, he returned to his victim, and threw the contents over Peter for a second time. It took longer this time for Peter to come round. Again he was assisted by a few heavy slaps from Ali, who was only too pleased to administer them

'We can play this game all night,' informed Ali.

'Enough!' instructed Sohail. 'I will handle this from now on. Just you shut up, and stay out of it Ali. The best you can do is search the room, and look *everywhere!*'

Peter's head was spinning once again. His shin and calf muscle were causing the greatest distress now, apart from his ribs. It was getting more difficult to breath. His neck was also causing unbearable pain as a result of the blows he had received, and jarring, when he was pushed back into the chair.

'Where is the book that you took from our room, Mr. Peter? Just tell me and we will leave you,'

Sohail asked in a soft voice.

Peter was gasping for breath. Tears of pain ran down his cheeks. He was a wretched hopeless mess.

'I—don't—have—it.' He managed to utter; his words coming out staccato style.

'But you know where it is, innit?'

Peter winced with pain. He felt that he was going to pass out again. There was a sick feeling in the pit of his stomach. Blackness was closing in on him again. Shooting stars formed by bright pinpricks of light flashed before him as they traversed in various directions. His vision was totally blurred through the tears of pain and the beating to his head.

'What—makes—you—think—that?' he rasped.

'Do you think we are stupid, Mr. Peter? We found the photocopies in your room.'

The engineer took a painful sharp intake of breath.

'They—were—given—to—me—by—someone.'

'*Liar,*' shouted Ali from the wardrobe as he was searching for the book. He rushed over, and was just about to deliver another fatal blow, when Sohail threw his arm out physically restraining the Asian from carrying out a further assault. The blow caught Ali across the chest. Sohail then pushed Ali firmly, and he fell onto the bed.

'*I'll deal with this. I told you to search the room,*' he said raising his voice to Ali. Then he muttered something angrily in Urdu. Both men were keen to get the book and appease their clerical leader, but Ali's remonstrative behaviour wasn't getting them anywhere. Neither man wanted to return to the training camp on the borders of Pakistan, but they knew they had to.

Returning to their victim, Sohail said slowly, 'We—know—that—it—is—in—your—possession—because—your—room—was—bugged. Your conversations have not only been heard, but also recorded.

He removed a small compact solid-state recorder from his pocket, and placed it on the wet table.'

Pressing lightly on a switch, the unit came to life.

'Peter, getting back to the book, yer say that yer still have it in yer possession?'

'Yes!'

'Where is it exactly?'

'Somewhere safe, and that's all I'm saying for the moment.'

The conversation was between Dudley and Peter. Both voices were clearly identifiable. The recorder was then turned off. Somewhere in the archives of his memory, the beaten man remembered the conversation; it was probably the same recording that Dudley had referred to in the villa.

'OK, Mr. Peter. For all our sakes, do not underestimate us or insult our intelligence further. You are in a hopeless, helpless, impossible, no-win, no-win situation, innit?'

It was painful for Peter to even think, let alone answer any questions.

He was in such unbearable agony, and he needed the toilet. He hadn't anticipated such an unexpected, vicious onslaught in his wildest dreams. He knew that he couldn't take much more. He was near to breaking point, and no longer cared as to what happened to him. His body was broken, and his spirit was at its lowest ebb. He thought that he was only one step away from death. His mind was disjointed; he managed a last logical thought. 'If I tell them, it will be my death sentence, and I have not prepared for that to happen. What can I tell them? What should I tell them? Why should I tell them? How could such a thing be of so much importance to another human being? But these people were not human. These were extremist fanatical thugs that carried out indiscriminate killings against innocent old people, women, and children in the name of religion. They are the scum of the earth; they are not concerned about my life or anyone that does not believe in their radicalism. I have to hang on a little longer. Nothing and no one mattered to them, except their weird, fanatical outrageous beliefs, and the ill-fated book.'

Sohail picked up the glass from the floor.

He again poured the remnants of the whisky from the bottle into it. He once again handed the tumbler to Peter interrupting his broken and fragmented thoughts.

'Here, drink this!'

Peter's hands were shaking to the point of spilling the contents, again not through fear but through such agonising pain. He looked at the glass, and with the last amount of energy, and defiance in his broken body, and mind, he managed to intentionally knock the glass out of Sohail's outstretched hand. The contents spilled over the man's wrist.

Sohail grabbed at the bedspread, as he wiped the devil's liquor from his hand and arm.

'Now then, Maynard,' it was the evil Ali once again trying to take control. 'I am the guy you insulted. You called me a wanker in front of everyone in the hotel lobby. You are in no position to argue with us or fight with us, do you understand you British bastard? Death is your only release unless you tell us where the fucking book is. Sohail, we have wasted too much time. It is not here, not even in the maintenance hatch. Finish it now.'

Peter remained silent; he treated the comments with contempt. The engineer was having a job to think logically. His head started swimming. Again the edges of his vision of his right eye started to dim. White, bright pinpricks of light broke the encompassing darkness within him once again. His left leg was painful; he leant forward in order to breathe. The pain seemed to shift, it was weird.

'By the time we leave here, you could have every bone in your useless body broken. We'll start with your toes, and then your fingers,' Ali continued; but his voice appeared to come from somewhere distant in the room, echoing, floating.

'I can't tell you where it is,' it was little more than a hoarse whisper. He had to play for time.

'Is it here?' asked Sohail trying to assist him.

'No, it is not with me,' his voice was getting weaker, and lower. He blacked out for a third time.

Cold water, together with facial slaps brought him back once again.

Wearily, Peter opened his right eye. The two terrorists were seated on the bed facing him.

They drifted in and out of his vision, for a moment, he thought there were four people in the room.

'We know the Dudley man doesn't have it, and the visitor you had here this evening never took it with him, we checked him in the car park. Now I hope you will help us. How are you feeling now?' asked Sohail.

'What a bloody stupid question,' Peter thought. He wearily and painfully shook his head. How could they know that Jim Grundy never had it unless . . . .'

He needed to get to the bathroom. He was completely disoriented. Instinctively, and shakily, he tried to stand up. His legs were like India rubber. His left leg ached so much, and couldn't hold the weight of his body. A rush of pain shot up from his left leg bone, nerve, and muscle as he tried to stand, the injured man surged forward, and crashed unconscious to the floor.

The victim of pain and torture was suddenly exiled from his body, and he was looking down on himself.

He was floating. Everything in the room appeared vapoury, unreal. He saw himself lying on the carpet, but felt no pain. It was as if his body had become so full of remorse, and his spirit, was topped with so much grief, that it had to leave the bounds of which contained it.

Somewhere, in the light of his inner mind, there was peace, and then, oblivion.

* * *

Ali and Sohail spoke in Urdu. They realised the punishment they had meted out had been too brutal. They would get no answers from the victim now. Peter could hardly breathe, let alone talk. He would surely take the beating as a warning, if nothing else. The terrorists would follow him everywhere, and watch his every move until he led them to their quarry. They knew that he had planned to go back to the UK for a three-day break in as many days time. What they underestimated was the level of the injuries the man had sustained. The Pakistanis had to either stop him leaving Saudi, or follow him back to England. Either way, he would eventually, and involuntarily, lead the vultures to their prey. They knew now that he had the book, but they still did not know where it was hidden. They would intercept him before he had a chance to contact MI5 or MI6.

Sohail turned off the TV so as not to draw further attention to the irate neighbour in the next room.

The Asians carried out a last quick search of the room in case the book was in Maynard's possession. Again no evidence of the book or anything of any use to them was found,

They looked at the lifeless, pathetic wet bloodied body of Peter Maynard, as he lay at an awkward angle face down on the carpet.

Sohail led the way to the door. Seizing the opportunity, Ali stamped on the injured man's head, and followed his colleague.

'You do not call me a wanker in front of people!' he uttered just about audibly.

'What?' asked Sohail.

'Nothing, I was just thinking out loud.' Ali lied.

The militants removed their balaclavas, and then cautiously left the room, quietly closing the door behind them.

*   *   *

At nine-forty-five the following morning, two houseboys stood patiently outside Maynard's room door. Beside them was a mobile trolley that contained clean laundry, and towels, a black plastic bin liner of dirty bed linen, and towels. There were also soaps, shower gels, body lotions, shampoos, boxes of tissues, toilet rolls, etc.

'Housekeeping!' one had called out cheerily, having knocked on the room door for a second time. There was still no answer. The voice called out again this time slightly louder, again there was no response. Assuming the room was empty, they entered with the use of their pass swipe card.

The sight before their eyes brought utter shock, fear, and disbelief. Never before had they witnessed a room in such a mess. It looked as though there had been a party.

Momentarily, they stood as if rooted to the spot.

Then they saw the broken, blue-clad battered body of a man sprawled on the floor in a mixture of dried blood, vomit, mucous, urine, and water. They took in the room trying to make sense as to what could have happened. The chairs, table, curtains, and carpet were soaking wet. The plastic toilet bucket was on its side in the room. An empty whiskey bottle and glasses were on the floor in total disarray. The counterpane was in a heap in the corner of the chamber, the air condition hatch had been opened. 'Whatever could have happened?' they independently asked themselves.

The room attendants determined that the man lying on the carpet was either dead or paralytic through alcohol abuse. They dared not enter the room further. Frightened out of their wits, the Tamil men backed out the room, closing the door behind them. The men entered an empty guest's room, and made a call to the duty manager, and housekeeping manager.

* * *

A small throng of people crowded around the doorway out of curiosity, and only stood aside as the hotel doctor made his appearance outside the room.

The man was an Egyptian, and a strict Muslim. At first glance, when walking towards the body, he glared in disgust. From a distance, he thought that this was another Westerner suffering from alcohol abuse in the Kingdom of Saudi Arabia, and the Holy Land of Makkah. He knew how the Western visitors liked their intoxicating beverages.

The doctor removed a stethoscope, and a pair of surgical gloves from his case. He put the gloves on in readiness to examine the patient. He knelt down beside the body, undone the pyjama jacket, and placed the microphone part of the stethoscope on the area of the man's heart and lungs. He could detect a very weak pulse, and hoarse shallow breathing. Dr. Mohammad observed the split on the man's forehead running into his scalp, broken nose, cut lips, and swollen, bruised face. He felt the body for broken bones. Apart from the nose, there appeared nothing broken, but only an X-ray would reveal broken bones and hairline cracks.

'These injuries had not been sustained by a drunken fall,' he figured.

'The injuries were symptomatic of the man having been savagely beaten, and he could be close to death. His breathing was shallow, and erratic, he needed oxygen. His pulse remained weak. He may be suffering from internal injuries.'

The doctor picked up the room phone, and called for an emergency private ambulance to come to the hotel immediately.

As the chief security officer and the duty manager entered the room, they observed the injured man lying on a stretcher about to be carried out by the paramedics. His neck was in a brace, an oxygen mask had been placed over his nose and mouth. He was also connected to an elevated drip feed bag, the other end of which was inserted into a vein on the back of his left hand, secured with a plaster.

The chief security officer found Peter's Saudi driving licence and iqarma, in his trouser pocket. The security officer was a Saudi national, also an ex-police officer. He made a call to the local police station.

SAAD HOSPITAL BASED in Dammam, is one of the most modern hospitals in the Kingdom of Saudi Arabia. There is a royal suite, in readiness for an emergency which is reserved for the king, visiting princes, princesses, and dignitaries. All the facilities at the Saad Hospital are the most modern and, up to date in the Kingdom.

The private wards resemble those of a five-star hotel rather than a sick bay.

It was at this hospital that Peter had been taken by private ambulance driven at high speed with sirens blaring. On arrival, the patient had been rushed into the Accident and Emergency unit.

His soiled pyjamas had been carefully cut and removed from his badly bruised and battered body. The patient was in a coma, and underwent a thorough medical examination. He was then taken to the X-ray department, where his body was checked with the radiation processes including a brain scan. After that he was hastily taken to the ICU, (Intensive Care Unit), and placed on a bed. His neck was placed in a brace; his nose had been reset, and held in position by a nose splint, and surgical dressings. Twelve dissolvable sutures were inserted into his forehead, and scalp. Clips had been carefully placed on his swollen lips. His left leg was in plaster and lay on top of the bed.

An intravenous drip had been inserted into a vein in his left hand. An oxygen mask covered his nose and mouth, and a ventilator rose and fell rhythmically assisting his breathing. A tube had been inserted in his nose, and down into his throat and lungs. Peter's face was a swollen black, yellow, and blue mess as he lay comatose on the snow white pillow and sheets of the grey metal-framed bed. Electrodes were fastened to his chest area and were attached to an electrocardiogram machine measuring his heartbeat. Plastic tubes came and went into and out of his body, and some disappeared under the bed covers.

* * *

Meanwhile, back in Brinsham Park, close to the small sleepy Cotswold market town of Chipping Sodbury, Kristine was beside herself with worry. She had not heard from her husband for four days. It was most uncharacteristic of Peter not to make contact.

Dutifully, he called his wife every day without fail, sometimes two or even three times. Intuitively, she knew that something was wrong—very wrong.

Kristine had tried calling his mobile phone many times. At first, the handset just rang unanswered. Now when she called, a recorded voice responded by saying, 'The person you are trying to contact has either switched the phone off or is out of the coverage area. Please try again later.'

The doting wife paced about the living room of the cottage in her little pink slippers willing for her husband to make a call. She prayed out loud to God. She begged Him to ensure her husband was safe and well, and that he would call her very soon.

Kristine had called Peter's mother several times in the days of silence. Mrs. Maynard had also confirmed that she hadn't heard from her son for a while. His mother suggested that she would phone the recruitment agency that Peter worked through to see if they could help. She would then phone Kristine back later with an update. Mrs. Maynard advised her daughter-in-law not to worry, as there was bound to be a simple explanation.

* * *

The secretary of STS (Saudi Telecoms Systems) AHT division in Dammam had called Riyadh several times asking where the consulting engineer was. The secretary wrongly assumed that Peter had returned back to Riyadh, and advised the HR person there that the engineer had previously arranged a meeting with the Project Director, Mr. Akram Abaras. He was the person responsible for the mobile telecoms network in that region. The engineer had not arrived for the pre-arranged morning meeting as scheduled; neither was he answering his mobile phone. It now appeared that the phone had been turned off. The PD was most disturbed about the issue. Riyadh had received no word from the engineer either, and had no knowledge as to his whereabouts. Riyadh HR (Human Resources Department) also had no idea as to which hotel the engineer was staying at in Dammam as Maynard had made his own booking.

The STS Head Office decided to send Dudley to the region and investigate further.

The colonel was the one person that could appease the client in a diplomatic way and assist in defusing the situation of Peter's apparent "no show." The colonel would also hopefully, be able to determine the engineer's whereabouts.

* * *

The following day, the girl at the recruitment agency in London received a call from a Mrs. Jill Maynard who was enquiring about her son. The employee was hesitant to give any details about the consultants that worked through the agency in case of breaching any protocols. Peter's mother had stressed the urgency regarding her son. She wanted to know exactly where her son was. The young lady said she would pass the message on to her boss, and he would call her personally.

Eventually, the manager at the bureau returned Mrs. Maynard's phone call. He informed the anxious mother that he had contacted the company (STS-AHT) in Saudi Arabia on her behalf, he further confirmed that nobody there had heard from Peter Maynard for about three or four days. The agency also had failed in their attempts to contact him themselves in any way. The manager did his best to reassure Peter's mother that there was probably nothing to worry about. It was more than likely only a communication problem. The executive suggested that her son could be in a bad mobile phone coverage area.

Jill Maynard was informed that a Colonel Dudley Coburn-Smythe, from the company would be visiting Dammam, and an appointment had been set for the following day. The colonel would be reporting back to Riyadh. The colonel was also a consultant employed through the same agency. The manager passed this information on to the distressed mother, hoping that it would pacify the woman.

Peter's mother requested the contact number of the person going to Dammam. The manager stated that it was against company policy to divulge that sort of information to an unrelated third party. Revealing personal details of staff kept on file, could be interpreted as a breach of company rules.

He also mentioned that it could possibly compromise the Data Protection Act.

'What nonsense,' Mrs. Maynard retorted indignantly. 'My son's working through your agency in Saudi Arabia. Now he's seemingly disappeared. You must take some responsibility; may I remind you that the agency has a duty of care.

'Let's forget the bureaucracy for once and just let me have the number of the person going to Dammam. I need to jolly well contact him myself if you will do nothing. His wife is worried sick, and so am I, come to that. Has anyone thought of contacting the British High Commission?' the urgency rose in Jill Maynard's voice.

The young executive at the other end of the line finally succumbed to the pressure. He gave her Dudley's STS company mobile number. At the same time, being a fairly new employee himself, he hoped that he had not broken any company code of practices in so doing.

Peter's mother thanked him, and then relayed the information to Kristine. Mrs. Maynard assured the young Filipina that she would make a call to the Dudley contact that she had been given. After that she would phone her daughter-in-law back—hopefully with some good news.

* * *

Dudley gradually managed to get over his past ordeal with the terrorists. He was doing his best in carrying on with his daily life. He tried hard to get things back to as near normal as they had been before the activist's unwarranted intrusion. There had never been any mention of the incident to a third party by him, and STS had no knowledge of the terrorists. The colonel rightly decided that it was none of their business, and best to let "sleeping dogs lie."

Unfortunately, the unjustifiable occurrence had badly affected his wife, and even more so their young daughter, Clarita. She had been experiencing nightmares, and had wet the bed in fright on two occasions. The memory of the event was with the family every time they had entered the villa.

Then Lisa dropped a bombshell. She told Dudley that she and Clarita were no longer happy to live in Saudi Arabia, and had decided to leave. First they would take a break in the Philippines to try and forget about their ordeal, and then return to England. Clarita would have to miss school until they returned home. Lisa felt that they both needed a complete change of scenery and environment.

The colonel had done his best to reassure his wife and daughter that the "hooded gangsters" would not be bothering them again, but it was to no avail; Lisa's mind was made up and she wanted to leave.

Dudley even suggested that the family moved into another villa, or even to another compound. Lisa would not be swayed. The little woman had started to pack some of her and Clarita's clothes in readiness for the departure.

Dudley reluctantly respected his wife's decision. As a result, he resigned from the company giving three months' notice. He planned to return to England for a short break, and then join Lisa and Clarita after their holiday in the Philippines. He then intended to look for work in Surrey at the end of his notice period. He would stay close at hand to give love, affection, support, and to enjoy a happy family life once again.

*   *   *

A flight had been booked with a Saudi Arabian Airlines bound for Manila, Philippines. Kristine and Clarita were due to leave at the end of the week. After their vacation in South-East Asia, they would return to the security and serenity of their home in a trendy part of Weybridge in Surrey.

If counselling was necessary, Dudley would ensure that they would receive it through his private medical insurance.

It had been a tearful farewell at Riyadh airport. Now all Dudley wanted to do was to totally immerse himself into his work and by keeping busy the time would pass quickly.

* * *

It was now five days since Peter's disappearance, and the unusual "silence."

Whilst Dudley drove along the four-lane highway to Dammam, many thoughts flashed through his mind with regards to his friend.

He could not help thinking why there had been no communication with Peter, and he wondered if the terrorist issue had something to do with the loss of contact. Or had the man had a nervous breakdown? Did he manage, in some way, to leave Saudi Arabia? Could he be travelling back to the UK? Had he been involved in a vehicle accident? The colonel shuddered at the thought that the engineer was injured, or even worse than that, dead! Or was he being held hostage somewhere, and being tortured by the desperate fanatics?

Then his thoughts turned to more positive matters. He was pleased that he would be leaving the Kingdom for a break soon, *but* he was most displeased that his family had left him, as a result of the terrible incident. Dudley was feeling like a fish out of water without the girls around.

'Oh, well! I will be out of this place soon, and back with the little women,' he thought as he turned up the volume of the CD. Beethoven's Fifth Symphony reverberated around the vehicle with the orchestral sounds of the string section playing.

* * *

Dammam is an up and coming city, bordering on the Gulf. Compared to Riyadh it is far more relaxed in many respects. Yachts can be seen in the harbour. Young Saudis speed around on jet skis churning up the water. The sea is a beautiful blue colour, and apart from the culture, and location, there is a Mediterranean feel about the place.

Dammam also has a number of five-star hotels. The company in Riyadh had managed to book the colonel into one of them, the Southern Sun.

On his arrival at the hotel, Dudley inquired as to whether a Mr. Peter Maynard was booked in. After checking the guest list, the clerk confirmed that Peter Maynard was not a registered guest. The helpful clerk suggested that he check some of the other hotels in the city. This Dudley intended to do later in the day.

* * *

The colonel went to his room and unpacked a few things from his holdall. He then drove along the Cornice to the STS offices. Unbeknown to him, he was taking the same route as Peter had driven five days previously.

On arrival at the offices, he met for the first time with Mr. Akram Abaras, and on behalf of the company, he gave apologies for Peter's absence. Then the two men immediately got down to business.

After the meeting, Dudley suggested that he take the project director out for dinner that evening. Akram readily agreed, and suggested they dine at the Sheraton Hotel.

At the conclusion of their business, and having completed their work for the day, the two men made their way in separate vehicles to the hotel. Dudley followed the PD as he didn't know the way.

Driving past the Sheraton entrance, they parked at the right-hand side of the building. As Dudley and Akram got out of their respective vehicles, the colonel stopped in his tracks. Peter's Cherokee Jeep was parked perfectly in a bay opposite to where Dudley had parked. 'So Peter *is* here in Dammam after all,' he thought to himself, feeling somewhat relieved.

The colonel pointed to the Jeep, informing Akram that it was his colleague's vehicle. He would enquire as to the engineer's whereabouts at reception after they had dined.

The two men on entering the building went directly to the restaurant. The colonel was bemused as to why the engineer had not made any form of contact. 'Maybe he was not feeling well or perhaps he was ill with Delhi belly, or some other form of gastric trouble. Perhaps the poor man was confined to his room. But then why had he not phoned? It was all very puzzling.'

Dudley had carried out a delicate PR job on behalf of the company. Peter, at that time was certainly not "flavour of the month" in Dammam. The sheik was displeased, especially after all the good work performed by the engineer up to that point.

The colonel, not having Peter's engineering experience, had to rely on the Eastern Region RF and transmission engineer's reports on progress, and made notes. He would have preferred an unbiased report from an independent engineer such as his colleague.

The two men made polite conversation over dinner, and continually returned to the project as this was a common denominator between them. Peter's name came up a few times, and the colonel did his best to sing the praises of the young man, and his achievements since joining the project. Akram agreed that he had heard only good reports of Peter, both from Jeddah, and Riyadh regions. It was therefore a disappointment not to have his presence, and technical expertise to the project in that quarter. It was also hoped that Maynard's presentation, risk management, risk assessments, and recommendations would be applied to the Dammam province. During the exchange, both men wrongly assumed that Peter was in his hotel room at the time they were dining and talking.

Akram smiled appreciatively having enjoyed what eventually turned out to be, for him, a mini feast. His corpulent girth was a good indication that said, "Here is a man that really enjoyed his food!"

After the small talk, the colonel decided it was time to enquire at the reception desk with regards to his colleague. He would then call Peter's room, assuming that the engineer was feeling better. If that was indeed the case, then all three men could sit down and talk together in the hotel lobby over a coffee. Dudley envisaged the following day that he would be on his way back to Riyadh. He excused himself to the project director, stood up, and walked briskly to the reception area. There he enquired if Peter Maynard was booked into the hotel, and if so, what his room number was. The reception clerk looked startled. He requested that the colonel wait for a few moments. Dudley looked across at his guest some distance away, smiled, and nodded, as if to say, 'Peter's here!'

The clerk reappeared after a while with a short man of smart appearance. He was wearing a stylish Western black suit, white shirt, and nondescript tie. The man strutted rather than walked as he was of a rotund, Humpty Dumpty build. His arms flicked out from his sides as he ambled forth.

His gait reminded Dudley of a pregnant penguin, and he couldn't help smiling at the comical figure.

The man was friendly, and he smiled affably. He introduced himself as Mr. Khalid Amadi, the General Manager. He placed one hand on the sleeve of Dudley's jacket, and then indicated with an outstretched right arm towards a quiet table in the foyer seating area. The colonel was offered coffee or tea, and he politely accepted the coffee, somewhat bemused at the unexpected hospitality.

The GM nervously flicked imaginary pieces of fluff from the dark suit, in an attempt to compose himself. He sat thoughtfully for a moment.

The GM raised his right arm and called to a distant waiter, he then ordered coffee for two.

The General Manager looked at Dudley, and he attempted a nervous smile. He then proceeded to inform the colonel, in slightly faltering English, about the incident, and the discovery of Peter's body in his hotel room some days earlier.

The blood drained from Dudley's face, and a chill ran up his spine in shock, horror, and disbelief. He listened intently, and in silence to the GM's delivery, hanging on to the manager's every word. He tried to picture in his mind's eye, the terrible incident that had taken place, as it was being described to him. Immediately knowing who was responsible for such an act of violence, and having witnessed similar himself, he knew how vicious and ruthless, these terrorists could be.

'So the bastards had finally got to him,' he thought when the GM had finished his account.

The colonel then enquired as to Peter Maynard's whereabouts. He was informed that he had been taken to the Saad Hospital. His condition was not good. Then the GM assured Dudley that it was the best hospital in the eastern province. Everything possible was being done to ensure that Maynard was receiving only the very best of treatment.

Dudley was informed that the injured man's belongings had been packed, and bagged, and were in the housekeeping store. He could collect them after showing his iqarma, (work permit) and signing for them.

Dudley was advised that the police had examined the contents as they searched for clues they found nothing to give any indication as to was responsible, or why the savage beating had taken place,

'If the police get involved, this could open up another can of worms.' Dudley thought. 'Oh, my! What a tangled web we weave!'

Being a complete stranger to the region, the colonel had no idea where the Saad Hospital was. Akram was still seated in a comfortable chair some distance away. He was well feasted, and was feeling rather mellow, and a little sleepy. He ordered a third cup of coffee in an attempt to stay awake. Whilst he waited, he casually picked at his teeth with a wooden toothpick. He also noticed that Dudley was talking to a corpulent well-dressed man in the corner of the foyer, and noted the colonel's body language, as he sat listening to the General Manager. He could not hear what was being said, but could tell that all was far from well.

Finally, Dudley stood up. He shook hands warmly with the GM, and thoughtfully returned to his seat back in the restaurant area. He sat opposite the project director, and was silent for some moments.

'Mushkela sadiq' (Is something wrong my friend?)

'Yes, sorry, a bit of a shock really, old boy. Something is very wrong.'

Gradually, he relayed part of the story from the manager's account. It was now Akram's turn to become visibly shocked. His mouth dropped open in awe. His coffee cup was held poised in his right hand, half way between the table and his mouth. Akram replaced the cup in its white china saucer without taking a sip.

He asked many questions of Dudley as to why and how such a thing could have happened. The colonel could only say that it was a total shock to him as well, which of course, it was. He could not tell about Peter's discovery of the terrorists, and in truth, that was what it was really all about.

Akram sat quietly and attentively. He nodded his head solemnly as he listened; to the story as was told to Dudley by the GM. He fumbled in his pocket and brought out a string of brown agate stone "worry beads."

In agitation, he transferred the beads from forefinger and thumb, one bead at a time, in a nervous manner.

Finally, the PD kindly offered to go with Dudley, and drive him to the hospital, wait for him, and then return the Riyadh representative back to his vehicle in the Sheraton Hotel car park.

* * *

Peter had had a full body scan and the doctor's report confirmed a hairline crack on Maynard's left shin bone. The patient's nose had been broken and had been reset. There was severe bruising to the head, body, and upper and lower limbs. Two ribs were cracked. Both eyes were badly swollen; the retinas fortunately had not been dislodged. The brain scan showed nothing untoward. There was activity, and luckily no sign of internal bleeding. Some of the organs were badly bruised but functioning fairly normally. His pulse rate was lower than normal, but steady. The patient was in a deep coma, and his condition was being closely monitored by both medical staff, and machines. Total bed rest was what was needed; also it was nature's best remedy to cure his injuries.

* * *

Dudley stood at the side of the bed in the Intensive Care Unit cubicle. He was in a shocked and stunned silence. The unfamiliar smells of disinfectant, mingling with wilting flowers, and body odour, assaulted his nostrils. A nurse stood unmoving just inside the doorway observing him, and the patient. Dudley was both bewildered and sickened by what he saw lying on the bed in front of him. The black and blue swollen face, bandaged head, scarred face, with leg in plaster lying on the bed was hard for him to come to terms with.

It was hard to believe that this battered, bruised, and broken piece of humanity was his friend.

The colonel had not seen such inhumane injuries since he had served with the army in the Falklands, in 1982.

Observing the drip, he followed the tube down to the needle inserted into a vein in Peter's left hand, which was secured by a plaster. He appeared to have plastic tubes everywhere, going into and out of his body, including his nose, and coming away and disappearing under the bed. An oxygen mask was placed over his nose and mouth and a ventilator made a noise as it rose and fell rhythmically aiding the patient to breathe.

Visibly shaken, the colonel turned and gazed out of the window. A lump came to his throat.

He stood in silence for some moments, alone with his thoughts. He turned, and again idly watched the ventilator rise and fall. He observed the wires attached to suction pads placed over the left side of the man's chest. These were cabled up to an ECG machine on a shelf above the bed. The luminescent green blips on the monitor ran evenly across the screen from left to right, indicating a weak but steady pulse rate.

Standing in a silent vigil, the ex-soldier was mystified as to what Peter had unwittingly got himself into. The words of George Fotheringaye echoed in his mind again, "these bastards will stop at nothing. Your life is in grave danger, Peter." That was true. The bastards were also "home grown." Born in the UK or brought over to England from Pakistan by their parents. The monsters would have been cared for medically by the NHS, and educated by the tax payers in Great Britain.

The young men had been corrupted in their mosques that masqueraded as holy places of worship at a young age. Mullahs and foreign militants lectured, and urged their Moslem brothers to take up arms, and make war against the

Christian West. Asians were flooding into Great Britain on a daily basis, and at an alarming rate. There were in excess of 400,000 Pakistanis coming and going in and out of the UK every year. It was too difficult to keep a check on them all.

The Immigration Service had been stretched to their limits, and had finally lost control.

How could such a vast amount of people be monitored and allowed to live illegally in the country, having contributed nothing? It didn't make sense, but then nothing in British politics or Government made sense any more. 'They've lost the plot,' Dudley mused. This was the result of a succession of weak British politicians that had allowed the influx of Asians to enter Britain unchecked over the years.

'What sort of a world are we living in?' he asked himself as he gazed out of the window, once again. 'We have sold our country to Europe, and what with Islam4UK we are heading to be a Muslim state just like America is becoming. The pathetic politicians together with weak governments were doing nothing about it. Apathy! Apathy! Sheer bloody apathy,' he pondered, 'Enoch Powell had got it right! Blair and Brown had got it wrong, and screwed up badly!'

He was suddenly aware of a pretty young nurse standing at his side. She coughed nervously indicating her presence. It was the same nurse that had not wanted to allow him into the ICU ward, as he was not a close relative. The colonel had been both authoritative and forceful, in a charming way, and had finally persuaded the young woman to bend the hospital's rules and regulations ever so slightly on this one occasion.

The friendly kind Irish girl from Dublin, had warned the colonel what to expect, even though her delicate words had not totally prepared him for what lay on the hospital bed before him. Eventually, she had conceded under gentle pressure to allow him "two minutes" by the bedside. Her head was covered, and her green eyes stood out against her pale, fresh-faced skin which was speckled with small attractive light brown freckles. The young nurse quietly broke the silence. 'Colonel, oi really do think it would be for the best if you would leave now. There's nothing that can be done. Only toime will heal the wounds.'

'Yes, yes of course, m'dear,' Dudley replied in a low voice.

'Cheerio, old boy,' he said, momentarily looking at his friend.

He walked around the bed towards the doorway. He knew full well that his voice had fallen on deaf ears. He stood at the entry for a moment looking once again at the motionless, helpless figure. It was so hard to believe what had happened to his friend and colleague.

In the corridor, outside the ICU cubicle, Dudley stopped in his stride, and asked the nurse, 'He will be alright, won't he? I mean, he will come out of the coma, and er, and he'll be OK?'

'Well, it's hard to say, sor. It's early days yet. He could be in a coma for several days, several weeks, or even several months. It all depends on how bad the beating affected his brain. Other factors are how he responds to the drugs, his inner strength, and his general state of health. The internal damage has to be repaired and then we have to hope that his mental condition won't be too adversely affected. We have to hope that there is no memory loss, constant headaches, or possible psychological problems. He is in a critical state, sure enough, but he *is* also in a stable condition. That is a good sign, to be sure. Well, what oi mean to say is colonel, his general health is not deteriorating, and he's comfortable.'

She smiled reassuringly. It had been an effort for her to put the words together. Her neat set small pearly white teeth glistened as she spoke. She was both comforting, and yet pragmatic.

Then she asked, 'Do you have any idea of how or why such a terrible thing as this has happened? The police will want to know.'

'*The Police*,' Dudley repeated in an unintentional, surprised outburst. Then he hurriedly attempted to correct himself, 'No, no, no, none whatsoever. It is a complete mystery,' he lied.

The colonel obviously could not give anything away. The story would sound too incredible for the authorities to comprehend. He would be questioned, hounded by the British press, and called to give account by the British High Commission. He may also be detained by the Saudi authorities, and charged under some archaic criminal Arabic law. George Fotheringaye would also become involved as Peter was a British national. Dudley could see a hornet's nest stirring up. The least said the better was the conclusion that he came to . . .

It was all too complicated; the best way, he thought, was to plead ignorance to any questions, and let the Embassy deal with it!'

In essence, he had no idea as to the terrorist's whereabouts. He only knew they could still be in Dammam, and close by. Maybe they followed him, or had overheard his conversation on the listening device planted in his room. That was the most likely explanation. Then a worrying thought struck him.

'What if there was an insider from the terrorist's side working in the hospital? God forbid.' He shuddered. No! He was getting paranoid.

'Does he have a woife and family?' the nurse asked, breaking his concentration. Just then a Saudi doctor in a white coat hurried past the couple. He nodded to them as he entered the small bay where Peter lay. Dudley and the nurse took a few paces back, idly watching through the window as the doctor checked the notes at the foot of the bed.

They observed the doctor checking various charts, also a range of electronic devices that gave visual information.

'Well, I know that he has a wife, and that she is from the Philippines, and she lives in England,' replied Dudley, 'and that's all I know about him and his family really.'

'Does his woife know what has happened to her husband?' the nurse asked quizzically.

'I have no idea, probably not. I don't have any contact with his wife or family. I've only known Peter Maynard for a short while. I'll have to try and contact the family somehow; probably through the HR Department of our company, or the British Embassy.'

'This is a bad business, and that's a fact,' the nurse added as she slowly led the way from the cubicle, down the highly polished floor of the corridor towards the main entrance.

'Yes, it certainly is,' Dudley agreed. He extended his right hand thanking the nurse for her help. She was surprised at the gesture. As the colonel felt her small, soft hand being drawn into his gravitational field. It was a wet-fish handshake he received from the woman. She smiled, slightly embarrassed. The colonel smiled too, grateful for her help. He nodded his head in respect, and walked purposefully out of the building.

'Hello, Dudley here,' replied the colonel answering his mobile phone having returned to his hotel room from the hospital visit.

'Hello! Am I speaking to Colonel Dudley, er, Coburn-Smythe?' A female voice enquired.

'Gosh! Yes, I am he. Who *is* this, please?' he asked the well-spoken woman.

'I am sorry to bother you, colonel, this is Mrs. Maynard. I am Peter Maynard's mother. I am calling you from England. The recruitment agency gave me your name and phone number. I do hope you don't mind my phoning you, and hope that I haven't called you at an inconvenient time.'

'No, no, no, not at all,' the colonel responded, 'and *please*, Mrs. Maynard, just call me Dudley. It makes things so much easier and far less formal.'

'Thank you, er, Dudley, then please call me Jill. I am phoning you because Peter's wife and I haven't heard from Peter for about five or six days now. Kristine, that's his wife, is worried sick. She's from the Philippines, you know, and she's on her own, and missing him terribly. She can't contact him by phone, and he hasn't contacted her or me, for that matter, not even by email,' then she added hurriedly with a slight laugh in her voice, 'but that's not unusual for Peter. His wife tried to call him on . . . .'

She was rambling on slightly embarrassed, when Dudley interrupted.

'Look, I'm sorry, Jill. I am going to have to stop yer there. Are yer at home?'

'Yes!'

'Are yer alone?'

'What a strange question,' she thought.

'No, my husband is here. Why?' She was slightly taken aback.

Dudley's mind raced. It was as if he was back in the army again, and having to inform a relative of a young soldier, some terrible news about her son having been killed, injured, or missing in action. 'Good,' he began, 'please sit down, Jill. I have something unpleasant to tell yer.'

He then elaborated on the circumstances that had brought him to Dammam and his visit to the hospital that evening.

'Oh, no!' she exclaimed choking back the tears. 'Oh! My goodness! No, no!'

Dudley heard a lot of coughing and choking distantly at the other end of the link.

'Mrs. Maynard, Jill are yer alright?' he asked.

'Hello! *Hello*! This is Jill's husband here, Michael Maynard. What's wrong? Has something happened to Peter?' he asked in an irate and concerned manner.

'Yes! Mr. Maynard. I am afraid something has happened to Peter.'

Dudley then relayed the account for a second time. He never discussed any of the details that had brought Peter's circumstances about. He did not want to complicate matters, or give reason to add further distress, or for the authorities to become involved. The colonel was in a bit of a predicament as he sought a diplomatic answer.

'But how could such a terrible thing have happened? Peter's not the type of guy that would get involved in a fight. Well, not since he left the army anyway. You say this happened in his hotel room? I mean why, I mean how? What sort of a hotel was he staying at? Who is responsible?'

The questions came at Dudley in a steady staccato stream, like the bullets from an automatic weapon. The colonel was not able to give any further explanation. He felt at that moment as if he was in some way responsible by having imparted the bad news. He figured the man at the other end of the line expected him to have all the answers. If the family knew the truth, they would be mortified. In ancient times, the messenger bearing bad news used to be killed; he felt that somehow he fitted that role in the present situation.

'Mr. Maynard, I am sorry. He took a very bad beating. I only got here in Dammam meself terday ter find out why Peter had not reported for work, or made contact with the client or the office fer the past five days. As soon as I heard about this, I went directly to the hospital ter see fer meself. I am sorry, Mr. Maynard, I am merely the messenger, and I have told yer and yer wife all I know. Please feel free to give me a call any time. I will do whatever I can.'

BALUCHISTAN IS A province on the west side of Pakistan fraught with problems. Terrorists have in the past blown up the water supply, and power lines to the towns and villages in an attempt to destabilise the Pakistan government.

In a mountainous desert area that borders Afghanistan with Pakistan, there is a small area of Iran known as Sistan. There in Sistan is a corridor where some of the Al Qaeda Islamic terrorist training camps are situated. Strangers can be easily spotted by Taliban lookouts if they wander into the region. These sentries are posted around the perimeter of the camps high up in the mountains. They are highly trained, and well armed. A six-hour walk along a narrow path that runs like a seam through Afghanistan's Urgun Mountains leads to a remote village near the Pakistani border. It is in these mountainous barren regions that Osama bin Laden and others like him had been hiding.

Grenades are lined up like sentries along a small patch of land. Nearby, weapons and explosives are piled high in readiness for action.

The Afghan warlord Gulbuddin Hekmatyar and his band of followers are ready to die in the drive to kick out the British, Australian, Canadian, Americans, and other occupying forces from his land. The Taliban is ready, and also capable of bringing down the despised pro-United States Government of the much despised Hamid Karzai, in Afghanistan.

The United Nations and other intelligence agencies had reported in the past a resurgence of terrorist training camps in the remote regions. These are along both sides of the Afghan-Pakistan borders.

The US military authorities in Afghanistan had stated several times that there are many compact fighting units in mobile camps starting up again. These can be on the move at a moment's notice. The camps have started to grow back after months of having lessened their activities due to US-led troop movements. The hunt for Islamist militants in the region continues relentlessly on a daily basis. The training camps have sprung up regularly since the *Taliban* fell in December 2001.

It is a well-known fact that Pakistan's banned Lashkar-e-Tayyaba militant groups train in a camp that is 150 kilometres west of Islamabad. Trainees learn how to make bombs by the use of ammonium nitrate, fertilisers, and aluminium powder. These chemicals are the basic ingredients for such types of explosive devices. The primitive bombs are set off by detonators, timers, and more commonly mobile phones.

The trainee terrorists prepare for terror tactics, and are instructed in the art of ambushing a column of moving vehicles. They can detonate a small bomb targeting foot patrols culminating in serious injury and death. They are masters in the laying of land mines, anti-tank, and roadside bombs. The activists are trained to become suicide bombers, and they target large groups of soldiers or police that are gathered together, in order to maximise death, and cause serious injury.

The trainees are "educated" in the techniques of hijacking airliners. They quickly learn which countries have weaknesses in their airport security systems, and those that are relaxed in their precautionary measures, and procedures.

The would-be revolutionaries practice the timing of when to hurl a grenade with accuracy. They also know when to clutch it to the body, and blow him or herself up, together with a nominated targeted victim, or victims. The training camps are evil places; they preach the gospel of death, destruction, and hatred on a continual basis. All are shrouded in "religious approval."

They believe in takfiri which is a reference to an extremist ideology that urges Muslims to kill anyone they consider to be infidels. This also applies to fellow Muslims who are thought to be a threat to the terrorist's fanatical beliefs.

The instructors in the main are Arab, Afghani, and Pakistani extremists. There are two Okai camps. One is in Islamabad, and the other is in a remote corner of the rugged North West Frontier province bordering Afghanistan. The natives of Afghanistan's *Paktika* province move regularly back and forth across the porous border. Their movements are very hard to detect even by satellite and therefore, they more often than not, remain undetected.

No one can stop these fanatics. As soon as they are killed, many more are ready to take their place and die for the Cause, their religious beliefs, their country, and ultimately for the Islamic terrorist brotherhood.

It was one such camp in Tora Bora, in Baluchistan, that hugs the Pakistani borders where Sohail and Ali were headed. The two men flew from Saudi Arabia into Islamabad. Then they went from the international airport to the domestic airport, where they took an internal flight.

A car was waiting on their arrival as they exited the arrivals hall. Then the men were driven at speed along the narrow winding road leading to the training camp nestled in the mountainous foothills and arid valleys.

The region is extremely remote. Gunfire on the rifle ranges can be heard by the villagers that reside some distance away. The firing of weaponry echoes around the mountains. Local shepherds and inhabitants ignore the retorts, and carry on with their daily mundane lives, barely eking out an existence with their chicken, sheep, goats, and farm produce.

* * *

On arrival at the training camp, Ali and Sohail were shown to their quarters which consisted of a four-man tent. Everything in the camp was collapsible. All furnishings were able to be carried away at a moment's notice. The caverns in the mountains also housed weaponry, ammunition, and explosives. The caves provided storage of weapons, limited cover, and protection from aerial bombardment by American patrols, and drone aircraft.

Donkeys stood disinterestedly in the relative shade of a few sad-looking trees. They were tethered to wooden posts. A number of camels lay on the ground in the shadow of the hills chewing the cud ignoring any activity around them.

Several Asian and Arab recruits were walking in a straggly line all heading in the same direction. It was prayer time, and they were making their way to a large tent that had been set aside as a mosque. One mullah was shouting through open hands, 'Allahu Akbarrrr!' (God is great), the call for prayer. The throng removed their sandals, and boots, and washed their feet before entering the makeshift mosque. They then filtered through the open tent flap entrance, and then stepped onto the carpeted area inside. They stood in silence for a few moments with their heads bowed in concentration. Some looked at their open palms as if reading a book. Ali and Sohail joined the assembly. Then as one, the congregation knelt, bowing, with their heads, just touching the carpeted floor.

After prayers, the religious leader singled out the two newcomers. He instructed them to accompany him to his private billet. Again they removed their footwear before entering the tent as a mark of respect. They stood in front of the mullah who was seated behind a makeshift desk. A well-worn copy of the Koran lay on the table. Two collapsible chairs were to the side of the desk, but as the men had not been invited to sit, both stood uncomfortably and passively before their leader. Ali and Sohail nervously looked at each other and then, as if in shame, looked down at the worn Persian carpet. There were no greetings or bonhomie.

'You have been very careless in your dealings,' the cleric began speaking in Urdu.

Then he raised his voice in anger, '*What are you going to say to me? That you are sorry?* You lost the manual, and now it is in the hands of Western infidels that have knowledge of our campaign. You are putting your brothers at great risk by your careless attitude, and the importance of our cause. The mission will continue with or without you.' He stood up and balled his right hand into a fist leaning forward in a threatening manner, putting his full weight on the table with his open left hand.

'I could have you both executed for losing an epistle of such high value. Our esteemed leader wants you put to death for your careless actions. I pleaded for your miserable lives, although I am not sure now why I did so.

'You all knew that the book is of such high importance. You knew that it had to be handed over to the newly appointed senior cleric in Riyadh. He has now had to postpone his visit to the UK.

'You have caused great embarrassment, and made trouble for us all, and in particular, for me!'

His voice was caged behind large clenched white teeth in his anger. Both Ali and Sohail swallowed hard; they could feel the man's wrath. The big man moved even closer glaring into their eyes, and into their very souls of the now startled terrorists.

'You gave away your position, and you lost the manual. You may have delayed our planned attacks, or worse, they may have to be cancelled.'

He pulled his face back from across the table, he breathed hard through his large nose. His wide-set eyes gouged into Ali's sheepish gaze back at the imam. His nostrils flared as he breathed. Ali felt the dark brown eyes peering down at him like the twin barrels of a shotgun.

The Asian's minds were blank. They were momentarily incapable of producing a single thought of their own. It was as if they were mesmerised. They knew that they had brought great shame upon themselves. Their destinies now lay in the furious heavy hands of the man, now seated, opposite them. He clenched and unclenched his hands at irregular intervals, and occasionally tugged at his long grey/black beard.

A pulse of remorse crept through the two chastised extremists.

'No one can stop us. You should *know* that. We will die for our beliefs, for our country, for our Islamic brothers, *for our rights, and above all for the great one!*' The cleric fumed. He stood up again and pulled himself erect. He was well above average height, around six feet seven inches tall. He levelled an angry, shaking, knurled finger at the men as they cowered in fear of his wrath.

'From now on you will do *exactly* what you are told, and to the letter. If you do not, you *will* be executed. The indignity, and disgrace will be carried across to Pakistan, and your homes, your families and friends alike, and to the country of infidels namely, Britain. They will know of your traitorous cowardly incompetence, and these will be broadcast throughout the Muslim world. You will die in shame, and *not* as martyrs in honour.

'Death comes with honour when fighting for the Cause of the Islam Brotherhood!' he continued.

'Good Muslims die as martyrs; with honour, and not with shame!'

The two men dare not speak. Their eyes were angled down again on the worn red and gold Persian carpet in the imam's makeshift office.

'But how will you fare in the next life? You will be like the snake, crawling on its belly—the lowest form of life.

'Fortunately, you have disabled the man that took the manual, this Maynard infidel. But he has succeeded in outwitting you all. His incapacity will hopefully delay his intended actions to contact the British or American security services. Reports from our intelligence have stated that he is now in a hospital in Dammam. He will be out of commission for a number of weeks. You had better pray that he does not die before we get the manual back. In the meantime you will undergo rigorous training again, as a punishment. You will have to graduate to an acceptably high level once again, and your progress will be monitored by the instructors. If you meet the expected level required, you will follow this Maynard, unseen, back to the UK, where you will intercept him before he can pass the manual on. That is, if it is not possible to get the item back before he leaves the Kingdom of Saudi Arabia. We know his address, in England, and once again his conversations will be monitored. Our brothers have already seen to that.

'One of our brothers in the British Embassy in Riyadh has managed to retrieve some photocopies of the transcripts, and others were retrieved from his room. You know this, *but it is not good enough!*' his voice rose again in anger.

'*You are both a disgrace to the Cause.* We have to get the manual back at all costs. Do you understand me? *Do you understand?*'

'Gee, gee!' (Yes yes!). They eagerly answered in Urdu, thankful that their lives had been spared. The Asians had been given another chance to placate their religious leader.

'While you are here you will study the Koran.' He touched the holy book reverently.

'You will master the training manual and terrorist methods and procedures again, and train with the new recruits from daybreak until dusk. Hopefully, you will become proficient in the making of explosives, enemy ambushes, and familiarise yourselves with the handling of weapons. Espionage and other clandestine activities will also be studied. This will enable you to carry out the mission that you have been given to 100, percent satisfaction. You will again learn sniper tactics, and if, or when you have become expert in all these crafts, only then will you be able to return to Arabia. Where it is hoped you can continue with your planned tasks. You will stalk this Maynard person, day and night until the manual is returned. Is that understood?'

'Gee, gee!' both men chorused, eagerly trying to please the mullah, and anxious to leave his presence as quickly as possible.

'Tariq and Asif have informed us that this Maynard plans to take the manual with him to England. There he wants to involve the British Intelligence authorities, and anti-terrorist agencies in London. It is our understanding that the manual is hidden somewhere in Riyadh.

'You will intercept him *before* his plan can be executed. You will then take custody of the manual. You will not allow him or anyone else to have the chance to hand it over to any of the so-called, British Intelligence agencies. You will give it to our leader at the Bradford mosque. Is all this clearly understood?'

The two men again answered in the affirmative, by shaking their heads from side to side in agreement, Pakistani fashion. 'Finally, you will carry out the execution!

'Our forthcoming attacks are listed in that manual. This is a jihad (holy war). We are at war with the West and with all the Christian infidels. We are the Brothers of the Islamic Cause. We shall avenge those brave souls that have given their lives so courageously in our name. Death to those that have occupied the Arab lands of Iraq, and Afghanistan. Death to those who have occupied and contaminated Saudi Arabia, and the most sacred holy land of Makkah! We will fight against them and drive them out. We shall heap devastation on those Westerners that have depicted our holy prophet; peace and blessings be upon him. Their houses and buildings will topple on top of them, and they will be destroyed by fire for what they have done.

'We will bring conflagration and terror to the cities of the western world. Our brothers in England are waiting for the world to rise up to the challenge, and take up arms. Christian blood will flow through the streets of all their capital cities. We will rise victorious by taking control. We will destroy their churches and bars, and replace them with mosques. This is the plan with Islam4UK, and it will be only a few years from now before we are victorious.

'You have been chosen to stand up and fight against the western ways. You have been chosen to fight against their filthy habits, their materialistic, demonic ideals. You owe it to your families. You owe it to your brothers in arms, and lastly you owe it to yourselves,' his voice rose and fell as he spoke.

'You should join the list of martyrs. *But* because of your despicable carelessness you are here. Allahu Akbar. (God is great). *Now get out of my sight. Get out!*'

Ali and Sohail walked hurriedly out of the tent in silence, their heads bowed in shame. They placed their feet back into their sandals and walked away, thankful not to have been made an example of in front of the new recruits under Shariah law. Their lives had been spared on this one occasion. The two men now had to succeed in the mission allocated to them, and prove their worth once again.

The following day, Ali and Sohail joined a group of newcomers. They were in uniform and had exchanged their sandals for socks and commando boots. Both men had an AK-47 semi-automatic rifle as they boarded a truck heading for the firing range in the hills and mountainous region. All the recruits were dressed in similar desert camouflage battle fatigues.

The trainees listened to a lecture given by a Pakistani ex-army weapons expert. The weapon they were being lectured on and using that day was, in fact, the AK-47.

'This is a semi-automatic assault rifle,' the instructor began, speaking in Urdu.

An interpreter was at his side relaying the sentences in Arabic.

'The is AK-47 is a *selective-fire, gas-operated 7.62 by 39mm assault rifle*, it was first developed in the *Soviet Union* by *Mikhail Kalashnikov*. It is officially known as Avtomat Kalashnikova. It is also known as a Kalashnikov, an 'AK', or in *Russian* slang, Kalash. Its final design was invented by another Russian by the name of *Avtomat Kalashnikova* designed in 1947, hence the letters AK. Semi-automatic means that it can deliver a single shot, and when switched to automatic, it can deliver a short burst or a volley of bullets at a speed of 600 rounds per minute. The clip itself holds thirty rounds. Another two clips of ammunition can be attached. This will give a maximum of ninety rounds. This weapon can cut a man in half at full volley.

'This is an excellent and accurate assault rifle, also extremely reliable in battle. It has a proven track record, and it is better than most similar western weaponry. Many of the enemy's weapons used to jam due to overheating, and bad design. More than fifty armies in the world use the AK-47,' he informed the class as he held the assault rifle above his head.

'The other weapon you will be using, and later become familiar with, is the AK-MP3 Kalashnikov machine gun. This weapon is designed by the same man. Both firearms use a 7.62mm bullet. The AK-MP3 is also popular with our brothers, the Taliban and most other organisations in our fight for freedom, recognition, and world dominance.' The lecture continued for another half an hour.

The AK-47 was stripped down by the instructor, and then put back together again. Each recruit had to carry out the same task having to remember the order in which it was to be reassembled. Ali and Sohail surpassed all the other recruits in speed and accuracy of this task. They had carried out the exercise many times before, also during training. It helped to remember that the first piece removed was the last piece to be reassembled. They also laid all the piece parts out carefully in an orderly line so as not to be confused, and to aid speed and accuracy of the assembly.

Ali and Sohail listened intently to everything that was being said. They had heard it all before.

The men had to achieve top marks in order to return to active service, also to appease their clerical leader.

After the lecture, there was another call to prayer. The group found a place on the desert floor, and they faced the east, bowed down, and prayed.

After prayers, another instructor spoke to the recruits about the art of killing with a single bullet. "The practiced art of the sniper" The lecturer had written in Urdu on a blackboard.

'During your practice, some of you have served well, but you can all serve better. Over the next few days you will learn how to hunt and stalk your enemy. It may be a politician, a monarch, and yes, the biggest prize of all, the world's number one terrorist. It may even be just that, the ex-president of the United States.

'Imagine that, my brothers, the honour to the Cause. Remember, death comes when it is least expected. You will kill the enemy when he makes the smallest mistake, when he and his goons are momentarily off guard. This type of killing is carried out with patience, and without the heat of battle. One bullet means one kill from a distance that is the skill of the sniper. You will wait until the target is in the centre of your sights ....'

The expert carried on for what seemed like an age. He was referring to the crosshairs of the telescopic sights. The lecturer taught how to conceal oneself unseen for long periods of time, and wait for the intended victim. He lectured on when to strike and when to run. He trained the recruits when to hide, and when to be exposed, while a second sniper took aim at the target. All through the address, he was continually making references to the enemy as infidels, enemies of Islam, a scourge on the face of the earth, and so on. This was not only an instruction on how to kill; but also a propaganda lecture on how to hate Christians. It built up revulsion against the West within the young hearts and minds seated on the dry desert floor. They listened attentively; taking in the instructor's every word.

After the lesson, Ali and Sohail attended target practice. Their marksmanship skills also exceeded those of the rest of the class, and were on par with those of their instructors.

The Asian's accuracy with the AK-47 in target practice, together with their knowledge of weaponry and ballistics was more than favourable to their teachers

When their achievements were reported to the mullah, the two men felt sure that he would appreciate that they had learnt their lesson well.

All the recruits were given instruction on chemical warfare attacks. These included the use of ricin and anthrax.

The trainees were informed that there are eighty-nine different types of anthrax. The one most commonly used by terrorists is the airborne variety that has an incubation period of forty-five days. There are a trillion spores per gram. The most common application has been used by letter. It is inserted into an envelope, and has been sent in the past to prominent MPs, Heads of State, and so on. If the bacterium is packed into a sachet, when opened, and the letter is removed, a cloud of fine white powder will be released into the atmosphere. When inhaled, after a short period of time, it will give flu-like symptoms. Chest pain will be experienced, after a time, plus shortness of breath. It affects both the lungs and the nervous system, and in most cases culminates in death.

The instructors were not only fanatical in their beliefs, but also highly educated and thorough in their evil teaching practices.

The imam had been pleased with the steady flow of new recruits that came in from Iraq, Iran, Afghanistan, and the Asian community, both from England and Pakistan. He warned the recruits of future infidel attacks on Afghanistan, and then went on to tell the trainees the story of an honourable Pakistani woman. 'She had brought her fourteen year-old son to the Balakot Camp. She had wanted him to fight, and to die for the Cause, and had wanted her son to avenge the death of his brother, who had been shot and killed by an American marine,' the cleric informed the mass. These were considered honourable parents, and heroic youths that were brave, young, and willing to serve.

The trainees were proud to live, fight, and die for the Brothers of the Islamic Cause; (the name of their new-found group), working beside Al Qaeda and the Taliban, and spear-headed by the imam . . .

The insurgents were informed of the sleeper cells in England, America, Asia, and right across Europe, and the Middle East, and even in Uganda, and Kenya in East Africa. This group is known as Al-Shebab. These activists are highly trained, and ready to strike anywhere, and at any time. They are fanatical in their beliefs and will rise up when the call to arms arises.

There are various specialists in each group, depending on the type of mission they are to be engaged in. The new recruits were being trained for similar clandestine activities.

The extremists on active service live near normal lives. Some lay in hiding in safe houses; others live in bedsits, and take on jobs in their chosen profession. Some are doctors, teachers, lawyers, software specialists, waiters, etc. All are skilled in the art of killing, and destruction. The terrorists integrate with the local community getting to know their enemy. The chosen targets range from railway stations, airport complexes, ministerial buildings, crowded shopping markets, and malls, airport control towers, unguarded civil aviation ground to air radar stations, and reservoirs. All are potential targets. The reward is that the terrorist's parents and families are looked after financially by the terror groups for the rest of their lives. It is the understanding that once the militant has carried out his or her deed, s/he is bound for Paradise!

* * *

Meanwhile, back in Riyadh, at the offices of STS and AHT, the conference room had fallen silent. All members of the meeting were held in awe at the grave news as Dudley concluded his report. He had given a full verbal briefing of his meeting with the Eastern project director. There appeared little interest in the update as it was overshadowed by the account of Peter Maynard's present predicament. Even the sheik was speechless, and failed to understand why the engineer was lying in a hospital bed severely injured.

'How had he got himself into such a situation?' he pondered.

The sheik then considered if the VIP connections could be involved. There was the Royal House of Saud, including the king and princes, the MODA (Ministry of Defence and Aviation). There were generals, and senior government officials, but these were no threat to anyone. There are no extremist organisations that would want to cause harm or hostility to the hierarchy, or interfere with the telecom project; he finally figured that it must be an unrelated incident.

Possibly there was another and a more feasible explanation. Maybe there was something the sheik was not aware of, something that he had not been told about, but this only added to the mystery, and intrigue.

TIME HAD PASSED since Peter's unfortunate cruel beating and his subsequent admission to hospital. Still in a coma, he had been moved to a small private ward. He continued to be wired to machines, and drip-fed. His breathing was still continuously assisted by the use of a ventilator.

*   *   *

The company had flown Peter's wife and mother to the eastern province. Dudley had met the ladies at the airport in Dammam, and presented them with the traditional black abayas that they were obliged to wear due to Saudi and Arabic customs. The retired colonel had driven the ladies to the Southern Sun Hotel, and once they had checked in and deposited their cases, he then drove them to the hospital. Dudley had briefly looked in at the young engineer, and noticed a distinct change in his outward appearance, thankfully for the better.

On their arrival at Peter's bedside, his mother and Kristine were both overcome with emotion at seeing their loved one unconscious, and in his present condition.

The bed rest had paid dividends, and the body was well into the healing processes, both externally and internally. His damaged organs had repaired with no apparent lasting ill effect. The visible signs of the bruising were clearing up, and the swelling of the face had gone down. His leg was still in plaster.

Both the medical staff and the engineer's relations wondered if there would be memory failure, or brain damage. This would not be known until he fully regained consciousness.

Then one day, about two weeks later, when the ladies were at the bedside, they experienced the first signs of outward change. There was a physical movement in the comatose patient.

It was Kristine that noticed it first. The forefinger of her husband's left hand had moved involuntarily. She instinctively held his hand tighter. His eyes were closed, and his face remained impassive.

'Peter. Peter,' she whispered. 'If you can hear me, squeeze my hand, my love.' She waited a few moments and then called his name again.

As she held her husband's hand in hers, Kristine felt a very light squeeze on her small delicate hand.

Her eyes opened wide in amazement. She turned to look at Peter's mother, with her mouth open in amazement.

'He can hear me,' she said excitedly, with tears in her eyes. 'He can hear me, Mum!'

'That is wonderful news,' Peter's mother replied. She had also witnessed the very slight movement of her son's hand in Kristine's. Although, she logically thought, it could have been an uncontrolled movement, and therefore, a coincidence. She stood up leaning over the bed, and quietly called out his name.

Then, unexpectedly, Peter's eyes flickered open. The movement lasted only for a brief moment, and then his eyes closed again.

Peter Maynard lay still and motionless as he had done before. His mother walked out of the small ward. She went in search of a nurse, or a doctor. Kristine kept calling Peter's name. She continued talking to him softly, still holding his hand and rubbing his finger with her thumb. His wife willed him to return to consciousness. She prayed softly, the Lord's Prayer, asking God to bring her husband back.

'Come back my precious husband,' she said. 'Come back to me, my love. I need you. We need you. We all want you back so much. I am here for you, my love. I am waiting for you, I need you.' Tears welled up in her eyes flowing uncontrollably in rivulets down her cheeks.

It was the same pretty, young Irish trauma nurse that Dudley had spoken to some weeks before. She accompanied Jill Maynard back to Peter's bedside.

The nurse checked on her patient. Kristine moved away dabbing at her eyes, and cheeks with a small, white handkerchief, mopping up the tears.

The nurse felt for a pulse on the patient's right wrist, looking down at the small fob watch on her apron, and noted the pulse rate. Then lifting the top of Peter's right eyelid, she shone a small torch passing the beam of light back and forth. The process was repeated on what had been Peter's badly bruised left eye. The pupil of the eye reacted to the light. The nurse nodded with approval. She also witnessed Peter's eyelids flickering. She dismissed the automatic movement, as it could have been only a reaction to the light.

Kristine carried on speaking gently to her husband, and continued to hold, and squeeze his hand momentarily.

'He is showing signs of coming out of the coma to be sure,' the nurse confirmed. 'Your being here and talking to him has obviously helped a lot. But please don't get your hopes up too hoigh yet, ladies. We still have a long way to go. It may be some toime before he comes round fully. His moind has to regulate, and register as to where he is, and what has happened to him. These will be "unfamiliar surroundings" to him sure enough. The memory of what happened to him may not be clear. Oi will see if oi can foind the doctor,' she said, smiling, and then hurriedly left the room.

In a short while, the nurse came back with a tall man. He was handsome with an untidy mop of curly black hair. Black stubble covered his chin, and beneath his nose, indicating that he had been on duty for some time. The doctor was in his mid to late twenties with a pleasant complexion. A stethoscope stuck out of the right-hand pocket of his long white coat.

'Good afternoon, ladies. I am Doctor Leturmy,' he spoke with a very pronounced French accent, whilst flashing a friendly reassuring smile at each of the females in turn as he spoke.

'Please, I would ask that you leave ze room for a short time. I need to examine ze patient in private. So if you don't mind, please. It will only be for a very short time.' He extended his arm to indicate the doorway.

'Yes, of course, doctor,' replied Peter's mother. She looked at Kristine, and nodded her head towards the open entryway.

Peter's wife let go of her husband's hand, and then stood up, and together the ladies left the room.

The doctor picked up the patient's chart hanging at the bottom of the bed and read the latest written report. He checked the graph, and wrote something on the papers. Then turning towards the motionless patient, the doctor noted the monitor as the regular light green blips passed the screen. Looking at the patient, the physician felt Peter's pulse, observing that it was marginally stronger than it had been before.

Peter's temperature appeared normal, and his heart beat was regular. The doctor placed the stethoscope around the patient's bare chest listening to his breathing. That too appeared to have improved. The unusual rasping noise had eased over the weeks, giving the impression that the patient's breathing was relatively untroubled. An oxygen mask still covered Peter's nose and mouth, as the ventilator continued making a quiet, reassuring noise of its own, as it rose and fell.

The doctor lifted the lid of Peter's left eye, and shone the torch back and forth across the pupil, as the nurse had done. He repeated the process for the right eye, nodding approvingly. The doctor took Peter's blood pressure twice; it was normal—120 over 84.

The physician's initial diagnosis was that the patient had made a significant improvement since he had last visited the bedside a few days before. He entered something on the chart, and then replaced it to its original position at the end of the bed. Leaving the cubicle, the doctor removed his stethoscope and stuffed it casually back into his white coat pocket.

'Ye-es, zere are marked improvements in 'is condition. 'E is still very weak of course, but Peter is making good progress; very good progress. I sink it would be good for 'im to see you when 'e wakes up fully, but only for a short while, as 'e will become tired quickly, and disorientated. It may not be today that 'e comes out of 'is coma, but . . .' the young doctor shrugged his shoulders, and his mouth dropped open. He extended his arms away from his sides.

'I sink quite soon now, we 'ave to 'ope for ze best, and maybe pray for 'is recovery. Please be tolerant, we will know more when 'e is fully conscious.'

The doctor then gave an infectious smile to each of the ladies, which was full, wide, white, and open. Kristine smiled happily in return at the news. The two women had listened to his account intently and respectfully nodded in agreement, so as not to interrupt the young doctor in his verbal diagnosis.

'So as I said, and on a lighter note, eet ees very good news for ze two of you ladies today,' he concluded. He smiled again, as he faced the two women. His manner was charming, reassuring, and inspired confidence. The tall, handsome practitioner had made a very favourable impression on both Peter's wife, and mother. Doctor Leturmy had also given them something they needed more than anything else in the world and that was, "hope."

'How long do these injuries take to heal, on average, doctor?' Jill Maynard asked.

'Recovery will be a slow process—normally, if a person is reasonably fit, maybe six to eight weeks. 'Is leg will take six weeks maximum to heal, we will probably remove the plaster in a few days. Zen 'e will need to exercise as zere will be muscle loss. Bed rest is ze only cure and zis is what 'e is getting, and nature does ze rest. Zese things take time.

'Zere may be memory loss, 'eadaches, dizziness,' again he made a face as he shrugged his shoulders. 'I don't know, but I don't sink zere will be any permanent brain damage, as zere is activity, when we last did a scan. 'Opefully, zere will be no long-term complications, we 'ave to 'ope, and wait and see.

'OK. I will check on 'im again later. Please excuse, I 'ave to see anozer patient.' They both thanked Dr. Leturmy warmly. He gave each in turn another broad smile, a flash of the teeth, and then he walked briskly away.

The nurse came back; she stood by the two women, having picked up the tail end of the doctor's conversation. She smiled at Jill and Kristine as the doctor disappeared around the corner, 'Glory be to God. It is good news, roight enough,' she began, 'and we must be thankful for small mercies.'

Two days later, the patient was showing the first real signs of recovery from the coma, and the injuries that he had sustained. Peter was able to move his eyes, flicker his eyelids, and move his fingers and the toes of both feet. The pain he had experienced before had now all but disappeared apart from his injured ribs.

Mentally, he was disorientated with regards to his surroundings. He sometimes had a problem focusing, and would close his eyes, and then try again.

Seeing his wife and mother at his bedside, Peter thought that he was back in England.

'But how did I get back?' he asked himself.

The engineer's mind was completely confused and full of unanswered questions. Even though he tried, Peter was unable to untangle the mess in his brain, or to form any logical thought pattern.

Kristine and her mother-in-law diligently continued their daily visit.

Peter gently squeezed Kristine's hand in his when he felt her touch. She noticed that his grip was slowly getting stronger, and this was a sure sign that he was well on the road to recovery.

The ladies gently spoke to the recuperating patient in turn. Again he would respond only by the squeeze of his hand.

'It was an odd way to communicate,' he thought as he sat up in bed, but it was the best he could do for now. He soon became exhausted in his confused state, and wondered why his mother and wife were wearing the black abayas in England!

The engineer had a memory of men wearing black balaclavas. Peter thought he remembered the sickening blow to his leg, or did he imagine it? He could sit up normally on his own once again.

'What had happened? Why did it happen? Where am I?' He thought his mind was playing tricks? Many questions came and went. They drifted in and out of his intellect, like the ebb and flow of waves on the seashore, only not so regular. Thoughts approached, and then receded before returning again. His disorganised memory teased him like a sort of mind game. The biggest frustration was not being able to hold on to the memory of anything for more than a few seconds.

As a result of the haze of his slightly bewildered mind, together with a minor delirium, he had a semi-permanent quizzical look on his face.

A nursing sister entered the small room. She was also Irish. Her light blue eyes peered out of a pleasant, pale, open face.

'Oi think if you don't moind, ladies, it would be for the best if you leave the room now. Peter has to rest, and to get his strength back. The doctor is on his way to carry out a few more tests. He may try and see if Peter can manage without the respirator.' Then looking at the patient, she said slightly louder, and with a strong Kerry accent, 'Would you loike to try that, Peter, would ya? Would ya loike to be able to breathe on your own, without that contraption thing beside you?'

The engineer could only raise his finger, and try a half smile. The oxygen mask and tube stifled and impaired any speech.

The engineer's wife and mother thanked the sister, as they got up to leave. Each in turn leant over and kissed their loved one on the forehead, and said goodbye. They squeezed his hand by way of reassurance. A smile, a wave, a kind word, and then they were gone.

MEANWHILE, SOMETHING WAS about to take place many miles away at Air Combat Command inside a US airbase. The location was just outside Kabul, Afghanistan. Four air crew, Larry Drew, Hugh Kelly, Ryan Clinton, and Bill Carey lounged in armchairs in front of a flickering television screen. The flyers were watching the Red Bulls verses the Dolphins football game on cable TV, live from the States.

The men booed and cheered as their teams scored or took a beating. It was something to take their minds off the boredom that had encompassed their lives. The work they did was considered to be 95 percent boredom and only 5 percent action on their current assignment. They had been in Afghanistan for almost four months. The last strike had been in Kunduz, a Taliban stronghold in the north of Afghanistan. That had been three weeks previous. Since then, they had only flown training missions, and carried out routine border patrols.

It was therefore like a breath of fresh air when the phone rang on the desk. The crews were told to report immediately to the briefing room. The upshot of it all was that an American intelligence report, together with back-up satellite photographs, revealed a new terrorist training camp. There was a lot of unusual activity in the area. The base was situated on a plateau close to a rocky mountain hillside, and was quite well hidden. The aircrew's mission was to fly low over the encampment, confirm that it was an enemy target, and then annihilate it.

The flight commander laid out a detailed map of the area to be targeted, together with latitude and longitude grid references. The four pilots studied the magnified satellite aerial view photographs of the camp. The crews familiarised themselves with all the data available. It was normal to look for landmarks such as rivers, mountain ranges, oases, roads, railroads, etc. The commander informed the four-man team that there were no reports of hostile aircraft in the region, or of any friendly troop movements.

The men synchronised their watches, picked up their helmets, and flight data, and then ran towards the waiting F-15E Eagle strike aircraft. The planes were perfectly parked on the black tarmac airstrip, fuelled, armed, and ready for take-off.

* * *

An observant Taliban lookout high on the mountainside saw, through his binoculars, two specks fast approaching just above the horizon. No sooner had he spotted them, when they were overhead, and had flown past him.

The Eagle's 30mm missiles were released, and almost immediately, made their first strike.

The ground shook, as the sandy surface erupted with an assortment of flaming tents, furnishings, clothing, provisions, and debris.

The second missile attack was more ferocious, and finished the camp off in its entirety. The innocent docile animals were blown apart. Their bodies were thrown into the air, and the carcasses became dismembered, as the bloody remains fell to the ground. Other debris came down to rest in a haze of dust and smoke.

Larry had observed that some of the Islamic extremists were desperately running to take cover into the mountain hollows. He pulled back on the controls of the aircraft, and obediently the craft sped upwards. The fleeing terrorist recruits from the firing ranges would be the next target, Larry decided. He spoke over the radio to Ryan, saying that he was going in for another strike. The Eagle flew up high into the clear blue sky, made a tight arc, and at high speed, the aircraft flew low as it roared back over the region. With the moving human targets in his sights, Larry released the second missile from the aircraft. It disengaged itself from the fighter, and snaked at a furious speed towards the running men.

The missile exploded. Bodies were tossed up into the air like rag dolls, falling to the ground with a sickening thump. Bones broke with such force that they shattered. Limbs were torn off and torsos ripped apart. Blood and intestines spurted out from the carcasses. Blood flowed in rivulets, making crazy patterns as it oozed and trickled from the torsos onto the arid desert sand. The firing range was a scene of slaughter, and utter devastation. The dying convulsed spasmodically. Some limbs twitched without coordination. Animal-like screams penetrated the air as life seeped out of the battered human remains.

Cries for help went unheard and unheeded as the men lay injured and dying. The deceased would be remembered as martyrs and heroes to the Cause by the Islamist extremists and their masters.

One man was seen running after the attack for a few metres with no feet. He eventually stumbled and fell. The young man cried out for his mother. The blood pumped out steadily from his open wounds. He became weaker, finally he bled to death. He was alone, unloved, and uncared for on the dirty, dusty, dull, yellow desert floor.

The horror of the attack was reminiscent of the devastation that the cowards had inflicted on their own people in the market places, malls and crowded places of worship.

There was no consideration given by the anarchists to the innocent Westerners' that went about their normal daily routine, or to their own kind.

'Eat your hearts out, you sons of bitches,' screamed Larry over the noise of the engines, and then he yelled in high spirits 'YeeHaaaaaa!'

Hugh laughed at his sudden and uncharacteristic outburst that he heard over the radio.

Meanwhile, high in the mountains, a Taliban militiaman held an SA-7 ground to air, heat-seeking Russian missile carried on his shoulder. He aimed ahead of his target, and squeezed the trigger. The missile snaked away from the mountain range leaving a smoke trail. It struck the belly of the aircraft that Larry and Hugh were flying.

Ryan had spotted the flash of the rocket launcher. He had a fix on where the missile had come from. He purposely overshot the target, and turned out of range of the missile.

Pulling hard on the joystick, the plane obediently lifted skywards. He made a tight arc in order to engage the enemy. Then flying low, he released his second missile. Again, pulling on the joystick to lift the aircraft up and away before the missile struck the Taliban outpost. His target was a group of militiamen.

He turned, circling high above the scene of destruction, and then reducing height he surveyed the damage.

Larry and Hugh's aircraft had spiralled out of control, as it fell to the ground. The fuel had ignited. The body of the fighter plane, the wreckage, and humanity were burning ferociously on the desert sand as one.

In the distance, Ryan spotted a flyer hanging from a parachute. It was Larry. He had ejected at the point of impact. For some reason, Hugh never made it. He went down in flames with the burning aircraft, and was incinerated with the rest of the craft.

Ryan, at the time, had no idea whether it was Larry or Hugh that was being carried by the wind down to terra firma. He flew past dipping his wings in a salute to whoever it was. The flyer parachuting down, would instinctively know that he had been spotted. A search team of Chinook helicopters would be scrambled. Ryan then turned the aircraft, and flew back in the direction of the airbase. He would be debriefed, and then would make his report.

* * *

The cleric and Ali had managed to enter the relative safety of the cave as the first missile struck. Both were thankful to be alive and uninjured. They had been walking together away from the main party when the rocket exploded. The remainder of the terrorists had been carrying out manoeuvres on the open terrain. They had been practicing firing from the hip, firing in a kneeling position, firing standing up, and firing lying on the ground. Only two out of the eighteen recruits, and the clerical leader, had survived the air strike. Sohail had been killed instantly. That now left Ali plus Asif and Tariq who were still in the UK to carry out the assassination and retrieve the book.

Ali, like the rest of his four-man team was of dual nationality holding both British and Pakistani passports.

The clerical leader, Ali, and another Pakistani named Abdul had run for cover as soon as they heard the aircraft approaching as they were not on the firing ranges . . .

When all was quiet, the three men cautiously walked back to the scene of the carnage. The view that met their eyes was horrific.

Bloodied, torn, and mutilated human carcasses, some with ripped off limbs, tattered uniforms, and scattered weapons, were littered on the ground before them.

Ali instantly recognised the twisted, lifeless face of Sohail. A fountain of blood had flowed from his mouth. Ali screamed out in both disbelief, and anger. *'Death to America! Death to Britain! We will avenge our brothers' deaths! You will be hunted down and killed wherever you go. The brotherhood will follow you. Death to all Christians! Death to Maynard! Long live Umrah!'* (The Islamic community).

Ali raved hysterically, shaking his fists in the air like a man possessed.

Ali blamed Peter Maynard for the death of his friend, Sohail. If the book had not been taken, the terrorists would not have had to return to the Pak-Afghan borders for retraining, and Sohail would still be alive.

He picked up a Kalashnikov lying on the ground, and fired the weapon erratically into the air. The rat-a-tat-tat continued until the magazine was emptied. Ali staggered about like a drunken man. He threw the empty weapon down on the ground. Tears streamed down his face. He sank to his knees in despair, hugging the lifeless body of Sohail, and holding the still warm hand of his dead comrade. Ali was stricken with grief, and in total shock. He wailed as he hugged the bloodied corpse. Ali then stood up, and picked up another AK-47 from the ground. It was loaded with a clip of twenty-two rounds. Tearfully, he carried the rifle, and joined Abdul, and the mullah.

Only one of the Taliban, who was concealed in the mountain hideout, had managed to survive the attack. Seconds before the missile had been fired from the American fighter plane, he had slipped into a crevice in his efforts to get away. That fortuitous action had saved his life. The other seven men weren't so lucky. Their blooded bodies lay face down over the rocks of the mountain peak.

Their torn bodies covered their weapons as they had fallen forward when the missile struck.

From his vantage point the Taliban had seen the American pilot parachuting. He then observed the pilot gathering up his parachute once he had landed. The Taliban picked up the damaged binoculars, and peered through the cracked lens once again. The flyer had landed far away, and was moving slowly from the scene of devastation. The militiaman also observed that the pilot was limping slightly.

'That would slow him down,' he thought. The terrorist looked for the sat-phone, but it had fallen into a narrow crevice, and could not be reached. He grabbed a Kalashnikov, then clambering down the mountainside; he went in pursuit of the pilot, with the intention of capturing him.

The pilot would be a trophy, and paraded around the Taliban's hideout. The terrorists would extract the information by the use of torture. The prisoner would then be stripped of clothing, and finally executed for all to see. The event would be video recorded and used as propaganda, and a victory against the West.

*   *   *

Meanwhile, the three surviving terrorists collected as many of the AK-47 assault rifles as they could find, that were strewn around the massacre site. Apart from the rifles, there was nothing of any use left. There were a few spare clips of ammunition, and some unexploded hand grenades. They took the weaponry, and spare clips into the caves, and hid them under rocks, and inside crevices. The armaments would be hard for the enemy to find.

The bodies of their dead colleagues could not be buried as the men had no tools to dig in the barren rock and sand.

There was also no time to hang around. All the trio could do was to drag, and drop the gruesome remains into a crater that the missile had made when it exploded. The birds of prey and desert animals would finish the task for them.

The clerical leader feared that the American assassins would be back, and hurried the two men in their grisly task.

The three survivors needed to get as far away from the scene of the destruction as quickly as possible. They considered it necessary to head off towards another terrorist camp some considerable distance away. Unless they could get a vehicle, the journey overland would take three or four days. In the distance they espied the smouldering ruins of the tent lines. The vehicle that had been operational before the attack, had been hit by the blast of the air strike, and knocked onto its side. Water, gasoline, and battery acid mingled together in the sand.

The mullah knew that the crashed, and burnt out American plane would yield nothing. Wisps of smoke continued to rise from the charred remains in the distance.

The men feared that American gunships would be overhead at any moment to carry out a reconnaissance of the area for a damage report, and to pick up survivors. They would almost certainly finish off any stragglers that had survived the air strike. The fundamentalists had no knowledge that a pilot had survived. They had been in the cave when the Taliban missile struck the American fighter aircraft. If they had known about Larry's presence, they too would have pursued him as the Taliban gunman was doing.

Chinook helicopters operate along the borders, and up into the mountains. They carry out seek and strike attacks, and other operations against the Taliban on a regular basis. The mullah expected, and feared their appearance at any moment. Luckily, the familiar engine rotor noise would warn the men of their presence well in advance. This would give the terrorists time to hide or play dead.

The three men walked in silence. Ali and Abdul were deep in thought, suffering from shock, and with their own view of events. They were slightly surprised at both the speed, and ferocity of the massacre. Ali was still quietly mourning the loss of Sohail. He secretly vowed to kill Maynard, personally, if it was the last thing he did, with or without the book.

The spiritual leader was also deep in thought as he hurried away from the scene. He was furious that the training camp had been destroyed; having a sense of failure, but retribution would come with a vengeance. Victory would be theirs eventually. Their brothers in arms that were killed by the murderous American scum would now be martyrs. Their lives would not have been lost in vain. Their deaths would be avenged. He was even more determined than ever.

The mullah would have to make contact, and give a report of the devastating air strike to his headquarters.

He would also have to get an update on the man—Maynard. Ali would have to follow him back to England. The new addition, Abdul would now make up the team of four on active service. The suicide missions would be carried out by two separate teams. He was sure that the Englishman would take the book with him; unless it was found in Saudi Arabia, before Maynard's intended departure.

* * *

Larry was in pain as he hobbled onwards trying to make as much ground as he could from the targeted area. His back ached due to a slight compression of the spine, resulting from the seat as he ejected to safety from the aircraft. He had also suffered a bad landing on the uneven desert floor. His limping got progressively worse, and he needed to rest, but he was driven on through fear of being captured in bandit country . . .

The pilot had urgency to get as far away from the area of destruction as possible, and wondered if a Chinook patrol had been sent out to look for him, as it was getting late.

'It would be a case of hide-and-seek,' he thought, 'and who would get to him first, the Americans or the Taliban?'

He wasn't going to hang around to find out.

His ears were listening intently for the comforting whirring noise from the rotor blades of the Chinook helicopters.

Larry knew that Ryan would have reported back to base that a flyer had survived. He wondered about his other colleague thinking that he had also ejected.

Larry was aware that he was being followed, or more like being stalked by one man.

The slowly moving figure on the landscape was still quite some distance away. The pilot figured that he was possibly in range from a high-velocity bullet. He could be shot in the back if the stalker took aim through the cross-hairs of the telescopic sights.

Larry had spotted the Taliban militiaman through his pocket binoculars shortly after his rough landing, as he was trying to hide his parachute, and had scanned the landscape. It was then he saw the unmistakable flat Pakol hat and loose fitting clothing of the Afghani in the distance.

The fundamentalist kept a safe distance between himself, and the pilot, waiting for him to tire, and come to a complete stop. He was waiting, Larry felt, for the right moment to pounce, or release a round or two. The enemy was still a fairly safe distance away, but closing in. The rebel had found the hurriedly folded parachute. It had been hastily concealed in a rock crevice. In Larry's haste to get away; he was not able to make a complete concealment. He knew that he had made a botched attempt to cover the parachute with torn-up dried brush weed, out of sight of the Taliban. His plan now was to put some distance between himself and the militiaman. He had to set a trap.

Larry's back continued to pain him as he stumbled on. Then he saw what he was looking for—a mountain pass to his left. The rock formation was hidden out of sight of his pursuer. Larry hurriedly made for it, and quickly removed his boots and one-piece light jumpsuit.

Hastily, he stuffed it with dried brush weed, fashioning the clothing in such a way as to make it look as though it was a person. He placed the effigy standing, and leaning forward against some rocks. The scarecrow figure appeared to be with the head angled down, and with its back towards the pursuing rebel. From a distance it looked as if it was "a man taking a pee!" A half smile crept across Larry's face at the thought.

The crashed pilot then took up a vantage point a short distance away from the dummy.

He crouched out of sight in a small rock-strewn area. Clad only in underpants, T-shirt, socks, and boots he looked an odd spectacle waiting patiently for the Taliban rebel to come into view.

In his right hand, he gripped the gnarled butt of his SIG arms M-11/P-228 9mm service revolver. Killing the Taliban was going to be his passport to freedom.

Suddenly, in the distance, he just could just hear the sound of what he took to be two Chinook helicopter gunships, searching for him, and they would destroy any survivors. There was no way that he could jump out and expose himself from his hiding place at this time. A revolver is no match for a high-velocity semi-automatic weapon such as the militiaman was holding. Apart from the Taliban stalker, he was totally on his own.

Eventually, the stooped body of the hunter, clothed in loose garments, approached nearer, and came into view. He cautiously and silently crept near to what he took to be the pilot standing with his back to him. The sun was setting quickly now, and visibility was dimming fast. This added to the realism of the mock person in front of the militiaman.

The terrorist was puzzled as to why the pilot had been standing in the same position for so long.

Suddenly, and unexpectedly, a shot rang out from the terrorist's weapon.

The retort took Larry completely by surprise. His gaze had momentarily shifted to the dummy. The round of ammunition had been purposely aimed above the stuffed jumpsuit in an attempt to startle the pilot, and then maybe he would be taken prisoner. The inert dummy remained upright, and motionless.

Larry knew his cover may have been blown. Had the Chinook's crew heard the gunshot? He guessed not as the choppers sounded so far away, and the noise of the engines would have muffled the gunfire from that distance.

The Taliban gunman was mystified as to why the "person" had not moved or reacted to the gunshot. Then thinking he may be deaf, as a result of the explosion, to the aircraft, the terrorist stood up.

He crept forward towards his intended "victim," in so doing, he left himself totally exposed.

'Something is not right,' his instincts told him. 'Something was definitely not right with the stationary figure in front of him.' He crept nearer.

Larry took careful aim at the crouching, approaching figure. The pilot's arms were fully extended, and resting on a rock to further steady his aim. The forefinger of his right hand was curled around the trigger. His left hand was around his right hand and wrist to prevent any movement. He now had the target perfectly in the foresight at the end of the short barrel.

A sixth sense made the terrorist instinctively stop. His animal-like instincts sensed danger. He immediately realised, too late that he was exposed.

Instinctively, he swivelled both his head, and the weapon, round to his left, raising his rifle as he did so in search of the pilot.

In a nanosecond, he saw the flyer behind the rocks. It was too late. Larry was slowly squeezing the trigger. The first bullet tore through the Taliban's left eye socket, and shot away part of the back of his head. His Pakol hat went spinning to the ground like a Frisbee. The second bullet was unnecessary, and caught the falling man in the chest. Larry clambered down over the rocks in his underwear, and boots, and walked towards the dead man. He picked up the AK-47 ignoring the body, and walked over to the dummy. He removed the bracken from his jumpsuit, and took off his boots, he then hurriedly dressed. His gaze then returned to the bloody mass of disfigured humanity lying motionless on the ground. He felt nauseous.

Blood flowed liberally out of the dead man's shattered skull, and chest. Apprehensively and fully dressed Larry forced himself to inspect the body. The sight of the once human being, and the fact that Larry had shot, and killed a man in cold blood, filled him with revulsion.

Slightly shaken, he wandered over to the rocks from whence he had come, and was violently sick. He retched until there was nothing left but green bile. Remembering a discarded water bottle lying near the body, he hurriedly went over, and retrieved it. His mouth tasted like a sewer from the residue of partially digested food, and stomach acid.

Through half-closed eyes, he returned to the butchery, and made a grab at the canvas carrying case.

The pilot unscrewed the top of the bottle, cautiously he smelled the contents; it was water without a doubt. He took a swig of the liquid rinsing his mouth, and then spat out the contents. Once his mouth was clean, he took a swig, and swallowed the tepid water gratefully; saving some for later Larry came close to the body, and picked up the discarded Pakol hat of the Taliban. Smiling, the pilot placed it on his head. It would add to his disguise when viewed from a distance, he thought. He removed the hat and stood waving his arms frantically in the dusk at the helicopters, but they were making their way back to base. He fired two rounds from the AK-47, but the choppers carried on without hearing the retort above the noise of the engines. The "Dakka Dakka" noise of the rotor blades grew fainter, as the helicopters became more distant.

The pilot then had no option but to continue his way on foot towards the relative safety of the Pakistan border. He had no GPS, but there was a small compass in the pocket binoculars that he was using, and a map in the pocket of his jumpsuit pants. He was now as lonely as a cloud, and an enemy, in a strange and hostile land!

*　　*　　*

The visitors dutifully arrived at the hospital the following day, and as they approached the cubicle, where Peter had spent the last four weeks, they found the room to be empty!

They were surprised, and feared that he had suffered a relapse. Jill Maynard asked a passing nurse if she knew where her son was. The nurse informed the mother, that her son had been transferred to a private ward on the next level, as he was considered to be recovering.

On arrival to the ward, they were pleasantly surprised to see the patient sitting up in bed, propped up by two crisp, white pillows. His eyes were open as he took in his new surroundings, but he still had a slightly bewildered expression on his face.

The psychiatrist's diagnosis had been that Peter was suffering from traumatic amnesia, resulting in short-term memory loss. He wasn't able to retain information about the incident that had led to his being hospitalised. The recollection he had was only of the men in black balaclavas, but his mind was in a total state of confusion, and he wondered, at times, if it was a film he had seen.

The psychoanalyst had told Peter that gradually the recall of past events would come back to him, although they may be disorderly at first. This mental state was not unusual in these circumstances, and it was nature's way of dealing with the series of traumatic past events.

'Peter, how lovely to see you wide awake and sitting up in bed' exclaimed his mother giving him a kiss on the side of his head. Kristine's face lit up on seeing her husband, she felt that he was now definitely on the mend. He was breathing without the aid of the respirator. The plaster had been removed from his leg, and he had taken his first unsteady steps over a long period of immobility, and quickly became exhausted.

Peter's mother asked him a question that was on every family member's mind.

'Peter, how did this terrible beating come about? What happened?'

The engineer told his mother and wife truthfully, 'I have no idea how or what had happened to me, and how I got here.' The engineer added that he also had no idea how he had been brought back to England either.

'They must have put me on a plane,' he said. He was then gently reminded that he was in a hospital in Dammam, and still in Saudi Arabia, and certainly not back in the UK.

The patient made a poor attempt at laughing. He thought his mother was joking, although both women sat wearing their obligatory black abayas.

His ribs and chest were still quite sore as he attempted to laugh, but this was normal.

'Maybe he will tell us the truth in his own time,' Jill Maynard thought.

She was still puzzling over how the appalling beating that he had endured, had come about.

It was a similar story for the Saudi police; they had followed the incident from the Sheraton Hotel report to the hospital, and carried out background checks. The police had traced the connections back to his work colleagues, and eventually the sheik. Due to the engineer's temporary memory loss, he was genuinely unable to assist the police in their enquiries. In fact, at one point the officers thought that the engineer was slightly demented!

The detectives soon lost interest in the Westerner. They knew that illegal stills were being used to brew, and sell alcohol. If, and when found, the muttawa (Saudi religious police), acted quickly, raiding the buildings, and pouring the contents into the street.

There had also been booze wars between rival distillers of Sid in Riyadh in the past. Without evidence, and no suspicion of him being involved in any way, the investigation was concluded and the case was closed. It was another unsolved crime in the Kingdom of Saudi Arabia!

* * *

A few weeks later when Dudley went to Dammam, he was pleased to see the progress that the consultant engineer had made. On this occasion he asked, 'How are yer feeling terday, old boy?'

'Not so bad thanks Dudders, ribs are still a bit sore. Try not to make me laugh. I think most of my memory has come back. Although of course, I don't know for sure. Some things are still higgledy-piggledy in my mind. I thought I was in England, with all these expat nurses and doctors around.'

'Ha! Ha! So yer are still feeling a bit ribby, eh?' Dudley joked. 'Yer are very lucky ter be alive. We were all very worried about yer. Any idea when yer'll be out of this place?'

'Probably in a few weeks time, I can't wait. I have been out of bed, and walking baby steps. That's what the nurses call it. But I am getting there slowly. I have to use that crutch thing there.' He pointed to a support by the bed. 'How's the project going?'

'It's finished. We had the launch, and it was a great success. The sheik was happy with the contribution that yer made ter the project. We are just getting all the site documentation up tergether, scanning it and making soft copies.

'By the way, the sheik insisted that yer were to be paid for yer time spent in hospital. Oh, and some more good news! Yer passport has an exit visa in it, and it is with HR. I can get it fer yer if yer want me to. I have yer iqarma (work permit), when I collected all yer belongings from the Sheraton.'

'Fine,' replied Peter. 'That's good of you, Dudders, thank you. By the way the hospital staff here are absolutely marvellous.'

'Yes, I've heard that too. By the way, I brought yer some wine.'

'Wine?' queried the patient, 'but I'm not allowed to drink, I am still on medication!'

'Yes, I know, but it's in its basic form, commonly known as grapes,' he joked as he passed Peter a brown paper bag containing the washed fruit.

Peter laughed, and then caught his breath in slight pain.

In a hushed voice he discussed, for the first time, events that had brought him to his unfortunate circumstances.

When he had finished unfolding the drama, Dudley said, 'Yer were very lucky, m'boy that it wasn't more serious. Yer were at death's door, as I understand. I hope yer are going ter drop this damn book nonsense now, and let the Foreign Office, or whoever deals with these things take over from now on. Just go back home to yer wife, and try ter forget about everything that's happened here, and this nonsense.'

'No Dudders, I can't! Not after going through all this? I am now even more determined to get the book and hand it to the authorities in the UK. I'm certainly not trusting George with it. He can't even look after photocopies in his well-guarded offices! No! Those terrorist bastards have got to be taught a lesson after what they did to me, to you and to your family. They're going to pay for this.'

Dudley almost exploded. He had a job controlling the level of his voice. His face became red, and his cheeks puffed up.

'*Have yer taken leave of yer senses, man? Can't yer take the beating yer had as a warning?*

'A *lesson?*' he postulated. 'Yer could have been killed all those weeks ago, and now yer persisting in this twaddle. I understand yer patriotism, and sense of righteousness, and doing yer duty, and all that bullshit, but don't yer think that yer loyalties are a bit misplaced after what yer have been through?

'Think of yer dear wife and mother and what they have been through as a result of yer being here in the hospital.

'Maybe yer medication or the knock on yer head is causing yer ter become mentally unhinged.'

The colonel paced around the small room like a caged animal in an effort to work off his nervous energy, and compose himself. He shook his head in disbelief as he stared out of the window.

Peter ignored the remark.

'I have had a lot of time to think, Dudley. Lying in this bed, and trying to piece everything together,' he said. 'God knows there's little else to do here but watch TV, fantasise over the nurses, and think about the terrorists. No, my friend, I've got this far, and now it's the final hurdle,' he responded, 'and I am on my way back to the UK fairly shortly.'

'Well, I disagree with yer entirely, but I have ter agree with yer mother.'

'My mother, why, what has she got to do with anything?'

'She says that yer as stubborn as a mule, and that's just what yer are! Where is the damn book now?'

'It is safe, but I need your help in getting it back to me when I return to Riyadh.'

'Oh, no.' Dudley protested. 'I want nothing more ter do with this damned stuff and nonsense. It's caused traumas ter my family, and ter me. Lisa and Clarita went back ter England weeks ago. I've resigned my position with the company. I stayed on because they asked me to. I want nothing else ter do with this balderdash. I've even fallen out with George over it.

'By the way, did yer know that the Embassy guys did a sweep of yer room at Radissons? They found that it *was* bugged, two devices they discovered, and I think that's what George said. That accounts fer yer being in yer present condition. Ferget it Peter, just ferget it! Those terrorist types probably know more about yer than yer know about yerself! I'm orf back to the UK soon, and the sooner the better! I've already stayed longer than I intended to help the buggers at STS, and make sure yer are OK.

'So now I don't want anything to hamper me leaving this place. I certainly don't want to end up in a hospital bed, or on a marble slab, come ter that. Besides, I have my family ter consider.'

'Yes I hear what you are saying, and you are quite right, Dudders, old mate, and thanks.' Peter interceded. 'I didn't know that Lisa and Clarita went back to Philippines, and then the UK. I am very sorry. I know that I was responsible for that. I hope they're alright now.'

Dudley nodded gravely as he slowly paced about the private ward once again. His head was bent forward as his mind pondered on other things. He had finally managed to regain his composure.

'Oh, did I tell yer, the bastards played a recording of a conversation we had in yer hotel room; on the unforgettable night that they came to my villa. Yer've had no more visits since being in here I hope?'

'No, Dudders, and the bastards must have played the same tape to me. I vaguely remember hearing our voices on their recorder; at least I think I remember. My memory is still a bit fuddled at times.'

Peter looked up at the ceiling as if searching for what had been recorded. His mind went blank as to the wording of the soundtrack.

Dudley shook his head. He took a swipe at a fly that had settled on the chromium bed frame. The fly gave a brief aerial display, and then made off to settle on the window pane.

'How can a fly settle on a vertical smooth surface,' the colonel mused.

'I have real regrets about you and your family, Dudders, believe me,' Peter continued, 'and for your present family circumstances come to that, but I have to finish what I have started. Now I only need you to do one tiny little thing for me. It doesn't involve any danger at all. Your association with me at this level is then finished.

'I can't do it myself because I no longer work on the project, and I am too weak to climb stairs.'

'D'yer mean to tell me that this damn book is somewhere on the project? Are yer out of yer tiny mind, Peter?'

'Yes, maybe I am. Maybe it is the medication I'm on, or the bump on the head, like you said. Maybe it is a lot of things, I don't know,' he reasoned. 'Look, old mate, all I need you to do is just one small thing. Pick up the book and then give it to me when I come back to Riyadh.'

'*No! I have already told yer*, I don't want any more involvement,' replied Dudley vehemently. He walked to the window gazing at the landscape, deep in thought. The fly had taken flight as Dudley approached. Cars were traversing in and out of the hospital parking area.

'My family was affected by this nonsense. I have been affected, both physically and mentally, and now as a result, I am living the life of a monk!'

The colonel stated. He had his white shirt sleeves rolled back, thus exposing his forearms. Peter could not help but notice the dark pink scar on the man's left arm. It was a living reminder of the evening when he and his family had been taken hostage in their rented villa.

'Oh! So you've stopped drinking then?' Peter joked.

'Well, OK, not quite a monk but celibate' Dudley conceded with a grin. 'Anyway, monks drink ale, and wine!'

'Well,' Peter began, 'it must be their habit. Ha ha ha. Oh, my bloody ribs.'

'Serves yer right,' Dudley said with a grin.

'I don't blame you for not wanting further involvement,' Peter said, looking at the red line on the sun tanned skin on the colonel's left forearm. 'I see the bastards have left their mark on you, same as me.'

'Oh! That!' the colonel replied casually, looking down at his left arm. 'It's just a scratch, nothing ter worry about. It will fade in time.'

'I will make sure the bastards pay for what they have done to you and your family,' said Peter.

'*Ferget about it, Peter*. How many times do we have ter tell yer?' Dudley repeated, trying to appeal to the engineer's last ounce of common sense, if he had any left.

'Put it all behind yer and move on with yer life. Yer are out of yer league, Peter. This is the material that books and films are made of. It's James Bond stuff.'

'I can't put it behind me, and that's it, and all about it. I won't stop until I meet with the people in charge of national and international security in London, Five and Six. What do they call them? The Spooks, yes, that's it. Sounds like the name of a rock band.' Peter laughed catching his breath as his ribs started to hurt once again.

Dudley could see that the engineer clearly wanted retribution for what the terrorists had done to him and to his friend, and more so to his friend's family. It was understandable, but there was one hell of a risk attached.

Dudley leant against the window sill with his back to the window. His kind face looked back at the patient with grave concern. The fly did a circuit around Dudley's head as it tried to land on the man's left ear.

'I mean look at this—damn flies in the hospital ward!' Dudley took a swipe, and missed. The fly flew upwards and away.

'Maybe the fly doesn't realise that this is a hospital, and a no-fly zone,' Peter joked.

Dudley smiled.

'Look, take George's and my advice, fer the last time. Get yer house checked when yer get back ter the UK fer those listening device things. George's theory is that someone entered yer house the night yer wife found the patio door open, and planted a bug there. It is quite feasible, because they need ter keep tabs on yer movements, and phone conversations. Is Kristine still here?'

'Yes, she intends to stay with me until I am well enough to be discharged, and so we can travel back home together. Mum's already gone back, now that she knows that I am on the mend. She has her office services business to take care of.'

'Hmm, well, getting back to yer Boy's Own adventures. Just take great care of yerselves, old boy. I mean you and Kristine.'

He moved away from the window.

'Well, I must be making tracks. Sorry, I can't help yer this time.' He straightened up, approached the bed, and shook Peter firmly by the hand. He then picked up his suit jacket from the back of a chair and nonchalantly slung it onto his left shoulder, and walked slowly out of the room.

'Bye, old boy, see yer soon. Tootle pip.'

'Can't, or won't help?' asked the engineer, calling after the retired colonel cheerfully.

Peter shifted his position from lying on top of the bed, and swung his legs so that he was in a sitting position. He was contemplating his next course of action. Maybe he should heed the advice that he had been given. It was, after all, sound common sense. Dudders was right. He ought to give up the book thing, but he couldn't. It had become an obsession with him. He struggled to get up, and grabbed the metal crutch hooked behind his bed frame.

'No!' his sub-conscious mind told him. 'To hell with it! He felt he could beat the terrorists at their own game. He had a strong impression that he must continue his quest, and get revenge on the people concerned. In addition, he had an obligation to see that the radical bastards and their organisation would pay dearly for beating him up. Not to mention the distress it had caused others.

Peter got hold of the metal crutch and stood up. He walked unsteadily around the small room, trying to exercise his legs. Eventually, he sat down heavily in an armchair. He stared at the floor, facing the doorway, and was once again deep in thought. Suddenly, his gaze came to rest on a pair of shiny patent black leather shoes. The colonel was back, he stood silently in the doorway leaning against the door-frame of the private ward. He looked at Peter seated in a chair.

'Forgotten something?' Peter asked, looking up.

'OK. I'll get the blasted book fer yer on yer return to Riyadh, and that's all I am doing!'

Peter smiled grateful at the gesture.

'Are you sure you want to do this, Dudders?'

'No!' replied Dudley. 'And that's why I'm here now, Goodbye.'

*   *   *

Larry had made it across the border into Pakistan. He wore a long brown loose-fitting jacket that he had stolen from outside a goatherd's tent one night while the man was sleeping. It had been drying on a makeshift washing line. He wore the Pakol hat, typical of the type worn by Pakistanis and Afghanis in the mountainous regions.

Larry felt odd at first in the strange clothes over his jumpsuit uniform, but it was important that he blended in with the local community in order to continue his journey safely. His back and leg still had a dull ache, but it wasn't too bad all the time he was moving. He had discarded the AK-47 and hidden it under some bushes. Now all he had for protection was his service revolver, and four rounds of ammunition.

The fighter-pilot already had three days' growth of black stubble on his upper lip and chin. This added to his appearance of being a local. 'Just as long as no one tries to talk to me,' he thought. He planned, that if anyone did try to engage him in conversation, he would pretend to be deaf and dumb, or a little subnormal, as he did not speak or understand Urdu.

Eventually, he left the barren outback behind him, and followed a road leading into a small town. After a short time, and sensing that there were no problems, he sat down outside a modest cafe. He was tired, and weary, and his back and leg were giving him pain after the long walk. Larry was asked if he wanted chai (tea), he grunted, and shook his head in Asian fashion. A small glass of sweet mint tea was placed in front of him.

It then occurred to Larry that he had no money to pay for the tea. He sat at the small table for nearly an hour resting, and taking in the activities of the local people. Eventually, he stood up. No one took any notice of him, and with an unsteady gait, he continued his journey following the narrow road ahead of him. Larry walked some considerable distance, it seemed like miles.

Every now and then he would move over to the side of the narrow road when a large vehicle approached.

He stopped only to rest. He still had the water bottle, and replenished the flask at regular intervals when he found water pumps in villages.

Eventually, as he progressed along the ever-winding busy lanes, he noticed in the distance the area getting denser, and more populated. The road widened at a junction, and vehicles passed on a main thoroughfare ahead of him from left to right, and right to left, they replaced donkeys, and oxen-laden carts carrying farm produce and country folk. The buildings and shops were taller, replacing shacks, and small dwellings. Here the people were slightly better dressed. There were many markets, and five, and six, storey buildings in contrast to the shacks and small stone dwellings that he had left far behind, and had become accustomed to.

As Larry continued deeper into the town, he saw a sign in Urdu and English, and could make out the word 'Islamabad.' He knew that if he could get to the capital, he would somehow be able to get a flight to Karachi, and then to the American Embassy. He was unaware that a US Embassy existed in Islamabad, at the time; also that it was now the capital, and not Karachi.

Larry reminded himself that he had little money on him, maybe twenty dollars at the most. He wandered around the streets looking in shop windows, and saw restaurants, and he smelt curry for the first time in days. Then he remembered that he hadn't eaten for a while, and had only been spurred on by the urgency to get to relative safety. He felt hungry, dirty, and exhausted.

As the pilot turned a corner, he saw to his surprise, a large building with a light blue fascia board displaying the word 'Citibank'. This was so unexpected.

He walked towards the bank, and opened the ATM room door. A guard stood passively outside taking little notice of him as he disappeared inside. Carefully, Larry took out his wallet, and removed his bank card. Praying, he entered his four digit pin code into the machine, and after a short while he pressed 'cash.' Lo and behold, his request was granted. The card was returned.

This was followed by a fistful of Pakistani rupees.

Larry was elated. It was as if he had won the lottery. Now he could get food, clothes, and transport without having to steal it.

The flyer bought a pair of jeans, a casual shirt, a holdall, and a pair of fashionable, casual shoes. The total cost was 455 rupees. Larry also purchased some toiletries as he hadn't washed or shaved for several days. He followed a European dressed gentleman into a reasonable looking restaurant, thinking this to be a recommendation if Westerners ate there.

When the waiter arrived, the pilot pointed to a chicken curry, pilau rice, yogurt, and papadums, all to be washed down with a bottle of water. Coffee completed the meal, and finally he requested the "check."

Feeling more at ease with himself having been well fed, the pilot left the restaurant. He then walked a short distance and made his way to a road bridge spanning a river. Instinctively he was drawn towards the centre of the bridge. He peered down at the fast flowing water.

'Why am I here?' he asked himself. Then he realised this was a good opportunity to rid himself of his service revolver. He looked around furtively. There was no one about, and no river traffic, only slow moving vehicles driving steadily over the bridge. Larry had his back to them.

Cautiously, he removed his United States Air Force issue side arm from the small of his back, and held it for some moments. It had saved his life. He looked at it one last time. Cautiously, he placed it on the parapet, and pushed it over the rim of the wall. As the revolver fell, it somersaulted once, and then there was a soft plop as it hit the water, finally disappearing from sight.

Larry retraced his steps back to the road from where he had come, and hailed a taxi to the main highway.

Once there he stopped another taxi, and informed the driver, who spoke some English, that he wanted to go to the Marriot hotel.

After checking in, he got to his room, and discarded his stolen apparel. He left it in the wardrobe.

He then took a shower, shaved, and dressed in his newly purchased clothes. Later that afternoon, the pilot asked the reception clerk if she could book a flight for him to Karachi the following day. The clerk readily agreed. Seats were available, and his flight was confirmed. He paid for both the hotel and airfare with his Citibank credit card.

The following day, Larry took a cab to the airport, and after a two hour wait boarded the plane. The flight took one hour and fifty minutes with Air Blue Airlines. The plane was flying at a height of 19,000 feet above the ground, and flew at a speed of 170 miles per hour, according to the aircraft captain.

Having taken instructions as to the whereabouts of the American Embassy in Karachi, from a fellow passenger, he decided on his next course of action.

On arrival at Karachi Airport, Larry hitched a lift with a Marriott Hotel courtesy bus. He alighted from the bus when the vehicle pulled up outside the hotel, and booked a room for one night.

It was getting late, and Larry needed to rest after his ordeal before his next planned appointment. He watched TV in his room, and eventually fell asleep.

The next morning, the pilot took a relaxing bath, shaved, and dressed in his new civilian clothes. He placed his flying suit in the newly acquired holdall, and went down for breakfast; he then collected his things from the room, and checked out of the hotel.

Once outside, he turned left out of the hotel entrance and strolled along the pavement to the next building, which was the American Embassy.

At the entrance, he was stopped by a Pakistani Police Ranger. The pilot tried to explain his situation, and showed his US Air Force identity card. Not fully understanding the pilot's English, the policeman made a call to someone inside the building. After a short wait, two American marines came out of the building to the front gate.

They checked Larry's ID and the contents of his holdall. They then observed his flying suit.

He was automatically allowed entry. The flyer was escorted by the marines to the officer in charge. After a fairly intense interrogation, a medical-checkup, and a short break, he relaxed, and then returned to the Marriot to await further instructions to be repatriated back to his unit.

*   *   *

Two weeks after Dudley's visit to the hospital, Peter had recovered sufficiently to be discharged. Kristine ran small errands for her husband, encouraging him to exercise, and fussed over him like a mother hen caring for its young. His ribs were still slightly sore, and sometimes he had to catch his breath as the pain came and went depending on the severity, or strain. His wounds had healed, but there was a visible scar on his forehead which would be a living reminder of his terrifying ordeal.

Dudley had arrived at the Saad Hospital, collected Peter, and his wife, and had driven the couple back to Riyadh with the sheik's consent. On arrival to the city of Riyadh, they booked into the Southern Sun Hotel, where Kristine and Peter's mother had been staying on their arrival in the Kingdom. The hotel was a short distance up the road from the Radissons Hotel, where Peter had resided before. He was very familiar with the area.

A few days later, the engineer visited the company offices for the last time and bade a fond farewell to his colleagues and the sheik.

The principal showed genuine concern for the engineer, and was sympathetic to the ordeal that he had sustained in Dammam. As a sign of appreciation, the sheik gave a small tea party in Peter's honour.

At the conclusion of the social gathering, the sheik presented the engineer with a commendation plaque for his services, and congratulated him for his contribution to the project.

Peter had felt that he did not deserve all the praise and fuss, and felt to some extent that he had let the sheik down.

Dudley was pleased to see the engineer finally out of the hospital and well on the road to recovery. Later that evening, the colonel suggested they had a bite to eat at Rafah's Restaurant, which was diagonally opposite, and across the busy main road from Peter's hotel on Prince Abdul Aziz Street.

Kristine stayed at the hotel that evening. Peter had told her a white lie that he was attending a farewell business dinner. He informed his wife that he had a lot to discuss with Dudley, all of which was work related. He intimated that she would be bored stiff sitting listening to their mundane talk. The engineer suggested that Kristine visited the hotel's hairdressing salon. She needed to get her hair cut and styled, and her nails manicured. That would while away a few hours, the engineer thought. Kristine was thankful for the break and felt that she needed to "spruce herself up a bit," having been through a very stressful time.

This was also her first opportunity to relax, and pamper herself as only a woman knows how, now that her husband was out of the hospital, and they were back living together once again.

It was essential for Peter to talk to the colonel alone; due to an urgent request that would come as a not too welcome surprise!

'So, good to see yer back on yer feet again, old boy,' Dudley said as they drove the short distance to the restaurant. He parked the 4WD outside Rafah's Restaurant, and both men alighted from the vehicle, and entered the building. At the time, Peter was now walking with the aid of a stick.

The two men found a quiet seat near the corner of the room, and sat opposite each other close to the window. Peter was idly aware of the traffic flow outside as he ordered two pint-sized glasses of orange juice. They then waited for their snacks to arrive.

'It's certainly great to be back in circulation again.' The engineer puffed, having walked from the car to the restaurant. Even exerting the smallest amount of energy was exhausting. He knew that it would take time to build up his strength, leg muscle, and stamina once again, and he was grateful to be in Riyadh. He interpreted his visit as a stepping stone back the UK, the flight was already booked.

Soon he and his wife would be home in England, and living in their cosy two-bed-roomed Cotswold cottage.

'Now my friend, I need one small last favour as I briefly discussed with you in the hospital. It is just this one last little thing that you agreed to help me with.' Peter began as he sucked through the straw at the pure, freshly squeezed orange juice in the pint sized mug. It tasted sweet and delicious.

A smiling waiter came to the table, and placed four chicken shawarmas (sandwiches), wrapped in grease-proof paper on two china plates in front of them. The Turk nodded, smiled again, and walked away.

'OK, old boy; fire away,' said Dudley as he tucked into his snack.

'I want you to go to site 262.'

'OK! But fer what purpose?'

'I need you to retrieve the book that is hidden there, and then bring it to me.'

Dudley almost fell off his chair. He coughed and spluttered loudly, almost choking as he was halfway through swallowing a mouthful of shawarma. His face reddened, and his eyes opened wide, watering slightly as he gasped, and coughed.

The Turkish waiter hurriedly returned to the table thinking the colonel was choking on a chicken bone. He gave Dudley a napkin. The colonel gave a brief nod in return, as he buried his face in the cloth, wiping his eyes and mouth.

He was too choked to speak. The waiter stood for a moment to ensure his guest was alright. Peter nodded assuring that his friend was OK. The waiter then returned back behind the glass display cabinet to attend to another customer's order.

'Are yer mental?' wheezed Dudley incredulously. His voice had gone up an octave due to the choking. 'D'yer mean ter tell me the book is on the *site?*'

'Yes. I'm afraid it is, Dudders, or at least it was!'

'Yer blithering idiot, why the hell did yer put it there of all places?'

'Because it would be the last place the terrorists, or anyone else for that matter, would think of looking for it. They've cleared out of there, remember? They, or someone, made a forced entry to search for it, and it wasn't there then.

'I cannot go back to the site again. Anyway, it's difficult for me to go there as I no longer work for the company any more. I suppose technically, I would be trespassing.

'Now will you do this one last thing for me or not, old chap?'

'Well, Oh my Lord!' The colonel placed his elbows on the table and held his head in his hands. He tried to clear his throat in order to speak in his normal voice. The silver mop of hair shook slowly from side to side in his hands as he stared disinterestedly down at his plate, and his quarter-eaten shawarma.

'Yes. I suppose so. But I am not bringing it back to my villa.'

'No! You don't have to,' Peter began. 'I will wait in the car. Then all you have to do is just bring it to me.'

'All I have ter do,' the colonel interrupted. 'All I have ter do, Peter?' He raised his head and rested his chin on his knuckles, with elbows on the table, and looked disbelievingly at his colleague.

'Yer make it sound as though I am going to the market ter buy some, some, Brussel sprouts or something, all I have ter do . . .'

Peter ignored the response and continued.

'Now, it is in a yellowish jiffy bag. It is sealed and hidden at the back of the BTS cabinet. It is wedged between that and the wall of the shelter at the top. You'll have to stand on the collapsible chair to see it. Then wiggle it free as it is firmly wedged in place. Whatever you do, promise me that you won't open it.' He paused and waited for a response.

Dudley again stared incredulously at his friend. Then looked at Peter in the eyes, and then looked away, he sighed raising both hands up at shoulder height as if in resignation.

'OK. I promise,' he said in what sounded like a heavy sigh.

'Please don't tell George or a third party about this.'

'No!' moaned the colonel. 'I'll bring the bloody thing straight down ter yer in the car. Trust me on this. I don't want the damn thing in my possession any longer than is necessary. As far as I'm concerned, it will be like handling red-hot coals. Is there anything else yer'd like me ter do fer yer, like fly to moon and back in a day?'

'No, Dudders, that will not be necessary, but thanks all the same.'

'OK I will do my best.'

'That's the spirit that won the war. I knew I could depend on you, Dudders,' Peter replied cheerfully. 'It's the trust you see, and that is why I am asking you to do this one last thing for me. 'OK. Now you must take your laptop and case to the site to make it look as if you are there for company business. Once you've removed the package, put it underneath your laptop in the carrying case and I'll be responsible for it from there on in, once I take receipt of it. Are you OK with that?'

'No!' again Dudley let out a low moaning sigh. 'Well, yes, just as long as the buggers aren't lying there in wait and watching—'

'Noooo!' Peter emphasised the word interrupting his friend. He looked around furtively to see if anyone was listening.

'They won't be there. That place is a no-go area as far as the terrorists are concerned. Trust me on this. They would not dare go back there in case the authorities were waiting for *them*,' he stressed. 'You see, they are not to know if one of us has tipped off the British Embassy or the Saudi security services.'

'So yer are still going through with this crazy notion of yers then?' The colonel asked.

'You bet your sweet life, I am Dudders,' Peter replied. 'What is it they say, "Revenge is a dish preferably served cold," or so I've been told. Hey, that rhymes,' he repeated it again for effect.

'If the Brits don't mess things up, then they, and the Yanks will be able to get the terrorist bastards.

'It will put a stop to their little game in good time before they can carry out their planned attacks. Just think of the lives it will save, Dudders.

'We will have our vengeance after what those bastards did to you and your family, and what I and my folks have been through.

'I want them picked up and incarcerated in hell. Actually, I want worse than that. I would like to string them up by the balls. Then watch the vermin plead for their pitiful lives. Martyrs! More like monsters.' he spat the words out in disgust.

'Hmm!' Dudley deliberated. 'I am not convinced with what yer saying, but I'll say one thing fer yer, yer are consistent. Ye're like a terrier and yer won't let go until yer get what yer want.'

'What's that supposed to mean?'

'In other words, yer are still as stubborn as yer ever were!' the colonel's kind, warm smile returned, lighting up his face. His voice had returned to normal.

The Turkish waiter returned to the table, and removed the empty plates smiling as he did so.

He asked if everything was alright, and would they like anything else. Both men agreed to another large glass of orange juice from the cheerful attendant, Peter was enjoying his friend's company . . .

'Mohammed Ali, the famous boxer came here once,' Peter informed the colonel.

'Oh! Really, how nice. How d'yer know that?' Dudley enquired.

'Because I saw him with my own eyes the very day he was here. I met him, and I have a photograph of him at home, that I took. I was working for Lucent

Technologies at the time. He was standing just there.' Peter pointed to the floor area, a short distance away, 'and look there, that is a photo of him taken with the waiters and the kitchen staff.' Dudley averted his gaze and squinted at the picture on the wall some distance away.

'What was he doing here?' he asked. 'It's a long way from the States to come for a shawarma!'

'This place is called Rafah's now, but it used to be called Ali's Restaurant before. That's just a coincidence, the name I mean. This restaurant is owned by Turkish people. Mohammed Ali was on his way to Jeddah, and to Makkah on a pilgrimage. The Hajj I think it was. He's a Muslim you know.' Peter explained, 'hence the name! He changed it from Cassius Clay.'

'Oh! I see, most interesting. Yer could do with a few boxers just ter take care of yer as bodyguards. I just hope that those rats don't come after yer again.

'Please think about little Krissie too. Yer don't want her dragged into this.'

'She won't be, bless her. I will cover my tracks. I don't think there will be a problem. I've had plenty of time to think things through lying on that hospital bed. I made a plan. What is it they say; perfect planning prevents piss poor performance! Anyway Dudders thanks for your concern. We will be fine, and we will probably go to Cebu to find our Shangri-la, in the Philippines, if that is what she wants.' He smiled cordially, and then extended his right hand across the table. The two men shook hands.

'I am very pleased to have you know me,' he joked. 'You can bring the family over for a holiday, well that is once we've found something suitable.'

Dudley shook the open hand firmly, still puzzled by the sentence, 'pleased to have him know him?'

The smiling waiter came back to the table with two pint mugs of fresh orange juice.

'I hope yer are right in what yer are doing with regards ter the little woman, and that she won't be involved in any way!'

'I hope I am right as well, my friend,' replied Peter dubiously. He looked down at the red and white chequered tablecloth; but he had his doubts. Then more to convince himself than the colonel he said, 'Yes of course I am right. I am sure that all will be well.'

THEY WERE BOTH completely naked as they lay side by side on the bed pecking each other on the cheek. Finally, their lips met, and they kissed passionately. Both wanted to give the other as much pleasure as possible. The need to satisfy their carnal desires was urgent. They had lain there for twenty minutes, playing, touching, caressing, fondling, feeling, and teasing.

He moved his head back as he looked into his wife's dark coffee brown eyes. Then his gaze shifted as he stared at her small, perfect round breasts. Her little nipples were erect with excitement, and anticipation. She wanted him. Her hand went down and grasped his hard erect penis. He moved his head down, and then flicked his tongue, teasingly over her erect nipples.

The throbbing sensation he felt was about to burst. Foreplay over, she finally let go of his stiff member. He climbed on top of her and inserted his manhood into her wet, velvety, waiting vagina. She was eager for him to enter her body, and to satisfy her burning desires. Kristine arched her back. She needed him as much as he needed his sweet wife. She let out a low moan as he slowly penetrated deep inside her. They rocked gently back and forth, both eagerly feeling the pleasure of each other's body, and not wanting the moment to end. The plunging sensation came and went rhythmically inside her. It was slow at first and so pleasurable, and welcoming. He thrust in and out, just teasing her clitoris, and finally penetrated deeply once again, thrusting so hard within her, and she moaned even louder. He started pumping faster and faster, and then uncontrollably, excitedly, and expectantly.

Suddenly, he felt himself burst with pleasure inside her as the semen shot forth flooding into her vagina. She felt the welcome warm sperm as she too reached her climax. Her legs were entwined high on his back. They groaned with ecstasy as they both enjoyed the satisfaction of the moment. Holding on to each other, she whispered, 'I love you, so much.'

It was what they both wanted, and a baby would make their marriage complete.

Peter's heart pounded. He lay on top of his sweet wife. Exhausted, and spent! His ribs, and legs were aching due to excessive exercise, but he had to savour, and to cherish this long-awaited moment. They kissed gently this time out of pure love for each other, and not out of fervor and lust. She held him tight, not wanting to let him go. Kristine could feel the hardness of his penis waning inside her, and the wet dribbling on the inside of her thigh.

He rolled off his wife and lay on his back.

She leant across and kissed him tenderly on the mouth, and then looked into his soft brown eyes. She pulled out four paper tissues from a box on the bedside cabinet mopping him and herself.

'I love you so much, my husband. I love you so very much. Promise me that you will never leave me again.'

'OK, boss, I promise,' he said as she moved away. His wife got out of bed, and hurried, dripping towards the bathroom. Peter watched her olive-skinned naked back disappear out of the room. He was a lucky man, he thought, and of that, there was no mistake.

He lay naked and motionless, with his hands behind his head, resting on the pillow for some minutes. His wilting manhood was now only a shrivelled, wet reminder of its former glory. He was happy, satisfied, and for once in a long time, content with his life. His ribs pained even more now. It was no good he would have to get up. Peter needed to get the circulation working to ease the muscle ache. Apart from the tender ribs, he was at peace with himself, and with life in general. He had everything planned out for him and his wife, and their future.

The engineer's thoughts were those of pleasure, satisfaction, and pure happiness, which were based on love. 'Bliss,' he thought. 'Bliss, it is the only word to describe the feeling! How many couples can honestly say that they are truly happy with their lives? Not that many.'

Peter listened to his wife as she sang softly in the shower. She sang against the background of the falling warm water. Her singing reminded him of the karaoke nights they had in her mother's house in Cebu.

The couple had returned to the UK, and to their small cosy cottage nestled just outside of Chipping Sodbury on Friday morning. They had the whole weekend in front of them to enjoy.

Peter was pleased to be back in England at last, and he was enjoying the comfort and serenity of his home. The ornamental garden was looking good, and becoming more mature with the shrubs growing, and spreading out.

'They needed a little attention, and tidying up,' the engineer thought. He would attend to that later in the week.

Peter was also looking forward to re-experiencing rural life once again. 'It will be good to see a few familiar faces down at the Golf Club, the Conservative Club, and the Royal Oak,' he thought.

Their lovemaking had been as good as ever it was. This time, it was enhanced by the long period of sexual abstention, and their decision to try for a baby.

For the moment, he had put the past behind him. Peter only wanted to enjoy their time together to the fullest, and experience a taste of "normality"— whatever that was. Something he had not been able to appreciate for months.

It was Saturday morning, and the engineer remembered that he had an appointment to keep. He informed Kristine that he would be going out, and would be back at home in about an hour. Then they would go to the farmer's market in Chipping Sodbury, and from there to the supermarket to do the rest of the week's shopping.

An hour and a half later, Peter was back in the cottage. He took the seven-week old, off-white struggling furry bundle of canine activity, from the pocket of his olive-green Barbour coat, and then placed the worried, nervous pup on the living room carpet. The small creature sniffed at the unfamiliar surroundings.

Kristine was upstairs vacuuming the carpets. She never heard her husband enter the house and Peter had not announced his arrival. After several minutes, he heard his pretty wife coming down the stairs. She was softly humming a tune to herself.

He had hid behind the living room door, watching the Labrador puppy walking unsteadily, and wagging his stumpy tail, greeting Kristine as she entered the room.

'Oh! What *is this?*' she asked in surprise. 'Peter, where are you? What have you done, you naughty man?'

'Der! Derrr!' Peter announced tunefully, as he emerged from behind the living room door with arms outstretched above his head.

'It's a little present from me to you, so you will never, *ever*, feel lonely again, my love.'

'Oh, Peter, he's so *sweet*,' she said. She bent down and scooped the soft, writhing pup into her arms, holding the bundle of furry activity to her bosom, and rubbing the side of her face against his tiny head. The puppy's tongue was licking Kristine's face, and his small tail wagged so uncontrollably, that it looked as though it would come off. Then in the pup's excitement, she felt the warm liquid running over her arms as the young dog wet himself.

'You see,' announced her husband laughing uncontrollably, 'That's his way of telling you that he likes you. Ha! Ha! Ha!'

She carefully placed the pup on the carpet, and ran back up the stairs to wash and change her clothes.

'What will we call him?' she called from the top of the stairs as she dried her arms.

'I thought about that,' her husband replied. 'Why not call him Pasko, after the Tagalog word for Christmas?' Peter suggested.

His wife agreed, and so Pasko it was.

*   *   *

Saudi Arabia and the terrorists had faded into the background of Peter's mind for the time being. He was determined to devote himself to family life, for the weekend at least. He remembered having read somewhere, "Like your job, but love your family," and that was what he intended to do without fail.

The engineer decided that he would find work locally at the Business Park situated at Aztec West, in Bristol, where a large number of the bigger international telecom companies have their main offices.

*   *   *

Meanwhile, the Islamic fundamentalists, unbeknown to Peter, were very active in the locality, and the engineer's activities were being closely monitored, by two of the Asian terrorists.

The road at the back of the family home, where Peter and Kristine lived, had been visited twice by the occupants of a light blue ex-British Gas van. It still had all its official markings displayed. The pre-owned company vehicle had been picked up cheaply by the Pakistanis at a car auction in London.

Being an "official" looking vehicle, it would not draw too much attention being parked in the street at whatever time of day or night. The van was parked at the back of the Maynard's house on a grass verge.

In the cab of the van, two shadowy figures were crouched in their seats listening to a VHF receiver.

All the conversations in the cottage were recorded, and listened to again and again, just in case anything was given away, and to ensure that nothing had been missed.

On one such occasion, they overheard a telephone conversation between Dudley and Peter:-

'Hello old boy. How are yer settling in?' the colonel inquired.

'Dudders!' exclaimed Peter, in surprise, pleased to hear his friend's "posh" dulcet tones once again.

'Very well thanks, all things considered,' he replied, and then went on to tell about acclimatising to everyday rural life, and the routine that he and Kristine had fallen back into. He spoke about the new addition, Pasko, and how the pup was chewing up everything in sight.

'Have yer made contact with yer know who, yet?' Dudley asked.

Peter replied in the negative. Then in a hushed, voice the colonel asked, 'Is the article with yer?'

'Yes, it arrived yesterday,' Peter replied. 'I have it locked safely in an aluminium briefcase on the dining room table.'

'Shh! be careful, old boy. Careless talk costs lives, and all that!'

Dudley's voice had lowered to a near whisper when he spoke.

'Don't take any chances, Peter, yer never know who is listening ter yer conversations. Remember what we said about yer house.'

'Yes! I remember; no prob's. I hope we can get things sorted out early in the week. Oh! By the way, is it still OK to come to visit you, and the family tomorrow morning?'

'We are looking forward ter it, old boy. If yer can get here fer around midday, we can pop over to the Crown pub by the river fer a pre-lunchtime drink. Bring young Pasko with yer. I know Clarita will love ter meet him. We'll take him fer a long walk along the towpath that should tire the little bugger out.' The conversation continued very matter of fact, and was just mundane small talk. Then, Lisa spoke to Kristine for the first time, in Tagalog.

*　*　*

Ali looked up at Abdul after hearing what they took to be a reference to their manual.

'So the book is in a locked aluminium briefcase in the dining room and on the table. That shouldn't be too difficult to find,' thought Ali, 'and the house would be empty the following day, Sunday.' The Pakistanis would have to check if the cottage was alarmed.

Ali decided that would be when the Asians would make their move, and finally retrieve their precious article during the couple's absence. Peter's death would follow shortly after, once the book had been retrieved. This would be designed to happen before the engineer could meet with MI5 or MI6 or whoever he was to meet with regarding the manual. The valued article would finally be back in their possession once again.

There was slight jubilation in the cab of the van. Ali would have exonerated himself to the mullah, and Maynard would be history!

*   *   *

That evening, while Kristine was sleeping, Peter crept downstairs. He picked up an aluminium briefcase packed with electronic parts. The engineer then emptied the contents on to the dining room table. Among the components laid out, were pieces of wire, a micro-switch, and other delicate pieces of apparatus, including a detonator, and a small timing device.

The engineer spent a long time getting everything just right, and fitted the pieces together inside the briefcase. He carried out some fine wiring, and soldered wires to various components.

One external essential item was set to a preferred angle for maximum effect, on the Welsh dresser that faced the patio doors. When he was satisfied that everything was ready, he then again turned his attention to the aluminium briefcase. The engineer removed several tubes of superglue and placed a book in a yellow-brown, jiffy bag, which he then positioned inside the briefcase.

The surprise he had prepared would be set off by a detonator once the case was opened, and that would trigger off a small switching device which, in turn, would activate the necessary component.

Carefully, he squeezed the superglue tube, and a clear, thin, evil-smelling liquid oozed out of its tiny conical aperture. He then ran the contents along the edges of the case, and used another tube to complete his task.

Peter then primed the small explosive, and carefully, and deliberately, he closed the lid. It would burst forth on opening, and at no other time. Then he glued the two catches together by squeezing the liquid into the lock, he then left the three combination lock tumblers as they didn't serve any purpose in any way. The engineer knew this would cause the fundamentalists added frustration in opening the valise. It would confirm their thinking that they had their prized item at last.

All this he had carefully planned from his hospital bed in Dammam, now his plan had turned to realism.

The arrangement for the coming week was that Peter and Kristine would be away from home, and staying in London. Peter had told his wife that they would make a cultural visit to include the Tate Gallery, Madame Tussauds, the Planetarium, and then have some fun on the Millennium Wheel. He was using this excuse as a cover. The main purpose of course was for the engineer to meet with the men from the Ministry alone. His plan was to contact MI5 headquarters at Thames House, Millbank, in London. It was a few hundred yards south of the Palace of Westminster; and his wife could wait for him there. George Fotheringaye had given Peter the contact name, and code word to contact a specific person at the Ministry of Intelligence. MI6 would also be involved. Their offices are based at Vauxhall Cross, a half mile upriver from MI5 offices. They would be in attendance at a meeting, also Special Branch, based at New Scotland Yard. The information he had, affected internal and external security to mainland Britain; this was why the agencies had to be informed. Peter had been clued-up as to what to say, at a secret meeting held with George Fotheringaye, before he had left Riyadh for the UK.

Maynard smiled at the thought of the shock the terrorists would receive on opening the case. His imagination ran away with him.

The engineer then fitted a small micro-switch to the patio door, and ran the cables from the switch, up the wall, along the picture rail, and finally to a camcorder on the Welsh dresser. The cables to the micro-switch were hidden by the patio door curtains, and concealed at the back of the dresser to the camcorder. He tested the electrical circuit. It worked perfectly.

Satisfied that everything was operational, Peter prepared himself for bed. He was weary through deep concentration, and once again exhausted. It had been a long and busy day.

The following morning, Peter instructed Kristine not to open the patio door as there was a problem with the lock.

By ten o'clock, they were ready to leave for the long journey to Weybridge, in Surrey.

Peter picked up Pasko and placed him on a blanket that covered the back seat of his Mercedes.

He then put a few of the pup's rubber toys beside him, and an old slipper for comfort, he also wanted to save the upholstery from being damaged.

Peter knew the pup would sleep for most of the journey. Then slamming the car door shut, he started the engine to begin their journey. He was looking forward to having lunch, and seeing his good friends once again.

The trip to Weybridge along the M4, and then onto the M25 was uneventful, apart from the varying traffic speed limits. The trip took approximately one and a half hours. Kristine sat with Pasko on the back seat, and Peter noticed, as he looked in the rear-view mirror, that they both slept for most of the journey.

* * *

It was ten minutes past noon when Ali, wearing surgical gloves and a hooded jacket, clambered over the wall, and on to the shed roof. His feet crunched over the Cotswold stone chippings of the back garden as he made his way unnoticed to the back of the house. He levered the door open without too much trouble and slid it back on its runners. There on the table, under some technical papers, was the aluminium attaché case that Maynard had referred to in the phone conversation. Ali tried to open the case, but the catches would not budge.

The Asian had finally got in his possession what he had come for. He was quiet, and very professional in his work. He stood for a moment, and fumbled, and fiddled with the tumbler locks, all to no avail. Finally, he walked out of the room with the case; he then slid the door shut, and tripped the lock. The Asian stood for a few moments, with case in hand listening for any movement outside. Only the sound of a motorbike somewhere in the distance, and a bird singing high up in a cedar tree to his left, broke the silence. Ali hurried to the bottom of the garden; and was elated as he climbed on to the ornamental wall. He swung the briefcase up so that it landed gently on the shed roof, and then clambered over. He crouched low, and scanned the local area for any motor vehicles or pedestrians. Satisfied that he had not been seen, he slithered down the wall directly behind the shed and landed on his feet. He opened the passenger side of the British Gas van, and whooped with joy. Abdul smiled as he engaged the vehicle into gear, and drove on to the road, and then back to their hotel. The terrorists intended to be back later in the day to finish the job off.

* * *

Just after eight o'clock that evening, Peter and Kristine returned home.

As they entered the dining room, the engineer observed that the aluminium briefcase was missing. 'So, they *are definitely* onto me,' he thought, 'without a shadow of a doubt.' He had suspected all along that the cottage was bugged, and as a test, he deliberately spoke about the case to Dudley over the phone. It was also the reason why he had carried out the intricate wiring job.

Peter never told Kristine about the missing case, or the unsavoury associations that he had with the terrorists in Saudi Arabia. She would have been worried out of her mind for his safety, if she had known the truth about the underhand dealings.

She and the family had been told that it was a case of mistaken identity, as a cover to what had really happened to him.

'Somewhere in this room the listening device must be planted,' he thought. For now, he would continue to play the terrorists little game. Once the case was opened, whoever unlocked it would be going nowhere for a while, and if he did, would be easily identifiable. Peter felt safe for the moment, and let out a chuckle at the thought of what was in store for the terrorists.

He checked the pine Walsh dresser, and noted the small counter on the camcorder, that had been placed on the shelf earlier. It was still wired to the micro-switch on the patio door. The counters on the camcorder indicated that there had been some activity. He then removed the wiring from the back of the unit, along the picture rail, and unscrewed the micro-switch by the door. Then with all the evidence of the wiring removed, he hid the items in the dresser cupboard. Peter was satisfied that the intruder or intruders had been captured on the video recorder. This may be required as further evidence for MI5 and MI6 if needed at a later date. He would view the contents later, when Kristine was asleep in bed.

Peter slid the door back to its fullest extent. The air inside the house still smelt a little musty. It was as a result of the cottage being unoccupied for the time that he and his wife had been in Saudi Arabia.

Kristine came back into the room.

'Darling, I thought you said the door was broken.'

'It's OK now, I just fixed it,' he lied.

'I am going to make some noodles. You want some?'

'No thanks. I'll have some cheese and biscuits,' he replied cheerfully.

He tried to sound as calm and casual as possible, just in case someone outside was listening.

*   *   *

The DHL package had arrived on Saturday morning. On Monday, he would call the number that George had given him, from a public phone box. Once he had made contact, he and Kristine would be on their way for their "cultural visit" to London.

While Kristine was busy preparing supper in the kitchen, Peter did a little unorthodox gardening. Pasko was getting in the way of everything, and wanting attention as he tried to play with the earth as the engineer dug the spade deep into the ground.

When he had completed the task, Peter decided to take Pasko for a walk. The pup still hadn't quite got used to the idea of having a collar round his neck, and couldn't understand why he had to be partially dragged along the path. He wanted to experience the interesting scents in other directions. The stubborn pup sat down sometimes, as he tried hard to resist the control.

*   *   *

There was triumph when Abdul and Ali got back to the MODA Hotel in Chipping Sodbury.

The case had been placed on the bed, and they did all they could to open it, but to no avail.

'The bastard must have the key,' said Abdul thinking the case was locked, and the tumblers on the locks had jammed.

'OK. Before we open the case, we will return to the house to finish the job off,' said Ali. 'We'll break into the case later. We have got what we want now. I will pick at the lock when we return. Where did you put the AK, Abdul?'

'It's under the mattress.'

'Right, get it out. We need to make our move now. Is it loaded?'

'Gee.' (Yes)

'Good. One shot should do it. Two if you think it necessary. OK?'

'Gee,' he agreed in Urdu for the second time. 'There is a clip of thirty rounds.'

'We won't need all that Abdul. We're not starting a fucking war!'

'Just to be safe, isn't it?' Abdul informed pulling on a pair of tight-fitting surgical gloves. He then removed the AK-47 from under the mattress, and wiped the weapon clean with a damp cloth, removing any trace of fingerprints. He then placed the weapon inside two black plastic bin liners.

'Ready?' asked Ali. Abdul shook his head from side to side in agreement. 'OK. I think it's time to go.'

*   *   *

Peter and Pasko followed the paths that formed the circumference of the cottage.

'OK, Pasko, you win,' said Peter, as he bent down and picked up the small pup.

Feeling the need to exercise, the engineer had walked as briskly as his aching ribs, and leg would allow him. He still got out of breath easily, and his local doctor had informed him, over the phone, to exercise as much as possible to enable the muscles in his legs to become strong.

As he was about to walk past the back of his house, he observed a blue British Gas van slowing down and mounting the grass verge.

On seeing Peter, in the rear view mirror, the driver had moved off.

The dog owner thought this strange, but then dismissed it from his mind. 'Probably out on a call,' he thought, 'and not sure of where they are.'

When he got back to the cottage, Kristine had prepared cheese and biscuits, and had poured a Guinness from a can. The beer, having been poured quickly, had effervesced in the pint mug. The contents of the glass were two-thirds froth, and only one-third dark beer.

'Coo!' remarked Peter on seeing the frothy stout. 'I think I need a shaving brush with all that foam?'

'What, my love?' asked his wife as she placed a hot plate of noodles on the table mat for herself.

'Nothing, my lovely, just one of my silly little jokes, you wouldn't understand.'

It was a warm evening, and getting dark, Peter decided to leave the patio door wide open, also to air the room to clear the musty smell, and to allow Pasko to run in and out.

The engineer sat opposite his wife with his back to the open door. He slurped the body of the stout through the froth. In so doing, it had left a foamy moustache on his upper lip. Purposely, he left it there for effect.

Kristine looked up as she was about to put a mouthful of noodles into her mouth, and laughed uncontrollably.

'Darling, you are *sooo* silly at times,' she emphasised.

'You know, Krissie, I am so happy. The most precious thing I have in all of my life—is you!'

'Me too, my love,' she replied with a coy smile, looking affectionately at her husband.

Pasko yapped at something at the bottom of the garden, he was standing outside on the patio, and looked a comical sight with his oversized feet for such a small body, an indication that when fully grown, he would be a large animal. The couple carried on eating, ignoring the pup's yapping. Feeling neglected, and in need of company, Pasko padded back into the living room.

He turned his attention to something else, then sensing something was wrong, he ran to the open patio doorway and looked up at something he either saw, or heard at the bottom of the garden.

Finally, disinterested, and looking for mischief, Pasko saw an open leather briefcase on the floor.

Playfully he burrowed into it. When he emerged, he had Peter's résumé in his mouth. His tiny, needle-sharp teeth had already made small indentations in the pages. It would soon be destroyed if the document wasn't rescued.

Peter fell to the floor to retrieve his curriculum vitae from the pup. 'Taking the very words out of his mouth,' he thought.

Then, everything happened at once.

It was impossible to comprehend, and without any prior warning.

The instant Peter had dropped to the carpet to retrieve his CV; an explosion seemed to rock the room. It startled him. He had a loud hissing noise in his ears, and he could barely make out the sound of a police car siren somewhere in the distance. It was getting louder, and then passed, and eventually became a distant sound. Peter tried to swallow hard, opening and closing his mouth in order to hear properly again.

Kristine had gasped. He looked up from the floor in total disbelief. Curious as to what the loud noise had been.

Kristine was sitting bolt upright. Her eyes were bulging wide open. A small hole had appeared in the middle of her forehead, and a trickle of blood ran down the side of her nose and mouth. There was a mess on the wall, and dresser behind her—she had been shot!

Peter looked outside and saw a figure disappearing off the shed roof. He was crouching. There was a clatter as something fell to the ground.

Peter got up from the carpet, and ran through the opening, and into the garden. He saw the Kalashnikov lying on the small white Cotswold chippings. He picked up the weapon, and scrambled on to the top of the shed roof. He heard the passenger door of the predominantly blue van slam shut.

The engineer stood on the shed roof, and fired wildly, hitting the back bumper of the van.

He was shaking, and knelt down on the roof. He pulled the rifle to his right shoulder, peered through the crosshairs of the telescopic sight, and held his breath whilst taking aim.

The van's back windows were blanked out. He was aiming at the passenger side back window area. It was clearly in his sights. He squeezed the trigger, and fired once, then again. The Kalashnikov had been set at a single shot, and not to automatic.

The bullets pierced the metal, and unbeknown to Peter, exited through flesh, bone and glass,

The van swerved uncontrollably across the road, and then the driver recovered control, and corrected the vehicle's positioning on the road.

Peter fired again, this time at the driver's side. The vehicle once again appeared to swerve out of control.

Then he threw the rifle on to the garden stones, and jumped from the seven-foot-high shed roof.

He landed awkwardly, and twisted his left ankle. Ignoring the pain he hurriedly limped back into the living room. The sight before his eyes was sickening.

His young wife was laying face down on the plate of noodles that she had been enjoying. Peter observed a gaping, pulpy bloody mess, where the back of her head had been. Blood pumped rhythmically, and freely.

Blood, gristle, and brain particles, stained the wall. Gruesome skull fragments mingled grotesquely with books and ornaments. The plaque commending the engineer for a job well done, from the sheik was also covered in human plasma.

Pasko whimpered as he stood on the carpet. He had wet himself again, this time in fright. The carnage that met Peter's eyes was too sickening for words. Vomit suddenly welled up inside the man's stomach. It was uncomfortably making its way up past his chest and to his throat. Peter took the stairs two at a time in spite of the pain in his leg and ankle. He only just made it to the bathroom. He spewed up freely into the open toilet bowl just as his left leg gave way. He lay half on the floor, and against the porcelain toilet bowl.

He spewed forth into the basin uncontrollably. He felt a blackness closing in around him. It was interspersed with tiny, bright needles of light reminiscent of when he had passed out in the hotel room in Dammam. Then again there was—nothing.

*   *   *

Earlier Abdul had stepped on the bonnet of the British Gas van, and heaved himself up on the wall, and onto the shed roof. The darkness of the evening hid his black shadowy figure from view. He lay flat on the shed roof, adjusting himself into a comfortable laying position, legs apart as he had been taught. From his vantage point, he could see the patio door was wide open. His target was in sight, and showed up well in the brightness of the living room. Peter was seated at the table, with his back to the would-be assassin.

A small puppy came out of the room, and gazed down the end of the garden and up at him.

The little dog yapped at the figure. No one had taken any interest, and completely ignored the pup. It then ran back into the living room.

Abdul stared through the cross hairs. There was no real need to use the telescopic sights. The back of Peter's head almost filled the sights from that close range. It looked as if he was only twenty centimetres away. The distance between him and his prey appeared uncomfortably close. He stared through the sights. He took his time as he steadied his aim. Then he experienced it again. Due to the length of time he had been staring through the lens, his right eye watered a little, and his vision had become slightly blurred. This had happened on the ranges in Afghanistan. He had not said anything to anyone about the condition.

He removed the telescopic sights, thinking it might be better viewing without the crosshairs. He stared down the foresight; a blurred image of the back of Peter's head was in view.

Then he heard a police car; its siren was getting louder.

Mistakenly, he linked his actions with the sound of the police siren, he panicked, as his concentration was fleetingly interrupted, due to the distraction, and his reoccurring blurring vision, Abdul hadn't noticed the target had moved. He fired one round. The job was done! He blinked, to clear his eye, and saw Maynard lying on the carpet. He quickly replaced the sights, and threw the Kalashnikov to the ground in case the police car stopped and questioned the Asians.

Abdul lay still on the roof for a moment listening, and looking at the road. Satisfied there was no one about, he rolled off the shed roof, onto the wall, and fell by the side of the British Gas van. The police vehicle was in the distance, lights still flashing, and sirens getting fainter. It was on a call to an unrelated incident. Abdul cursed his action, of discarding his weapon, and opened the van passenger door, and got in.

'Where's the gun?' was the first thing Ali asked.

'I dropped it in the garden. I thought the police were after us,' replied Abdul, pulling off his surgical gloves.

'You idiot, did you kill Maynard?'

'Yes. I think so.'

'What do you mean you think so? You either killed him or you didn't innit?'

'I had him in my sights. The cop car came, and I fired. Yes he's got to be dead. I saw him lying on the floor. Come on let's get away from here before the cops come back. We need to open the case.'

As a result of recent showers, the wheels spun on the wet grass, and mud then the tyres finally gripped, slowly the van edged forward. As soon as the vehicle was on the road, there came a sharp crack and a whine as a bullet hit the rear bumper and ricocheted off.

'What the fuck was that?' asked Ali.

The second and third shots entered the back blanked-out window area, and went through the back of Abdul's skull. The bullets exited through the windscreen making two neat holes. A long crack appeared on the windshield. Human bone, tissue, gristle, and blood, instantly spattered the glass inside.

'*Fuck!*' screamed Ali. The van swerved erratically. The fourth bullet whizzed past the Asian's right ear, and exited through his driver's door window, shattering it as the bullet exited. Ali was deafened by the noise. He tried to swallow, but still he could not hear properly.

Ali again lost control, as the vehicle veered across the empty road once again. He automatically corrected it back to the left side of the road, as he did so, he punched the glass several times, but he could not break the reinforced windscreen. There was only a small clear area that he could see through as he crouched in his seat; the rest of the window was covered with human remains.

Abdul's body had slowly fallen across to the driver's side of the van. Blood continued to gush out of the fleshy pulp.

Fortunately, Ali was not able to see fully the mutilation in the passenger seat next to him. It was dark and his concentration was on driving, and getting away from the area as fast as he could. He had to dispose of the vehicle and the body quickly.

Ali turned the van round at a small roundabout. The body fell towards him, and rolled away from him as the steering wheel turned.

The Asian took a chance, not seeing anyone about, he sped past the rear of Maynard's house. He had no idea from where the shots had been fired, or who had fired them or from which direction they had come from. Abdul's inert body finally lodged itself against the passenger door, held in place by his seat belt.

The driver remembered a quarry a short distance away. It was back the way they had come earlier in the direction of the hotel.

His stomach turned over at the carnage, in the passenger seat next to him. There was also an awful overpowering, putrid smell emanating from the still warm corpse. He needed air, it was hard to concentrate, and keep himself and the vehicle in control. Still slightly deafened by the gunshot, Ali drove up Peg Hill, and finally saw what he was looking for.

The quarry entrance had a sign in large writing; "WARNING QUARRY." Then another depicting, "THIS IS NOT A CHILDREN'S PLAY AREA. KEEP OUT."

Ali ignored the warning signs, and swung the vehicle into the entrance at full speed, smashing through two strong white metal gates that were secured with a padlock and weak chain, at the unmanned entrance. The gates flew back on impact, as the thin chain broke. The white gates rebounded back on the sides of the van, as if in anger. The van drove through the opening. Ali hadn't noticed the CCTV camera sign. It wouldn't have made much difference if he had. He needed to get the van, and body dumped, and out of sight as quickly as possible . . .

It was dark along the quarry road, there were no lights, and there was no one about. With headlights full on, he followed the unmade road, not knowing where it was taking him. Then he saw what he was hoping for. Ali got out of the van and walked to the edge of the quarry. He peered down.

Below him there was a huge drop. The light of the moon played on the near still water of the man-made lake. It appeared peaceful in the lunar light. There was no way of knowing how deep the water was. 'It will have to do,' he thought; as there was no other option.

Unthinking, his gaze fell down to the passenger window. The gory mess of the faceless, nigh on headless man, was pressed against it. Ali staggered away in utter disgust, and disbelief. He leant on a tree for support, and retched.

'This was worse than the slaughter of his colleagues in Afghanistan,' he thought.

Finally, he had recovered sufficiently, and forced himself to get back into the driver's seat. He moved the van forward to the edge of the excavation. The front wheels were at the brink of the grassy verge. He put the van into neutral gear, and then released the hand-brake. Ali got out of the van, and again surveyed the scene. The verge was slightly inclined downwards in his favour. He moved round to the back of the van. With his back to the rear doors he took hold of the chromium-plated back bumper, and heaved and pushed. He had all his weight at the back of the vehicle as it edged slowly forward. Centimetre by centimetre, the van moved closer to the edge. The front wheels eased over the ebrink of the land. With his back to the van, and the heels of his commando-style boots gripping the ground, he heaved, and pulled upwards with all of his might, on the back bumper.

Finally, the weight over the edge was greater than that on the ground. Gravity took care of the rest.

He watched the vehicle slowly somersault, and fall down the cliff. The wheels moved the vehicle forward, as it came to rest in the lake.

In the moonlight, it was apparent that the van hadn't sunk fully, it was front down, and only the front of the vehicle was fully submerged. The back doors were visible, also the yellow reflective rear number plate.

'Maybe the water will seep into the cab, and eventually sink the vehicle,' the radical thought, in an effort to reassure himself. He took off his denim jacket. The blood and mucous from Abdul's body had stained the left sleeve, when the body lolled against him momentarily. He hurled it with all his might down the abyss, but the wind got behind it, blowing it onto the stony side of the quarry. It came to rest halfway down the cliff face on a small shrub. There was nothing he could do about that. Ali took a final look at the van, and then cautiously made his way on foot from the quarry.

He walked cautiously past the broken gates, and back towards the main road. The memory of the mutilated body was still fresh in his mind.

There was a footpath running parallel to the Wickwar, Road, and it was partially hidden from view of the road by large hedges and shrubs. He could see security lights in the distance of the Chipping Sodbury Rugby Club, as he made his way to the old market town. Fairly soon, he would be back to the relative sanctuary of his hotel room. The Asian's mind was in turmoil, there were so many questions that remained unanswered.

'Who fired the shots? What firearm was used? Was it the police? Had someone been lying in wait at Maynard's house? If not, then how did it happen? Could it be Maynard? Could it be that he was still alive?' He remembered Abdul had said that he "thought" he had killed Maynard. Abdul then corrected himself, and confirmed that he had. He said that he saw Maynard's body on the floor. But what if he was wrong? No, he must be right if the body was on the floor, and he would have fired at close range, therefore, he would not have missed.' These thoughts and many more troubled him and haunted his mind like ghosts as he made his way back to the MODA Hotel.

*   *   *

Peter came round slowly to the frantic whimpering, and yapping of Pasko. The engineer's neck was aching as it had been resting at an awkward angle on the white porcelain basin of the toilet bowl. The smell emanating from the bowl was rotten. His throat burned due to the soreness, and fiery stomach acid. His mouth was dry, and acerbic. He flushed the contents in the toilet away, and half-heartedly, he did his best to clear up the residue of mess with the toilet brush. Finally, he rinsed his mouth under the tap of the wash hand basin, and made a vain attempt at cleaning his teeth.

Nothing seemed to matter anymore, as the memory of his dead wife came flooding back to him. He stood up. His ankle ached so much where he had taken the bad fall in the garden in his haste to get back to the house, and it barely could take his weight. Peter limped unsteadily towards the stairs. He looked down, and saw Pasko. The little dog had made it three-quarters of the way up the carpeted staircase. The pup was struggling with the next rise, and fell back to the carpeted tread of the previous step in his attempt to climb up. Just as Peter was about to place his left foot on the tread, and descend the flight of stairs, in an effort to avoid stepping on the pup, the engineer had transferred the pressure from his right leg to his left, but the pain in his ankle was not capable of taking his full weight.

He missed his footing as his leg gave way, and he fell headlong down nine stairs cracking the top of his head on the corner of the telephone seat-shoe cupboard in the small hallway. He lay motionless.

Some time later, Peter was aware of something wet against the side of his face. The little Labrador pup was licking his ear. Groggily, Peter came round, and got to his feet. He made his way painfully into the living room. He had no idea how long he had been lying on the small hallway floor. His head ached considerably; his vision was slightly blurred. It was difficult to walk, and he needed something to lean on to take the weight from his left side.

A red congealed mess of what had been Kristine's skull with long bloodied black hair still attached confronted him as he entered the room.

He felt nauseas again as he limped into the kitchen. This time he managed to keep it in control. There was nothing more to bring up. He grabbed a glass, and filled it with water. He drank the contents greedily, and then opened a drawer and removed a neatly ironed checkered, red and white tablecloth.

Tearfully, and out of decency and respect, he covered his wife's disfigured remains.

The body of his wife was slumped forward in the chair, her face resting on a cold plate of noodles.

Picking up the phone in the living room, Peter dialled nine-nine-nine.

'Emergency, which service do you require?' the voice immediately responded.

'Police,' Peter replied hoarsely.

'What is the nature of the problem sir?'

'My wife's been shot. She's, dead.' His voice trailed away. He never believed that he would ever have to put those words together in a sentence. His body convulsed as he cried uncontrollably.

'Hello sir. Hello. Sir, are you there?' The engineer couldn't bring himself to speak. His words were choked in the back of his throat.

The voice on the other end of the line became urgent, and then distant as he moved the phone away from his ear and replaced it on the unit. His mobile phone was in need of charging . . .

He knew the call would be traced back to his house. Now it was just a matter of time.

He managed to open the front door, and sat down heavily on the staircase waiting for the police to arrive.

Silently, he comforted the confused, frightened little pup. He sobbed quietly. The tears ran freely down his face. His head was throbbing. His leg ached as did his ribs. He was still nauseous. Peter only once went back into the living room. He had to be sure that what happened really *had* happened, and that he had not imagined the trauma.

The engineer looked across at the table. He observed the redness of the table cloth where it had made contact with the body. Kristine's right hand was visible as it lay palm down on the table. The gold bangles he had bought, and that she had treasured so much, were on her slender olive wrist. He fell to his knees on the carpet in despair.

Two young constables were the first officers on the scene. The inexperienced, keen, and youthful men were not prepared for what lay before them at the dining room table. All they had been told was that someone reported that "his wife had been shot dead," and then the line was cut. One officer hurried outside after seeing the human remains on the wall, floor, and dresser. The other spoke briefly to Peter but was unable to get a coherent response. The officer thought the seated man was either drunk or drugged.

The policeman then made an urgent call to the police station, and requested to speak to a member of the Serious Crime Squad.

*   *   *

Detective Inspector Jerry Hemmings of the Avon and Somerset Police Murder Squad was an experienced officer of some twenty-three years service. He was a little over six feet two inches tall, with broad shoulders that any rugby player would be proud of. His once black hair was turning grey at the temples. His complexion was rugged, and his countenance appeared serious. The manner of the man was brusque, no-nonsense, and professional.

'What have we got here?' he asked one of the constables waiting by the front gate.

'Blood and crud, guv, it looks like the victim was shot in the head. There is a male suspect that I think could be the worse for drink, or maybe drugged up. He's sitting on the stairs just inside the door.'

The inspector looked at the young PC; he was clearly not impressed by his verbal account or assumptions.

'Has anyone touched anything?' the inspector asked.

'No, sir. As soon as we saw that it was a murder case, we came outside and called for assistance.'

'It is so hard to put an old head on young shoulders,' the inspector thought; 'but then, they were only probationer plodders, and had done the right thing in contacting him directly.'

Before the detective inspector entered the house, he donned a pair of polythene overshoes, and latex gloves. He observed Peter who appeared to be in a state of shock. He was sitting motionless on the stairs. The man was holding a nervous pup for what appeared to be for comfort. The young dog struggled to free itself upon seeing another person entering the room. The DI ignored the seated man, and continued to make his way inside the house. The second officer came from behind a tree in the front garden, and stood passively by the front door having finally discharged the contents of his stomach.

DI Hemmings partially lifted the tablecloth, and observed the remains beneath. He then made a call on his PR (personal radio). The inspector then dialled another number requesting a medical examiner to be on the scene without delay. He needed to know the approximate time of the victim's death. He then dialled SOCO, (Scenes of Crime Officers).

Then the DI called for an undertaker's vehicle.

Twenty-five minutes later, SOCO arrived in two white vans. The head-to-toe-white-clad officers placed polythene over their shoes and latex gloves over their hands. They entered the front door of the cottage carrying a variety of plastic bags.

One team erected floodlighting in the back garden. They then proceeded to thoroughly search the area for clues. A police photographer arrived, and photographed the spent cartridges on the flat roof of the shed. He photographed the assault rifle that was still lying on the ground, and then made a few notes on a pad.

Plastic sheeting had been erected at the front of the house, and tape cordoned off the crime scene at both ends of the street.

The DI made another call and requested a firearms expert to come to the house to examine what he thought could be an AK-47 assault rifle, and make it "safe".

In the living room, similar activity was taking place. One of the SOCO officers walked into the room from the garden. He was carrying a few white plastic bags with black felt-tipped pen writing.

When the firearms expert arrived, he observed the weapon, and its position on the ground. With surgically gloved hands, and similarly attired as the SOCO team, he put the safety catch on. He then carefully removed the magazine clip, and placed both items in separate white plastic bags. The weapon, cartridges, and spent bullets, would be sent to a forensic laboratory for examination of fingerprints, and DNA tests. When the lab had finished with the weapon, further tests would be carried out. The spent bullets, and cartridge cases were needed to establish the signature of the weapon, also to establish whether more than one firearm had been used. The ballistics officer would accompany the weapon to the lab and sign it over into safe-keeping . . .

The detective inspector gave a curt nod as a man in white walked through the house to the SOCO van. Plastic bags were catalogued, each containing a spent cartridge case, and writing on the bags indicated where the cartridge cases had been found. Circles had been drawn on the shed roof.

The projectile that had killed Kristine was embedded into the thick plastered wall of the cottage. It would take a lot of effort to retrieve the bullet due to the velocity from the weapon being fired at a fairly close range. It would have to be dug out of the plaster, and matched to the AK-47.

Jerry Hemmings turned to the accused, and spoke to him softly. Peter had a look of disbelief on his face, and was clearly in a state of shock. He absent-mindedly stroked the pup more for comfort to himself than for the young dog. The engineer remained seated on the stairs throughout the police activity. His mind was a complete blank, and his head was still throbbing. He may have been suffering from concussion, as his mind appeared to have shut down.

The policeman was a steady, old-time copper. He had seen similar signs at murder scenes in the past.

The DI knew only too well that it was a foolish assumption to jump to conclusions. The engineer stared idly in front of him, not hearing the question.

'What is your name, please, sir?' he asked the traumatised man for a second time.

Peter replied.

'Have you been drinking, or taken any drugs or noxious substances?'

'No!' Peter replied wearily. 'None.' The voice seemed to come from somewhere distant.

'Peter Edward Maynard, you are being arrested on suspicion of the murder of your wife Kristine Reyes Maynard. You are being cautioned, and you are not obliged to say anything, but it may harm your defence . . . .' The caution trailed on. Peter was not listening.

The DI then spoke quietly to a policewoman. He advised her to go easy on the prisoner. She gently eased the dozing puppy from Peter's lap. Softly she persuaded the engineer to leave the house with her. Peter was like an automaton. It was as though it wasn't happening. He limped rather than walked. His head ached incredibly. It was the second blow he had received to his skull in a matter of months. Once outside, a male officer handcuffed Peter's wrists behind his back, and the trio walked slowly down the path, to a waiting police car.

Pasko yapped, as he saw his master leaving him. One of the constables was holding the small dog. Pasko would be taken to police kennels, and looked after for the time being.

As the police car reached the end of the road, a PC removed the tape to allow them to leave, also for a mortuary van to enter the crime scene area. Peter bowed his head; tears flowed down his cheeks, he wept uncontrollably, as he sat in the back seat of the squad car . . .

*   *   *

At the police station, the handcuffs were removed. The duty sergeant asked Peter to empty his pockets. The engineer obliged in silence. He was still in a daze. Without argument, he removed his belt and shoes. He had to be helped. As he bent forward, his head pained so much. He was not able to continue, as his movements became uncoordinated.

The sergeant asked the prisoner to confirm his full name, address, and date of birth. All the details were entered into a computer. Peter just stared blankly at the man wearing a black tie, white shirt, and chrome sergeant's chevrons, on dark blue epaulettes. Nothing seemed to mean anything anymore.

'Has he been cautioned?' asked the sergeant to the policewoman.

'Yes Sarge,' the female PC replied. 'He's been arrested on suspicion. Mr. Maynard is just helping with the investigation at the moment. The guv' said to detain him, and we'll question him in the morning,' then she whispered, 'he is the prime suspect.'

'So he has been charged on suspicion?'

'Yes Sarge.'

The desk sergeant informed Peter of his rights. 'You are allowed to make one phone call. Is there someone that you want to contact or to let know that you are here; a solicitor, a close member of the family, a friend, your wife-?'

'Sarge,' hissed the policewoman interrupting the officer from his delivery. She frowned, and shook her head. The custody sergeant had not been informed that it was Peter's wife that had been killed. He had only been told that the body of a female had been found, and that Peter was the main suspect.

A WPC wearing surgical gloves took Peter's DNA by use of a swab, sampling saliva from inside his mouth. His fingerprints were taken, and he was then photographed.

Peter stood silently, still in shock. He hopelessly shook his head, and at the time was not capable of thinking straight. Very confused, the engineer felt completely dehumanised at the alien surroundings, and police procedures.

The prisoner was led back to the front office in his stocking feet. Then without warning he felt his legs about to give way. He tried in vain to hold on to the counter, where the sergeant stood at the computer. He missed his grip, and started to fall.

'Are you feeling unwell?' a distant voice asked him 'Do you need to see a doctor?'

Peter passed out. It had all been too much for him. It was the young female police constable that got to him first as he was falling. The sergeant came from behind the desk.

The WPC stopped Peter's lifeless body from hitting the floor, but she wasn't strong enough to hold him up. The officer, and the lifeless body, sprawled unceremoniously, and almost comically, to the floor, The WPC had managed to keep Peter's head up in the struggle as she fought to keep her balance.

'Call an ambulance,' she said to the custody sergeant. The officer had returned to his desk and picked up the landline phone, punching in the 3 nines.

Two male officers entered the front office. They stepped forward, disregarding a drunken handcuffed prisoner in their care. They lifted Peter off the female constable, one officer either side, of the inert body and then they laid him carefully on the wooden floor, in the recovery position. The young woman took over as the officers returned to their prisoner who was by now noisily complaining to the custody sergeant about wrongful arrest, and his rights.

Within seven minutes, an ambulance crew had arrived at Old Bridewell Police Station, one of the two police stations in Bristol, those being Old Bridewell, and New Bridewell.

'What happened?' a female paramedic asked of the custody sergeant.

'He just seemed to pass out, and fell' the sergeant replied

'Did his head hit the floor?'

'No! The PC managed to prevent that from happening.'

'What's his name?'

'Maynard, Peter Edward Maynard.'

'Hello, Peter, can you hear me?'

The female paramedic asked, kneeling on the floor next to the patient, and trying to coerce the comatose man back to consciousness.

'Hello, Peter,' she called again lifting each eyelid in turn. 'He's unconscious,' she declared.

The paramedics propped him up against the wall, the female then checked his breathing, his pulse, and then placed an oxygen mask over his face. Soon the engineer was breathing normally, and the colour returned to his face.

'Has he been drinking, or taken drugs, do you know?' the paramedic in control asked.

'Not sure,' replied the custody sergeant. 'He was very quiet, and looked confused. I suppose he could have taken a noxious substance.'

'Can one of you get this man a glass of water?' she requested.

Two gawking constables had just entered the room, as Peter began to come round. They were the same officers that had attended the scene of the crime earlier.

The medics managed to assist Peter from the floor, and sat him in a chair. Peter slowly came round to a barrage of questions, and hoarsely whispered 'no' to each one.

'Are you on any medication, Peter?'

'Have you taken any drugs?'

'Do you take drugs Peter?'

'Have you been drinking?'

It was painful for him to shake his head. A plastic cup of water was produced. The oxygen mask was removed. Peter's hands were shaking as he took the cup. The paramedic removed the cup from his grasp, and raised it to the engineer's lips. He drank the tepid water. His mind flashed back to the hotel room incident where he was given a scotch by one of the terrorists.

'Are you in any pain, Peter?'

'Yes,' he whispered hoarsely.

'Where is the pain?'

'My head, ribs, and my leg ache.'

'Did you suffer a blow?'

'No! Well, yes. I tripped on the stairs, and fell. I hit my head on the corner of a piece of furniture.'

She felt his scalp. A bump had already formed. Peter winced when she touched his head . . .

The paramedic noticed the fresh looking scar on his forehead.

'Have you had a blow to your head recently?'

'Yes.'

'How long ago, Peter?'

'About two or three months ago, I can't think.'

'And is the scar on your forehead from that blow?'

'Yes.'

The male paramedic was taking Peter's blood pressure while the line of questioning continued.

'This man is going straight to the hospital,' the female paramedic informed the desk sergeant. She folded a stethoscope and put it back in the medical holdall.

'He may well have sustained a fractured skull, concussion, or have internal head injuries.'

'Yes ma'am,' the sergeant replied. 'Morgan, accompany the prisoner to the hospital.'

'Is it really necessary for him to have a police escort?' the female paramedic asked.

'I am afraid it is, ma'am. He is under arrest on suspicion of a serious crime that we are investigating. He could be dangerous,' the sergeant informed the medic. 'It's wise to be cautious in these matters.'

The desk sergeant was feeling a little smug as the authority had returned from the paramedics back to the side of the police once again.

Peter was carried out on a stretcher, and taken to the ambulance, followed by PC Marc Morgan.

*   *   *

Ali made it back to his small hotel. He was exhausted, and mentally fatigued due to concentration, and the terrible carnage he had witnessed, and the aftermath of the shooting. The faceless bloody gory mess of Abdul was etched in his mind. He shuddered as he sat on the bed contemplating his next move. The aluminium briefcase lay unopened on the bed. He would unlock it later in the morning. The terrorist had strict instructions to make a call on the sat-phone, to his superior in Pakistan with a full report.

Ali felt unclean, and needed to wash any remains of Abdul both from his hair, his body, and his mind. He took a shower, and then dried his hair, and upper body. He then walked to the bed. He stood there for a moment, giving his hair a final rub. Water ran from his hips, down his legs, and soaked into the carpet.

Being mentally drained, Ali needed to rest. He threw the towel across the room close to the door.

Then he climbed into bed between the crisp white bed sheets. His eyes closed, and he was soon deep in slumber.

*   *   *

Somehow, the faceless, gory specimen of the once complete human form of Abdul had managed to open the door of the van, and get out. He stepped into the lake.

Like a monster in a horror movie, he emerged slowly from the water, clambered up the stony cliff face. He finally made it to the main road. Again, in some way the faceless corpse had succeeded in finding its way to the MODA Hotel.

He entered the lodge and trudged up the carpeted staircase. The door of the room Ali and he occupied opened easily. Abdul's gruesome remains entered the room, and stood at the bottom of the bed. Blood and water dripped from his body. The fleshy, bloody, grisly spectacle stood motionless by the side of the bed. He waited for an indeterminate time.

Ali's body twitched uncontrollably on the bed, worried by the torment in his mind. His eyes fluttered open momentarily, and then closed again.

The faceless body came slowly nearer, nearer, and nearer to the bed. He wanted to say something, but could not speak. He stood there for some moments. The corpse loomed over Ali.

'Aaaarrgh!'

The loud scream filled the room. Ali sat bolt upright in bed. His heart was pounding rapidly.

He could clearly see a form looking at him. He was sweating profusely through horror, and fear. He backed away as he sat up in bed, and felt the headboard, and wall at his back. The hair on the back of his head stood on end. He was aware of an unfamiliar, prickly sensation running up his back, and neck. It went up and down his spine. Goose pimples appeared on his arms. For an instant, he could still see the horrific vision standing in front of him in the room.

Then, slowly, the dawn of realisation came to him. He was looking at his own reflection from the magnified wardrobe mirror door that had swung open in the semi-darkened room.

It had been an unbelievable dream. It was the mother of all nightmares. Not only had it been such an extremely frightening experience, but it seemed all so real. Ali jumped off the bed, and turned on the light. He moved the curtains peering outside into the misty gloom.

Rounceval Street was very quiet, there appeared to be very little traffic about.

'The sun would be coming up in a couple of hours,' he thought.

He then got out of bed and stood on the carpet where the corpse had been standing in his nightmare. He could feel the dampness of the carpet, where the "corpse" had been.

In his startled, confused state, and partial disorientation, he convinced himself that Abdul *had* come back. He felt that the man was somewhere in the room, as he could feel the wetness of the carpet.

The Asian was oblivious to the fact that he had taken a shower earlier. It was not the water from Abdul's body, but the residue of the water from his own body left after taking a shower a short time earlier!

He searched the room under the bed, in the wardrobe, in the toilet shower area—nothing! Then he saw the crumpled towel, and remembered the shower he had taken earlier, and having not properly dried himself.

Oh! The relief at the realisation! He sat back on the bed, and laughed. How stupid could he be? His mind returned to almost near normal. He stood up, and held one hand to his forehead deep in thought. It had all been too much.

Ali needed something to take his mind off the horrendous images of Abdul that were still in his mind.

He entered the small bathroom, and ran the water once again. Setting the temperature, he entered the shower unit, pulling the plastic curtain across. The rapid stream of hot water tingled on his head, and body. He stood under the hot spray for some moments. He then energetically lathered his body with scented soap. Ten minutes later, he stepped out of the shower. Vigorously he dried his hair, and body with the damp towel retrieved from the floor. He then put a dry towel around his waist, and secured it. 'The case,' he thought as he turned on the television set. It was time to open it, and take his mind off the drama. This would indeed give him a high, and make him feel a good deal better.

Ali was now more at ease with himself. He made a cup of tea, and put the television set on. India was playing cricket against Pakistan at the Madras Cricket Ground in Chennai. He checked the score. India, were all out for 215 runs. 'Pakistan has a good chance of winning this,' he thought approvingly. Although it was a repeat of earlier that day, but Ali still had not watched the match or heard the final result.

Now that the book was back in his possession, his next move would be to make contact with the imam, and deliver the item intact.

The Asian would call the mullah with the bad news of Abdul's death, and would then give the good news about the repossession of the book. He would then inform the mullah that Peter Maynard was dead. By doing this, he would redeem himself in the eyes of his masters.

After several minutes, Ali gave up trying to revolve the tumbler combination catches. The locks appeared to be jammed. He lifted the case, and on close examination, he saw a clear smear of something around the outside of the locks, and around the rim of the case where the two halves met.

He tried to figure out why the case had been sealed in such a manner, but came to no plausible conclusion.

Pakistan opened the batting. Muzhar, the opening batsman hit the ball with such force that he scored six runs. 'A boundary,' thought Ali. 'Six runs, what a good start. Now if only this case would open as easily as the opening bat.'

He picked up a screwdriver, and scored around the case to break the seal. He then tried to force the blade of the tool into the case, to separate the two halves apart. Slowly, and methodically, he eased the join apart on one side. He needed another implement. He looked around the room for a suitable tool. On the table, there was a knife on a plate close to a small bowl of fruit on the bedside table.

The terrorist managed to wedge the two implements into the case close to the locks.

With all his force, he prised the lid up.

Suddenly, and unexpectedly, he was hit full in the face. It took his breath away. His face, upper body, arms, and hands were all covered in a purple colour. A purple wet cloud seemed to fill the room, and envelop him. Ali was partially blinded. Not knowing what had happened, he stumbled in the direction of the bathroom. The Asian removed the towel from his waist, and rubbed it hard over his face.

He splashed cold water into his eyes from the running tap at the bathroom sink.

Gradually, his vision came back, although slightly blurred. Then to his horror, as he gazed into the bathroom mirror, through a blurred haze, a purple face stared back at him. He looked at himself in total disbelief, at his hands, chest and arms. They too were all covered with the purple dye. Ali went back into the shower unit for the third time in almost as many hours.

Again he ran the water, this time at full pressure. He stood there in the steaming water, hoping the heat of the water would wash off the dye. Grabbing the soap, and flannel, he rubbed his arms and chest. It did no good. Stepping out of the small shower unit, Ali picked up a nail brush from the sink, and scrubbed so hard that his skin became sore. The dye had penetrated deep into the layers of skin. The membranes of the three layers were covered by the purple dye. No matter what he did to his face and body, the dye could not be removed.

Dejected, he wandered back into the room. The once cream duvet cover was partially purple. Part of the carpet, wallpaper, and towels, were splattered in the purple dye. He grabbed at the dyed stained large A4 Jiffy envelope in the case, and removed it.

Dejected, Ali sat heavily on the bed, and opened the package.

He felt the hard cover of the book inside, and pulled it out expectantly. His eyes prominently bulged in disbelief in his purple face. The shiny cover of the book depicted purple-faced animated characters. He read the title:—'THE PURPLE PEOPLE EATERS!'

A yellow Post It label was stuck to the front with the written words "Eat your heart out you terrorist bastard."

'Fucking bastard! Fucking, fucking bastard,' Ali screamed. He kicked at the furniture in the room, as if it was in some way responsible for what had happened. The ball of his right foot suddenly pained him.

There was a loud knocking at the door.

'Mr. Patel. Are you alright in there? Is something wrong?' asked the hotel owner as she stood outside his room. The lady was on her way to the kitchen to prepare breakfast for the guests when she heard the sudden outburst. She knocked again on the door. 'Mr. Patel?'

'I'm OK,' Ali replied irritably. He sat on the edge of the bed completely dejected, and in total silence, he was searching for a solution to the problem.

Ali and Abdul had given the false name of Patel to the owners when they had checked in.

The landlady stood outside the Pakistani's room for a short while listening for any more unusual noises. She was still puzzled as to what the cause of the commotion inside the room was about. Then, satisfied with the silence from within, that all was apparently well, she continued along the landing towards the stairs.

*   *   *

Jill Maynard had been really busy on Monday morning as she pottered about in the greenhouse. Both she and her husband lived in the quaint Cotswold village of Hawkesbury Upton.

The little shoots were emerging through the potting compound. Peter's mother had decided to take them to her son, and Kristine's cottage. It was only a few miles away across the common, and off the Wickwar Road. When the buds blossomed, they would add colour to the small front garden of Peter's stonewalled cottage.

As Jill Maynard turned the car into the road where her son and daughter-in-law resided, she was more than surprised to see a uniformed police officer in a yellow fluorescent jacket cradling a black Heckler and Koch semi-automatic weapon. The area was cordoned off with yellow tape. The bold, blue writing on a yellow background announced, "POLICE CRIME SCENE DO NOT CROSS—POLICE CRIME SCENE . . . ."

Jill nervously got out of her car, and walked up the narrow path . . . When she arrived at Peter's cottage she could make out some activity behind the officer. There were odd looking white clad-people inside the cottage, seemingly very busy.

'What's going on?' she asked the policeman with a sense of urgency, and apprehension in her voice.

Just then, DI Hemmings emerged from the doorway. He removed the pale blue overshoes, and latex gloves. He stopped for a moment as he walked down the short garden path, and then placed them in a bag he was carrying.

'One moment, ma'am,' the armed officer advised. Then turning to the senior plain-clothed officer, he said, 'The lady is enquiring about the incident, guv.'

The detective inspector nodded to the officer as he neared the open gate that led onto the pavement.

'And you are ma'am?'

'Jill Maynard. Peter's mother—Peter Maynard's mother,' she volunteered. 'Is there something wrong?'

'Mrs. Maynard. When did you last see or speak with your son?'

'Well only Saturday. We spoke early evening. Peter and his wife were going to Weybridge in Surrey, in the morning to visit friends. Everything seemed perfectly normal when we last spoke.'

'You are obviously not aware that a tragic incident took place in the Maynard's household last evening.'

'Peter,' she gasped, her left hand went to her throat, as her right hand held on to her handbag. She then grasped the gate post for support.

The armed officer moved forward in case Jill Maynard fell.

'No madam, not your son, he is OK. Unfortunately, it was his wife.' The officer spoke slowly, softly, and deliberately.

'But how, why, what's happening, what happened to Krissie?' her voice trailed away. 'Oh! No!' she moaned; as tears welled up in her eyes, and the blood drained from her face.

'Mrs. Maynard. I am very sorry to be the bearer of bad news, and I do not want to add to your distress, but it would be most helpful if you could come to the police station to answer a few questions, if you don't mind. It will also be of great assistance to your son if you cooperate with us fully. It may well clear up some very loose ends. I think also, that you should sit down Mrs. Maynard.

'By the way, I am Detective Inspector Jerry Hemmings of the Serious Crimes Squad.'

He took from his pocket a visiting card with the Avon and Somerset police insignia, and handed the card to the distressed woman. Jill absent-mindedly took the card, glanced at the writing without reading the content, and dropped it into her handbag.

'I am the investigating officer in charge of the enquiry. Your son, Peter is or was, at Bristol Royal Infirmary. Once he has been thoroughly checked out, he will be returned to the custody suite at Old Bridewell Police Station in Bristol. We need him to assist us with our enquiries.'

'Of course I will cooperate all I can. I will come right away,' Jill Maynard replied, 'anything to help my son, and his dear wife. But *the hospital, again,* what happened this time?'

'Yes, he is alright. Possible concussion, that's about the extent of his injury, plus he appears to have a bit of trouble walking from what I could see.'

'He has hit his head again? Oh, no, not again!' she exclaimed.

'Again?' enquired the DI.

'Mrs. Maynard, I really do feel that you *should* come with me to help clear up the matter. You need to tell us what you know. You can leave your car. I can see that you are understandably upset by the terrible news. Your car will be quite safe here. We will take you to the station, and an officer will return you to your car, or to your home, as you wish.'

'Thank you officer. I need to call my husband,' remonstrated Jill.

'Of course,' replied the DI. 'Lift the tape, and let Mrs. Maynard through,' he instructed the armed officer.

Peter's mother parked her car near to the house. Then walked a few paces with DI Hemmings to the waiting squad car with a blue lamp on top.

DI Hemmings opened the rear door of the police car in readiness for the lady to enter, and then promptly closed the door when she was seated.

Jill Maynard made a call on her mobile phone to her husband, as the car moved forward.

The DI sat next to the driver.

'New Bridewell Nick, and at the double,' he ordered the young constable at the wheel.

'Righto, guv,' the PC responded. Then putting on the police warning lights, and siren, they sped off. No one spoke during the twenty-five minute journey. Jill Maynard sat in a trance; her husband was also on his way to the police station in Bristol.

Mrs. Maynard wondered what had happened to her son and daughter-in-law. She was perplexed as to what could have brought the unexpected situation about, and wondered, not for the first time, if her son was involved in something sinister.

*   *   *

Peter spent the night in the hospital under observation. Once again he found himself in intensive care. He had a brain scan . . . His left ankle had been X-rayed, and the diagnosis was that it was no more than a serious sprain, with possible torn ligaments, and would heal in time. He was advised to rest as much as possible.

His blood pressure was normal. His breathing and heart rate were regular. After twenty-four hours of being detained in Bristol Royal Infirmary, the doctors decided there was no reason to keep him hospitalised any longer.

A young Scottish doctor entered the small room.

'Hello, Peter. Ye are being discharged, and returned into police custody. Ye may be suffering from delayed concussion. It may last for two or three days, maybe a wee bit longer. If ye have bad headaches take two paracetamol every four hours. Maximum eight tablets in twenty-four hours, d'ye ken? If the pain persists after that, ye are tae come back here, is that understood? I'll have a wee word with the PC about this also.'

'Yes, thank you doctor,' Peter felt like a schoolboy in front of the headmaster once again. Everything was so surreal. Maybe it was nature's way of dealing with the situation—that and possible shock.

'These tablets are fairly strong, and should do the trick. Be careful as too many tablets may upset ye're stomach,' the doctor advised. 'Ye are lucky not tae have fractured your skull again, or suffered more damage. Ye must be a bit of a hard nut, Peter,' the Glaswegian doctor tried to make a joke to ease the concern on Peter's face, but to no avail. The patient could only manage a weak smirk.

'Try and get as much rest as ye can and avoid stressful situations.' Then looking over his shoulder at the waiting officer, he hastily added with a half smile, 'Well, if that is at all possible, Peter.

'If ye are having trouble sleeping, see ye're GP, and he may give ye something tae help ye sleep. If ye're vision becomes blurred see a doctor immediately, as it could be a displaced retina, but I doubt that will happen, ye appear normal with ye're vision. OK that's me done. Ye can go now, Peter; and guid luck.' He winked and gave another smile to the anxious man

'Get plenty of rest, avoid stressful situations. He must be joking,' Peter thought, and now he had to face the music. He got off the bed, and limped in his stocking feet to the entrance of the cubicle. When he cautiously peered round the corner, PC Marc Morgan was not there. Another policeman paced slowly about the corridor. Then the doctor appeared, and had a whispered conversation with the constable.

When the doctor had finished speaking, the officer turned to Peter who was slightly out of earshot, but still waiting by the opening of the cubicle.

'Alright, mate?' the constable asked. He had a cheery London accent, and a hint of a smile.

'Yes. I guess so,' replied Peter, 'under the present circumstances, as they say.'

The officer removed a pair of handcuffs from the side of his belt.

'Is this really necessary?' Peter asked. 'I'm hardly going to run off without any shoes on my feet, and with my ankle the way it is.' He was still suffering pain from the events in the back garden. 'I am not resisting arrest, but-' his sentence was interrupted.

'Look, mate, it's a precaution.' The officer looked at the engineer, and then felt a twinge of compassion. 'OK. Give me your word you won't do anything you'll regret?'

'Yes, of course, you have it,' replied Peter. 'It's degrading enough being like this, and under arrest, without the humiliation of being handcuffed. I've already refused a wheelchair to deposit me to the police car. I would like to keep what little dignity I have left.'

'I understand Peter, OK then, let's go, mate. The car's just outside.' The officer put the handcuffs back on his belt. The two men walked slowly towards the exit. Peter was walking with a very pronounced limp having rested for so long.

The police car was parked close to the main door. An officer sat reclined in the driving seat. As the two men approached the vehicle, the driver looked up in surprise seeing his colleague, and the prisoner. He adjusted the seat to the upright position, and then enquired, 'What about the handcuffs, Barry?'

'No. He's OK,' replied the officer, as he opened the nearside rear passenger door for Peter to get in. 'He's had enough problems for one day, and has to face the music.' The policeman then walked round to the other side of the car, and getting in, sat beside the prisoner in the back seat.

'OK, Kev, back to the nick.' He said, and they drove back to Bristol and Old Bridewll Police Station at near normal speed.

* * *

'Can I offer you a cup of tea or coffee, Mrs. Maynard?' the detective inspector asked Peter's mother in the interview room.

'No, I'm fine thanks. I just want to get on with this, and get it over as quickly as possible, maybe a glass of water?' she added suddenly changing her mind.

'Yes, of course. I fully understand that this is most distressing for you.' He asked a female officer to bring a cold glass of water for Mrs. Maynard.

The DI pulled up a chair and sat opposite Peter's mother.

Karen, the female PC re-entered the room with a plastic cup of chilled water. She placed it on the table, and then stood passively with her back to the interview room door.

'OK, Mrs. Maynard, this is an informal interview. I just want to get an idea of Peter's background. I will make a few notes as we proceed. Also I would like you to fill in the gaps that have led to this unfortunate tragedy as we proceed.'

'I will help you all I can, sir, but I am sure that I don't have much information that will be of use.'

'Well, OK, but let me be the judge of that.'

The officer had a large notebook open on the table in front of him. The door opened, and another plain clothes man entered the room. He carried an open laptop computer in one hand, and a cup of coffee in the other. He sat next to Jerry Hemmings.

'This is Detective Sergeant Roger Pertwee.' He will take your statement on the laptop. This is Mrs. Maynard, Peter Maynard's mother.'

The detective sergeant nodded to Mrs. Maynard, and then voiced a soft 'hello' with a hint of a smile from across the table.

'OK, first, we will start with Peter's occupation. What does he do for a living-?'

'I am sorry to interrupt you inspector, but please can you tell me what all this is about? What really happened in the house last evening?' she asked.

'Sure! Sorry, you have not been informed? At twenty-one twenty hours approximately, that is er, nine twenty in the evening of Sunday, Mrs. Kristine Reyes Maynard was shot through the head at a fairly close range. The bullet passed clean through her skull leading to her immediate death.

'A weapon was found in the rear garden of the house together with some spent cartridge cases. The weapon a,' he flicked through his notes, and referred to a piece of paper from the forensic laboratory, Kalashnikov AK-47, serial number AK, well that's not necessary to know, was found discarded in the back garden. Peter's hand and fingerprints were found to be the only ones on the weapon. It looks as though the AK was fired from the rear garden area, possibly on the shed roof. That is according to our ballistics expert. This is as much as we know. Peter is obviously the prime suspect due to his fingerprints being the only ones found on the weapon. He was also most probably the last person to see his late wife alive.

'There appears to be no witnesses. The house is fairly secluded, with no immediate neighbours either. No one has come forward as yet, and there have been no reports of noise or even gunshots being reported-.'

'But Peter wouldn't be involved in shooting his wife,' Jill Maynard interjected, 'er, late wife, they adored each other.'

'That is for you to know, and for us to verify. I hope you are right, Mrs. Maynard. For now, we have to assume that person, or persons unknown that came into contact with the late Kristine Maynard last evening, are under suspicion of the crime until proven otherwise. Once Peter is eliminated, our enquiries will take a different route.

'All the evidence we have at present, is what I have told you. We will make our enquiries and eliminate those with alibis, once they are checked out, and confirmed as genuine. We can then close the net; and basically that is how we work.

'I hope that once we start putting all the pieces of the jigsaw puzzle together, suspicion will be removed from your son. We can then move forward from there, and focus on finding the real culprit. For now we have to establish if it may have been premeditated, an accident, or nothing at all to do with Peter.'

Jill Maynard sat back in the chair. She mopped her eyes at the thought of Kristine being killed, and Peter in police custody. She was at a loss to understand what could possibly have brought about the tragedy. More to the point, Jill Maynard asked herself again, 'What had Peter got himself into this time? What with the injuries he had sustained in Saudi, and now this tragedy. Were the two incidents related?'

'OK, Mrs. Maynard, I can see that you are understandably upset, and this has come as a bit of a shock.

'Are you ready to continue with the interview, as we really must get on?" the DI spoke in a friendly but businesslike manner.

'Yes, please go ahead with your questions. Sorry to have interrupted you. It's just all so, so, incredibly sad and hard to digest.'

'I understand, and you have a right to know why you are here. OK where was I?'

He looked down at his notes once again.

'Peter's occupation,' prompted DS Pertwee.

'Oh, yes. What is Peter's occupation ma'am?'

'He is a telecommunications engineer. He works abroad a lot. I don't know much about his job.

'Peter never tells me anything. He and Krissie have recently come back from Saudi Arabia.'

'OK.' The DI jotted down something on his pad.

Fingers clacked down lightly on the laptop keyboard as the interviewee's words were recorded on the screen by DS Pertwee.

'Peter would never have killed his wife. They were devoted to each other.

'He suffered a terrible beating in Saudi Arabia. He could have been killed. We, er, that is Kristine and I were at his bedside every day for about four weeks.'

'And how did it come about that he suffered a terrible beating, Mrs. Maynard?'

'No one really knows. Although I have an intuitive feeling that Peter knows a lot more than he is letting on. All he will say is that it was a case of mistaken identity. If it was something more sinister, he would not have wanted Kristine to know, or to become involved, come to that. He would have protected her from any danger, of that I am certain.'

'Why did you not believe what Peter said was the truth, Mrs. Maynard? I mean about it being a case of mistaken identity?'

'It was something Dudley, that is er, *Colonel Dudley* Coburn-Smythe, said in a conversation we had. He unintentionally let something slip, but I picked up on it.'

DI Hemmings made a note of the name on his pad. It was also included in the typed statement.

DS Pertwee interrupted the interview for clarification of the name spelling.

'And who is this gentleman, Mrs. Maynard?'

'He is, or was, a work colleague of Peters, as I understand, in Saudi Arabia. This was the person that he and Kristine, went to see on Sunday, well, Dudley's family in Weybridge.'

Then the DI wrote the name on his notepad.

Jill picked her handbag up from the floor and placed it on her lap, she pulled out her purse, and opening the wallet removed a business card. On the back was written in blue ink the colonel's UK home number

'OK thank you, and what was it he said that made you suspicious at the time?' asked the DI.

'I cannot remember verbatim inspector, but it was enough to convince me that other powers were involved. I really cannot remember, sorry.'

'Is there any way that you could let us have this colonel's home address or contact details, Mrs. Maynard?' DI Hemmings asked.

'I do not know his home address. Peter and Krissie went down to visit the family over the weekend, as I said. Weybridge it is in Surrey, I believe. Peter will have Dudley's details.'

The inspector looked at the business card and copied the Saudi mobile number down. 'He may still be contactable on the number,' he thought.

He then handed the business card to DS Pertwee. The number was entered onto the statement.

'OK. Were the Saudi Police involved at all, do you know, Mrs. Maynard?'

'Yes, they were initially. But Peter was so genuinely disorientated at the time, as he had only just come out of a coma. He was suffering memory loss due to the brutal attack in his hotel room. I believe that he told them it was a case of mistaken identity, and he could not remember anything. As the police had nothing to go on, he heard no more from the Saudi authorities.'

'Does your son own a firearm, Mrs. Maynard?'

'Peter? Good heavens no. Well not that I am aware of. Apart from his time in the army, he never showed any interest in guns as far as I know.'

'He lives in the country, so he could own a shotgun, or maybe he is a member of a gun club. Does he have anything associated with guns or firearms at all? For instance, is he a member of the Territorial Army, Army Reserve, or a Cadet Corp, does he go clay pigeon shooting?'

'No. He is too involved with his home, and work life. Well, that is when he is at home. He works overseas a lot. I believe this was to be his last out of the country position, as he and Kristine wanted to start a family.'

'So you have no way of knowing how he came to be in possession of the AK-47 assault rifle, or the Kalashnikov, as it is known, and you have no knowledge as to how it came to be in his possession?'

'None whatsoever, officer, and that is the truth. It is a total mystery to me.'

'OK that's fine. What was Peter's relationship like with his wife?'

'Well, sir, as I said, they were devoted to each other. He just bought her a puppy for company a few days before. Saturday, I think it was. Peter told me over the phone that it was to be a surprise for her.' Jill Maynard responded. 'Krissie was devastated to learn that Peter had been hospitalalised during his time in Saudi. As of course, we all were. She would not have left his bedside had it not been for the strict Saudi customs and hospital rules.'

Further questioning carried on for another half an hour. DS Pertwee noted down everything that was said. DI Hemmings had also made many notes, leading to questions to ask her son. Again he asked the interviewee if she would care for refreshments when the meeting was over. Once more Jill Maynard declined the offer, only asking if she could use the ladies room to freshen up as she was about to leave. The policewoman escorted her, and then waited outside the room. On Mrs. Maynard's return, DI Hemmings, stood up out of respect.

DS Pertwee made a few last minute notes, and read the report. He then took his laptop out of the room to print out the statement. A few minutes later he re-entered the room with four A4 pages. He asked Mrs. Maynard to read through what he had written. When she had finished checking the statement, she nodded her head in approval, and as requested, signed each page in turn, and the last page immediately after the last word printed.

The DI extended his right hand, 'Thank you very much for your assistance. You have been most helpful, Mrs. Maynard.'

DS Pertwee also shook her hand, and excused himself as he left the room.

'By the way Mrs. Maynard your husband is waiting in reception. I believe he wants a quick word with me,' the DI informed.

'Can I see Peter?' Jill Maynard requested.

'Not at this time. He will be at Old Bridewell, and I understand he is on his way back from Bristol Royal Infirmary today at some point.

'It will be possible to see him quite soon. Please do not worry too much. He'll be quite safe here.

'We will go easy on him.' The officer did his best to give the woman reassurance, with a hint of a smile.

His normally serious rugged countenance did not convey fully his warm intentions.

He was a good judge of character, and could see that Jill Maynard was a decent sort of woman.

She stood in silence. The officer then interrupted her thoughts.

'That will be all for now, and thank you once again for your assistance. Oh! Let me escort you to the reception area, as that is where your husband is waiting.'

*　　*　　*

It was late afternoon when Peter returned back to Old Bridewell Police Station. He was again booked into the custody suite, and after the procedures, he was taken to a holding cell.

On arrival, the engineer was offered food, tea, or coffee from the canteen, but he refused, only requesting a glass of water. Peter then asked to see a doctor as he knew he would not be able to sleep.

A plastic cup of water was delivered to his cell, and he sat on the makeshift bed and drank the contents. He felt that he was dehydrated as he kept feeling so thirsty. It would be morning now before anyone would come to interview him. The DI and other officers were still following up additional leads of enquiry relating to the murder.

*　　*　　*

Peter had complained that his head was hurting.

Forty-five minutes later, a police appointed doctor came to visit the prisoner in his cell and examined him. He gave the prisoner a mild sedative to help him sleep, and calm his nerves. The blood pressure reading was slightly higher than normal. This was to be expected, and nothing to be too concerned about due to his anxiety and stress-related problems. The doctor also prescribed two paracetamol pain killers.

*　　*　　*

The prisoner idly counted the thick glass window bricks once again, forcing his mind to focus on something. There were twenty-eight glass bricks in total. Seven ran lengthways and four in height. The density of the thick glass only allowed daylight to penetrate their depth. The ten-by-eight-foot cell was very basic, and contained only essential amenities. A stainless steel lidless toilet stood in the corner of the room. Positioned beneath the thick glass window bricks stood a rigid enclosed wooden bed frame that was fixed firmly to the wall and floor. A thin green plastic mattress covered the top of the fabrication. The walls of the cell were painted a drab green colour, interrupted only by crude graffiti from former inhabitants.

A strong steel grey reinforced door was the only way in and out of the alien space. The door's austerity was interrupted only by a small round glass inspection window, and an oblong sliding grille. There were two odd things about the room. There was no handle on the inside of the door, and the toilet was un-flushable from inside the room. 'Must be to check on druggies,' the man idly thought. He lay down on the hard thin plastic sponge, closing his eyes. Every time he did so, he saw her sweet smiling face, and then the horror and the realisation of what had happened returned.

His heart was pumping fast. His head still ached from the fall. He could not concentrate on anything. He had been released from hospital, and brought back into police custody. His heart raced as the adrenalin surged through his veins and arteries fighting the numbing effect of the tranquiliser. He heard a noise, idly turning round he saw a police officer peering in at him through the round inspection window. Peter glared at the intrusion. The man turned and walked away.

The prisoner lay still on the bed for a short time willing sleep to rid him of his living nightmare. As he did so, his mind became tormented once again. Swivelling to a sitting position, he put his head in his hands, and moaned aloud. The tears welled up in his eyes once again; and his body shook as he wept uncontrollably. He felt weak, broken, defeated, and robbed of the woman he loved.

After all that he had been through. The innocent victim had now become the accused!

The allegation was too much to bear. The penalty for murder and the repercussions were an even worse fate to consider. His memory of the incident was so vivid, and yet he could not accept the reality of the situation or his present confinement to a prison cell. It was all so weird.

With mixed emotions, he stood up and paced round the room.

In frustration, and anger, he punched the walls until his knuckles became red and sore; it was almost as if the walls were somehow responsible for his present confinement. The man wanted to feel some pain. His future prospects were bleak. He knew the police had found the weapon. He was aware that his finger and handprints were on the barrel, and trigger of the high-powered semi-automatic rifle. Unless the truth came out in full, and the police believed him, and events leading up to his wife's death, the prisoner was looking at a life sentence at the very least. Time would have no meaning in the confined surroundings of a Category 'A' prison such as HMP Belmarsh.

The present detention to a police cell was only a taste of what he could expect. 'Prison could not be an option,' he thought, as he sat down on the bed.

In his tormented mind, he decided that he would kill himself if he were sentenced to life imprisonment.

A tangled web of despair engulfed his troubled mind once again, as he tried to grasp the situation and make sense of it. The man was unable to comprehend, or apply any logical thought with his emotions running so high. Rest was the only answer. He needed to recuperate, and have the chance to regain his strength, also his logical thinking. In the morning he knew he had to be sharp at the interview, and therefore he would need a clear mind.

The sick feeling returned to his stomach once again. It was the same feeling he had when the bullet struck his wife. It had been over an hour after the incident before he phoned the emergency services. He had not been able to bring himself to report the incident immediately. His mind had been in turmoil, hampered by his injury. If there was ever a time that he needed her, it was now.

'Krissie' he called out in despair, softly at first and then again, slightly louder, as if she could hear him and would return to his side.

The custody sergeant heard the woman's name being called out. He took no notice. It happened all the time when prisoners were in custody.

The man knew that the interview would start in earnest sometime in the morning. He imagined the police were searching for evidence in order to find him guilty or not guilty of the serious crime. After all, he was the prime suspect. In the meantime, the processes of the law would be run by the book, but then again, he thought, probably not by the book. How many times had police evidence been fabricated in order to frame a suspect, so that a case could be closed, especially by the Met? (Metropolitan Police in London). James Hanratty sprang to mind. He was an innocent man that was sent to the gallows in Bradford, Yorkshire in 1962.

He imagined men and women in white one-piece suits, hands and shoes covered in plastic, trawling through his house. They would be searching through the personal possessions of his and his late wife. They would be taking photos, and piecing the whole tragic incident together. As he sat alone with his thoughts, the coming day stretched ahead of him like an expanse of featureless desert. The engineer knew that he would be questioned and cross-examined by professional police officers who were used to dealing with murder suspects and serious crimes. He would be no match for them in his present state of mind. The custody sergeant had advised him to get a good lawyer.

He lay back on the bed tormented once again by his thoughts.

An hour later, when the policeman checked on him, the prisoner was sleeping peacefully.

The tranquilliser had finally overcome the adrenaline coursing through his veins.

ALI SPENT THE worst day of his life in the confines of his hotel room. Every time he looked into the mirror to see if the dye had faded, a purple face stared back at him. He had called the clerical leader earlier on the sat-phone informing him of Abdul's death. Ali relayed the story about the book, and the purple dye. The mullah at the other end of the link went berserk. His expletives and derision were too much for the Asian to bear. Ali realised that he was no longer able to fulfil his mission. Further, the clerical leader had informed him that Maynard was still alive, and that it was his wife that had been shot and killed, and *not* the engineer.

This was total incompetence, and Ali was held responsible for the charade. The cleric informed that Maynard was in police custody, and therefore would be extremely difficult to get at. More frustratingly still, no one knew the whereabouts of the fated book!

The mullah was sending Tariq and Asif to replace Abdul and himself. Ali was a disgrace to the Cause and was ordered to return back to Pakistan immediately.

The Asian had a final plan, and if that plan failed, he would take matters into his own hands.

During the night, he left the hotel wearing an Arab headdress as a scarf wrapped around his face. He took with him a few belongings, and walked to the outskirts of Chipping Sodbury town, and then back down the Wickwar Road. Ali came to St. John's Church where to the right of the house of worship, there was an open car park.

He saw the vehicle he needed. It was fairly easy to break into. He went over to it. The lock tripped easily. There was no alarm fitted to alert anyone of his actions. Ali ignored the CCTV warnings as he bent down to remove the ignition lock. He cut the wires, throwing the superfluous ignition switch into some foliage.

Ali then connected the wiring to the appropriate lead, colour for colour, when the final wire was connected, the engine burst into life.

The Asian drove slowly back to Peter's house intending to break in to search for the book.

As he approached the residence, he was surprised to see a police officer standing at the road entry, and yellow plastic tape cordoning off the area. There were several bouquets of flowers adjacent to the outside wall of Maynard's cottage.

Ali then drove round to the back of the house. There he observed another police officer standing unmoving on the pavement between the road and the grass verge. The Heckler and Koch semi-automatic pointed upwards as he cradled it in his arms.

Ali's luck was out. It was then that he made the fateful decision, and drove to Clifton Suspension Bridge in Bristol.

Ali parked the car on the bridge. There wasn't much traffic about, and there was hardly anyone around. The failure for him to recover the book, his purple face and body, plus being summoned to return to the Afghan borders for possible execution, was too much for him to bear.

It would be easy. The death threat he had received from the clerical leader was excruciating.

Ignoring the Samaritans signs, with phone numbers, he climbed on to the framework at the centre of the suspension bridge. He ignored the barbed wire deterrent as it gouged into his leg. Then balancing himself, he looked down on the watery mud flats below. His final thought was that as he fell, the watery earth would rise to meet him, thereby ending his life. It was low tide.

A builder's flatbed truck, screeched to a halt at the side of the kerb. Two burly men got out and shouted for him to stop. It was too late. Without looking back, Ali, still perfectly balanced, stretched out his arms upwards, and above his head, he then hurled himself forward.

The builders stood in awe, unable to stop the Asian.

One of the two men was frantically calling the emergency services on his mobile phone.

'*Allahu Akbarrrrrrr.*' Ali screamed as he tumbled down towards the watery grave at speed.

His body clawed the air just before it hit the water and the mud floor.

His spread-eagled broken body lay face down, and motionless in the muck. He had saved himself from the disgrace of returning to the Pakistan-Afghanistan borders where Shariah law would have been imposed upon him.

The builders looked down in disbelief. A small crowd had gathered, their cars parked by the sides of the road. Many people were dialling the emergency services on their mobile phones.

*   *   *

Peter woke up at 0600 hours feeling drowsy. The sleeping draught hadn't totally worn off.

There was a lot of noise and activity outside his cell. This was due to police officers changing shift. Cell doors were being opened and closed releasing an assortment of drunk drivers, brawlers, prostitutes, and inebriated party-goers that were being released after a night in the slammer.

The engineer felt dirty, dishevelled, and disorientated.

Finally, a police officer came and unlocked his cell door. Peter was escorted to the wash area. The officer stayed with the prisoner whilst he showered and towelled himself dry. Peter's head still ached. He was surprised that someone had brought fresh clothes from his house. He quickly changed into them, placing the dirty clothes in a polythene bag. He thought the garments would be examined at the forensic labs for possible clues. He felt slightly better after having washed and shaved. The prisoner was then escorted to an interview room, having refused breakfast.

Two plain-clothed police officers stood waiting as Peter entered the sparsely furnished room.

'Hello, Peter, this is Detective Superintendent Ian Barrington. He will be conducting the interview. I am Detective Inspector Jerry Hemmings. We met briefly at your cottage, you may remember.'

'Hello,' Peter replied disinterestedly.

Superintendent Barrington looked to be in his mid to late forties.

He was of medium athletic build, tall, and with a slight scholar's stoop. The smallish head was covered with thinning salt-and-pepper hair. It was combed to one side in a boyish style.

His features were regular, and yet too delicate to be considered handsome. He appeared pleasant nonetheless. There were no friendly handshakes. Peter nodded to the superintendent who in return gave a curt nod back.

'Please sit down. I understand that you have refused breakfast, Peter. Would you care for tea or coffee?' DI Hemmings enquired.

'Coffee with both, please,' the prisoner replied. He then asked, 'Do you have any painkillers? My head is aching like hell.'

'We cannot give medication without a doctor's advice. Do you want to see a doctor before we proceed with the interview?'

'The police doctor gave me two pills last night to kill the pain. I was advised by the doctor in the hospital that I can take two paracetamol tablets, also to avoid stressful situations. There's a fat chance of that happening here!'

'I will ask you again, Peter, do you want-'

'No! Just get on with it,' the prisoner replied irritably.

Peter was not looking forward to the interview. The thought of not knowing what would happen to him, and the unfamiliar bureaucratic police procedures unsettled his troubled mind. He stared past the officers looking at the drab green wall opposite. His intellect was still in a confused state. He felt anger mixed with grief and guilt. The engineer had to control his emotions that were now taking over any logical thoughts once again. Peter placed his head in his right hand, elbow on the table.

Both officers looked at each other, slightly taken aback. His report up to that point by the custody sergeant had been described as passive and cooperative. That was to say, with one exception where the prisoner attempted to beat up the cell wall! All had been recorded in the custody suite log book.

DI Hemmings, asked the young, uniformed officer standing with his back to the door to bring three coffees, then, having second thoughts, he got up and spoke to the uniformed officer privately.

The DI re-entered the room and returned to his seat . . .

Within minutes the beverages arrived. Peter noticed a white plastic beaker with water, and what looked like two paracetamol tablets on the tray. These were passed to him still in their airtight seal. He took the tablets, read the description on the back of the silver backing, and then satisfied with their authenticity he took the pills washing them down with the water provided.

He then picked up his coffee cup, and greedily sipped the hot brown liquid.

'I was only just informed that we had received a note from the hospital to say that you are allowed to have the pain relievers . . . .' DI Hemmings stopped mid-sentence, and then hastily added, 'Are you feeling well enough to carry on, Peter?'

Looking up from the weak coffee, the prisoner replied, 'No, but I guess as well as can be expected under the circumstances, for now.'

A recording device was turned on. 'OK, let us commence.'

DI Hemmings then spoke into the microphone giving the day, date, time, and place of the interview.

'I am Superintendant Ian Barrington of the Serious Crime Squad, and I am accompanied with Detective Inspector Jerry Hemmings.' He then looked at Peter saying, 'please give your full name.'

'Peter Edward Maynard.'

'And you reside at-'

Peter gave his home address.

'You have refused to see a solicitor, and a doctor. Are you feeling well enough to continue with the interview?'

The engineer nodded his head.

'Please, Peter, answer the question, as a nod cannot be recorded. By the way, for your information, this is not a video recording of the procedures either.

'There is a two-way mirror outside, you may be under observation.' Peter shrugged his shoulders disinterestedly.

'I have nothing to hide,' he advised.

'Good! That is good to hear. Now you have refused to see a solicitor twice. Is that correct?'

'Yes, officer,' Peter replied.

'If at any time during this interview you change your mind, and require a solicitor present, then please inform us.'

'I will!'

'By the same token, if you are feeling unwell, please let us know.'

Peter nodded, and then remembering the recorder said, 'Yes!'

'OK, let us continue. Now the purpose of the interview is to establish, your whereabouts and actions on the night of the assassination. Also we are looking for any possible motive that you may have had for the murder of your wife, Mrs. Kristine Reyes Maynard. Basically, if you have a plausible explanation as to what happened that evening, and it checks out, you may be eliminated from our enquiries. We will then proceed with other possible lines of enquiry.'

'I never killed my wife!' Peter protested.

'Well, that's for you to know, and for us to verify,' the DI informed.

'Am I being charged with the murder of my wife?' Peter asked incredulously.

'No!' the superintendent replied. 'You have not been charged of anything at this time. You have only been arrested on suspicion and cautioned. You are the number one suspect, pending our enquiries.'

'Then I am free to go,' Peter asked.

'No, you are *under arrest* on suspicion, *pending* police enquiries. When we are satisfied, then you will be free to leave. In the meantime, your full cooperation in this matter is requested and expected. You are not obliged to say anything without the advice of a solicitor. However, anything you do say will be of your own free will, and without counsel's advice. In addition, everything you say will be recorded and may be given as evidence in court, at a later date. The sooner we have all the answers, the sooner you will be at liberty.

I repeat once again, *provided* we are satisfied. Also if you feel happier to have legal representation, then you can still request the same. We will delay this interview until then.'

'I am OK at the moment, and prepared to help you all I can.'

'Good, then we shall proceed.'

DI Hemmings interjected.

'Sorry sir. Peter, our job begins and ends with the gathering of evidence and information.

'You are the prime suspect at this time, as this is all we have to go on. We need to establish exactly what happened on the evening of Sunday the sixteenth of April. We hope that you will tell us precisely what occurred, and in truth, what brought about the death of your late wife.' DI Hemmings voice was both fair but firm.

Peter felt the tears welling up in his eyes again at the thought of Kristine. He wrung his hands as if for comfort. The thought of Kristine lying on a cold mortuary slab somewhere filled his mind with dread and torment. He put his head in his hands again. The wave of emotion came and went. He had virtually no control over his feelings. There was no way of knowing when the panic attacks would sweep over him.

'Can you cope, Peter?' It was DI Hemmings again.

'Yes! Just give me a moment, please.' The voice was both weak and hoarse. He lifted the plastic cup to his lips and drained the remnants. His hand was slightly shaking, and his eyes were wet with tears. After a brief moment he managed to compose himself, and responded.

'I'll do my best,' he replied clearing his throat.

'Right,' replied the superintendent, 'If you are sure you are OK, then we'll proceed once more.'

The questioning went on for two hours. Progress had been made. Then there was a break. The sophisticated recording device was turned off. Peter was asked about the beating he took in Saudi Arabia and the reasons why. The engineer was surprised.

'How could they know about that?' he asked himself.

At the time, he had no knowing that his mother had been to New Bridewell and questioned by DI Hemmings.

Peter told the police what he knew.

The officers had repeated some of the same questions, only in a different way as to why it was that his prints were found on the AK-47. They asked over and over again, how the weapon had come to be in his possession. The engineer repeated many times the story of the Labrador pup taking the papers from his bag, and the instant he fell to the floor, plus the noise of the retort reverberating around the room, and the instant his wife was hit. He informed the officers that he knew the bullet was meant for him, and it was only a miracle that he hadn't been hit.

'Why did she have to die, she was so young?' he had asked the officers ...

'If the bullet was meant for you, and you had been seated in front of your wife at the time, and someone outside had pulled the trigger, you would both have been killed, Peter.' Superintendent Barrington advised.

'A bullet at such close range and of such high velocity, would have passed through you both as easily as a hot knife going through butter. Then the missile would have carried on, as it did and finally embed itself into the wall, or maybe ricocheted around the room,' the officer spoke knowledgeably. Peter thought that maybe he had been in the forces before being a policeman.

'As I said, after the bullet hit my wife, I heard a clattering noise outside, Pasko, er, that's the little dog, was yapping at a noise previously. The patio door was open, as it was a warm evening. I heard a noise outside and saw the weapon lying on the stones. As I ran forward, I heard the sound of a vehicle engine the other side of the wall, revving up. I knew it was them.

'I also faintly remember hearing an emergency services siren somewhere in the distance. It was approaching, as the sirens were getting louder.

'My guess is the guy panicked, and dropped the weapon. But I could be wrong.'

'Who do you think it was?' asked Superintendent Barrington.

'I know who it was. It was the terrorist bastards. I knew it was them come to get me and the bloody book.'

'A book you say? What book? What is this about terrorists?'

'The book I found on a rooftop in Riyadh with all the notes and dates written in it. There were newspaper clippings, notes written in Arabic or Urdu, I am not sure. I thought I mentioned it earlier. Anyway, as I said, I think I heard a police car or ambulance siren passing close by as I got up from the living room floor after retrieving some papers from Pasko. My hearing was affected, but I have a vague memory, maybe even before the shot rang out. I had a sort of hissing in my ears after the bullet entered the room.

'After seeing my wife had been shot, I acted on instinct. I ran outside, picked up the rifle, and climbed on to the flat roof of the shed. A blue British Gas van was just pulling away. I had seen the van parked there before, but took no notice of it. Instinctively, I knew it was them. Without thinking, I pointed the weapon at the back of the van without taking aim, just as it was driving off.

'I had never fired a Kalashnikov before. The first bullet went wide hitting the back of the van I think. I then knelt down on the shed roof, and took aim through the telescopic sights. I fired two shots one after the other. I think I hit the passenger but cannot be sure. The back windows were blanked out. Anyway, I saw the van swerve erratically across the road. I fired again, this time at the rear blanked-out window on the driver's side. The van was swerving again. I dropped the weapon, and jumped off the shed roof, and ran back into the cottage to attend to my wife. She was, well, it was too late,' his voice trailed off, 'and that is how my prints happened to be on the weapon.'

The two senior officers exchanged glances. DI Hemmings let out a loud sigh. 'It sounds too incredible for words, but it was possible,' he thought.

Both officers made notes. The DI requested a break in order to get CID to follow up various leads relating to what they had just been told.

Half an hour later, the officers returned. Again Peter was offered tea or coffee. He opted for coffee, and water. The recorder was again turned on, and the interview resumed.

'Getting back to the incident at the cottage, why was there such a long delay between the time your wife was shot, and you dialling the three nines?'

Peter then went on to explain his passing out in the bathroom after being sick. Then he informed about his coming round and tripping over Pasko on the stairs, as a result of his weak ankle, and then falling headlong into the shoe cupboard and knocking himself out.

Superintendent Barrington questioned the engineer about the incident in Saudi Arabia once again.

He enquired, as to why Peter had been beaten up, and why he had not mentioned earlier a possible Al Qaeda terrorist link.

After a while, the incredible story unfolded, this time in detail. Peter began the narrative with his discovery of the book on the flat rooftop of Site 262. The two senior officers sat in stunned silence. The story was most unexpected giving a strange and sinister turn.

As Peter listened to the sound of his own voice trailing on, he also felt the account was almost too incredible to be believed. Then again, this wasn't something that he could make up on the spot.

He described everything in as much detail as he could remember, explaining about the bugging of his hotel room, also the cottage. Peter mentioned the electronic wiring he had installed from the patio door to the camcorder. He then went on to elaborate about the aluminium briefcase, plus the purple dye. He told about the theft of the case from his house whilst he and his wife were in Weybridge, Surrey with their friend and his wife.

Both officers listened intently to the prisoner's every word, almost mesmerised. The account given was almost inconceivable. Everything was being recorded. The recording would be played back over and over again to various police officers, and agencies involved in the war on terror. They would look for evidence to substantiate the verbal account . . .

Terrorism in the Avon and the Somerset Constabulary had never been experienced at such a high level before. There had been an incident, where an Asian had been taken away from a housing estate on suspicion, as bomb making materials were found in his room, but nothing to the scale that was being explained so graphically.

Another incident in the Bristol area had involved two Afghanistan men who were acting suspiciously, and found to be high on drugs. When their premises were searched, hydrogen peroxide was found. This gave the police cause for concern. Hydrogen peroxide was used on the seventh of July 2005 in the London bombings.

DI Hemmings was very much aware of the terrorism groups around the world that were seemingly growing in numbers.

Another incident that came to mind, was the IRA bombings in Bristol in 1973, also London, plus more recently, the attempted strike at Glasgow Airport, but what Peter Maynard was relaying, was too terrifying, and too close to home.

There had not been any Al Qaida type terrorist activity to the scale as described by Maynard in the Avon and Somerset police division. But now, if what Maynard was saying was true, there was real cause for concern and alarm bells had already started ringing!

The officers noted all the details down including the named British Embassy contact, George Fotheringaye. CID would check him out with the Foreign Office.

The Colonel Dudley guy was also to be interviewed. The police officers needed to establish that the account the prisoner had given them was 100 percent correct, and without fabrication.

The engineer tried to relay everything in as much detail as he could, and as it had happened. Then questioning and cross questioning began again in earnest, followed by a few trick questions. At one point, Peter had to start his account from the very beginning again. He laboriously went into as many finite details as he could remember.

After the interview, both DI Hemmings, and Superintendent Barrington returned to the CID suite. 'Come into my office a minute, Jerry, please,' the superintendent, invited.

DI Hemmings entered the room closing the door behind him. The senior officer stood for a moment deep in thought.

'What do you make of all of this, Jerry?' he asked.

'In a word, worrying, if we are to believe what we are being told, sir.'

'I guess we move in different circles here than other forces, but, it sounds unbelievable, and maybe even improbable, but I think not impossible.

Maynard sounds genuine and convincing enough for this story that he has told us, to have happened

'Sherlock Holmes was supposed to have said, "when you have eliminated the impossible, whatever remains, however improbable, must be the truth?" I guess this is where we are at now, Jerry.'

'Well, sir, it may *sound* impossible, but not improbable, so he could well be telling us the truth. Anyway, why would he lie? The only reason would be to cover up the killing of his late wife. How could he have fabricated such a story? I mean, we tried to trip him up several times, but he stayed cool, and gave the same answers as before. My gut feeling is that he *is* being truthful with us, sir.'

'Would you put your pension on it, Jerry?'

'Yes, sir, I think I would.'

'Tell me, how many sets of prints were found on the weapon?'

'Only one set, sir, Maynard's.'

'Then we must follow up all the leads and see where they take us, the superintendent informed.

By the way, just a thought, could there be an ulterior motive to the murder? If, in fact, he did kill his wife, then the story he has given us is fantasy, and a cover-up to throw us off the scent. Get one of your CID guys to check to see if he had taken out a hefty life insurance on the deceased. Also we need to find out if his late wife had an inheritance due, or if she had money or property in the Philippines. In addition, try and find out if the deceased had made a will recently. We need to detain Maynard further until our enquiries are complete. In the meantime, get on to Special Branch, also the anti-terrorist team, they will need to become involved, and get one of our lads to find out if the anti-terrorist guys have any knowledge of such activities in the Chipping Sodbury area, for example has anyone reported anything suspicious, or if other stations know of anything.

'Set up an Incident Room here, for the murder enquiry, and separately, for now, one for possible terrorist activities in the area. We must collect and collate *all* the information we have to date, and as we get it. Get your lads working on this ASAP, like now. This is red hot!'

'Yes will do, sir. Let's hope this is not a wild goose chase, but my gut feeling is that is not.'

'I accept that but at this stage, we have to keep an open mind. If there are terrorists working in the Avon and Somerset patch, we have to know about it PDQ.' (Pretty damn quick)

* * *

It was the quarry foreman that noticed the exterior gates had been smashed and broken early the next morning on his arrival for work. Out of curiosity, the foreman proceeded along the top of the unmade quarry road on foot.

As he was approaching the lake, he saw in the distance, a blue van partially submerged with clearly identifiable British Gas decals, and the registration plate displayed.

Due to the acuteness of the cliff face, he was unable to clamber down the side of the quarry to take a closer look.

On entering the office the supervisor informed the manager of the incident. The manager asked to see the video footage from the CCTV camera. He was informed that there was no tape installed.

The manager then reported the incident to the local police. The call went through to the Bristol police control centre; the report was then diverted to a central police station at Staple Hill. The call finally went from there through to Chipping Sodbury Police Station. The local police would deal with the reported incident.

British Gas at the Bristol depot was also contacted. They had no reports of any vehicle being reported missing or stolen. The registration identification never checked out with their fleet of vehicles either.

The police checked with DVLC Swansea. After a while, they were informed that the vehicle had previously been registered to the British Gas Board Battersea, London. They were informed that as the vehicle was outdated; it had been sold on to a local dealer. The dealer in turn had sold it privately to a Mr. Mohammed Patel of what turned out to be a fictitious address in Bradford.

It was therefore untraceable back to the purchaser, and without an authentic address.

* * *

The Incident Room had now been set up at New Bridewell Police Station, in the CID suite. On a wall was a large whiteboard with many notes that had been made in felt-tip pen.

A light blue British Gas van, with possible bullet holes, and probable other damage was also being sought.

Detectives were checking Kristine Reyes Maynard's bank account, also her financial details in order to ascertain whether there was a large amount of money on deposit, or an inheritance due to her. So far, they had drawn a blank.

Peter Edward Maynard's bank accounts would also be checked, and investigations would be carried out to verify if Maynard had taken out a sizeable insurance policy on his late wife, as a possible motive for her murder, or if he owed large amounts of money. No stone would remain unturned!

George Fotheringaye of the British Embassy in Riyadh, KSA was to be contacted, also the Colonel Dudley Coburn-Smythe person, of Weybridge in Surrey.

STS in Saudi Arabia, and Techno Staff, the recruitment agency in London, would be contacted in order to verify that Maynard was working in Saudi Arabia legitimately as a consultant.

The anti-terrorist team, and other intelligence agencies including Special Branch, had already been contacted, and investigated Peter Maynard's background. Nothing untoward had been found.

* * *

The following morning, Peter resumed his session with the two senior police officers. He had again informed them of his work in Saudi Arabia, and described in detail how he had discovered the book. The engineer explained the involvement of the British Embassy in Saudi at the time. He then went on to describe for a third time, the bugging of his room, the beating he had received, and the kidnapping of Dudley and his family and the trauma that they had independently suffered. This had been carried out by the terrorists in an attempt to recover their precious article.

The engineer then repeated how he had rigged up the video recorder, explaining that he had not viewed the clip, but had noted that some activity had taken place, as the counter had registered a recording. He retold the story of the decoy book in the attaché case with the explosive purple dye, and so on.

The officers listened to the account intently. Even though the interview was again being recorded, both men occasionally scribbled notes. This was for cross-referencing, and possible further questioning some time later as both officers were having difficulty in keeping up with Peter's account of events. They interrupted him several times with trick questions, but all to no avail. Peter Maynard's account was watertight, and as consistent as it had always been.

Suddenly, the interview was interrupted by a sharp knock at the door. The uniformed officer in the room opened the door slightly. There was an urgent request from the person outside to speak with DI Hemmings. The superintendant spoke into the recorder, announcing the interview was suspended, and he gave the time. The recorder was then turned off while the officer conversed with his colleague outside the room.

The DI had been informed by a CID sergeant, that a body had been recovered from the River Avon, beneath the Clifton Suspension Bridge. The appearance was rather puzzling as the face and hands were purple in colour. The man appeared to be of Asian origin.

After a short while the senior officer returned to the table. He sat quietly for a moment, and looked at the prisoner for quite a few seconds without saying a word.

Peter felt very awkward, and was puzzled as to why there was no immediate conversation, and instinctively feared the worst.

Then the DI turned towards the superintendent and said, 'There has been a new development in the case, sir. We need to postpone the interview at this time to discuss further, and investigate.'

'Right, inspector, we will leave it for today,' the senior officer replied. 'By the way Peter, is this Dudley person still in the UK, or has he returned to Saudi Arabia?'

The prisoner had not been informed at that point that DI Hemmings knew of the colonel's whereabouts.

'To the best of my knowledge he is in the UK, and can be contacted by phone. I am not sure if he is aware of Krissie's death, unless, of course he has read about it in the papers.'

'Where does he live, again?'

'Burwood Park, Weybridge in Surrey,' replied Peter. 'Krissie and I visited him and his family on Sunday. I have his number in my wallet, but it's with the custody sergeant.'

'OK. We will look into that later. In fact, I see no reason why you should not have your personal possessions back, Peter,' informed the Superintendent looking at DI Hemmings for a reaction.

'No. None that I can see, sir,' agreed the DI. 'I will have a word, but for now, you will have to remain in police custody, at least until we clear up this mess. It looks as though these, er, interested parties are still around. Detaining you here is for your own protection more than anything else.

'Also, we need to check out various points given in your statement. It is certainly a most incredible story. Only time will tell if what you have told us checks out 100 percent. But something new has just come to light, and I have to go to a crime scene, it may or may not be connected to this case. It's obvious that if these people are out there, they still could be armed, and extremely dangerous. Also, we have informed Special Branch, and the Home Office. They will want to interview you,' then he added, 'Well it will be more like an interrogation than an interview!'

'Oh! Incidentally, sir, here is the Dudley guy's phone number.' He had gone back about eight pages in his A4 notepad. The number had been written down a day or so before when he had interviewed Peter's mother.

Again Peter was mystified as to how the DI had managed to get the information.

'The police certainly did work in mysterious ways,' he thought.

Unfortunately, the engineer had to remain in custody at Old Bridewell Police Station. If he was released on police bail, and stayed at his parent's house, he would need to be guarded night and day. He wouldn't be able to return to his house for a while, unless he had an armed guard there all the time . . .

On the other hand, he had not wanted to spend another night in the cottage ever again.

He could never see himself sleeping in the bed that he and his wife had shared, and made love in. Never!

Superintendent Barrington interrupted the prisoner's thoughts.

'It is our duty to inform you, Peter that the Special Branch, and anti-terrorist team are being brought in on this, also possibly MI5, MI6, SIS (Special Intelligence Service). They are based in London. I am fairly certain they will be very interested in what you have told us. This is a matter of both national and international security, and of the highest importance. You will be interrogated by them and this,' he said as he indicated the room, and the recorder, with a sweep of his hand. 'This is a walk in the park, compared to what those guys will put you through.

'Do you feel that you are up to it?'

The attitude of the police towards him had changed for the better. Not only were they solving a murder mystery on their patch, but thanks to him, they had also uncovered a terrorist network operating around the sleepy hollows of Chipping Sodbury.

'I guess I will have to be up to it,' declared Peter, and then raising his hands, he added, 'Whatever! I had planned to give the book to MI5 in London some time during this week. I have a telephone number that is also in my wallet. It was given to me by George Fotheringaye at the British Embassy in Riyadh.'

'That's fine. The Special Branch guys will sort out all the nitty-gritty.' The superintendent advised. 'Once they catch these insurgents, they will be taken to Paddington Green Police Station for interrogation, and detained there for a while. By the way, where is the book now, Peter?'

'Being guarded by your police officers, I shouldn't wonder.' The merest hint of a smile crept on Peter's face, but it only lasted for an instant and disappeared as soon as it had come.

'Good. OK, that will be all for now. Try and get some rest. We will talk again tomorrow. I'll see that you get your shoes and personal effects back. We will get you some reading material. And *try* and get some food down your neck. You have to keep your strength up. The canteen grub isn't that bad here, is it, Jerry?'

DI Hemmings agreed he had tasted worse.

'Oh! By the way, Peter, your mother phoned. Naturally, she is worried about you. I told her you were being well looked after. You will be able to see her soon. She has taken possession of your little dog.' The DI then spoke to his superior, 'Incidentally, sir, as I said earlier something has come up relating to this case. I need to have a word with you in private, and then get going.'

The superintendent nodded his head.

Peter was escorted back to the custody suite for yet another night in the slammer!

* * *

A tractor had been lowered by crane to drag the vehicle out of the water. When the police rock climbers got to the vehicle they put shackles around the axles of the vehicle. The van was then lifted by the crane and placed onto the road in readiness to be loaded onto a low-loader. At that point it looked as though it was vandals who were responsible for damage to the gates, and the dumping of the vehicle.

It was only when the van was examined that the gruesome remains of Abdul became visible. The police then realised this was not just a common vehicle theft, but something a lot more disturbing.

'There is a body in the passenger side of the van, skipper,' one of the rock climber PCs at the scene reported on his PR (personal radio) to his superior.

'Can you confirm if the person is alive or dead?' the sergeant at the end of the connection asked.

'Dead, Sarge,' replied the officer peering in at the sickening remains. He felt slightly queasy looking at the mess; he had seen dismembered bodies in the past, but none as gruesome as the one before him.

'Can you confirm that? Maybe there's an air pocket.'

'Affirmative, Sarge, it looks as though his head has been blown off!'

There was silence at the other end of the link. Then a female in the background giggled. The sergeant must have felt foolish; the connection to the PR went dead.

The matter was now a murder investigation. The Serious Crime Squad at Bristol was informed, and DI Hemmings had been requested to attend the scene. Now there were two murders on his patch, and one apparent suicide. The DI instructed DS Roger Pertwee to accompany him to the quarry at Chipping Sodbury. Jerry Hemmings had a hunch that the British Gas van was the one that the prisoner had described in the interview room.

The British Gas van stood on the makeshift road, from whence it came, water dripping off the body of the vehicle . . .

A low-loader had been brought to winch the vehicle and take it to a police compound. The near headless body was slumped forward in the passenger seat, and was hard pressed against the shattered windscreen.

SOCO officers took photographs of the van, the bullet holes, and the corpse.

On his arrival at the crime scene, Jerry Hemmings carried out a meticulous check of the vehicle and cross-referenced with the notes on his pad. Incredulously, everything that Peter Maynard had described in the interview room about the van incident checked out perfectly.

There was an indentation on the back bumper that 'could' have been made by a bullet, he assumed. Two small entry holes were on the passenger side blank panel at the back of the van, and one in the blank panel on the driver's side. This was exactly how Maynard had described the shots he had fired.

'Incredible!' the DI thought.

The police now had the van plus two Asian bodies. The pieces of the jigsaw were beginning to fit into place.

The body that was retrieved from the river Avon, a short distance from the Clifton Road Bridge was on a mortuary slab.

The DI had visited the remains, and confirmed it as being that of an Asian male with purple dye over his face, hands, and upper body. His identity at that time was unknown.

In the Incident Room, Peter Edward Maynard had been eliminated as the prime suspect for the murder of his late wife. All the CID checks on Kristine's finances and background checks on Peter Maynard had revealed nothing.

The Gas van had been found and the bullet holes tallied to the shots fired as Maynard had described

DI Hemmings was focusing his thoughts on the muddy footprint found on top of the shed roof in Maynard's garden, and the boots worn by the headless passenger in the van. If that checked out, it would then put the man at the scene of the crime, and the possible killer.

'I found this, guv, on my way back up the cliff face. It might be nothing, but it may be linked to the investigation. That brown stain on the sleeve *could* be dried blood.'

The safety-helmeted rock climbing PC, handed the DI a faded blue denim jacket. DI Hemmings called to one of the SOCO team.

'I want this bagged and tagged, then sent to the forensic lab. We need to check if the blood on the jacket matches that of the remains in the passenger seat. Check the pockets also, and let me know if you find anything.'

The SOCO expert rummaged through the pockets. He had found something.

'Here, sir; that's all there was in the pockets. I checked the lining on the collar also, nothing there.'

The SOCO Officer handed the DI a folded grubby white business card. DI Hemmings opened it and was surprised to observe *Peter E Maynard BSc MBA* AHT Division Saudi Telecom Systems.

The address was in Riyadh, Saudi Arabia. On the reverse side of the card, everything was printed in Arabic. This was further evidence that his prisoner had been telling the truth.

'The engineer was definitely off the hook now apart from being guilty of the murder of a terrorist suspect. But then, that would be construed as an unpremeditated attack, heat of the moment, or a crime of passion.

There were no witnesses. The only evidence was the finger and hand prints found on the weapon in the back garden. It would be for the Crown Prosecution Service to decide, if it ever went that far; which it probably would not.' The officer thought.

The DI had considered all along that the prisoner was a decent sort of guy, and not capable of such a crime. Maynard had given a good account of himself and his actions, albeit an incredible story. During the interviews, Maynard had conducted himself in a helpful and dignified manner.

Occasionally he was overcome with grief at certain parts of his story.

A pattern was now beginning to emerge. Back at the Incident Room in Bristol, many items on the whiteboard had ticks and notes written in felt-tip pen. On another board there were photographs, and newspaper cuttings

All the evidence obtained, would be available for Special Branch and the anti-terrorist squad to view before they conducted their interview with the prisoner. The expert interrogators would dissect his story attempting to pull it to shreds. Then they would examine the engineer's account in more detail for any inaccuracies. There was no doubt that the DI's evidential report would confirm the recorded interview was factual.

'Sir?' it was the young Scene of Crime Officer standing patiently waiting for an answer. He interrupted the DI's train of thought.

'Hmm? Oh, yes. No I'll hang on to these for now,' the DI replied, placing the business cards in his wallet.

The gruesome spectacle of the corpse had been removed from the British Gas van after having been photographed, and placed in a body bag. An undertaker's black van had reversed along the path and parked. The headless body would be taken to a police mortuary for close examination, and autopsy. Fingerprints, blood, and swab tests would be taken to establish the identity of the deceased.

The British Gas van was winched onto a police recovery vehicle, covered with a tarpaulin, and the vehicle would be transported to a police compound for forensic testing. All that remained of the incident at the quarry was wheel tracks, and two damaged gates.

DI Hemmings and DS Pertwee made one last stop before returning to Bridewell Police Station. They returned to the scene of the crime.

'Is this the house guv?' asked DS Pertwee, looking at the array of flowers wrapped in cellophane.

'Yes, this is it, Roger, a bit of a giveaway really,' the officer replied referring to the floral tributes. 'There's something I need to collect from the house, Rodge.'

The tape had been removed from both ends of the street, and residents and passersby once again had free access to the quiet road.

On entering the house, the DI made his way to the living room. There on the dresser, as Peter had described, and still undisturbed, was the video camera. It was facing towards the patio door and garden. DS Pertwee witnessed the removal of the camera with mains lead attached. The DI hoped this would give him further supporting evidence, and possible clues with regard to the terrorists operating on the Avon and Somerset patch. The DI remembered the engineer saying that he hadn't viewed the content and only confirmed that the counter had moved, indicating that a recording had been made.

It was getting late.

'Drop me off at home Rodge, and then get yourself home. It has been a most tiring, and yet interesting and fruitful day, also a day full of surprises. Tomorrow is looking to be even more eventful,' the DI said as he entered the unmarked police car.

'Maybe we'll have a celebratory drink if we crack this one, guv,' the sergeant suggested hopefully.

'Ha-ha! Maybe, Roger, maybe!'

'But we still have a way to go yet before the champagne corks start popping out of the bottles!'

Having had his tea, the senior detective sat in his den at his neat red brick house in Bradley Stoke, locally referred to as "sadly broke!"

'Would you like a cup of tea, dear?' his wife asked before the DI settled down in his armchair.

'Ah! Yes, er, on second thoughts, no. I think a scotch would be more welcoming.'

'Large and on the rocks?' she asked.

'Yes, good girl; you know it makes sense,' he replied, mimicking Del Boy from the *Only Fools and Horses* series, which was one of his favourite comedy shows.

Plugging the mains lead into a power socket, the DI pressed rewind. The video camera whirred into life giving a low click as it came to a stop. Taking a lead from his own video camera, he plugged one end into the camcorder, and the other end into the flat screen TV set in his study, and then pressed the "play" button.

A shadowy figure wearing a hood appeared on the outside of the house. He was sliding back the patio door. The man was of Asian origin. He entered the room, stood cautiously for a few moments presumably listening to see if the coast was clear and it wasn't a trap, and looked around furtively. He appeared relaxed and to be in no apparent hurry. Then espying what he came for, he strode purposely towards the table, and stood directly in front of the camera. The Asian was completely oblivious to his every action being recorded. There was no mistaking the clear image—it was the notorious Ali.

At that time, the DI could not confirm, if it was the same man that lay on a mortuary slab. That one had a purple face. Jerry Hemmings would put money on it that it was the same man.

The figure of the intruder moved some papers, revealing an aluminium briefcase. He then played with the tumbler locks for a short while but never managed to open the case on camera.

The figure then walked back towards the patio door carrying the briefcase. He went outside and slid the patio door shut. The machine stopped recording.

The DI now had further verification. Evil forces had intruded on the engineer's house more than once. The inspector played the clip back six times, and made the odd note on a writing block.

Contented, he sat back in his chair, placed a set of headphones over his ears, and listened to the strains of Brahms, as he sipped his scotch. He was more than satisfied with the day's outcome.

*   *   *

New evidence had filtered through from the Chipping Sodbury Police to New Bridewell at Bristol. There was every indication that the crime would be solved sooner than anticipated.

A detachment of armed anti-terrorist police had been stationed at Chipping Sodbury Police Station.

This was a precaution by the Intelligence Services against any further possible terrorist activities in the area.

*   *   *

The following morning DI Hemmings entered Peter's cell. The engineer had been trying to concentrate on reading a book given to him by one of the police officers, Marc Morgan. The prisoner was finding it very difficult to focus his mind and concentrate. He stood up when the DI entered the room.

'Please,' the inspector said, motioning Peter to remain seated.

'We've found your British Gas van, Peter. My first evaluation of the evidence is that everything you have told us to date checks out perfectly. You may be interested to know that a body was found in the passenger seat, or should I say a nigh on *headless* body was found,' he continued, correcting himself. 'The van had been dumped in a disused quarry along the Wickwar Road near Brinsham Park.

'The man appears to be of Asian origin. It seems that the man's head had been blown off possibly by the shots you said you fired from quite a close range!

'Also the broken body of a purple-faced Asian male was found washed up somewhere near the mud flats down by Clifton Suspension Bridge. It looks as though this was a suicide. These two bodies resemble the description of the two terrorists you described at the interview. We now have to establish their true identities.'

'Good,' the engineer responded. 'I know it all sounds such an implausible story, but it proves that what I have been telling you all along is the truth. Initially, you put two and two together and made five. I was guilty of my late wife's murder by association, because the Kalashnikov was there with my prints on it.'

'That is true, Peter, but that was all we had to go on *at the time,* as I had told you before. Police procedures and our lines of enquiry may seem a bit complicated to you. By the process of elimination and detailed checking of what you gave us on the statement, and on the recorded account, plus what we found, has proven your innocence of the murder of your late wife. Our ways may seem a bit long-winded, time consuming and unfathomable at times, but we need to get the answers we require, and have to be thorough. You were informed of this at the preliminary interview stage a few days ago. Anyone and everyone that came in contact with your late wife on that fateful day was a suspect, and you were our prime suspect as your dabs were found on the rifle. The AK-47 was found in your back garden. Do you follow?' The engineer nodded his head. 'You are an intelligent man, Peter. If you were in my position, what conclusions would you have drawn?'

Peter shrugged his shoulders; he thought for a moment and then replied. 'The same as you, I guess.'

'Exactly, so once we checked out your story, it was evident that you were telling the truth, you were gradually eliminated as the prime suspect. It all follows a pattern. Police work is based on guilty and not guilty.'

'I am sure the guy in the passenger seat was the one that killed Krissie, so that's two down and two to go. Well there may be others,' replied Peter with a strong hint of resentment in his voice.

'We are looking to see if there is a match to the boots he was wearing, also the muddy footprint we found on your shed roof. Incidentally, the headless terrorist was wearing surgical gloves. We found them in the van, near where he was seated. That is probably why there are no other prints on the weapon. We think the other man, the one with the purple face, is the one you refer to as Ali.

'Yes, he was the one that gave me the beating when I was being questioned by the bastards. It was him that was the most violent of all.'

'Well, I have given this matter a considerable amount of thought. I viewed the clip from your video cam yesterday, several times in fact. Someone *did* enter your house and take the briefcase as you described. He could be clearly seen. That was a very clever piece of work on your part, Peter.'

'Not clever enough. It won't bring my wife back, will it, sir?'

'No, unfortunately it will not, nothing will. We will continue our lines of enquiry back to Saudi Arabia to see if we can trace any leads through Interpol, the Foreign Office, and the Saudi Police.' I need you to view the video clip with me, and confirm if the person on the recording is the person we think it is, and known to you.'

'Yes, out of interest, I would like to view it,' Peter replied

'In the meantime, we have to interview the Colonel Dudley, er, whatever his name is, and try to make contact with Fotheringaye from the British High Commission in Riyadh. That shouldn't be too difficult as we have his number, and our guys are on to it.

'Oh! One final thing, you have an interview. As I said earlier; it will be more like an interrogation with the guys from the anti-terrorist or intelligence services this morning. I advise that you stay very cool throughout. Those guys have a reputation for being intimidating, and are masters at grilling suspects and so on.

'They have been informed that your wife has been killed and that you are not the guilty party in our view. These lads are only interested in the terrorist activities. The anti-terrorist people will go as gently as they can, but they are not known for treading on eggshells lightly. However, I feel sure that you will give a good account of yourself.

'When you have finished with the anti-terrorist guys, we will have a better idea what to do with you.'

'What's that supposed to mean?' Peter asked querulously.

'Well, you cannot stay here forever, and your life is still in grave danger all the time the terrorists are on the loose.'

'Where have I heard that before?' the engineer asked, thinking out loud, and interrupting the DI.

'Oh! So this is not new to you then?'

'No sir! Both Dudley and George told me. I should have listened. If I had maybe Krissie would be alive today.'

'Well, in hindsight, they were right, weren't they? But you were not to know that at the time"

'With hindsight—as you say, yes, sir.'

'DS Pertwee, that's one of our CID boys, is going down to meet this Dudley fellow at Addlestone Police Station in Surrey. He will take a statement from him, and get his side of the story. The Anti-terrorist Branch will probably want to interview him also, but this is merely a formality, and they will only do so if they feel it is really necessary.

'We've already contacted him, and he is more than willing to cooperate and back up your account with what you have told us. He sounds a pleasant sort of guy.'

'Yes, he is. Good old Dudders.' Peter mused thinking of happier times.

'Right, well the London boys should be here in about an hour. Is there anything you need, Peter? Oh! I brought a copy of today's paper. Sorry to see your house is on the front page.' Peter took the newspaper from the senior detective. "Who killed Kristine Maynard?" the headlines read.

A photograph of the suspect Peter Maynard was featured on the front page.

Peter sat staring at his picture in shock. A chill ran up his spine.

'It didn't take those bastards from the press long to get on the case,' he said, referring to the headlines.

'Unfortunately, that's life. Bad news sells, Peter.'

'How much do they know?'

'Only what we have told them, and what they misinterpreted, the rest is supposition.'

'Parasites,' Peter spat the word out. 'They're as bad as lawyers, making money out of other people's demise and misery.' He sat with the paper opened in front of him reading the account.'

'OK, we'll see you in about one hour, Peter.' The DI wasn't going to be drawn into a discussion. 'Once you have finished with the anti-terrorist guys, and if you feel up to it, I would like you to view the video clip in my office. I need a positive ID of the guy that entered your house, as I said.'

Peter nodded in agreement.

'It will be a pleasure. I have a pretty good idea who that was,' he assured the detective inspector. Jerry Hemmings stepped through the open doorway, and then he was gone.

The young cockney PC that had collected Peter from the hospital looked through the entryway as the DI left, and gave the prisoner a paperback book to read. Giving the thumbs up, he smiled, winked then closed the door. The key turned as the lock clunked loudly shut. The footsteps faded along the corridor of the custody suite. The prisoner once again sat alone with his thoughts, he now had a novel and a fictitious account of his activities from the newspaper to read.

An hour-and-a-half later, the cell door was opened. It was another officer about to escort the prisoner to the Interview Room with the anti-terrorist representatives.

When the engineer entered Interview Room 3 (IR3), he saw DI Hemmings standing with two smartly dressed, plain-clothed officers. Peter stared at them. Their hard faces appeared to have been chiselled out of granite. 'They look more like criminals than criminals,' he thought.

DI Hemmings introduced the men to Peter, but their names were forgotten as soon as they were given. The interviewee wasn't really that interested in who they were. He was apprehensive and just wanted to get the interview over with. There were no friendly handshakes, just a brief nod of the head, and the officers sat down. One indicated that Peter should also sit in the chair opposite.

The two men had their own recording apparatus, with a video recorder.

They also placed notepads on the table in front of them. They had presumably been briefed by the DI, Peter thought.

'Very well, I'll leave you gentlemen to it,' the senior CID officer informed the interviewers, feeling slightly out of place in his own police station. Both men stared at Peter for a few moments, and then silently set up their equipment.

Peter sat upright on the hard chair, he was feeling very uneasy. He was also conscious that he shouldn't fidget or be nervous; as this may be misinterpreted he wasn't telling the truth. He also knew his body language would be taken into account, at the time, and when the recording was played back later.

There had been no offers of beverages, and the atmosphere appeared tense, and to the point of being hostile.

Once the officers checked that the equipment was working satisfactorily. One asked the other 'OK?'

The other officer answered in the affirmative.

One of the officers spoke into the microphone introducing himself, and then the other did the same . . . .

'State your name.'

'Peter Edward Maynard.'

'Date of birth?'

Peter obliged.

'You reside at?'

Peter answered the question.

The purpose of this interview is to investigate the allegations you have made with regards to terrorist and criminal-linked activities on the Avon and Somerset patch. Namely, Chipping Sodbury.

'If what you say is true, then these activities could be a threat to the British government. You have reported this in a previous interview to Detective Inspector Hemmings and his boss, Superintendent Barrington, we are given to understand. As a result, this is the purpose of why we are here to investigate further. Do you agree, comprehend, and can you confirm this?'

'Yes, I do and can confirm.'

'We have listened to your taped interview, and read your statement. To save our time and yours is there anything that you have told the police officers that you wish to add to or retract?'

'Nothing whatsoever at this time,' Peter replied, noticing a small red light on the video recorder. He instinctively knew that he was being recorded.

The meeting was intense, also frequently interrupted with questions. Notes were scribbled on writing blocks. Then things started to heat up as they took a faster pace.

Peter was questioned repeatedly as to how he had stumbled onto the terrorist cell. Why had he assumed the things he had discovered were linked with a terrorist organisation or terrorist activities? Had he connections with terrorists? Was he sympathetic to their cause or to any other? Was he a Muslim? What were his religious and political beliefs?

When Peter mentioned the discovery on the rooftop in Riyadh, he was asked continually what was stored in the small room. Where was the building? Could he pinpoint the place on a map? To this question, Peter replied that he could as he had the coordinates stored on a GPS in his briefcase at his residence. He also advised that they would not find anything on the rooftop now as the terrorists had moved on. George Fotheringaye of the British Consulate in Riyadh, and Colonel Coburn-Smythe could vouch for that.

The two men made notes.

Peter was then asked if there wasn't anything in the room now, was he sure there had been something there in the first place? Peter thought this to be a stupid question, and informed them that the British Embassy guy could confirm there was nothing in the room when he visited the radio/telecom site. The interrogators then suggested that he had made the whole thing up to bring attention to himself, or maybe for some other reason or reasons to hide the truth about a murder enquiry?

Peter felt the anger rise up inside him.

'Piss off!' he responded.

Both officers were taken aback at the outburst. Peter remembered that he had to keep his cool. Finally, he shrugged his shoulders.

'You will believe what you want to believe,' he replied. 'I couldn't give a toss if you don't believe a word I say. I only know what I saw, and what I have in my possession. You can ask George and Dudley about the smell of Semtex or some other plastic explosive that we witnessed on the rooftop.'

There was a short, silence at this unexpected outburst. The interviewee had been passive, almost humble up to that point. The anti-terrorist officers were the ones on the attack, now the interviewee had changed his tactic. They wanted the suspect to bite, goading him further.

'Maybe you put the Semtex there yourself,' one of the interviewers said.

'Oh, yes! I do that all the time.'

'OK don't get smart with us, Maynard. Let's go back to the beginning again.'

'How do you know about these things, like what Semtex smells like?' the officer asked. Until that point he had remained silent but attentive throughout.

'I served in the *British* Army for six years, the *British* army,' he emphasised. 'I spent a lot of time in Northern Ireland; I also did a ballistics course.'

The engineer was cross-examined with more vigour and intensity. More questions were fired at him from both directions, as he was given the third degree. He was told that he could be wrong about what he thought he saw. Maybe the weapons found were a store for security guard.

After all, he had stated that there was a guard on the rooftop.

Peter advised that the guard was not armed.

The engineer sat still in the chair refusing to be drawn or intimidated into any plan to try and catch him out. He folded his arms. He knew how his body language would be interpreted.

He sat poker-faced, and stuck to his story. The engineer knew that he had the winning hand and spoke slowly and deliberately across to the microphone. The book was in his possession. He sat back and smiled at the officers out of contempt, and at their crazy assumptions. He knew they were trying to break him down, but he was not going to change his story or be drawn.

'What does it contain, this book of yours? Maybe you were mistaken? Where is it now?'

Peter explained the scenario as it had happened, more or less verbatim over and over again. The officers were not able to trip him up on any point, although they did their best. The engineer did not give the whereabouts of the manual. He decided to play them at their own game for a while and just answer their questions, sort of cat and mouse style.

Once they saw the manual, together with the written notes, they would believe him. He knew he was holding all the aces.

Two hours later, the officers abruptly and unexpectedly stopped the interview. They were seemingly satisfied with the outcome, and the prisoner's answers. They spoke into the microphone, stating that the interview was concluded, and then turned the video recorder off. The two men packed their equipment, and then left the room.

A police officer entered the interview room and stood in silence with his back to the door.

After about fifteen minutes the two men re-entered.

'We need to see this book you refer to. Where is it exactly?' the officer in the blue suit asked.

'It would be best if I showed you where it is,' Peter proffered. 'I need to be sure that it is still where I hid it.'

'OK, that's fine by us. We need to speak to the custody sergeant and get you transferred into our charge. There will not be a problem. They've more or less finished with you, as I understand.

'You will be happy to know that you are no longer under suspicion of your late wife's murder. All we need now is to get on to these terrorists.'

* * *

And so it was. Peter entered an unmarked police car with a radio, an internal blue light, aerials, and the mysterious world of the anti-terrorists. They sped off in the direction of the empty cottage close to Chipping Sodbury.

After half an hour the car pulled up outside the residence. Peter was surprised to see an armed police officer standing outside the house. There were many flowers wrapped in cellophane along the front wall.

A few members of the press were outside, and Peter was photographed as he alighted from the back of the unmarked police car. Questions were being fired at him by reporters. He had had enough for one day.

Peter gave a scornful 'Fuck off.' He was still angered at the press headlines in the newspaper, and his photograph being displayed on the front page of an international tabloid, also his recent grilling at Old Bridewell Police Station.

The plain-clothed officers smiled at his unexpected expletives as they flashed their warrant cards to the uniformed officer.

'Anti-terrorist unit,' one of the officers informed.

'OK sir, we are expecting you,' the armed policeman replied.

Peter led the way down the short path. He opened the front door with his key. He took one step inside the hallway and froze. His mind pictured the scene of the devastation in the living room. He felt that he could not go on any further.

'Are you OK?' the officer in the blue suit enquired.

Negative energy had taken over once again.

'No! I don't feel too good. It's a bit of a shock coming back here. I haven't been back since my wife-'

He stopped short unable to finish the sentence. The dry feeling was back in his throat. He couldn't go on, but he knew that he had to. He sat heavily on one of the stairs as he had done on the night of the murder. He felt dizzy. 'This isn't happening,' he thought.

'Get him a glass of water Mike,' the officer in the blue suit instructed.

The officer proceeded further into the house, and found the kitchen. He picked up a glass from a cupboard, ran the water for a while, and then filled the glass.

'Sorry,' Peter said hoarsely, with tears in his eyes, and feeling foolish.

'It is understandable mate, considering all that you've been through. It's a wonder you haven't cracked sooner.' This was completely unexpected, as it was the first sign of compassion that his interrogators had shown towards him.

Peter drank the water greedily and slowly started to feel a little better. He rubbed his head, ruffling his longish brown hair, and then stood up.

'Thanks,' he said.

'Do you feel you can continue Peter?' Dave asked. The silent officer as Peter had thought of him to be.

'Yes! Yes, let's get this over with,' he said 'It has been a bad day for me, the sooner it's over, the better.'

The engineer led the way through to the dining room. He was surprised to see that the house was tidy, and had been thoroughly cleaned. Even the carpet had been shampooed, and the furniture had been moved around.

'Whoever has done this is very thoughtful,' he told himself. He walked to the patio door, unlocked it, and stepped outside. The officers were taken aback. They had wrongly assumed that the book was hidden somewhere inside the house, and not outside.

They followed their charge to the bottom of the garden. Peter lifted Buddha from his pyramid of stones. He then removed the pile, stone by stone, while both officers looked on, with both curiosity and interest.

When he had finished, he unlocked the shed (office) door and picked up a spade. He carefully dug for about five minutes. Then on his hands and knees, he cleared the rest of the earth by hand. Carefully, he lifted a package well wrapped in polythene. He removed the plastic wrapping letting it drop to the ground. A yellow jiffy bag with DHL written in large red letters was exposed. The engineer opened the package for the first time since it had left Saudi Arabia. He pulled out an oblong object wrapped in a white plastic bag with the words in blue print "*Jarir Bookstore, Olaya, Riyadh, KSA*."

Peter then extracted a reddish brown coloured book from the plastic bag and opened it.

Flicking through the pages, he nodded his head in approval. For a brief moment, he had a feeling of triumph over his insurgent enemies. He had managed to outwit them at their own game. The book that had caused so much grief was safe and in the UK. Then the realisation of his loss rebounded back to him. The book was the reason for his late wife's death. He quickly passed the book to the blue suited officer.

'It's all there,' he said, 'even the newspaper cuttings.'

*   *   *

Dudley drove the short distance from Weybridge, to Addlestone Police Station, and presented himself at the front desk. The police support officer rang a couple of numbers, finally tracking down DS Pertwee to the canteen.

The colonel was shown to an interview room. After a short while, DS Pertwee entered holding a steaming cup of hot coffee in one hand, and a laptop case in the other. He placed the items on the table, extended his right hand, and introduced himself cordially. He then asked Dudley if he would care for a beverage. The colonel politely refused the offer.

'Right, colonel, taking a statement from you is purely a routine matter. At first, we thought this unfortunate incident was a run-of-the-mill murder enquiry. We have since discovered something a lot more life threatening and disturbing, so we have to delve into the matter a little deeper. Well, quite a lot deeper in fact,' he said, correcting himself.

'To bring you up to date, sir, we are making good progress with the investigation. Well, that is according to my governor, at any rate. Now we just need to establish and confirm certain things that we have been informed of. We need to tie up a few loose ends that your ex-work colleague a, er, Mr. Peter Maynard has already helped us with. The episodes that have unfolded need to be confirmed by you. So let us begin with when you both first met, how you met, where, when, and events leading up to his having been badly beaten, then hospitalised. We also need to confirm for what reason his beating had come about?

'Also, your own unfortunate confrontation, your version of events, and what actually happened. Finally, I would like you to inform me of anything else that you think we need to know. Are you OK with that?'

'Yes, that's fine by me, sergeant. Can I ask before we proceed how Peter is? Lisa, er-that's my wife and I were both devastated to hear the tragic news. Our thoughts are with him at this time. Poor chap, what with all he's been through.'

Dudley stared deep in thought at the metal table. Thinking about his friend banged up in some police cell.

'He's bearing up quite well under the circumstances. He's not under arrest any more. He is in police custody for his own safety and protection. It's only a matter of time when we can get safe and secure accommodation for him.'

The sergeant slurped his hot coffee loudly, savouring the flavour, and then was silent.

Suddenly, as if remembering his purpose in the Surrey Constabulary territory, he reached into his laptop case and pulled out his computer, and a recording device.

'I just need to have your report first-hand, so to speak. Do you have a socket your side of the table colonel?' the sergeant asked.

'Auto-suggestion,' Dudley thought.

'Yes, here, give me the plug,' he said, and taking the electrical connection he then pushed it into the power socket and pressed the switch. The detective then turned on his laptop.

'We're cooking with gas, colonel.'

'No, please, Dudley will suffice.'

'Right Dudley, no problem with that.' The DS agreed smiling broadly at the colonel as he took another sip of coffee.

'Sergeant, before we begin, please can you see that Peter gets this?' He handed the officer a smallish flat, white envelope. 'I didn't seal it in case you chaps have to check what's inside,' Dudley volunteered.

'That's very thoughtful of you, sir. No worries, I'll make sure Peter gets it. Right then, down to business,' he said, putting the envelope into the inside pocket of his jacket.

Dudley gave his delivery. After the story was told, the questioning began which was frank, friendly, and to the point. All the relevant issues had been highlighted in yellow on the DS's notepad. He steadfastly typed Dudley's report of the incident on the laptop as the story unfolded. He also included a description of the visit the colonel had received by the terrorists. Dudley removed his jacket, and rolled up his shirt sleeve, revealing the long scar made by the knife on his left arm. The detective winced, and reported it on the recording. Everything that the man in captivity had told the police checked out, including the scar that the colonel displayed on his left forearm.

Finally, DS Pertwee went outside to print off a copy of the statement. On his return, he requested the colonel to read it, and if he was happy with what was written, he was to sign the document. Four minutes later, Dudley put pen to paper giving his autograph.

* * *

The room cleaner knocked on the Pakistani's room door.

'Mr. Patel, are you in there?' she enquired. There was no reply. She knocked again, and then for a third time. Finally, she used her pass key and entered the room. The sight that met her eyes was the worst she had ever encountered in the seven years she had been employed by the MODA Hotel.

There was a purple colour over part of the bedding, the carpet, and the wall. Water seemed to be everywhere in the room. The towels had purple dye on them; the place was a mess.

Mrs. Cummins padded down the patterned red carpeted staircase in her soft, flat shoes, striding purposefully to the reception desk.

'Room four is in a dreadful state, ma'am. An utter disgrace,' she informed Mrs. Wilcox, the joint owner. 'It looks like that Paki chap, Mr. Patel, and the other one have run off.'

'I'd better take a look,' Mrs. Wilcox declared. He owes nearly two weeks rent, him and his brother.'

'Oh! They are brothers are they? Well, that explains it! I didn't like the look of them when I first set eyes on them. Shifty that's what I thought. Their eyes are too close together, I said to my Sid-'

'Yes, well, let's take a look at the room, Mrs. Cummins, shall we?' the lady owner interrupted.

The two women trudged up the stairs, and stood in the open doorway of the Pakistani's room.

'I said to my Sid, they look a right strange pair-'

'My goodness,' the owner declared, interrupting the cleaner again, 'whatever has been going on in here? Where did that purple colour come from?'

'Search me, Mrs. Wilcox. Do you think we should inform the police?'

'I'm not sure,' the owner replied. I mean we don't know for certain that they are not coming back. 'Some of their clothes and things are still here,' she said looking into the open wardrobe doorway.

'Oh! And the suitcase is on top of the wardrobe, and what's this metal case on the bed? There's a purple colour here too, and a book.'

'Yes, but—I mean, well, should I tidy the room up best I can, that is?'

'No, best leave it until tomorrow, and see if they come back, or call. If not, then we'll decide. I'm sure Raymond will know what to do.'

Raymond was Mrs. Wilcox husband. He was a retired police officer, and had taken early retirement after winning 464,000 pounds on the lottery. With the winnings, and his police pension he thought the hotel to be a good investment, so he bought it. Someone in "the job" had once told him, "Bums in bed make money!"

* * *

Peter at first had feared the worst, thinking it may have been intercepted in Riyadh. After having flicked through the pages, he confirmed that everything was intact and had not been harmed.

'Well, officers, er-gentlemen or whatever you call yourselves, the book and contents do not appear to have been interfered with in any way. It looks to be as I remember it from Saudi before I sent it to myself by DHL.' Peter passed the book across, happy to be rid of it.

The officer took the manual, and slowly went through it. Dave stood at his side. The officer's eyes widened at something he'd seen, and then he resumed his normal countenance as to being expressionless. He did this when he realised that Peter was closely observing him. The officer opened his briefcase and inserted the book. He played with the tumblers until the case locked.

'Well done, mate,' the officer said to Peter. 'Let's hope it is the genuine article, and not some sort of decoy to throw us off the scent. But from what you've told us, it would appear to be genuine as per the beatings you and your colleague took. We will need to get parts of the transcript translated by the looks of things as there are notes in what appears to be a foreign language.

'Probably Urdu,' Peter offered, 'as the bastards are from Pakistan.'

'Yes, you could be right.'

'Is it too late to have a bite to eat around here?' his colleague asked. 'I mean, have we missed lunch?'

'No it's only just gone one forty-five guv,' replied Dave.

'Very well, you're a local Peter, can you suggest anywhere close by?'

'Yes the Royal Oak, in Chipping Sodbury. The food is excellent and reasonably priced,' the engineer replied.

'Very well then, the Royal Oak it is on your recommendation. We'll follow your directions.'

The establishment was very mature, dating back to the seventeenth century. There were heavy oak beams, formerly ships timbers, that supported a lath and plaster ceiling. There was a huge inglenook fireplace to the right hand side of the large bar room, and a very welcoming log fire burning in the hearth, as it was a cold, crisp day . . .

A very smartly dressed attractive grey haired lady was sitting with an elderly gentleman with a shock of white hair. They looked up as Peter and his associates entered, and both nodded in recognition. Peter nodded, in return.

'How long are yer back for this time?' the elderly gent asked the engineer in a broad Yorkshire accent. Obviously he hadn't been informed of the engineer's sad loss.

'Sorry to hear about-' the smart, grey-haired lady began.

'Thanks,' replied Peter. Then the two returned to their conversation. The engineer knew the lady was informing the gentleman about the recent tragic events.

The two anti-terrorist officers were suitably impressed with the establishment. They picked up a menu from a table, and without looking at it, one of the men asked Peter if he could recommend anything.

'The fish and chips are very good. The fish here is fried with bitter or lager, giving the batter that extra crispiness. Well, so I'm told. My wife doesn't like English food as a rule, but she-'

He stopped speaking. Suddenly he realised that he was talking in the present tense.

He bit his lip as hard as he could. The tears welled up in his eyes, and the dryness returned in his throat once again.

'Excuse me,' he said in just over a whisper. He walked quickly through the bar, and up the plush red-patterned-carpeted staircase. Then Dave indicated with a nod to his colleague that he should follow Peter. Casually the man followed the engineer at a discreet distance through the bar and up the carpeted stairway, and waited outside the Gents toilet.

Peter threw cold water over his face. It had happened again. He never knew when the wave of emotion would sweep over him. The police doctor had informed him that these emotional sensations were known as panic, or anxiety attacks. The doctor had offered to prescribe Bromazepam to help reduce the tension, also the nervousness, but Peter had politely refused the drug.

When the engineer emerged from the toilet, he was surprised to see the officer waiting for him.

'Did you think I was going to do a runner?' Peter enquired.

'No, mate, but you are our responsibility until we get you back to Bridewell. Are you feeling a little better?'

'Yes I will manage, thank you. I just miss my wife so much. It's too hard to bear at times. I cannot come to terms with it.' He felt it happening again, and swallowed hard.

'I understand. Let's see if my colleague has got the beers in, that might help,' he suggested good naturedly.

'Three pints of best bitter, that is what I have ordered, and one pint is all *you're* getting, as you are driving us back to the smoke. Come on, mate, where shall we sit?' he asked Peter.

The engineer led the way through an archway to a table for four near the window. Blue suit placed his briefcase containing the book, between him and the wall. Peter began to mellow. He warmed towards the anti-terrorist officers for the first time.

He said, 'You know, when I first met you guys in the interview room, I thought you were a right evil pair of bastards.'

'We are, mate, don't underestimate us. We have a tough job to do, and need to be downright nasty sometimes.

'We do what we have to do to get the information we need out of suspects. There are a lot of wicked people and organisations out there, bent on death and destruction of others. Our job is to catch the bastards and lock them up, before they carry out their evil intentions.

'Anyway, *today* thanks to you, we may have struck gold, without being the pair of bastards that we usually are, hence the beers, and the fish and chips. You've seen our bad side, now you see our good side.

'So tell me, Peter, where did you learn about electronics, and being able to fire a high velocity weapon and so on?'

'In the army,' Peter replied. 'I was six years in the Royal Corps of Signals, Para' attached-'

'Fish, chips, and peas three times?' an attractive, tall, young blonde female enquired, interrupting the conversation.

'Yes that's us,' replied Dave. 'Cheers Peter, and bon appetit,' he said raising his glass.

'Salut,' Peter responded in the vernacular, then, 'Cheers.'

They consumed their meals in relative silence. Pinstripe, or Mike, as Peter now knew him, stood up after he finished his meal and went back to the bar. He purchased another two pints of Courage best bitter, and bought himself a small lemonade shandy.

'Will I hear anything more about this?' Peter asked, indicating to the briefcase.

'Yes, keep a sharp look-out in the newspapers,' Mike replied with a smirk, placing the drinks on the table. 'Hopefully, there'll be some arrests. We'll be handling this from now on. I expect the carrot crunchers have told you about protection and all that?' He was referring to their police counterparts in the Avon and Somerset Constabulary, in a joking manner.

'No, not in any depth, but I heard a whisper,' replied the engineer, thoughtfully.

'OK, I will have a word with the DI on your behalf when we get back. Be advised that we or our colleagues *will* most certainly want to question you again at some point. It will be regarding issues relating to the book, and events leading up to the book incidents. Don't worry, it will not be as intense an interview as you had today, but you are not totally off the hook yet, Peter.'

'No problem for me,' the engineer responded. 'I just want those bastards to suffer for what they have done. Catching them and locking them up is not good enough. Two are dead, and there are still at least two more at large to my knowledge, maybe somewhere around here. I think they work in a cell of four people.'

'Yes, well, I cannot disagree. Incarceration is too good for them,' replied the man in the blue suit not wanting to express too much of an opinion. 'Are you aware that there is an armed rapid response unit here in this town or village, or whatever you call it?'

'Town, I think. Yes I was told at the police station. How do you guys work?' Peter enquired.

'We work with MI5, or the Spooks as they're known, and Special Branch at Scotland Yard, and all that. In a civilian war where terrorists are mixing with the population both inside and outside of the UK, military intelligence is supplemented by police intelligence. This is also dependent on sources among the civilian population.' The officer stabbed at a fat golden brown chip with his fork.

'This comes through two divisions,' he began, holding the chip on the fork midway between table and mouth. 'Everyone knows, and can see what CID does. For example, they make arrests; follow suspects, scenes of crime investigation, surveillance, giving evidence in court and so on.

'In counter-terrorist operations, and espionage for example, police effort must be covert. Like Military Intelligence (MI5 and MI6), they are covert. This is where Special Branch fits into the equation. When terrorists operate from a safe haven in neighbouring countries, SB interests follow them. This is known as "going external." There are many examples of this, Northern Ireland, Pakistan and now Saudi. MI6, SIS, SAS, and C15. They all play their part in different ways. Incidentally, there is always a Special Branch presence close to immigration at the air and sea ports. This is in case of suspicious persons, forged passports, wanted terrorists, and so on. Those Islamic fundamentalists will do anything to get into the UK to help destroy our structure, and of course live off the state.

'So you see Peter, how important something like this book you stumbled upon, in all innocence, is of such high importance to us? It will help in the war against terror. You may not realise what a great contribution you have made, albeit unknowingly.'

Peter sat listening in silence. This was poles apart from what he did for a living.

'Maybe you should think about a future with one of the intelligence gathering agencies. You are not that far from GCHQ at Cheltenham. I am sure they could use someone with your skills.'

'It's a thought, but I have too many other things on my mind at the moment. I have to bury my wife, and return to the Philippines at some point. Thanks anyway, I'll think about it!'

The three men finished their beers, and then headed back to Bristol.

* * *

'Ah! Peter, DI Hemmings wants to see you in his office,' the desk sergeant said as the engineer was escorted back to his cell.

The custody sergeant walked behind the desk and then picked up some papers. Then turning to a young PC he instructed, 'Barry, take Peter to the DI's office in the CID suite.'

'Right ho, sarge.' The officer released the electric door lock, and indicated for Peter to go through.

Once inside he pointed towards a staircase. 'Follow me mate,' he instructed as they walked up the bare stone stairway. Then they entered an open office area. Many eyes were staring at computers, phones rang, and there was a general air of activity.

Barry stopped outside a door marked DI Hemmings, knocked and waited. 'Come!'

'Peter Maynard is here to see you, sir.'

'Show him in. Hi, Peter,' the DI greeted, 'how did it go?'

'Better than expected, sir thanks. We even had a couple of beers, and fish and chips, after I presented the guys with the book.'

'Well, better than expected, sounds very good. OK, Peter, take a seat. Now, I have the video from earlier on the day that your wife was murdered. I would just like to run through it with you, and see if you can give a positive ID.'

'OK, I'll do my best.'

The DI switched on the camcorder. It was already wired into a flat digital television in the large office. The screen flickered. A figure was attempting to enter the patio door. He entered the room and stood in front of the video camera completely oblivious that his every move was being recorded.

'That's the bastard.' Peter nearly jumped out of his chair. 'That's the guy I threw out of Radisson's Hotel in Riyadh. He's the main guy that beat me up, and kicked my leg afterwards!' He watched the end of the short clip, and saw the Asian walking out with the aluminium briefcase, closing the patio door. Then the screen went blank.

'You are sure that is the man?'

'Absolutely! Not a shadow of a doubt. His name is Ali; at least that's what the others called him.'

'Thank you Peter, that is most helpful.' He stood up and walked to the door. 'For your information he is the guy that was found on the mud flats near Bristol. His face and hands were purple. This all fits in with what you have told us to date.'

'Well, I am pleased to hear that,' the engineer replied.

'Good. I am fairly certain that this is the same man with the purple face that is in the mortuary. Now we have to identify him, also the faceless one. OK, thank you, Peter, you have been a great help.

'Tracey,' the DI called, looking at a young blonde girl of about twenty-four years of age.

'Take Mr. Maynard back down to the desk sergeant please.'

'Hmm! So Ali is confirmed dead,' Peter thought as he descended the stairs.

*　*　*

'And just look at the state of this room. I mean who's going to pay for the damage, and all this purple paint or whatever, it is?'

'Then there's the unpaid room rent,' Mrs. Cummins interrupted, as she reminded her employer of the outstanding amount.

'Yes, they ran off without paying, I mean it is just not good enough. What are you going to do about it?' Mrs. Wilcox asked the young looking, ruddy-cheeked constable.

Both women stood in the doorway of the Asian's rented room.

'Yes! Well! I will make my report, and then pass it on to my superiors,' PC Dennis informed the ladies, trying to sound official, and in control.

'My hubby says we shouldn't touch anything in case your detectives want to take a look. He was in the Metropolitan Police in London, you know?' she said proudly. 'That's where we're from.'

'*I'm* from around here, in Bristol, that's where I am from.' Mrs. Cummins remarked, not wanting to feel left out of the conversation. 'Shifty eyed they were.'

'Then there's that funny looking phone they left, there on the bed,' informed Mrs. Wilcox. She was referring to the Satcom phone, and indicating it to the young officer. He nodded in response.

'Right then; I would imagine that you can claim the damage on the insurance. I am not sure about the loss of your room rent money. It will be best to check your insurance policy. We will give you a crime number, and I will have a chat with CID about the room, and the missing occupants. Your husband is quite right saying not to touch anything. I think it's best for now, to leave *everything* as it is just in case there is more to this than we know at present. If the occupants return, please let us know as they may need to be interviewed.'

He walked down the stairs, on arrival in the small hallway; he put his notebook in his tunic pocket.

He was puzzled about the situation. Something was not right.

'On the one hand, it could be a case of vandalism, and running off without paying the bill, but on the other hand, there was an anti-terrorist armed response unit stationed at the Sodbury nick. He had heard that terrorists were operating in the area, and wondered if there was any connection between the Pakistanis, the room with the purple dye, and terrorists, but then probably not,' he thought. He picked up his helmet from the hall table, turned to the landlady, and said goodbye. The PC then walked the short distance back to Chipping Sodbury Police Station, still deep in thought.

* * *

He sat on the bed holding the card, and read the hand-written message for the third time.

> "In Deepest Sympathy
>
> I know that even the most sincerest of words cannot alleviate the pain and sorrow that you are currently experiencing, and we want to express our deepest sympathy. Our thoughts, love and prayers are with you at this time."

It was signed, "With all our love, Dudley, Lisa and Clarita."

'What lovely people,' Peter thought amidst a mixture of emotions.

His mother and father had visited him the previous evening at the police station. They sat together in a vacant interview room. Pasko was growing, and still very mischievous. He greeted Peter affectionately. After licking his master, Pasko started gnawing at the engineer's knuckles. He hadn't taken to his new surroundings with the engineer's parents easily; they had guessed he missed Peter and Kristine.

*   *   *

'Yeah! And there was this purple dye all over the bedspread and carpet. The old biddy wasn't too happy. The buggers had made such a mess, and ran off without paying.' He sat back in the chair balancing it on the two back legs in the canteen of Staple Hill Police Station, as he faced two of his colleagues.

'It was the MODA hotel near Sodbury nick. That's what you get for being too trusting, you see?'

'So what did you say to her?' asked another PC sitting opposite as he unclipped his tie. He placed it on top of his flat-peaked cap on the table, and proceeded to roll up his shirt sleeves.

'Well, I agreed with her old man that they should not touch anything until they had a report from CID. Her old man's an ex-copper, Met, I think she said. Let them see what they make of it,' informed PC Dennis.

'So what did CID say?' asked PC Barry Orgman.

'Dunno, I haven't made the report out yet,' replied the young constable with a snigger. 'It doesn't seem *that* important.'

'Slurp! Slurp!' the coffee was steaming hot. DS Pertwee eyed the three young probationers over the top of his brown coffee mug.

The DS was sitting quietly in the corner of the room unnoticed, thinking, and listening to the conversation

Finally, having heard enough, the officer placed the large coffee cup down on the table. He stood up and walked over to the Formica-topped table where the three young PC's were seated. The detective sergeant placed both hands heavily on the table top and leaned forward, staring directly into a surprised PC Dennis's pair of hazel brown eyes.

'Then I think that you *should prepare your report, and pronto, chummy, like now*! Allow me to introduce myself, DS Pertwee from New Bridewll nick. *Now get that report typed up, and let me have a copy, and be quick about it!*'

'Yes, sarge, right away. Sorry.' The young officer almost overbalanced on the two legs of his chair. He got up from the table, grabbed his helmet, and without saying a word, hurried back to the main office.

DS Pertwee returned to his seat, stirring his coffee thoughtfully, as he sat pondering. There was an uneasy silence in the room.

'Purple dye?' he mused, 'Hotel guests absconding? There was a purple faced Asian's body found washed up by a suspension bridge near Bristol, and then possible terrorist activity near or around the Chipping Sodbury area. Hmm! Interesting, most interesting.'

He made a call on his mobile phone 'Hello, guv, Pertwee here. I'm at Staple Hill nick. I was on my way back, but I might be on to something. I just overheard one of the young uniformed PC's talking about a hotel down in Chipping Sodbury; purple dye was found on the furnishings. The occupants have apparently done a runner. The local copper had visited the scene a short while ago, and I've just told him to make out his report, and get it back to me PDQ. As I'm over this way, do you want me to make a visit, and investigate guv?'

'Yes, it may well be worth your while Roger. It's not far from the quarry either. Hmm maybe they were holed up there. Where is the hotel?'

It's at the top of Chipping Sodbury Street apparently. I think I know the one MONA or MODA, something like that. It shouldn't be hard to find, the PC will tell me. I am pretty sure it's Rounceval Street.'

'Hmm, it's not too far from Maynard's house either, if I'm not mistaken. That could have been where the Asians were staying. OK good work, keep me informed.'

'Yes, will do, sir!'

* * *

Peter got out of the car and entered his house for the second time since the murder. The uniformed PC was no longer on duty outside the cottage. The engineer took time to look at the labels on the cellophane-wrapped bouquets of flowers along the front wall. He stood and read the dedications. *"In deepest sympathy, you were a good friend and will be sadly missed, love from Nell and family." "Peace at last to our sister, from all of us at St. Paul's Church." "In* loving memory of a wonderful daughter-in-law, rest in peace, Love from Mum and Dad." It was all too much for Peter to bear.

'Shall we go inside Peter?' the female police constable counsellor, named Yasmin suggested, sensing the engineer's anguish.

'Yes. Yes, aren't people lovely?' he asked, quietly standing outside the house and looking at the colourful array with tears in his eyes.

'Some are Peter; some are, but not all.' She looked towards the road at the young PC in the driving seat. He met her gaze, and made a thumbs up sign, and then thumbs down. She nodded that everything was satisfactory, giving a thumbs up in return.

They entered the house together. Peter went straight upstairs, and pulled a suitcase off the top of the shelf from inside the built-in wardrobes. He let it fall onto the bed. It was the same suitcase he had taken with him to Saudi. He threw his clothes into the valise. It reminded him of the last time Kristine had packed in preparation for her husband's trip to the Middle East. He felt he had to do it quickly. Underwear, socks, shirts, trousers, T-shirts, jeans all went into the case. He felt compelled to get out of the room and out of the house as quickly as possible. He knew that it was Kristine that had washed his clothes, and folded them so lovingly and neatly after having been ironed. Memories flooded back to him as he looked at the bed, that she had made that fateful Sunday.

'I have to go,' Peter said. He was at breaking point once again.

'It's OK, Peter. It's alright, I understand. Be calm.'

'I don't think anyone understands. I don't even understand myself anymore. I have no future, I know that. Maybe I am cracking up. I just don't know any more.'

'I read on my course, Peter, that if you think you are cracking up—you probably are not.' The young blonde policewoman offered her advice. It was an effort to try to make the distraught widower feel better about himself, and his situation.

'People that *are* cracking up act irrationally in many cases,' Yasmin said.

'You are not like that. You are grieving, and that is normal. It is also healthy. It's all got to come out. It is nature's way of dealing with the loss of a loved one.'

Peter looked at the young woman. She couldn't be much more than twenty-four or five.

'What could she know about life?' he thought. He appreciated her explanation as he placed his right hand on the top of her white uniform bloused arm.

'Thank you,' he said looking into her pale blue eyes, knowing that she was doing her best for his sake.

He then picked up the suitcase and carried it down the stairs, not bothering about it hitting the wall or balustrade. Not much mattered anymore; only getting out of the house was important. He could not see a future for himself. He would carry out his wife's dying wish.

She had wanted to be buried in Cebu beside her elder brother in the cemetery. There was no knowing when the body would be released. There was so much red tape involved, formalities, paperwork, and so on. Both the Philippine Embassy and the British authorities were required to authorise the release of the body. It had to be placed in a lead lined coffin. The authorities had to check that drugs were not concealed in the casket, or bundles of banknotes, before sealing the lid. Peter shuddered. 'Such beaurocratic rigmarole,' he thought.

He led the way out of the house and hurriedly walked to the car. Yasmin pulled the front door shut behind her, ensuring that the house was secure, and removed the keys from the lock.

The boot lid lifted easily as Peter heaved the suitcase into the near empty space.

The two passengers got into the car, and the driver accelerated away from the house. Yasmin handed the house keys to the engineer.

The driver noticed in the rear view mirror, a white car pulling out of a driveway of a house at a discreet distance behind them. It had similar police decals from what little he could make out. The occupants appeared to be in uniform. They wore what looked like white police shirts with blue epaulettes, and the men were wearing black ties. After several miles of being followed along winding country lanes that led from Gloucestershire to Wiltshire, the driver of the police car became suspicious.

'Have we got an escort Yas?' he asked of the WPC.

'Not that I am aware of, Kev. No I don't think so.'

Kevin spoke into the hands free radio, 'Hello, control, can you put me through to DI Hemmings please? This is an extremely urgent request,' the PC informed.

'DI Hemmings,' a voice snapped into the receiver.

'Hello guv,' PC Kevin Adlam here, Have we got an escort, sir? Only we have been followed since we left Maynard's house.'

'Not that I am aware. Where are you now?'

'Coming into Devizes, sir.'

'OK. You need to go to the nick, and stay there until you get further instructions. Wadham's Brewery is on your left. The police station is just past there on your left-hand side. I think there's a pub just before the nick, The Crown, I think it's called. I will get the Wiltshire boys alerted. Get into the station and wait there until I give you word to move.'

'Affirmative, sir will do.'

'What's up?' asked the rear passenger wearily. He had fallen asleep on the back seat, and suddenly woke up hearing the tail end of the conversation.

'We've got company, Peter. We've been followed ever since we left your house. We are not taking any chances. We are pulling into the nick here, somewhere.

'Look out for a police station on the left, Yas,' Kevin instructed as they turned the corner. 'There's the brewery, now where is the nick?'

'OK Kev,' the WPC responded.

'Fuck!' exclaimed Peter looking through the back window. 'It's them. I am sure of it.

'Sorry I didn't mean to swear,' he apologized to the female officer who had been so helpful earlier.

'It's OK. You get used to it in this job, Peter,' the PC informed the engineer good naturedly.

The radio crackled into life.

'Whiskey alpha, did you request a vehicle check a short time ago?'

'Affirmative.'

'The car is an ex-police vehicle sold to a London dealer by the name of Carter and Bonner Used Cars Ltd.'

'Is it still registered in their name?'

'No, it was recently purchased, and it is in the name of a Mohamed Khan.'

'Thank you,' replied the driver, 'you've been a great help.'

'There Kev,' said Yasmin pointing to the police station. 'The reddish brick building, left, left, left.'

He overshot the turning, missing the service road immediately before the police station. Kevin checked the rear view mirror, reversed, and then swung the wheel hard towards the left, and then turned the wheel to the right into the police car park.

'Right,' he said as he braked hard. 'You two get out, and go in the back entrance. I hope the door is not locked.'

A white car with police trappings pulled into the police car park, and stopped at the entrance. It reversed, and then the passenger window wound down. A shot rang out as Kevin got out of the police vehicle, then another.

'Come on, Peter, run,' Yasmin instructed as they made for the rear entrance. Kevin lay down by the side of the car hidden from view of the bogus police vehicle.

Heads appeared at the windows at the back of the police station.

The ex police car reversed, and then quickly sped off. Kevin stood up unhurt, and walked briskly to the rear door of the station, brushing himself down as he entered a small room.

Peter and the female PC were safely inside.

'What the *hell's* going on?' a uniformed inspector asked, seeing the trio as he came out of his office after hearing the gunshots.

'You had better speak to my guv, sir,' advised the young PC slightly out of breath. He went to auto-dial, and handed the inspector the handset. 'We have been followed from South Gloucester, and fired at. I need to speak to the DI when you have finished, sir.'

*   *   *

Asif wound the window up, as he put the Magnum revolver back in the glove compartment.

'Why did you shoot at them?' asked Tariq.

'I wanted to wound Maynard, and then we could have taken him. The cops would have backed off. I don't think they were armed,' replied Asif.

'Think, you don't think? You think nothing. Now we're in deep shit if they follow us, or put out an alert, which they are bound to do.'

'They knew they were being followed. OK, we wait, but we have to get rid of the car. Our plan has failed.'

Asif tried to sound convincing. 'We'll get him, don't you worry. We'll have to wait until they leave the police station.'

'We can't do anything now, he will be too well protected,' Tariq informed. 'We wait our time. We will get him, and the book! At least we know where he is. Now we have to find where they are heading.'

*   *   *

SOCO were at the MODA Hotel. Two white-suited people were examining the room in detail. They took photographs, plus samples of the dye from the carpet, and dusted the room for fingerprints. The satellite phone was bagged and tagged; boots and clothing were bagged. Hair samples were carefully lifted from the pillows by the use of clear adhesive tape, and tweezers. These were also bagged and tagged.

Spare clips of AK-47 ammunition were found at the back and underneath the wardrobe. A glass with fingerprints on was removed and also bagged and labelled.

DI Hemmings viewed the scene of the Asian's room from the doorway. He sipped the complimentary hot coffee from a mug. The two individuals from SOCO busied themselves like white worker ants in front of him.

The inspector had mixed feelings as he stood thoughtfully for a moment. On the one hand, he had a possible success story as far as the solved murders were concerned. On the other side of the coin, he shuddered to think— terrorists on his patch. It had happened only twice before he thought . . .

It could have gone badly wrong for him. He may have been forced to resign, or take early retirement. Perish the thought! What an oversight on his part. There should have been at least two vehicles shadowing Maynard with armed officers. He could have used the armed anti-terrorist team from Sodbury to shadow them. He mentally kicked himself.

'Am I losing my grip on things?' he asked himself, 'and what a stroke of luck that DS Pertwee had overheard the conversation when he did at Staple Hill Police Station. That in itself was a bonus.' The assistant commissioner of police had been more than pleased with the DI's performance on the case to date. Even DS Barrington had patted him on the back when he left his office. It was not every day that an investigation was solved so easily, especially one with such sinister under currents. All police procedures had been carried out to the book, with positive interesting results.

Jerry Hemmings knew that he would be in line for promotion once the case was concluded. The Maynard car incident had been covered up. So there was no loss of face on his part. The engineer was unharmed, and out of immediate danger; for the time being anyway!

He was now the responsibility of Wiltshire Police, and would be accompanied by armed officers to his destination.

'Sorry?' Lost in thought for the moment,' he said as he was interrupted by a softly spoken female.

'Sir, I said we have just about finished here. We've got our shopping bags,' she joked holding up a variety of clear, thick plastic envelopes, and plastic bags.

'Very good, that just leaves me to placate Mrs. MODA, or whatever her name is. She can have her room back now,' he said as he surveyed the space, 'although it is in a bit of a mess.'

'Don't forget the suitcase on top of the wardrobe; that may reveal something of interest,' he added.

* * *

Wiltshire police had taken over the escort duties of conveying Peter to the village of Durrington not far from Salisbury Plain, Stonehenge, and the city of Salisbury.

Two cars with armed officers from Wiltshire's crack firearms squad Armed Response Group (ARG) accompanied the main car with strict instructions to look out for a fake police vehicle with two armed Asian male occupants.

The ARG officers were armed with the Heckler and Koch G36 semi-automatic assault rifles.

* * *

The two Avon and Somerset officers were reasonably happy with the outcome, as they wound their way down the narrow country roads of Wiltshire that would eventually lead to Bristol.

'This will be something to talk about back at the nick,' Kevin said as he drove the police car . . .

'They'll never believe us, Kev,' Yasmin said, 'and being shot at, of all things.'

'Yeah, never a dull moment in this job, ha ha,' Kevin joked as they came off the M32 and filtered left towards the Bristol police station.

Then suddenly he exclaimed, 'Oh! Shit!'

'What Kev?'

'We've still got Maynard's case in the boot!'

* * *

The house was a five bedroom spacious detached abode in a quiet location. It was known as a "safe house." It was the sort of place that police use to shelter informers, who had assisted the police with their enquiries, in order to get a lesser sentence, or to have their sentence quashed. The "grasses," as they are known, sang like canaries in court against their colleagues for serious crimes, and were usually given a safe house and a change of identity.

Peter was introduced to the two plain-clothed armed officers of the Police Protection Unit by one of the Wiltshire escorts. The protection officers were to be his guardians until further notice.

They did not appear over friendly at first, although they shook hands and introduced themselves to their new charge. Peter felt that the two men in casual clothing were weighing him up.

One of the Wiltshire Police escorts had a quiet word with Peter's guardians, and their attitude towards him immediately changed.

Then, quite unexpectedly, one of Peter's custodians asked if the engineer would like a brew. The man was standing in the kitchen just as Peter was about to go with the other officer to view his room.

The kettle was just coming to the boil.

'Yes, please,' the engineer replied. The two men walked up the stairs, and Peter was shown his accommodation.

'All mod cons here, mate, even an en-suite bathroom,' he was casually informed.

The engineer had also been told that his suitcase was back in Bristol, and would be delivered in the next few days.

The picture window of his bedroom overlooked open ground, and Peter Maynard thought it was either farmland, or on the perimeter of the army ranges. The ranges were used by the Royal Artillery, Royal Tank Regiment, and Territorial Army, and Cadets Corps.

The garden was flanked with three, eight-foot-high walls. New shingle covered the open area at the back.

The stones glistened in the weak afternoon sunlight. There was a patio paved area immediately outside the back of the house which was adorned with green plastic garden furniture.

Peter then saw the trip wire. It was barely noticeable. A fine fishing line ran across the width of the garden. 'Very clever,' he thought. 'When tripped, it would set off an alarm in the house, alerting the occupants of intruders.'

The bathroom had a full length white bath, plus a shower unit. He tested the bed, and was content with his comfortable surroundings which were a vast improvement on his small cell at Old Bridewll Police Station. Satisfied with his room, he went back downstairs.

One of the officers was watching the Manchester United verses Chelsea football match on the television. Peter sat in an empty chair, and as he did so, he was handed a hot mug of tea. He thanked the policeman, and was just about to place it on a small occasional table when suddenly a loud shout rang out.

'*Yes!*' screamed the other officer who was seated. He looked around excitedly.

Peter was startled for an instant, some of the hot tea spilt over his hand, and onto the table. His nerves were still quite raw. The tea maker (whose name was Andy) came into the room with mug in hand, 'Chelsea scored, Tim?' he asked jokingly.

'Bugger Chelsea, you Wal, no—Man U. Oh! Yessss, come on my son!'

'Well, at least they're human,' the engineer thought.

'Which team do you support Pete?' Tim, the other policeman sitting down asked.

'Well, as I was born in London, it has to be Chelsea, I guess,' Peter replied.

'You've got *no* chance,' Tim replied, as he fidgeted in his chair, then he asked, 'Hey Andy, where's my tea?'

'It's in the pot. Sorry, mate, I gave yours to Pete, the other Chelsea supporter here.'

'You're having a laugh! Isn't it right, a? I have to keep my strength up, and protect a Chelsea supp—did you see that. *Foul!* Bloody *foul*, ref, he should be sent off for that.'

The good-natured banter continued throughout the continuation of the game.

Peter had a security briefing, after the match. He was informed that the two officers worked a shift system. One would sleep at night, while the other officer stayed awake and on duty during the day, and vise-versa. They would overlap in their waking hours, eat, and then would resume their mundane routine. Two other PPO's would be joining them over the next few days, so that would mean four officers to guard him day and night, in order for Andy and Tim to get a break. Peter was grateful, but felt that to some degree, he was still a prisoner.

* * *

DI Hemmings mulled over the hard copy lab reports on his desk from the forensic team. The findings were both positive and constructive.

The satellite phone proved to be worth its weight in gold. After forensic had finished with it, the communications device had been sent to MI5 and MI6. They then downloaded all the call information. The Spooks were able to pinpoint the exact location of the mullah at the time the calls had been made from the UK to the other end of the link. It was as the MI6 team had expected. The calls had been made on the Paki/Afghani borders. This information had been forwarded to the Ministry of Defence, and they in turn forwarded the information to the Army Intelligence Corps, better known as the Slime!

There were also telephone numbers stored on the device. The mobile switch (telephone exchange) was able to download the call data (numbers and times) which were of interest to the anti-terrorist squad, C15. They were also able to trace the calls back to addresses in the UK, which would be followed up.

* * *

The boot of the dead man, Abdul, had matched the muddy footprint on the shed roof. The soil samples confirmed the location, where the wearer of the boots had been. In this case, it was from the muddy grass verge at the back of Peter's house.

The purple dye taken from the hotel carpet matched the type that was on a skin sample of Ali's.

The DNA of hair follicles taken from the hotel pillows matched those of Ali when DNA tests had been carried out. Boot prints at the quarry matched those that Ali was wearing when his lifeless body was hauled out of the water. The blood group on Ali's jacket was directly related to that of Abdul, putting them both in the vehicle, and at the crime scene, the quarry, and finally the hotel.

The police now knew there were at least two other Asian suspects on the loose. They were very much alive, armed, and highly dangerous.

The evidence obtained, supported Maynard's account of the four Asians on the rooftop in Riyadh. Other cross referencing of information-gathering sources was also found to be accurate. Special Branch traced the two men back to Riyadh through their passports that were found in the suitcase at the MODA Hotel.

Positive identifications were made, and finally traced back to family home addresses in Bradford, Yorkshire.

As a result of the case being solved, there was jubilation in the CID suite at New Bridewell Police Station that day. There was also a series of ticks, and crossings out made in coloured felt tip pens on the white board. The officers knew there would be a celebratory drink at the local pub on Friday evening.

* * *

The ex-police car had been found by military police on the edge of Larkhill firing ranges at Salisbury Plain. The car had been set on fire, and was a burnt out wreck by the time the SIB had carried out their investigation before contacting the civilian police. There were no clues as to the vehicle's identity other than the engine number. The Asians had been thorough in destroying evidence. The index plates had been removed. The vehicle was uncomfortably close to where the protected man was being housed. The armed protection team had been informed to keep a sharp lookout for the men.

The whereabouts of the Asians was unknown, and their descriptions were vague. The police rightly believed the suspects were no longer in the Avon and Somerset Police region. The terrorists were possibly shadowing their target around the Durrington, Aymesbury, and Salisbury, areas of Wiltshire.

* * *

DI Hemmings concluded his report, and added it to the folder. He closed it thoughtfully and then placed the folder in a filing cabinet drawer. The murder enquiry was complete; and that case closed. Two murders and a suicide had been cracked. Two dead terrorists identified, and the mystery of the innocent female that had been shot and killed by terrorist gunmen was also solved.

Another commendation was about to come the detective inspectors way.

'I may even get promotion *before* retirement,' he thought, as he sat back in his chair.

* * *

Peter Maynard was standing on a narrow ledge looking down at a maze of traffic and small buildings. The ledge was about 100 metres from the ground. He could see vehicles passing beneath him, their headlights, and rear lights coming and going in the darkness as they weaved their way along the busy main road.

He looked down at his feet on the off-white stone ledge where he was standing. He ignored the passing traffic for the moment, and just stared at his feet; the ledge was just wide enough for him to stand. The engineer was aware of the open window behind him, and could feel a warm draught on his back in the cool evening air.

He seemed to be on the outside of what appeared to be a tall hotel or office building.

He looked up. She was there in front of him, floating. She was smiling, happy, complete, and at peace. Her long black hair moved slightly in the light evening breeze. She wore a long white dress, and hovered before his eyes. How could she do that? He thought. She seemed to be in no danger of falling—yet, there she was.

'Krissie,' he called her name. 'You came for me.' She held out her hand for him to take—he held it gently in his. It felt warm and soft. She was back with him once again. He felt elated. She came close. Her hair brushed against his cheek tickling his face. He placed his arm around her slim waist as she stood on the ledge next him.

He could feel the warmth of her body. He was happy for the first time in weeks. They kissed briefly.

'I love you so much. I've waited for this moment so badly. I did not want my life to continue without you.'

'I know my precious husband. I came back to tell you not to have those thoughts. I am at peace. I feel no pain, only my undying love for you. Please don't take your own life. You have a purpose here on earth. God has a purpose for you, my dear'

'But I cannot live without you, darling Krissie.'

'I will always be by your side no matter what, no matter where you are. You will always be my precious husband. I will be with you forever, even if you can't see me, I am with you.' Then she started to fade.

'Don't leave me, Krissie,' he pleaded in a panic.

'I have to go back—you have to go back too, darling,' she spoke the words as she let go of his hand; Kristine looked at him as she gently floated away.

'I want to come with you; I want to be with you.'

'You cannot, my darling. Your time is not yet come. I will go now to prepare a place for us.' She smiled such a sweet smile as she was becoming fainter.

'Go back, go back through the window of life,' she insisted. She started to fade even more.

He took a step away from the wall towards her, and then found himself suddenly plummeting towards the ground. The cars were getting bigger, their lights became brighter. He was falling as the realisation of his action came to him in his final moments. He shouted her name. Where was she?

'**Krissssie,**' He shouted, as he landed with a resounding—thump!

*   *   *

Tariq and Asif had fled the scene of the burning wreck, and had broken into the forecourt of a Peugeot dealer in Durrington. They chose their vehicle carefully. Asif made a forced entry. He then managed to disengage the steering lock, and then hot-wire the electrics.

Once the engine fired up they sped away from the area driving into the small town of Aymesbury.

It was early morning, and there were not many people about. The Asians found a car park and drove close to a Gents toilet, where they parked the vehicle and alighted.

Leaving the Peugeot, they walked briskly towards the restroom, where they removed their police epaulettes and ties. They then dumped them inside the water cisterns of the cubicles. The men returned to the car, and slept until nine o'clock in the morning.

On awakening, the Asians walked the short distance from the car park into the small town of Aymesbury, and found a charity shop. They rummaged through the casual clothing, and went into the changing rooms. They then changed into their newly acquired temporary casual clothing, and placed their uniform shirts and trousers on hangers on appropriate racks. The elderly lady assistant had no knowing of what was going on, as she was pricing a bundle of books that had been donated by someone, and the Asians then left at the front door of the shop without paying.

They soon found a car spares dealer, and requested a set of front and rear number plates to be made up. The Asians then returned to the car park with their purchase, and checked that there were no CCTV cameras operating. The men then removed the original number plates from the vehicle, and hid them in some bushes. Finally, the two men fixed the false registration plates to the front and rear of the stolen car. The two men then split up and independently took residence in two small local hotels, awaiting further instructions from the clerical leader.

*   *   *

Night had fallen, and Tim was again seated in the living room. He had the TV set on low watching the end of a documentary about Uganda on the National Geographic channel.

He stood up, stretched, and yawned.

'It is still early hours,' he thought. 'Andy is probably pushing up the zeds,' Tim then wandered around the ground floor and peered into the gloom of the back garden through the kitchen window. He decided to put on the outside lights, thus overriding the proximity detector. Everything was quiet and still outside.

'Pete isn't a bad sort of a guy,' he mused, 'apart from being a Chelsea supporter.'

A smile spread slowly across his face at the thought of the new guest spilling his tea at his outburst when Manchester United scored the winning goal.

Andy had leant the engineer a T-shirt, also a spare pair of jogging bottoms. Peter's clothes were due to be delivered sometime in the morning.

It made a pleasant change looking after a decent sort of a guy instead of the usual criminal types that had turned supergrass and reluctantly had to be protected.

Suddenly his thoughts were interrupted by a shout, and then a loud thump upstairs!

The noise came from the upstairs bedroom. He raced up the carpeted staircase two at a time and almost collided with Andy, who was dressed in a T-shirt and shorts on the landing. Both men had their Smith and Wesson revolvers drawn.

Andy stood to one side, his revolver pointing upwards in two hands holding the weapon steady in readiness. Tim threw back the door of Peter's room, and stood in the opening. The door hit the wall. Standing in a crouched position he moved his extended arms around the room pointing the weapon in a sweeping movement. The room was partially illuminated by the landing light.

Peter was seated at an odd angle on the floor; he had a shocked expression on his face.

'*What happened?*' Tim demanded as he lowered his revolver, now assured that no one else was in the room.

'Krissie—she—was—here—somewhere . . . she-'

'There is no one here, Pete. You must have been dreaming, and fell out of bed.' Both men were relieved as they put their weapons away.

'Or sleepwalking,' added Andy.

'But she *was* here, I tell you. I held her hand—she was warm I was on the ledge.'

'What ledge? There is no ledge here.' Tim moved round the room, cautiously and peered out of the window.

It was dark, and the night air was still. The garden was illuminated by the light that he had turned on some moments earlier.

'The ledge was high up, I—I was going to jump. No I jumped or fell. She came to me—she—I jumped. I—Oh!

'Hell! I don't know any more, what is real and what is not.' He sobbed uncontrollably into his bare crooked arm. He was by now sitting up straight, his back still against the wall with his elbows on his knees which were drawn up to his chest. His body shook.

Andy and Tim exchanged glances. They did not know what to make of it, or how best to deal with the emotional situation.

'Go back to bed, mate,' Tim said softly. 'Everything will be different in the sober light of day.'

'I ca-can't sleep now. I need to get out—get some air. Do you mind?'

'Well, we're all awake now,' began Andy. 'I might as well make a brew. You can keep your eye on Pete if we sit out the back?' he said, looking at Tim.

'Yes, no problem. He'll be alright.' Tim helped Peter to his feet. Peter put on his jeans and T-shirt, plus a pair of Moccasin shoes that belonged to Andy.

'Here, you had better put this on,' said Tim handing over the heavy body armour beside Peter's bed as they stood in the hallway. 'It's a precaution, as we have been warned by the local police that the Asians are on our patch now. Therefore, we have to be more vigilant.

Peter placed the armoured sleeveless jacket over his head attaching the Velcro straps to their mating halves by the side of his waist. He hadn't worn body armour since he had been in Belfast.

Tim pulled the patio door open, then he and the engineer went outside, taking their seats at the patio set. It was a pleasant morning, the air smelled sweet. The Moon was full. A misty translucent cloud crept slowly across the yellow glowing sphere.

Tim sat facing the end of the garden. Peter noticed that he had placed his revolver on a spare chair.

It was to his right hand side, the engineer sat on Tim's left.

Andy came through the patio doors with a tray of mugs. 'Here we are,' he said. 'Just like muvver used to make!'

'Right, I'll be mother; tea vicar?' Andy asked of Peter.

'Yes, please.' The dream was beginning to fade. Everything appeared so alien to him. The last time he had sat on the patio set with a hot drink was with his wife before leaving for Saudi Arabia. 'Would you like milk?'

'Yes just a splash please.'

'And sugar?'

'No! On second thoughts, yes, I think I will. Maybe hot sweet tea is what I need right now. That and a brain transplant!'

'Shit happens, Pete,' said Andy placing the hot mug of tea on the table in front of him. 'I made you coffee Timothy old chap, with both.'

'That's OK, as long as it's wet and warm like a welcoming pussy.'

'Coo! Dream on mate,' replied Andy, smiling. 'Shag happy this one, Pete.'

Peter managed a smile. The thought of Kristine was still playing on his mind. He knew she was there. He saw her. He touched her. He felt the warmth of her body. He tried to replay the message in his mind. "Your time is not yet come. I will prepare a place for us. Go back through the window of life." The window that was behind him when he stood on the ledge, maybe it was a message, a sign, even maybe a prophecy.

'But where *was* that building with the ledge on which he was standing? It was all so strange but also, so real.'

'Feeling better mate?' Andy asked after about ten minutes of relative silence, and tea sipping.

'Marginally, thanks. I feel such a fool now. I am very sorry.'

'It's alright mate. You've been through a lot from what the guv' said from Avon and Somerset.'

After a second cup of tea, the dream had faded into the distance of his mind, and became nothing more than a fading memory.

'Nice evening,' remarked Tim.

'Morning you mean,' corrected Andy. 'It is four thirty-five; it will be getting light soon.'

'Are you going for a run this morning?'

'Is the Pope a Catholic? Of course, I am,' replied Andy. 'In fact, I will go for my run early and then you can get your head down. I doubt if I will be able to go back to sleep now.'

'How are you feeling now Pete?'

'I am OK I guess. I don't know what I am going to do all day here.'

'Better than sitting in a police cell, and you've got muvver here to make you tea-'

'Watch it, mate, or I'll piss in yours next time, bloody Man U supporters!'

'And who won?' asked Tim winking at Peter

'Yeah, well, you were lucky.'

'Lucky?' The teasing continued.

'We'll have a nice hot breakfast fry-up after Andy's run, and then I'll get some kip,' informed Tim.

'Did you make the call?' Andy asked.

'Yes.' Tim replied, 'just before Pete fell out of bed.'

'OK that's good, or we'll have the buttons from Handcuff House round here.'

They had to make a call to their base every hour on the hour or they would get a call, or a visit from the local constabulary. The Wiltshire Bobbies stopped by at times usually during the night for a cup of tea and a chat. It broke the monotony of their shift. It was also no bad thing for a police car to be seen parked outside the house in the small hours.

*   *   *

The mullah in Afghanistan was furious when he learnt that the book had still not been recovered, and that Maynard was still breathing. The English infidel had outwitted his people so many times.

He could not believe that the man had turned the terrorist's weapon on Abdul, shooting and killing the activist, as Ali had described to him earlier.

He had also been informed that Ali had committed suicide out of shame, as he had failed to retrieve the article. Abdul's death and the suicide of Ali were both directly related to Maynard, as was the death of Sohail on the arid land in Afghanistan.

The Americans had sent another 3,000 troops into the country in an effort to wipe out the Taliban, and their training camps, but they had failed miserably in their apparent attempt!

An Al-Qaeda spokesman, Suleiman Abu Gheith had gone on record stating that the objective of Al-Qaeda was "To kill 4 million Americans—2 million of them children, and to exile twice as many, wound, and cripple hundreds of thousands of men women and children!"

New followers were being recruited daily on the Afghan-Pakistan borders. More would follow Abdul, Ali, and Sohail; their deaths would not have been in vain.

Asif and Tariq had strict instructions to capture Maynard, and then torture him into submission. They were to go to any lengths necessary to recover the manual. The men were to lead the ruthless terrorists to the person or persons that had the volume; even if it had been transferred to a third party. After recovering the book, Peter Maynard's execution had to follow swiftly, brutally, and without delay, and there was to be no more loss of activist's lives, or further injuries, or calamities. The attacks had been planned as scheduled at New Year celebrations such as The Brandenburg Gate in Germany, Trafalgar Square, in London, UK, and the Eiffel Tower in Paris. The war on terror would be won, and the Islamic militants would be seen as victorious.

Asif and Tariq had alerted as many of the sleeper cell activists living in London, Leeds, Bradford, Birmingham, and Manchester to move to other locations. They had to seek alternative secure accommodation as a precaution before the police closed in. They were also to change their identities, places of work, and then continue as normal. The cell members were instructed to wait for further orders, and the men were to be ready for action at a moment's notice.

If British Intelligence had the information in their hands, arrests at their current locations would be imminent.

Two more cells of four had been instructed to be transferred to Wiltshire to support Asif and Tariq.

This would bring the total strength up to ten men. It had been reported that Maynard was living in a house in Wiltshire, and was guarded by at least two armed policemen. He had to be captured and questioned fast.

* * *

'Would you like a full breakfast, Pete?' Andy asked on his return from his early morning run, mopping the sweat from his brow and neck with a face flannel.

'Yes, fine, thanks,' replied the engineer as he stood in the kitchen doorway. No one had called him Pete since he was in the army. He didn't object to Andy and Tim's good natured shortening of his Christian name, and he smiled at the thought.

'Oh! By the way, here's a copy of the morning paper.'

'I see there is another mention to the terrorists *and* to you, Pete, regarding the Wiltshire Police Station incident. You are in the limelight again. Something of a celebrity! Your face is on the front page. You're getting more publicity than Wayne Rooney,' he joked.

'Me? A celebrity, that's something I can do without.' The engineer picked up the newspaper, and his mug of coffee, and went back to the patio area.

'Mind if I join you?' he asked Tim

'No, be my guest.'

The breakfast sizzled and popped in the frying pan on the stove as Andy prodded the sausages around with a spatula.

The engineer read the headlines, and began reading the journalist's account of what had happened. The heading in a national newspaper described the incident in Devizes as a chase by " . . . *extremists in a fake cop car. The real cops scurried off to the safety of the back of a police station with their prisoner Peter Edward Maynard. Shots were fired at the fleeing occupants and the real cops were unarmed and therefore unable to retaliate, or give chase. No arrests were made . . . ."* It went on; *"The man being protected by the police is Maynard who was previously suspected of his wife's murder in their home in Brinsham Park, near Yate, in Bristol . . . ."* The account continued

'Wankers!' Peter announced. Tim was startled at the sudden vehement vocal outburst.

'Where do they get their misinformation from? They should be sued!'

'If we don't, or will not tell them anything it is down to supposition, and speculation on their part.

'As in war, Pete, with the press, the first casualty is always the truth. I do know that the powers that be and the police have been pretty tight-lipped about this case due to the terrorist connection. There is a press conference due to be given by the superintendent of Avon and Somerset Police later today. The truth will be out, and I feel sure the press will announce your acquittal of your late wife's murder. I can assure you of that, from what little I know.

'Moves are afoot to catch, and detain the bastards. That is why I sit here, waiting for the tossers.

'Waiting for them to come to Daddy over the wall, and meet "The Equaliser,"' Tim said, smirking as he glanced down at the revolver on the plastic patio chair next to him. 'This is "Old Faithful", he said, holding the weapon so that Peter could see it clearly, and then he placed it back on the chair.

Peter glanced at "Old Faithful." It was a Smith and Wesson revolver. Peter smiled,

'Do you think they would dare to come over the wall?'

'You never can tell, Pete, in this game. I spend a lot of time trying to get into their heads. Trying to figure out how they think. I spent five years in the army with the Special Forces, mainly on covert operations. I learnt that the best way to outwit the enemy was to try and think like they did. We had to anticipate their actions. It is a bit like chess, trying to work out your opponent's next move, and counteract it. We just have to be one move ahead.'

'I was in the army too,' informed the engineer, 'Royal Corp of Signals, Para' attached, four-five commando. Disbanded now, I think.'

'Really? I didn't know that. I started in the Para's at Aldershot in the old days at North Camp. I went to Hereford for selection,' Tim informed.

'Did you get into the SAS?' asked Peter.

'Yes. I did nine years in total. Four years with two Para.' I served two tours in Iraq, three in Northern Ireland, and two tours in Afghanistan, mainly behind enemy lines.'

'Hmm!' Peter mused. 'I did five tours of Northern Ireland and missed the Falklands by a few weeks. That was pretty clandestine stuff that you were involved in.'

'Yes, you could say that. It was mainly blowing up communications sites, and oil dumps. Makes work for telecoms guys like you,' he laughed. 'Then I felt I was getting too old to keep playing at soldiers, so I joined the boys in blue, and now I am doing this police witness protection for my sins.'

'Yes, Pete, and he *loves* it. Now make some room 'because these plates are hot.' Andy had come from the kitchen with two large white dinner plates filled with an appetising fry-up.

He placed the plates in front of Peter and Tim on the oval patio table.

'Can you sit in the middle Pete?' Andy asked, 'then we can each keep a lookout one at the back of the garden and me looking at the house—just in case.'

Peter did as he was bid, and sat with his back to the wall. Andy returned with the cutlery, condiments and his own breakfast.

The engineer then noticed they were all wearing flak jackets.

'You enjoy cooking, don't you, Andy?' Peter observed.

'Yes. I did all the cooking when my wife was alive. Well, I had to.'

'Oh! You lost your wife like me then?'

'Spookily, yes, Maisie was shot in crossfire. She was a WPC in Blackwall on a drugs raid at the time. The bastards had been tipped off, and there was no escape. She was badly wounded. I nursed her for five months, but she never made it. Spleen gone and liver damaged. Sorry to be morbid.'

'I'm sorry,' Peter responded. He looked down at a sausage, prodding it thoughtfully with his fork.

'Life is so cruel at times,' he thought.

'Tim I forgot to ask, tea or coffee?'

'I'll get it Andy,' Tim replied getting up. 'Finish your breakfast, and I'll fire up the kettle.'

Peter sat deep in thought. Once again he felt embarrassed about the dream he had, wondering again if the message was an omen? He wanted to talk to Andy more, but now was not the time, or the place.

'Is there any chance of me going into town today?' Peter asked. 'I need to get some shaving things, and socks. I hurriedly packed some odd ones I think, and my stuff has still not arrived yet.'

'Yes, we can take a drive into Salisbury while Tim gets his beauty sleep. You must wear your flak jacket under a jumper or coat,' he said stuffing his face with half a sausage. Andy then pierced a slice of tomato balancing it on his fork as he chewed.

Tim returned from the kitchen.

'Here we are three coffees with milk, and sugar on the tray. Oh, and a winder. Help yourselves.

'You know, I am really grateful to you guys,' said the engineer, hurriedly swallowing an unchewed mushroom as he spoke. He then realised too late it was hot, and caught in his gullet. He made a grab at his coffee mug on the tray, in an effort to wash it down.

'That's what we're here for, mate,' Tim remarked, glancing at the wall. 'We are professional killers, and domestic maids, so to speak! That's what they used to call us when I was in the army, especially with all that spit and polish.'

'Yes I have heard that reference before. Well, thanks anyway.'

'No, Pete, you shouldn't thank us for doing our job. That's what we're paid for. In a way, I guess we should thank you for helping our country fight the war against terror,' Andy interjected.

'I never looked at it like that, but in retrospect, the cost to me has been too great. I'm no bloody hero.'

'OK,' Andy did not know what to say, and wanted the conversation to end at that point, thankfully it happened.

SALISBURY IN WILTSHIRE is an ancient city steeped in history. It was once surrounded by a wall in the fourteenth century. The city boasts of a beautiful old cathedral in its centre, the spire of which can be seen for miles on the approach to the old municipality. Nestled a short distance away is Stonehenge. The ancient stones stand as they have for hundreds of years like sentries. The site is shrouded in mystery as to why they are there, and the formation of the stones and why they are in the particular configuration is unknown to this day. For centuries the ancient stones have been visited by Druids at the Solstice, which is a yearly pagan festival.

The streets of Salisbury are narrow, and were never designed for the high volume of modern day traffic, or heavy vehicles that rumble through the streets daily. Lorries and vans keep the shops stocked up with regular deliveries. The council does its best in keeping through traffic out of the main town by the use of a ring road that bypasses the narrow main city thoroughfare.

Andy and Peter got out of the car, and after paying the parking fee, the two men walked through an archway that led into the main town, that was full of activity with shoppers, business people, and passersby milling around. The engineer saw Boots the Chemist shop. He indicated to Andy that he wanted to go there.

It was while he was browsing through the toiletries that his gaze happened to fall on two Asian men. They were standing at the outside of the store peering in through the glass doors. Peter immediately recognised the two Asians as being Tariq and Asif.

'*Bastards!*' Peter hissed through clamped teeth.

Andy turned and stared in the direction his charge was facing. He instantly recognised the problem. The two Asians to whom Peter was referring were standing a safe distance away, outside the shop. Andy turned his back on them, and faced the engineer blocking him from their view. The Asians were dressed in army battle fatigues. Their hair had been cut short in a military style.

'So that is their cover now,' mused Peter, 'blending in with the military in and around Salisbury.'

'I want to go and smash their stupid heads in,' Peter said with both hatred and venom in his voice. He tried to move away from Andy.

'No! You'll do no such thing! Just take it easy Pete, or we will be in trouble, serious trouble,' Andy instructed as he held the engineers arms at his side.

'Do you think they saw you?'

'I am not sure! Maybe they followed us here.'

'It is a possibility; most likely a coincidence.'

'No it is not a coincidence. We were followed by a dummy police car after we left Bristol to come here. It was in the papers, remember? Also we were shot at in Devizes at the back of the nick there. They have their intelligence sources.'

Suddenly, and without warning, Andy grabbed Peter roughly by the back of the collar, and spun him round. He grabbed hold of the engineer's right arm forcing it up behind his back, causing the man slight pain. Holding Peter by the back of his coat collar, and in an arm lock, he force-marched the engineer towards the rear of the shop.

'What the hell are you doing? Where are we going?'

'Out of here, that's where, and quick. Just play along with the situation,' Andy said as they neared the rear entrance.

'Police Officer,' Andy said to the manageress as she stood in the entrance marked "Private" blocking their exit. He roughly pushed Peter against the wall, holding him with one hand.

Andy removed his wallet, and flipped it open, thus revealing his warrant card. He flashed his ID to the woman. She glanced at the official police identification.

'Has he been shoplifting?' she asked.

'No ma'am, it's a bit more serious than that I'm afraid. I have just arrested this man and need to get out the back entrance to the car park area.'

Peter was nonplussed.

He stood passively with a bemused expression on his face, never knowing what was going to happen next in his life.

'Right officer, you had better come this way,' replied the smartly dressed young woman. She gave Peter a distinct look of disapproval. The men followed her down a corridor, past some offices, and out to a loading bay area.

'Thanks love,' replied Andy, then to Peter he said, 'Come on you,' giving him a rough shove in the back.

The two men walked some distance, and as soon as they were out of view of the staring manageress, Andy released his grip. He turned to Peter saying, 'Sorry about that. I have to call the local police. I need backup. I have to go back to the front of the shop to find out where those guys are going. We need to follow them at a discreet distance. The hunters are now being the hunted. Pete, I beg you, do not do anything foolish; they may be armed. I have my revolver, but I cannot risk an incident in the street. Give me your word that you will—'

'Yes, yes, yes,' Peter interrupted. 'You have my word. All I seem to do these days is to give my word to police officers!'

'Right,' said Andy, 'follow me Pete.' He quickly led the way back into the main street.

In the distance he saw the two camouflaged "army" Pakistani men hurrying away from the store.

'Code Red,' he announced into the mobile device. Andy identified himself and gave a brief accurate description of the situation.

At the other end of the phone, in the control room at Wiltshire Police Headquarters, the officer had identified the street. CCTV cameras were already searching for the Asians. An armed response unit had been alerted and was on the way.

The PR was still on. Andy said to the engineer, 'We will follow them to see where they go. Backup is on the way. They will be arrested then taken away for questioning. This is not our business from there on in. We only protect you, Pete.'

The Asians seemed to be in a hurry as they turned the corner, and walked into the same car park where Andy had parked his vehicle. The Pakistanis were way in front, then suddenly disappearing into a car and driving off at speed.

'Damn! Suspects driven off very fast in a blue Peugeot registration number Whiskey Lima . . . .' He then gave the index number and his location.

Just then a white unmarked police car swung into the car park, and turned round. A magnetic single blue light flashed on the top of the vehicle. Andy ran up to the car, identified himself, and pointed in the direction in which the terrorists had fled. The white police car then drove off in hot pursuit. The light continued to flash, as the sirens burst into life.

* * *

During the evening, Andy was relaying the incident to Tim when there was a sharp rap at the front door. Both men turned and looked at the small screen on the TV. The CCTV showed two Caucasian uniformed police officers standing outside. Tim walked down the hallway, and cautiously opened the front door.

Andy stood behind the kitchen door. He was hidden from view as he peered through the narrow opening between the door and the architrave. His right hand rested lightly on the butt of his Smith and Wesson police revolver in his opened shoulder holster.

'Good day sir. I have a delivery for you. I need to see some ID before I can hand over the goods?'

'Sure,' said the police protection officer as he flashed his warrant card. He looked at the uniformed policemen, then at the car. Everything appeared as it should.

Peter was seated on a wooden stool by the breakfast bar in the kitchen in full view of Andy, the hallway, and the front door.

'Now let me see your warrant card,' he informed the uniformed officer.

'Here,' said the man as he pulled his ID out of his side pocket in readiness.

'OK. What have you got in the bag?' Tim asked the officers before allowing them to step inside the house.

'It's a gift from Wiltshire Police HQ, the instructions came from London apparently, two Heckler and Koch semi-automatic weapons and two clips of 30 rounds of ammo.' You are requested to sign for them. Oh, and a case of clothes, plus a laptop for a Mr. P. Maynard. They were dropped off at Devizes nick this morning. They're in the car. I will go back and get them.'

'OK,' remarked Tim. 'Go through,' he said to the second officer, as Tim took receipt of the concealed weapons.

Andy emerged from behind the door just as the second uniformed officer was walking into the kitchen. He was startled by Andy's sudden appearance.

'Sorry mate,' began Andy with a smile, 'can't be too careful.'

The bulge of the revolver under his loose-fitting shirt was suddenly apparent to the officer.

The policeman nodded, and smiled.

Tim read the contents of the document and then signed for the consignment. Peter's case and laptop were brought inside the front door.

The engineer sat feeling slightly out of place.

'All this is because of me,' he thought.

Finally he took advantage of the pregnant silence and asked, 'Anyone fancy a brew?' It seemed to be the custom in the house, and so he automatically fell in with it.

The uniformed officers and his protectors looked at him as he held the kettle. The men murmured their approval.

Peter turned on the cold water tap, and then proceeded to fill the kettle.

While the water was boiling, he lugged the suitcase, with laptop case strap over his shoulder, up the stairs to his room. He dumped the case unceremoniously on the bed. He would unpack after he had made, and distributed the tea.

The two hatless uniformed police officers sat in the back room at the dining table.

They undid their dark blue protective vests, and the atmosphere became a lot more relaxed.

Peter was surprised at the support the police protection guys were getting from the local police.

Obviously, the Wiltshire Constabulary was taking no chances. This was more apparent now that the terrorist activity had transferred from Avon and Somerset to the Wiltshire police patch. All the emergency services in the area were on high alert.

The local and international press was having a field day, as they continued to exaggerate and speculate on recent events.

Referring to the incident in Salisbury earlier, one uniformed officer said, 'I think that is part of the reason why London has beefed up your armaments,' he then continued, 'thinking about it, there are not many weapons to equal the Heckler and Koch semi-'

'Oh! I don't know,' replied Tim knowledgeably, and interrupting his uniformed colleague. 'There's the AK-47, the Uzi sub-machine gun, used by the Israelis which is capable of delivering 600 rounds a minute, the Gyurza. That weapon fires tungsten-core armour plated bullets-'

'Yes, yes,' interrupted the young officer, 'I was thinking more of hand-weapons in general. Like the illegal ones the gangs use in Britain today. They wouldn't be a match for the H K the weapon can empty its thirty-round magazine in a very short time, when on automatic.'

Peter walked into the room carrying a tray with five mugs, sugar, milk, and chocolate digestive biscuits.

'Here we are, gentlemen, help yourselves,' he said, placing the tray on the coffee table. Tim introduced Peter to the uniformed officers who were by now on first name terms. The weaponry conversation trailed off, and the dialogue then focused on Peter Maynard. This was the face that had been seen on every national newspaper and television screen in the country over the past week.

Peter was the most sought after terrorist target. For a short time the engineer felt like a famous personality; although, he would have much preferred to have anonymity for everyone's sake.

*   *   *

During that afternoon in Salisbury, Asif and Tariq had recognised Peter, as he and Andy walked from the car. The Asians followed the men at a discreet distance, and had stood outside Boots the Chemist, not knowing what to do next. They stood in the shop doorway trying to plan their next move, whilst keeping an eye on their prey.

The terrorist's intelligence information was that the engineer had been taken to somewhere near Salisbury Plain in Wiltshire, at a place called Durrington. At that time they did not have an exact location.

Having recognised their prey, they were surprised to observe Maynard being roughly manhandled, and marched out of the shop by the rear entrance. They knew they had been recognised by the engineer and had decided to make a strategic withdrawal and backtrack. But who was the guy that shoved Peter through the shop and acted so aggressively towards him, and why?

Having posed the question, they wondered had Maynard been targeted by another organisation? If so, the terrorists had to find out, and get him into their custody. Maybe the two factions could work together for a common cause.

Entering their stolen car, the Asians had driven out of the car park, and round the one-way system. They went twice round the roundabout, to ensure that they were not being followed, and returned to the car park to a different entrance.

Both men observed the police car with flashing headlights, blue light, and siren when it left in pursuit of the Asians. They had also observed the unknown person with Maynard talking to the police. They then realised that the unknown person was connected with the police and in their custody. They had also observed. Peter was standing casually a short distance away. He could easily have run off, but he didn't. This indicated that he may have felt threatened by the police, and the man standing close by to him, either that, or the man with Maynard was friendly.

The Asians waited for the police car to leave, and then tailed Peter and Andy at a discreet distance. They needed to find out where the engineer was hiding.

* * *

At that time, Andy was at the wheel of the car. He pulled into the driveway of the house. He hadn't noticed that he was being followed. The terrorists had kept a cautious distance allowing other cars to overtake.

The Asians parked their car at the top of the road but were unable to see the occupants of the vehicle alight due to the high brick wall running from the side of the house. They decided to move on and stake out the place later, and check for a weak access point. They would need backup. Mohammed, and Faisal, two new recruits had joined their team. This brought the total back up to four men. There was another support cell of six Asians close to hand, and they were on standby to assist in an operation as and when required.

Just as they were about to drive off, the Asians observed a police car pulling up outside the house. Two uniformed officers stepped out of the vehicle. One was carrying something fairly bulky and indistinguishable in a black plastic bag. Then the same officer returned to the police car and retrieved a suitcase, and what appeared to be a laptop bag. He then carried the items into the house. Asif handed the binoculars to Tariq.

'What do you think they are taking into the house?' he asked.

'Not sure, but we have to assume a weapon or weapons in the black bags,' responded Tariq. 'We know there are a minimum of two men that are staying there, Maynard, and the other guy. Maybe it's his bodyguard. It looks like Maynard is in police custody still. Perhaps the cops are moving in as well. That would make four.'

'But if only two persons are guarding Maynard, then it will be easy for us to take him out, and get the infidel.'

'Yes, but we have to be certain, and not assume. We cannot make assumptions.

'We will check the area around the house, back, and sides. Also we have to find the Achilles heel,' informed Tariq. He then spoke into a sat-phone in Urdu to the clerical leader on the Afghan-Pakistan borders.

There was mild jubilation at the other end of the phone that Maynard had finally been tracked down.

Then the instructions were delivered clearly to Asif. The neighbouring cells were to join forces, and pose as British soldiers and appear as if they were on military manoeuvres close to the house . . .

* * *

It was 0600 hours on Thursday morning. Ten Asian males well armed, and dressed in British Army battle fatigues alighted from an army truck. The "soldiers" had noted that there was only one car in the drive. The police vehicle was absent from the location.

They parked the army lorry on open ground behind a row of hedges, and trees to avoid being observed from the road.

The men advanced in a disorderly formation across a field some distance away, on ground which backed on to the house where Maynard was staying.

Each man in turn peered through a pair of army field binoculars to familiarise himself with the surroundings.

The house was isolated inasmuch that it stood in its own grounds, and was only bordered by high brick walls. There were no immediate neighbours. The leader (Asif) estimated that there were three or four occupants in the premises at the most. There were two tall trees close by; they would serve as excellent vantage points to overlook the garden, and rear of the house. The plan was that once the occupants had been identified, the insurgents would pick them off one by one. Then once the "guards" had been eliminated, the fundamentalists would make their move to capture Maynard.

The arrangement that had been suggested by the mullah in Afghanistan sounded more than feasible. It had sounded simple and straightforward in the briefing. There were ten terrorists, and a maximum of four people in the house. The general consensus was that with their strength in numbers, plus the fire-power, they could easily overpower any resistance. Conversely in the briefing they received; the men were to "expect the unexpected."

'Whatever that was supposed to mean!' Asif and Tariq independently thought.

The remark was intended for the team not to misjudge their quarry as they had done previously.

Maynard was remembered for being responsible for the deaths of the three activists, Ali, Sohail and Abdul, and Asif was reminded of this.

Maynard had been evasive, elusive, and unpredictable in the past, and hard to capture. In reality, and unbeknown to the mullah, this was more by luck than something that had been planned.

At no time did Maynard ever know about the death of Sohail in the air strike on the borders.

Asif had looked at Tariq, who smiled back in a confident manner. The group considered the attack would be a pushover! Maynard would be captured, the book would be retrieved, and they would be well respected by the clerical leader.

Once Maynard had confessed under torture, he would then be executed. It sounded simple and straightforward.

*   *   *

Earlier that morning, Andy had got up at his usual time and went for his early morning run. As he ran past an open area close to the house, he observed several armed soldiers. They were wearing what appeared to be balaclavas, battle fatigues, and steel helmets. He assumed they were carrying out manoeuvres. The "soldiers" looked like a detachment on some sort of training exercise. He continued with his run.

That morning Andy had pushed himself really hard to do six miles instead of the usual five. He was determined to run in the London Marathon and intended to increase his running distance by a punishing training schedule on a daily basis.

As Andy was running, something gnawed at the back of his mind. He had a hunch that all was not well. He had never seen the military on exercise so close to the house, and at such an early hour. Neither had he ever seen the military wearing balaclavas with helmets. The SAS wore balaclavas he remembered, but looking at the "platoon" something did not seem right.

Artillery gunfire, tank engine noises, and vehicle movement sounds were commonplace to those living on the edge of the ranges. Again, he dismissed the idea as nothing untoward, about to happen. He concentrated on his breathing as he ran up a steep hill. When he reached the top, so as not to break his rhythm, and to satisfy himself, he ran on the spot watching the small figures in the distance. They were bunched together, and one by one peering through binoculars. They then fanned out as they trekked further forward into the field. The "soldiers" held weapons that were indistinguishable due to the distance that Andy was from the assailants. They also appeared to be a rabble, and not in any orderly formation. 'Maybe the army's changed,' he thought as he continued with his run ...

*   *   *

Tim had made a coffee, and was sitting in the garden. Old Faithful was on the chair beside him as usual. He was not wearing body armour. This was unusual as he always took precautions.

It was a pleasant morning. The sun had risen over the hills, and the air smelled sweet and fresh as a result of a light drizzle earlier. Birds in nearby trees sang, but they suddenly made a fuss.

Tim was looking forward to a long weekend off, and the other two Police Protection Officer joining them.

He picked up his coffee mug, and took a sip of the hot brown liquid. There was a sudden movement in the two trees close by. An assembly of birds suddenly flew off together as if having a single mind. After their unexpected evacuation everything appeared normal and quiet once again.

Straining his eyes at the trees he wondered what could have made them panic. Animals and birds were often the best giveaway of human or enemy activity in thickets and jungles. His army training had taught him that. He watched, waited, and listened. His senses were highly tuned, and alert. He got up, entered the house, and put on the body armour over his head and shoulders, sensing that there could be a problem.

Crack!

The bullet hit him on the body armour near his shoulder. It was a glancing blow doing no more than bruise the muscle.

He fell back. Instinctively, as Tim fell he grabbed the revolver and rolled. The sniper in the tree was too well concealed. His camouflage suit merged in with the leaves and branches of the tree.

The officer made a dash for cover, and ran back inside the house. He reached the kitchen just as a second shot was fired. This time it missed. He was partially deafened by the noise made by the bullet as it whizzed past his ear. Instinctively, he knew where the shot came from. He would get a fix on the target.

Tim left his revolver on the kitchen work surface. As he got to the front door he grabbed the Heckler and Koch leaning in the corner of the hall. He slammed a magazine inside the weapon, and set it to automatic. He took the stairs two at a time, entering Andy's empty bedroom.

Peering from behind the partially closed curtain, he eventually saw the target moving slowly. He was camouflaged and barely visible, and seated on a limb of the tree. Tim was hidden by the curtains. The window was open. He pointed the barrel through the narrow gap between the window and the frame, and adjusted the lens of the semi-automatic sights. The target was clearly visible. Aiming for the chest he squeezed the trigger, and fired a short burst of two shots.

The body jerked upwards, and then lurched forward, falling to the ground.

Suddenly there was movement. Two persons wearing camouflage clothing, crouching as they ran, quickly disappeared from view behind the wall of the house.

'Come on Andy, where the hell are you?' Tim asked out loud.

Peter was rudely awoken from his slumber by the retort of the gunfire. He jumped out of bed, pulled on a pair of jeans. Then dragging a T-shirt over his head, he left his room, and ran downstairs, and through the open hallway door. He saw the patio set overturned. There was a broken coffee mug, with the spilled contents on the ground.

Old Faithful lay unattended on the kitchen worktop where Tim had left it, as he had opted for a more powerful weapon.

Peter picked up the revolver, ran through the kitchen and into the hallway.

From upstairs, Tim called out. He had left Andy's room and was hurriedly running down the stairs, two at a time. Peter then returned to the kitchen doorway holding the police revolver.

'Put the flak jacket on, and get in the cupboard under the stairs,' instructed Tim.

Peter slipped on the heavy waistcoat. A shot rang out, just as a head appeared over the parapet. The scary helmeted, black balaclava, masked face, concealed the man's identity. He was in the process of heaving himself up, in an effort to get into the garden

The engineer knelt in the kitchen doorway holding the revolver with both hands, arms fully extended. He took careful aim, and fired a single shot. The bullet hit the Asian in the face. Losing his balance he toppled forward into the garden. Peter fired again, and a third time. The man lay still.

'Nice work, Pete.' Tim said, 'now get inside, mate.'

Another man had climbed the tree which was the best vantage point for the house. He took aim and sprayed the yard with bullets.

Tim rolled across the kitchen floor pulling the engineer down with him, out of the line of fire. By now, seven terrorists had surrounded the back of the house, with one at a vantage point in the tree, making eight in total, with two dead.

Two men were clambering over the wall. Peter turned; he saw the enemy. Instinctively he aimed the weapon at the man. He hit another one in the face through the mask, and he fell back. The second man dropped back down unhurt. Gunfire erupted from the tree once again. Peter retreated inside the house just as the patio window panes shattered.

Tim went back to the garden, taking aim at the tree. A bullet hit him in the upper arm close to his shoulder. The shot knocked him backwards. He struck the side of his head on the corner of the wall by the open kitchen door. Peter couldn't get to him as a hail of bullets sprayed the yard again this time, shattering all the kitchen windows.

Peter dropped the hand gun and picked up the Heckler & Koch semi-automatic rifle.

Andy heard the exchange of gunfire as he ran down the road back towards the house.

On entering the hallway, Andy slammed the front door shut. He picked up the second H & K and placed a clip of ammunition into the weapon. He called out Tim's name as he entered the kitchen. Peter was holding the other semi-automatic weapon

'What the fucks happening?'

'Tim's been hit. I can't get to him. We've got to get the bastard in the tree; he's holding us down while the other bastards are trying to get over the wall.

'Get further back in the house Pete,' Andy instructed.

Andy went back into the hallway and ran up the stairs. He entered the engineer's bedroom. The windows were open, the partially drawn curtains moved slightly in the early morning breeze. He took careful aim behind the curtains, firing two short bursts at the tree through the opening as Tim had done earlier.

The body lurched forward, hung to the limbs of the tree for a brief moment, and then fell out of sight, obscured by the wall.

The engineer took advantage of the situation. He tried to lift Tim, but he was too heavy. He was losing a lot of blood. Peter foolishly removed his flak jacket placing it over Tim's head and chest.

A terrorist was in the garden.

'Maynard, give yourself up,' he ordered in a deep Pakistani voice with North Yorkshire overtones. He pointed the weapon in the engineer's direction, and then lifted his balaclava so that Peter could recognise him. It was Tariq. Peter held the weapon that Tim had used. Tariq yelled, 'I am your friend!'

A single shot rang out. It was Andy, from the upstairs window. Tariq fell to his knees.

'Nehey! Nehey!' (No, no), he cried as he fell.

The Asian tried to hang on to his life—it was over. The Kalashnikov slammed down loudly on the stones as the dying man fell on top of it.

An unseen terrorist had raised himself up on the other side of the wall, firing one shot in an effort to cover Tariq. It was not only too late, but also a badly aimed attempt. The retort from Andy's weapon caused the Asian to miss his target. The terrorist dropped back over the wall unhurt.

The bullet had grazed Peter's left leg. The smell of burnt flesh, and cloth was nauseating. The wound made by the bullet hurt, even though it was only a graze.

The engineer was in a lot of pain. He held on to the semi-automatic, dragging himself in front of Tim, shielding him as best he could. He had witnessed Tariq falling forward.

Once Andy was satisfied that there was no one else in the trees, he ran down the stairs to rescue his colleague. He saw the engineer sitting on the ground in front of Tim by the back wall, Heckler and Koch in hand. The firing had stopped. Andy guessed the enemy was re-grouping.

'Pete,' he shouted, 'Are you OK?'

'I'm OK, thanks; it's only a graze on my knee. We need to get Tim inside quickly.'

Andy saw the blood seeping through the knee area of the engineer's jeans, also the pool of blood from Tim.

'Get in here, now,' Andy ordered.

'I can't leave Tim. I have been hit in the leg. I don't think it's too bad.'

'I'll take care of Tim. Keep low but you get your arse in here. I'll cover you.'

Peter rolled over, towards Andy, almost crying out in pain as the wound in the knee made contact with the stone patio slabs, and splinters of glass. He then stood up and limped painfully through the open kitchen door.

'OK, now cover me Pete,' Andy instructed as he grabbed Tim underneath both arms. Peter moved to one side spraying the tree with bullets in case there was someone hiding. There was no movement. Once Tim was safely in the hall, Andy got on the radio calling for the armed Rapid Response Unit on twenty-four hour standby.

Twenty minutes later he heard police sirens of the RRU.

'Thank God!' he said out loud.

'Well done, mate.' Andy said with encouragement; then, 'you daft bastard, you put yourself in the firing line, and in grave danger. Where the fuck's your flak jacket?'

'I used it to cover Tim,' Peter replied. 'I told you.'

'You daft bastard,' Andy uttered the words with a certain amount of respect. 'We have the RRU, and an ambulance coming. Those sirens are probably them now, not before time either.'

Suddenly there was an almighty crash as the front door burst open.

'*Armed Police! Armed Police! Freeze! Freeze! Drop your weapons. Drop your weapons. Get on the floor. Get on the floor. Now! Now!*'

'You fucking idiot, we **are** the police!' Andy shouted in defiance. 'Keep your weapons down.

'Pete put the weapon on the floor.'

The engineer did as he was told, instinctively raising his hands.

There was a moment of utter confusion as the RRU sergeant tried to assess the situation.

'OK. We didn't have too many details.' The officer informed without apologising.

He and his colleagues were wearing dark blue body armour, steel helmets with visor, and Robocams fitted to the side of their helmets. Each man was heavily armed, and tear gas canisters were attached to their belts. Two men had stun grenades. They lowered their weapons.

'OK, I need a statrep?' (Status report), informed the sergeant. The other officers deployed themselves around the house.

Andy gave a quick briefing to the officers. They noted the two camouflaged bodies in the back garden. Andy had given the report of ten armed men seen in the field. Peter confirmed three kills, not knowing that Tim had killed a sniper in the tree. Andy had killed two. The body count came to six, but could not be verified as one may have only been badly injured. In fact only five of the terrorists remained alive.

'My guess is they are at the other side of the wall at the back of the house, and re-grouping.' Andy informed the RRU sergeant. 'You guys need to be aware of the trees where they have cover, and a good vantage point.'

He pointed through the shattered patio door windows, 'I shot one down from there. I don't think they are wearing body armour.'

Two armed officers carefully picked up Tim from the hallway, and carried him into the front room laying him on a long sofa. One of the officers took out a field dressing. They undid his body armour carefully removed his shirt so as to administer first aid. The wound was cleaned, and padding and a dressing was applied to the injury.

Tim was drowsy. He gradually came to his senses, unaware of what was going on around him.

The officers were very professional as they took control. It was obvious to the engineer they had done this before, or had certainly trained for it.

'The paramedics are outside, with instructions, not to enter the house until it is safe.'

The sergeant informed the group. Then he turned to Andy and Peter, and instructed, 'You guys stay in here with your mate. Keep the curtains closed.'

Two of the anti-terrorist RRU officers had entered the loft, managing to dislodge some roof tiles in order to gain a better vantage point than the trees. The two men were concealed, with an excellent view of the open field at the back of the house.

'We will take over from now on,' informed the sergeant to Andy. 'Well done for your actions, all of you.'

'Thanks,' they mumbled.

The silence outside was unnerving. Andy, Peter, and the officers, agreed that the enemy was either planning to leave or considering other tactics. Either way, they would be finished off.

* * *

Asif was the senior member of the group. The five men had to make a decision as to what course of action they should take. The men huddled by the back wall of the compound, hidden from view. They were now outgunned as there were six RRU men, plus the three inhabitants, one injured, or dead. They were not to know that the three men were now not involved with proceedings. The H & K rifles were in the back room, leaving the three men in the lounge, unarmed.

A police helicopter hovered overhead. Two gunshots broke the silence. The bullets struck the bodywork, piercing the outer shell before exiting, but the missile did not bring the chopper down. The pilot, worried about his safety, and manoeuvred the craft to a safer distance.

The Asians did not have grenades; they would therefore have to rely on marksmanship, and strategy. They considered a frontal attack. Their plan was to keep up the fire power at the back of the residence. Two members of the team were to run round the side of the house to the front, and injure or kill as many of the RRU guys as possible. They would then snatch Maynard holding him, while the lorry came back to collect the remaining fighters.

*　*　*

The paramedics were instructed to enter the house, as it appeared that the fighting was at the back of the residence.

Tim's injury was checked again, an oxygen mask was placed over his nose and mouth. Peter's wound was cleaned, and dressed by the ambulance personnel, after they had finished with Tim. The plan would be to take Peter and Tim to a nearby hospital. This action could not be carried out until all the terrorists had been defeated.

Suddenly all hell broke loose again. The Islamists had used logs, and tree branches to stand on. Their heads and shoulders were barely visible over the top of the walls as they fired a volley of bullets into the back room and at the rooftop smashing roof tiles, and partially exposing the two RRU men.

One officer was instantly shot dead. A bullet had caught him full in the face.

Without warning, two armed terrorists entered the hallway through the broken front door. A hail of bullets sprayed into the kitchen. Two RRU men were shot in the back, buttocks, and legs rendering them seriously injured.

Asif had entered the house, and stood in the open doorway of the front room. The paramedics looked up from their patient. Asif held the AK-47 in a threatening manner. He pointed the weapon, and waved it at Andy to move. The paramedics continued to monitor Tim's breathing, and blood pressure.

The Asian beckoned for the engineer to come forward. They had removed their helmets. Peter looked at Andy, whilst a fierce fire-fight still ensued at the back of the house.

'*Fuck off!*' Peter shouted defiantly. The second terrorist had returned to the hallway. He was facing the back of the kitchen. The rescue team were down to two in the smashed up dining room, out of sight, and now only one RRU man was upstairs. Andy had managed to get an H & K earlier, after reasoning with the RRU sergeant. It was hidden from sight and contained a number of rounds.

Asif fired one round close to the engineer. The noise reverberated around the room, surprising them all. Finally, Peter stood up unsteadily. He didn't want any more deaths on his conscience.

Asif asked the paramedics where the keys to the ambulance were.

'In the ambulance,' replied the blonde-haired female as she dealt with her patient.

'Good, come on Maynard, we're going for a little ride.'

Peter again looked hopelessly at Andy. The policeman was helpless to do anything for the moment without putting lives in danger. He had already formulated a plan; he winked, and nodded at the engineer to go.

Peter was escorted down the path as he hobbled towards the waiting ambulance. He got in the back with one of the masked terrorists.

Asif got in the front, and was preparing to drive off, but the keys were not in the vehicle. He cursed, and then shouted something in Urdu to the other Asian holding Maynard prisoner in the back.

Cautiously, the Asian returned to the house. He entered the front room. Andy had observed the terrorist returning to the house from behind the net curtains in the front window. He was ready for him, as he hid from view behind the broken front door.

As Asif entered through the doorway, Andy appeared behind the man, bringing the butt of his H & K crashing down on the back of the man's head. Asif's legs buckled. He fell forward. The remaining RRU man had come down the stairs. Andy advised the anti-terrorist men about the situation. One RRU man, dead and two badly injured. Andy's charge was now in enemy hands in the back of the ambulance that was going nowhere for the moment.

Outlining his plan, the two men stripped Asif of his outer clothing. Andy donned the camouflage garments. Finally, he removed the black balaclava from the unconscious Asian, and pulled it over his head, adding to his disguise. Only the colour of his hands gave him away.

Andy collected the keys to the ambulance. Then, covered by the RRU man by the front door, Andy walked down the path carrying his H & K weapon. He entered the cab of the waiting ambulance.

'Did you get the keys?' the Asian shouted. Andy adjusted the rear view mirror. He could clearly see the terrorist, and the prisoner. They were sitting opposite each other.

'Yes,' replied Andy as he put on his best Pakistani accent, revving up the engine to partially disguise his voice. Then he drove off at speed.

Suddenly, and without warning, he braked furiously, throwing both bodies in the back to the floor. He accelerated, and braked hard again. The vehicle had stopped.

Grabbing the H & K he got out of the cab, and entered the adjoining doorway between the main body of the ambulance. He had the Asian covered.

'Grab the weapon Pete, it's me.' Andy pulled off the balaclava. Peter grabbed the AK-47 which had fallen out of the Asians hands when Andy had braked hard.

'Right, open the back door Pete, and walk towards the house. There is a policeman covering you, and I have got you covered from this side.

Peter got out of the ambulance, and walked in a crouched position, as he limped towards the front of the house. He suddenly realised that he still had the enemy's weapon in his hand. Instinctively, he held it away from his body. He felt exposed but safe when he saw the dark blue uniform of the RRU man, with his weapon at the ready.

Andy couldn't kill the terrorist in cold blood. The activist lay on the floor of the ambulance cursing, and pleading for his life. He was whimpering in the corner of the vehicle waiting for the fatal shot. The officer ordered the man out of the ambulance. As soon as the Asian was standing on the road, Andy brought the man down by a stunning blow to the back of the skull with the butt of the H & K. He pulled off the camouflage top, walked to the front of the vehicle, and placed his weapon on the passenger seat. He then returned to the back of the vehicle, and dragged the limp body into the back of the ambulance.

He closed the door, and returned to the cab. Andy turned the vehicle round in an arc, and then drove the short distance back to the house. He grabbed his weapon, opened the back doors and dragged the limp body of the terrorist unceremoniously to the front of the house.

'Nice work mate,' the officer said to Andy as he helped him to bring the body in through the doorway.

The firing had stopped. The paramedics were now attending to the two RRU anti-terrorist men that were injured, in the kitchen. The men's injuries were serious. The officers needed to be transported to hospital. The medics called for an air ambulance, as the injuries were life threatening.

More armed police backup arrived at the house, alas too late. A team of six officers went down the side of the house. As the lead officer rounded the corner a wounded terrorist, propped up against some logs by the back wall, opened fire. Tosh had returned to the loft, after Peter was secure in the house. He could not see what was going on as the wall at that point was too high, and the enemy was hidden from view.

The bullet ricocheted off the officer's helmet. On impulse, the policeman fired two short bursts back. Blood spurted from the man's chest and mouth.

He lay motionless. Another terrorist that appeared dead fired two short bursts from where he lay. Instinctively, two officers opened fire at the same time, killing the man instantly.

The officers cautiously continued to check the remainder of the bodies. All were confirmed dead, including the one that had been hiding in the tree. The remainder of the bodies would be carried away by funeral directors to the mortuary.

Nine terrorists were accounted for. Was there a tenth or had Andy's count of ten men been wrong?

Handcuffs were applied to the two Asians inside the hallway. The men had gradually come to, and were aware of not only a throbbing pain in the back of their head, but also their fate. They would be transported to Salisbury Police Station, and then on to Paddington Green Police Station, in London for intense interrogation the following day.

The injured men lay on stretchers waiting for the "all clear" from the patrol. They would be airlifted to a specialist hospital that dealt with back and spinal injuries.

A third ambulance had arrived at the house, and the two paramedics were talking to the surviving police sergeant in the kitchen.

Tim was carried out on a stretcher, he feebly raised his arm to Peter, who responded by briefly holding the injured man's hand, speaking softly, and assuring him that all would be well.

The engineer sat alone in the front room. All was relatively quiet apart from the murmur of voices.

Feeling out of place, Peter stood up. He also needed to exercise his heavily bandaged leg as it was causing him pain. He was to be taken to hospital in the third ambulance under escort. He limped into the kitchen and was amazed at the destruction that met his eyes. This had been his home for a brief spell. There were shards of glass, broken crockery, splintered wood, and damaged furniture which littered the room. Rich red plasma stained the off-white tiled kitchen floor.

Peter walked through the open back doorway. Funeral attendants were dealing with the Asian corpses, and placing them in body bags.

The RRU sergeant and Andy were standing in the living room by the kitchen assessing the gravity of the situation.

Peter stood thoughtfully on the patio. His leg and knee were paining him. He yawned, stretched, and thought what a terrifying day it had been. He had fond memories of him and Kristine in the early mornings, and evenings as they had spent time together on the paved patio of their cottage. He missed her so much. She was his inspiration, and his reason to live. He felt the wave of emotion coming over him again. His life was nothing without her. Then he remembered the dream.

He heard the crack from the near still silence, but it was too late. He fell clutching his chest. The RRU sergeant and Andy instinctively dived for cover.

Two retorts hit the camouflaged body in the tree. Another two rounds were fired off from Tosh, the policeman in the loft. The body twisted in a spasm, and finally fell to the ground.

'Medics!' Andy shouted, seeing Peter on the ground.

Two green clad figures ran into the house. They had been waiting by the front entrance for the "all clear" before transporting Peter to the hospital to have his leg attended to.

Peter was partially aware of bodies around him. There was a burning pain. Blood poured from somewhere in his chest.

Concerned, worried, and anxious, faces peered down at him.

A blonde woman with a kind face in a green uniform knelt down beside him. She was saying something. Andy knelt down beside Peter on the other side. His face was in full view, strained, concerned, then everything became blurred. Peter barely felt his hand being held. Voices were distorted and distant, they came and went. He was slipping away, he knew, his time was up. He was weak. Frantically, the green clad people were working on him, calling his name.

'Peter, can you hear me? Are you with us? Don't go, Peter!'

He moved his head slightly, and looked at Andy. Was Andy crying? He was a good man. The engineer's lips opened partially. He tried to say thank you. No sound came out. A tear rolled down his cheek. A trickle of blood ran down his chin. An oxygen mask was placed over his nose and mouth. The medics frantically worked on his limp body. The injury was too serious.

Everything was fading and the visions were getting fainter. There was blackness with pinpricks of bright silver light . . . .

'He's going,' someone said faintly in a seemingly distant voice.

* * *

The officer came down from the loft.

'All appears quiet out there now skipper,' he informed the sergeant. 'Tosh is still up there covering. Should we do a damage assessment?' They looked into the dining room, and took in the gravity of the matter, and then saw the body on the floor with the paramedics.

'No we'll hang on for the second team to return, and get their report. You guys can stand down.'

'OK Sarge.'

The police helicopter had reported no further activity on the ground so the paramedic helicopter hovered at a safe distance, and landed by the side of the house. The injured RRU men would be transported to a specialist hospital.

Andy sat down heavily on a dining room chair. It had all been too much. What was he to do now? The man they were protecting was dead. His colleague was injured, but thankfully alive. Had it all been worth it? What price can be put on a human life? That was the most precious of God's gifts.

'No! Peter! Stay with us!' The voice was getting more distant, more urgent, and more unreal.

The people around him looked very foggy now. Nothing was authentic. He felt himself lifted out of his body. He was at a vortex between two worlds as he looked down seeing, but not recognizing himself on the floor. People became blurred, almost vapoury, and were fussing over his body. Then he realised it was *his* body he was looking at . . . .

It was no good, he couldn't go back.

He hovered for a while, and then drifted onwards and upwards. He saw rooftops, then something that resembled a long tunnel of light. He felt drawn towards, and inside it. Then he saw her.

'Krissie!'

'Yes darling, I am here. It is your time now my husband. I have prepared a place for us.'

They were floating together, there was no pain.

He was with her, she was so real, but where would this beautiful yellowish, lime green, tunnel of love, and light eventually take them?

* * *

'He was a bloody hero,' Andy announced holding back the tears 'I think the poor bastard wanted to die, the way he tried to protect Tim.'

'There is nothing we can do for him now,' said the paramedic sympathetically.

'He is at peace.' said someone.

'What a bloody mess. What has it all been for?' Andy was overcome with grief, having a hard job to regain his composure. The hatred for the terrorists welled up inside him, counterproductive to his police instructions. He was human after all. Then the feeling eventually subsided as logic, and his training once again prevailed.

'Why wasn't the guy wearing body armour?' the sergeant of the anti-terrorist squad asked.

'He took it off to cover Tim's head and upper body while he protected him as he lay injured until I got back from my morning run. There was so much going on at the time. I was upstairs firing at the bastard in the tree. Pete grabbed an H and K and picked the bastards off as they tried to come over the wall.'

'OK. You did all you could, don't blame yourself, old son.'

Andy looked into the tired eyes of the forty-something-year-old police sergeant. He carried the same rank as Andy.

'Thanks.' Andy sniffed trying to hold back the tears once again. As hard a man as he was, he had built up a lot of respect for the engineer in a short space of time.

'He was a bloody hero, the stupid sod!' he said to the mixed assembly as they stared down at the lifeless body.

He left the room.

EPILOGUE

THE BRITISH SECURITY services acted swiftly on the information received. With names, numbers and addresses, they were soon able to round up many of the cell members. The captured, injured terrorist suspects were taken to Paddington Green Police Station, where they were routinely interrogated.

Arrests were made in many cities throughout the United Kingdom.

A small number of the sleeper cell terrorists had fled from their lodgings and disappeared.

* * *

Riyadh, Jeddah, and Dammam were vigilant with compound wardens liaising closely with the British Embassy staff. The American Intelligence Agencies were on high alert. Anniversaries such as The American Day of Independence, Thanksgiving, and 9/11 were boosted by a strong police presence, roadblocks and extra Saudi Arabia National Guard, were attentive on European and American compounds.

* * *

Andy continued with the Police Protection Squad, and then went back to the Metropolitan Police in London. He requested to be stationed at Paddington Green. He continued his private war against terrorism by being one of the interrogation officers after training.

Shortly after his posting, he met a female constable whilst on duty, and they later married.

* * *

Tim partially recovered from his injury, but was invalided out of the police force as he lost some movement in his injured arm. Tim received compensation, and an early retirement pension, some of which he had received as a lump sum. Tim married a nurse, sold his house, and bought a Bed and Breakfast establishment in Polperro, Cornwall.

* * *

Dudley and his family moved to the West Country also. He and Lisa opted for a quiet life. They bought a small shop that Lisa ran, and the colonel started a consultancy business supplying resources to telecoms companies in the UK, and overseas. He never really got over the loss of a good and trusted friend

* * *

Peter? He had nothing to live for, and was so much in love with the woman he married. Did he have a death wish? Well, we can only speculate and wonder! We will never know for sure—or will we?

THE END

Remember, Al-Qaeda spokesman Suleiman Abu Gheith went on record stating Al-Qaeda's objective is: "to kill 4 million Americans—2 million of them children—and to exile twice as many and wound and cripple hundreds of thousands."

Printed in Great Britain
by Amazon.co.uk, Ltd.,
Marston Gate.